Glittering pa...
passio...

Regency

HIGH-SOCIETY AFFAIRS

They're the talk of the Ton!

Lord Calthorpe's Promise
by Sylvia Andrew

&

The Society Catch
by Louise Allen

The Regency

HIGH-SOCIETY AFFAIRS

Regency

HIGH-SOCIETY AFFAIRS

Sylvia Andrew &
Louise Allen

*M&B™ and M&B™ with the Rose Device
are trademarks of the publisher.
Harlequin Mills & Boon Limited, Eton House,
18-24 Paradise Road, Richmond, Surrey TW9 1SR*

First published in Great Britain in 2000 and 2004

REGENCY HIGH-SOCIETY AFFAIRS
© Harlequin Books S.A. 2009

The publisher acknowledges the copyright holders of the
individual works as follows:

Lord Calthorpe's Promise © Sylvia Andrew 2002
The Society Catch © Louise Allen 2004

ISBN: 978 0 263 87551 5

052-0609

*Printed and bound in Spain
by Litografia Rosés S.A., Barcelona*

Lord Calthorpe's Promise

by

Sylvia Andrew

Sylvia Andrew has an Honours Degree in Modern Languages from University College, London and, before ending up as Vice-Principal of a large comprehensive sixth-form college, taught English for foreigners in Switzerland, Cambridge and in Compton Park, an international finishing school for young ladies which was housed in a beautiful country mansion leased from the Devonshire family. The house and grounds have provided inspiration for several settings in her novels. She and her husband Simon now live in a small market town in the west of England, which is full of the Georgian architecture which they both love. And just a few miles from their home is the marvellous Dorset Jurassic Coast World Heritage Site. In 2000 Sylvia wrote a historical celebration of the town's splendid fifteenth-century parish church in a millennium *son et lumière*, which was a great success.

She and Simon belong to the Georgian Group, the National Trust and English Heritage, all of which help them to satisfy their love of historic houses and wonderful landscapes. Simon lectures all over the place on architecture and wild orchids, while Sylvia tries to do nothing, and usually fails, since she is heavily involved in the local museum. She just can't keep away from old maps, newspapers, photographs and census returns! Her other passion is theatre performances of Shakespeare. She and Simon have one married daughter, whom they visit quite often, and a very precious grandson called Joe.

Chapter One

June 1815

Adam Calthorpe stood in the doorway of the Duchess of Richmond's ballroom and surveyed the scene. The Duchess had spared no effort to make this ball one of the season's outstanding events, and it looked as if she had been successful in spite of considerable competition. Ever since the Duke of Wellington, Commander-in-Chief of the Allied armies, had made the Belgian capital his headquarters, pleasure seekers from all over Europe had been gathering to enjoy the brilliant social life to be found there, and for weeks Brussels had been a whirl of parties, concerts, dances, picnics, musical rides and a host of other entertainments. Adam wondered briefly how long it would last...

With an effort he dismissed all thought of the worrying news coming in from the French border. Time for that later. He and the others were here to spread confidence, to reassure. He looked down the ballroom, and smiled. Everything seemed to be as usual in the Duchess's ballroom. Tom Payne was galloping down

the country dance set with more enthusiasm than
grace, Ivo Trenchard was leaning over the beautiful
wife of a Belgian diplomat as if she were the only
woman in the world for him. As she was, thought
Adam cynically, for the next half-hour. They were all,
so to speak, on duty—detailed to represent the Duke's
staff at the ball—and were all wearing full dress uniforms. It was a very hot evening. Adam felt uncomfortable enough in his high stock and black cravat, his
scarlet and gold lace, Tom's face was shining with his
exertions, but Ivo looked as cool and controlled as
ever in his magnificent Hussar uniform. All the same,
that fur-trimmed pelisse must be unbearably warm.
Even as Adam looked, Ivo offered his arm to the lady
and they walked out through the long windows into
the garden...

'Lord Calthorpe!'

Adam turned. An elderly lady in a blaze of diamonds caught his arm anxiously. Adam took the claw-
like hand and kissed it. As he straightened up he
smiled reassuringly. 'How may I help you, Countess
Karnska?'

'The Duke. He is not here?'

'Not yet, Countess. But you know how much his
Grace likes dancing. He'll be here presently.'

'But what does it mean that he is late? Is it true
what they are saying? That Bonaparte has crossed the
Belgian border? Is the Duke aware of this? Should we
leave Brussels while we can?'

Mentally cursing the busybodies who ferreted out
the latest news from the frontier and spread it among
the anxious populace, Adam smiled again and said,
'You may be sure, Countess, that the Duke is fully

aware of the situation. But there is really no cause for alarm, I assure you. Brussels is in no danger.'

'It's all very well to say so, *milor'*.' The Countess had been joined by her son, a florid gentleman in a puce coat. 'But Bonaparte is a genius. A genius! And, as far as I know, the Duke of Wellington has not yet ever faced him in battle. How can you be so sure?'

'Comte, Napoleon Bonaparte may be the genius you say he is, but I fancy the Duke has his measure. You and your mother should forget Bonaparte and enjoy the ball. The Duke has everything in hand. Now, may I fetch you some wine, Countess? You will see his Grace very soon, I promise you. He is merely dining late.'

Adam fetched some wine for the two guests, and then made his escape. He hoped he knew his duty, but enough was enough. The air in the ballroom was stifling, and the thought of even two minutes of reassuring yet another aristocratic visitor, who had come to enjoy the brilliant social life in Brussels and had stayed to regret it, appalled him. In the past hour he had had a dozen such conversations and for the moment he was tired of concealing his own anxieties.

He saw that Ivo and his lady had returned to the ballroom and decided to have some air himself. But even out in the garden at ten o'clock at night it was still very warm, with not the slightest hint of a breeze. Adam stood watching the dancers for a while through the wide glass doors. It was a splendid sight, dominated by the scarlet and gold of uniforms, the ladies in their light muslins and silks fluttering like moths around them. But the laughter was more highly pitched than was normal, and more than a few of the faces round the ballroom were anxious.

For all his reassuring words to the Countess, Adam knew the situation to be even more disquieting than they suspected. News of Bonaparte's sudden advance against the Prussians had come late to the Allied headquarters, and, far from dining late, the Duke and his aides were closeted in the Richmonds' library, conning maps and writing sheaf after sheaf of new orders. Soon Adam and others like him would be galloping to deliver them all over the Belgian countryside, wherever the Allied troops were encamped. It looked as if Boney might have stolen a march after all on the Allied Commander-in-Chief...

Oddly, Adam had no doubt of the outcome. After seven years of campaigning with Wellington he had absolute confidence in the Duke's ability to get the better of his enemy. But the battle ahead was going to be a tough one, of that he was equally certain. He sighed. It would probably be his last. The Army had been good to him—promotion had come quickly, and at thirty he was on the Duke's own staff, seconded from his regiment with the acting rank of Major. But once this campaign was over, he must think seriously of going back to England. Inheriting his uncle's estate had been an unexpected piece of good fortune, but it also brought its duties. The estate was large and had been neglected—it would need a great deal of his attention. And it was time he set about finding a suitable bride...

It was certain to feel strange at first, after ten years of marching, fighting and bivouacking all over Western Europe. Ten years ago it had been perfectly in order for a young man with no hint of future riches, no prospect of a title and estates in England, to take a commission in the British Army. Ten years ago he had had two lusty cousins between him and the handsome estate near Bath which was now his. It was ironic that Adam had survived ten years of some of the toughest fighting in Europe, while his cousins had both died in the pursuit of pleasure at home—one in a brawl outside a tavern in London and the other on the hunting field. Quite unforeseen, Adam had come into a title, as well as a substantial fortune. He owed it to his family to return to England and to look after the inheritance which had so unexpectedly come his way. The excitement of life in the Army, the cameraderie, the fights, the celebrations—one last great battle, and then they would be over.

He turned towards the ballroom again, but stopped short when he caught sight of a young couple coming his way. They were a handsome pair—the lad's distinctive uniform of the Blues was a wonderful foil for the girl's white dress and guinea-gold hair. They paused in the doorway... Adam drew a sharp breath and his heart gave a thump. *Julia!* What in the name of all the gods was Julia doing here? For a moment he couldn't think—he was transported back ten years to a glade in the woods which surrounded the Redshaws' estate...

He had a vivid picture of himself at twenty, just down from Oxford and passionately in love with Julia Redshaw. He had met her often in the woods which separated her home from his, the secrecy of their meetings adding to the romance of their affair. It had all been touchingly innocent. But the day came when he had kissed her, kissed her with all the ardour of a lover… They had drawn back from each other, gazing in wonder, mixed with a touch of fear, he remembered. The whirlwind they had raised between them had astonished them both.

It wasn't surprising that his voice had been a touch unsteady as he said, 'I…I shouldn't have done that. I'm sorry, Julia.'

Julia's eyes had sparkled blue fire at him. 'Don't you dare say you're sorry, Adam Calthorpe!' she had said. 'How could anyone be sorry about a…a kiss like that? To know that we love each other like that? I'm not sorry! Kiss me again, Adam!'

Adam smiled. At twenty he had been so serious, such an idealist! He remembered feeling slightly shocked, saying, 'N…No. Not again. Not before you'll say that you'll marry me.'

That was when disillusionment had set in. Julia's eyes had widened and their sparkle diminished. '*Marry* you? Why?'

'Well, of course we must marry! It's what we've always wanted…isn't it? I know I fell in love with you the minute we met. Are you saying you don't love me after all?'

'No, no! I do, I do!' She had flung her arms round his neck. 'You know I do!'

How hard it had been to ignore those arms! But he had put her gently aside. 'Well, then…?'

'But marriage is something different. I couldn't possibly marry *you*, Adam. What on earth should we live on? No, no, when I get married it will be to someone rich!'

The memory of his disbelief was still surprisingly

strong. But he hadn't been able to move her. She had remained as affectionate as ever but adamant. Julia Redshaw was determined to marry into a fortune, and though she loved Adam Calthorpe as much as it was in her to love anyone, she was not going to change her mind. She would not even promise to wait. In one short summer Adam Calthorpe lost his love and his ideals, and grew up. He refused to stay and watch while the love of his life pursued her goal of marrying a wealthy man. Instead, he had persuaded his uncle to buy him a commission in the Army, and had left England. It had been his good fortune that the regiment he had chosen eventually turned into one of the crack fighting machines in the Peninsula…

He stole another glance at the girl in the doorway. How stupid of him! This couldn't possibly be Julia. This girl was hardly more than seventeen, and Julia was only three years younger than he. Julia would be twenty-seven now, certainly a married woman, no doubt a *wealthily* married woman. He shook his head, impatient with his own folly. How odd that the sight of guinea-gold hair, a tumble of curls over a heart-shaped face, still had the power to disorient him! He would have sworn he had forgotten Julia Redshaw. Certainly, for the past six or seven years, he had seldom given a thought to the girl whose rejection had first sent him into his present career.

He smiled wryly. How oddly it had all turned out! Would it have made a difference if Julia and her father had known that Adam would one day step into his uncle Calthorpe's title and riches? Hardly! Time waited for no one, and ten years would have been a long time for a girl of seventeen to wait! He himself had changed in those years. He was no longer the hot-headed romantic who had joined the Army in despair when Julia Redshaw had rejected him. He had since enjoyed several quite lively affairs, with no thought of marriage on either side. And now, at thirty, he was all set to look for a wife with whom he hoped to enjoy a more mature relationship, with less passion and more sense! There would be affection, he hoped, and re-spect, but not the headlong folly of that first love. Julia Redshaw would remain in the past and he would find a modest, well-bred girl to take her place—in his life, if not in his affections.

He watched the golden-haired girl floating away on the arm of her partner, and felt a last momentary pang. Then he shook his head and made for the ballroom again.

He was met at the door by Lieutenant Tom Payne. The country dances were finished and Tom was alight with excitement.

'I say, sir, isn't this a splendid do? What a send-off for the troops, aye!'

Adam smiled. It was impossible not to smile at Tom. Six feet tall, fair hair that was usually falling over one eye, fresh-faced and full of enthusiasm, he reminded Adam of a large puppy and aroused in him the same amused affection, tempered with respect for his qualities as a fighting man. Tom had been a mem-ber of Adam's company ever since Spain, and his de-votion to Adam was second only to his devotion to life in the Army generally.

Adam asked, 'Any news, yet?'

'No, I've just been to enquire. The Beau is still

stuck in his papers with De Lacey and the others. Lord, I wish they'd get on with it.'

'"The Beau" is no way to refer to our revered Commander-in-Chief, you graceless young dog! How ready are you to ride off when the orders do appear? I can see you're dressed as unsuitably as I am for a swift ride through the night.'

'It won't take me long to change, I promise you. What about you, sir?'

'It might take me a fraction longer, but I'll manage. I wish the Duke had chosen someone else to do his entertaining for him, I can't say I've enjoyed it.' There was a short silence as they paused to regard the dancers circling round.

Then Tom Payne said, 'I know I have to leave the Army after this is all over. But I'm not looking forward to it. It'll all seem a bit tame after Spain and now here. Y'can't hunt and shoot all the time, and what else is there at home?'

'You and the Army might have been made for each other, I agree. But your grandfather's death was bound to put an end to it all, Tom.'

'That's true! I should have gone back months ago. There's the estate, and there's my sister, too. Heaven knows what would happen to her if I left her to herself. What she needs is a husband, of course.'

Adam laughed. 'That's a coincidence! I have just been deciding that I need to settle down and look for a wife!'

'You're not thinking of leaving the Army, are you sir?' Tom's face was a picture of astonishment. 'Not when you don't *have* to?'

'But I do have to. You're not the only one with

responsibilities, Lieutenant! And I'm a good bit older than you. No, we shall have one last glorious fling, and then we shall both knuckle down to a sober, industrious life at home!' He laughed at the expression of disgust on Tom's face. 'It won't be so bad. And you know, Tom, once we've settled Napoleon Bonaparte once and for all, life in the Army in peacetime could get very dull.'

'There'll always be a fight somewhere, sir! You know I'm not very good with words, but I've never been as happy as I am now. I've never fitted in anywhere as well as I fit in here.'

Adam looked at his junior. Tom was right. By temperament and character he was an ideal soldier. Whether he would have reached the top was more questionable. He was a man of action, not of thought. In battle there was no better fighter, no one more daring, or more loyal. But inactivity bored him, and when he was bored he tended to get into mischief. During quieter periods in Portugal and Spain, Adam had more than once been forced to defend Lieutenant Payne against a charge of misconduct—usually successfully, for everyone liked Tom. What would happen when he was forced to lead the quieter life of a country gentleman? The high spirits and daring, which made him such a brilliant soldier, might well turn to recklessness. Or would he move to London, where he would find even more dangerous adventures? From what Adam knew of his family, there was no one to check him. The two Paynes, brother and sister, were alone in the world. He was so deep in thought that he did not at first hear Tom's hesitant voice.

'Sir...sir!'

'Tom?'

'Sir, are you definitely leaving the Army?'

'Quite certainly.'

'Sir, may I ask something? If you don't like it, you only have to say no…'

Adam knew that pleading tone. Tom was about to ask something outrageous. 'Out with it!' he said with a resigned smile. But even he was not prepared for quite how outrageous Tom's request would be.

'Sir, if you liked the idea…I mean, if you are really looking for a wife… Would you…would you consider my little sister? I'd like nothing better for her than to marry you.'

Adam was speechless with astonishment. 'Tom! Are you out of your mind?'

Tom's desperation gave him the courage to pursue his goal. 'Oh, I realise that you would need to meet her before you considered such a thing. But… but…if…if you liked each other… And you did say that you wanted to marry… And as sisters go, she's not at all bad. She's fun to be with, and she is very good-tempered and…and patient. Usually. She's had a rough time these past years with my grandfather being ill, and me away in Spain. And she *needs* someone—someone like you, to look after her!'

'I thought that was to be your job,' said Adam sternly.

'Well, I will. But she must marry some time!' When Adam continued to regard him in the severest disapproval Tom went on, 'She's a very pretty little thing, too. And…and very understanding. Tolerant.' He stopped and looked at Adam with the air of a starved puppy looking for a bone. Adam began to be amused at his persistence.

'What is this, Tom? Why are you so keen to marry your sister off?'

'Well, I thought...I thought that if I could find someone I could trust to look after her I might be able to think of the Army again...'

'The idea is absurd! Give it up!' Adam started to walk back to the ballroom. 'Come on! It's time we reported for duty.'

'Well, would you think about coming down to Herriards? Just to meet her?'

'I'll agree to that. Not with the idea of meeting your sister with an eye to marriage, Tom—but I'd be pleased to visit you once we're back in England. Come!' Tom looked crestfallen, but obeyed the dismissal in Adam's voice. Together they walked briskly through the ballroom and up the stairs to the small 'den' which had been allotted to the Duke's staff.

Here they found several others, waiting for orders. Any minute now they would be given their assignments, to ride into the night with new commands for the regiments stationed in the countryside round the Belgian capital. Adam hoped he'd be given a chance to change out of his full dress uniform before leaving. White breeches, gold lace and silken sashes did not stand up well to the sort of hard riding which would be expected of him. His regiment was stationed almost as far from Brussels as it was possible to be.

He turned as Ivo Trenchard came in, resplendent in his pelisse and fur. 'You look warm, Ivo!'

'It must be the hottest night yet! But that's not it, my dear boy. If I look a trifle flushed, it's through hard work. I've been reassuring all the ladies that Boney ain't going to capture the lot of them and haul 'em all off to Paris.'

'I'm sure you reassured them every one... splendidly,' drawled Adam. 'Madame de Menkelen seemed particularly impressed. But does she realise that Bonaparte might not be the only danger she faces?'

There was a shout of laughter. Captain Lord Trenchard was Brussels's worst flirt. His exploits with the ladies—who were most of them, it has to be said, only too willing—were legendary. Adam knew him for a cool, resourceful fighter, and a ruthless opponent in the field, but no one observing his indolent figure and lazy charm at work in the drawing rooms of Society would have suspected as much. He had a number of advantages, of course. He was not only rich and related to half the top families in England, but was tall, with dark brown hair, sparkling blue eyes and a slow smile which wrought havoc among the female population wherever he happened to be. Perhaps it was this ease of conquest which had made him somewhat cynical, certainly in his attitude to the fair sex. Be he never so charming, no woman had as yet managed to hold his attention for long, and the matchmaking mamas of Brussels had long regarded him as a hopeless case. But though Adam might deplore Ivo Trenchard's more outrageous affairs, the two men were good friends. Adam found it significant that the men in Ivo Trenchard's company had enormous respect and trust in him as a leader.

'How is it that you're still with us, young Tom?' Trenchard asked now. 'I thought you had decided to leave us to fight without you? Or have you changed your mind?'

The Lieutenant coloured up. 'It wasn't because I was tired of fighting,' he began defensively. 'I wish I needn't leave at all—' He stopped. Adam intervened.

'Leave the poor fellow alone, Ivo! He really ought to be in England at this moment, but he decided to postpone his departure from the Army when he heard about Boney's escape. Wasn't sure we could finish this job without him, were you, Tom?'

The ready colour surged once more in Tom Payne's cheeks. He ignored Adam's teasing words and said, 'But this is going to be the greatest fight ever! Boney has never faced the Duke directly before! He's bound to lose, of course, but think of the challenge! I couldn't have missed a battle like this. I think I'll just slip downstairs to see if anything has cropped up. We can't have to wait much longer. Excuse me.' He gave a slight salute and hurried out.

The two older men smiled at the Lieutenant's eagerness. 'All the same, Adam,' Ivo said, 'the boy is right. It's going to be a battle between Titans. Let's hope we survive to tell the tale afterwards.'

'We shall, Ivo, we shall. Only the good die young. But I hope Tom manages to keep a cool head. He's apt to let his enthusiasm run away with him, and take unnecessary risks.'

'While you, as we all know, stand back and let others do the dangerous work?' said Ivo with a mocking smile.

'I don't lose my head, Ivo! I'm too old for that. But Tom… The trouble is that he's so sick at the thought of leaving the Army that he might well decide to go out in a blaze of glory.'

'Why *is* he leaving? Or am I being indiscreet?'

'Not at all, it's very straightforward—I'm surprised he hasn't told you. Tom and his sister were brought up by their grandfather. They haven't any other close relations. The grandfather died last year, and Tom really has no choice but to go back to England and look after his sister and what, from all accounts, is a substantial estate. But he put off leaving when the news came through that Napoleon had slipped the leash on Elba and was marching through France, ready for another campaign.'

'What about the sister?'

'There's a governess or companion—something like that. She's looking after the girl until Tom gets back.'

'Let's hope he does…'

Adam frowned. 'Amen to that! The Payne estate is entailed. If Tom dies without an heir it goes to a distant cousin. I wonder what would happen to his sister then?'

'If she has half of Tom's looks and charm she will probably marry some local squire and be perfectly happy,' said Ivo with a cynical smile. He stretched himself and yawned. 'Lord, where the devil are those orders?'

In fact, it was half an hour before Tom returned. His eager informality had vanished, for he accompanied Colonel Ancroft, the commanding officer of their group. But underneath Tom's rigidly correct manner Adam could see that the young man was still ablaze with excitement.

'Well, gentlemen, it looks as if we shall all be in

action tomorrow. The last checks are being made and as soon as the orders are brought you will be dispersing at speed. Meanwhile, shall we drink to Boney's downfall? Tom?'

Tom went over to the corner table and poured out some wine. He served them all round, and they solemnly toasted the King, each other, and lastly, but most heartily, they drank to death and destruction to Napoleon and his troops. Then Colonel Ancroft nodded and they sat down. There was a moment's pause, while they all tried to think of something to break the silence. Their commanding officer had an air of authority which came from more than his rank. Adam knew him to be not more than five or six years older than he was himself, but the Colonel's coal-black hair had silver wings at the temples, and under the severity of his gaze was a hint of pain, disciplined, suppressed, but there. He was generally held to be a cold man. He was certainly austere. Though he had the trust of all the men under him, and was known to be absolutely fair and impartial, it was not easy to like him. It certainly wasn't easy to make light conversation with him. But Adam had known him for a long time, and, acquainted as he was with some of the Colonel's history, he understood and respected the other man's reserve. However, perhaps because of the tensions of the night, their commanding officer seemed to be in a talkative mood.

'So, what are you all planning to do with yourselves after this is over? I hear you're leaving the Army, Tom? Reluctantly, I gather.'

'Sir.'

'You too, Adam?'

'I'm afraid so, sir.'

'Are you taking part in this wholesale exodus, Ivo? There'll be one or two sighs of relief among the husbands in Europe if you do!'

They laughed, Ivo as well. Then he looked down into his glass and said, 'To be honest, I don't know. sir. I have one or two bits of unfinished business in England. It's time I put things right with my father, for a start.'

'That's good! Lord Veryan will be pleased to see you again.'

'You think so? When I last saw him he was shouting that he never wished to set eyes on such a villainous, unnatural monster again.'

'I shouldn't let that deter you. People often say things in a rage that they don't really mean.' Colonel Ancroft stopped short. 'And do things, too,' he added, almost to himself. The curious little silence that followed was broken by the arrival of one of the Duke's aides. He had a sheaf of papers in his hand which he handed to the Colonel, who read them through, then gave them out. Most of the men were to rejoin their own regiments carrying the orders with them.

'The news is as bad as it can be, gentlemen. Napoleon has attacked the Prussians in force, and it seems likely that they will not be able to hold. To save Brussels we must concentrate our forces at Nivelles—these are the orders. God speed to you all!'

Ivo was the first to go, bound for Ninhove where the bulk of the English Cavalry could be found. Tom was given the task Adam had expected for himself, sent off to Ath to deliver the orders for the Light Divisions. His turn came immediately after.

'Wait outside, Lieutenant. Major Calthorpe will join you in a moment.'

Adam waited while his superior fidgeted with some papers. 'I've given you the hardest assignment, Adam. You're to deal with the Belgians—the King's generals can be touchy if they think their royal prerogative is being undermined. Tact and charm are needed, but above all they must move quickly!' The Colonel looked up with a gleam of humour in his hard grey eyes. 'I'd have sent Trenchard, but since his escapade with the Comtesse Leiken he's *persona non grata* at the court. But you have plenty of tact—you can deal with them. Get them to accept the Duke's commands—we can't afford debate, they're damned urgent.'

'Sir!'

'And, Adam—!'

'Sir?'

'You and young Payne will ride together for some of the way. Do what you can to calm him down. He's in too much of a death-or-glory mood.'

Adam gave a nod of understanding, saluted and left.

He found Tom outside, practically hopping with impatience. Together they set off to the west.

For a while they rode in silence, concentrating on getting out of Brussels as expeditiously as possible. But then they dropped the pace to a trot to allow their mounts time to recover. The cooler air outside the capital seemed to have a sobering effect on Tom. He said eventually, 'I'm not altogether a selfish villain, sir.'

Adam looked in surprise at him. 'I never thought you were. What is on your mind, Tom?'

'Asking you to consider my sister. It's not only that

I want to be free to rejoin the Army. But…but if anything happened to me—I know it's unlikely, but it could happen—she'd be left without protection from my cousins.'

'She would need protection? From members of your own family? Surely not!'

'Sir, she's by way of being a bit of an heiress. If anything happened to me, she'd be even more of one. The Payne estate is entailed on a distant cousin, but not any of the money. Henry Payne would have the house and lands, but not much to support them. I…my grandfather never trusted him and nor do I. And he has a son of my age—single and free to marry someone like Kate. I knew him at Eton—he's a bit of a worm.'

'Whew!' Adam felt growing anger at the extent of Tom's irresponsiblity. 'In that case, why the devil did you risk staying on for this battle? You'd better make damned sure you come through it, my boy!' He stopped before he said something he might regret.

Tom was suffering from a belated attack of conscience. 'Kate always said I laughed too much and thought too little. I'll go back to England as soon as the Army releases me. But if anything should happen to me, sir, would you…?' He turned a worried face to Adam. 'Please! If she was married to you, she'd be safe.'

Adam said in exasperation, 'I can't promise to marry your sister—apart from anything else, she may not want to marry me! Have you thought of that? But I'll make sure she's looked after. And now we must push on. I turn off at the next crossroads.'

They rode on again at speed, pausing only briefly

where their ways parted. Adam wanted to urge Tom to caution, but found he couldn't. That was no way to send a serving soldier into battle. So he merely nodded and called 'Good luck!' as he turned on to the road to Braine le Comte.

Behind them, on the other side of Brussels, the Prussians were fighting a losing battle against the massed forces of the French. It would soon not be enough for Wellington's troops to wait at Nivelles. Before morning the Army would be ordered to Quatre Bras to meet Napoleon, and the final battle would be fought outside a small, as yet unheard-of village called Waterloo.

Chapter Two

July 1815

Katharine Payne stood at the window of her sitting room, a letter loosely held in her hand. The room had been hers ever since her grandfather had decided that she was old enough to leave the nursery and have her own set of rooms on the first floor. Till now, even in her most difficult or tempestuous moments, she had found calm and consolation in the view over the garden and beyond to the Hampshire countryside. But today she was blind to the flower beds, bright in the colours of high summer, the beautiful specimen trees, planted by her great-great-grandfather, the wide lawns, vividly green after a recent shower.

Tom was dead. Killed in action.

She had been told several weeks ago, of course. But throughout all the dreadful formalities, the visits from the family lawyers and all the rest, she had lived in a daze, still half expecting Tom to come bursting in through her door, his handsome face alight with laughter, mocking her for having fallen for one of his tricks.

Now this letter had brought the bitter truth home to her at last. Tom would not come back. Not ever... The letter fluttered to the floor as she hid her face in her hands.

'Katharine! My dear!'

Katharine straightened up at the sound of Tilly's voice.

'It's all right, Tilly,' she said, turning round. 'I'm not about to break down.'

'It might do you good if you did,' said Miss Tillyard gruffly. 'You can't go on as you are, Katharine.'

'No, I know. I must pull myself together and make some plans.'

'That's not what I meant! But I agree you need to think of the future.' She came over and picked up the letter lying on the floor. 'Is this what has upset you?'

'Yes. It's from one of Tom's friends in the Army. A Major Calthorpe—Lord Calthorpe. I've heard Tom talk about him. It is...it is very kind. He obviously liked Tom a great deal.'

'Was Lord Calthorpe with your brother when...?'

'No, but he has spoken to someone who was. He tells me that Tom...died bravely.' She paused. Then she went on, 'Lord Calthorpe saw Tom for the last time on the evening before Waterloo. They talked of me...' Her voice died again, and again she rallied. 'He is coming back to England for a short while and would like to call here. He knows I have no one else and offers to help me in any way he can. It's a very kind letter.'

Katharine's voice broke again, but Miss Tillyard resisted the temptation to put her arm round the girl. She knew her pupil of old. When Katharine Payne was hurting, any attempt to comfort her would be instantly rejected—she would regard accepting it as a sign of weakness. So Miss Tillyard kept her distance and asked instead, 'When will you see him?'

'I shan't see him at all. I don't want to see anyone.'

'But you ought—'

'It's very kind of Lord Calthorpe, but what could he do?'

'Katharine, he has taken the trouble to write. You ought to see him.'

'No, Tilly! No! I couldn't bear it. I shall write to thank him for the offer, of course.'

'Don't put him off completely, my dear. You might find you need his help in the future. Why not say that you would see him in a few weeks, when you are feeling better?'

'He wouldn't be able to come. From what Lord Calthorpe says, he is still on the Duke of Wellington's staff, and on duty with the Duke in France. And I really can't imagine what help a perfect stranger could give me. But if you think it is more polite, I'll do as you say.' Katharine turned back to her contemplation of the view. There was silence in the room.

Then Miss Tillyard asked quietly, 'When is your uncle due to arrive?'

'Any day now.'

'Have your guardians decided what is to happen to you?'

'General Armitage told me to wait till after my uncle has taken over here at Herriards. Sir James, of course, agreed with him.' She added with a touch of bitterness, 'I think those two old men are hoping that

Uncle Henry will offer me a home. They wouldn't know what to do with me otherwise.'

'The system of entailing property is a monstrous one!' Miss Tillyard said with uncharacteristic heat. 'You're the one who has really looked after the Herriards estate, Katharine—not just while your grandfather was ill, but for all the time your brother was away in the Army.' She stopped and thought. 'And now that I consider it, you were the one who saw to the estate when your brother *was* here, as well! All Tom ever thought about was the Army and how soon he could get back to it. And now, just because you are a female, you are effectively homeless, and Herriards is to go to someone who has never taken the slightest interest in it! It isn't right!'

Katharine gave a rueful smile. 'It's not exactly Uncle Henry's fault that he hasn't ever been here. My grandfather wouldn't let him come!'

'And why was that, pray?'

'I never knew. Uncle Henry isn't really my uncle. He's a distant sort of cousin, so Tom and I never had much to do with him. I think there was bad blood between the two branches of the family. Grandfather always called him "that villain Henry".'

'And look what has happened! Herriards now belongs to this same Henry Payne, simply because he is next in the male line after Tom. It is all his—farms, lands and this house as well.'

Katharine's face closed up. 'Yes. I've lost my home, as well as my brother,' she said. She spoke in such a detached tone that only someone who knew her as well as her former governess did could detect the heartache behind those briefly spoken words.

There was a pause, then Miss Tillyard said briskly, 'We must look on the bright side, Katharine. You know very little about Mr Henry Payne. I doubt he is the villain your grandfather called him. You told me that he has a family—a son and a daughter about your age. They could be ideal companions for you. You've lacked company of your own age for years.'

'I never wanted it. You were company enough for me, Tilly.'

'An old governess!'

'And now a friend,' said Katharine with a look of affection. 'I cannot say how grateful I am that you came back to live with me after Grandfather died. I know how much you love your little house in the village.'

'It's still there,' said Miss Tillyard. 'And, as soon as Mr Payne and his family come, I shall move back into it. You won't need me then—and your uncle won't thank me for staying. Now, why don't you write that letter to Lord Calthorpe? Are you sure you don't want him to come?'

'Quite sure. I already have two guardians to tell me what to do. I don't need advice from another elderly gentleman, however kind he may be.'

'Katharine! Lord Calthorpe is a serving officer. He can't be all that old!'

'He's on the Duke's staff. You noticed that he was not in action with Tom during the battle? He was probably safely back at headquarters. Tom used to call staff officers a lot of old women—and that was when he was being polite! No, I don't want some bewhiskered Army Major coming here to tell me how my brother died. And I certainly can't imagine that I would ever need any help from him.'

A week later Katharine sat in the saloon with Miss Tillyard. Both ladies were listening with an air of determined calm for sounds of arrival. Mr Henry Payne had announced his intention of coming that afternoon to take up his position as owner of Herriards. A crunching of gravel on the drive, sounds of bustle in the hall, then the door of the saloon opened and a large gentleman strode confidently in, brushing the house-keeper aside as he did so. Katharine was fascinated to see that his eyes were blue like Tom's, that his colour was high, as Tom's had been, and that his hair, though touched with grey, still had traces of Tom's reddish-gold. But his features were coarser, harder, in spite of his broad smile.

'No need to announce me! I'm not a guest.' He came over and took her hands in his. 'And here is little Katharine! My dear, I am delighted to meet you at last!' Then his face grew solemn and he added heavily, 'Though, of course, the circumstances are very sad for you. Indeed, for us all, for us all. How are you, my dear?'

'I am well, Uncle Henry, thank you. But where is Mrs Payne? Is she not with you?'

'Your Aunt Ellen and the children are arriving to-morrow. They can hardly wait to see their new home, but they couldn't leave Cheltenham when I did.' He looked inquiringly at Miss Tillyard. 'And this is?'

'This is my former governess and a dear friend, Miss Emily Tillyard. Mr Payne, Tilly.'

Henry Payne's smile diminished. He gave the briefest of nods in reply to Miss Tillyard's curtsy and said, 'Your governess, eh? Aren't you a little old for governesses?'

'You mistake me, Uncle. Tilly isn't my governess any more, she came back to live with me when Grandfather died.'

'Ah! Your companion! Well, there'll be no need for that now, my dear. Miss Tillyard will be free to look for another post as soon as your aunt arrives. Which is tomorrow.' He beamed at them both as if he had conferred the greatest of favours. He added, 'Sit down, sit down, my dear! There's no need to stand on ceremony with me. You, too, Miss…er, Tilson—unless you wish to go to your own quarters, of course. To pack.'

Katharine was outraged. Annoyance at the insult to Tilly was added to strong resentment at being invited to sit down in what had been till now her own home. But a warning glance from Tilly restrained her from responding too hastily. After a pause she managed to say calmly, 'Miss Tillyard has no need to find another post, Uncle Henry. She is a friend, not a paid servant, and has a home of her own in Herriard Stoke.'

Henry Payne was not listening. He walked round the room, examining the pictures and ornaments on display with a proprietorial air. At length he turned and said, 'You know, there's some damned valuable stuff here. Mrs Payne will be delighted. As soon as she is here tomorrow you must show us both round the rest of the house. I shall leave it to her to choose rooms for the children and herself. But don't worry,

Katharine, my dear. If you wish to stay with us, I'm sure we can find room for you, never fear! Somewhere.'

After this experience with her uncle, Katharine was better prepared for making Mrs Payne's acquaintance. That lady arrived the next day in a showy barouche, her daughter at her side. They were attended by several grooms dressed in elaborate livery.

Feeling in need of some moral support, Katharine had persuaded Tilly to delay her departure for Herriard Stoke until after Mrs Payne's arrival, and they now both waited a little behind Henry Payne on the steps at the front of the house.

The carriage came to a halt, the grooms came round to the doors, and Mrs Henry Payne descended. Rather stout, of not more than average height, she was an impressive figure all the same. She wore a striped silk jacket over an elaborately ruched and padded robe of bright blue silk. Both garments were obviously new. Two of the largest feathers Katharine had ever seen curled round the brim of her matching bonnet. She paused before coming up the steps. A pair of rather hard blue eyes surveyed Herriards's graceful frontage, its wide flight of steps leading to the door, its beautifully proportioned windows to either side, its handsome balustrading.

Mrs Payne frowned. In a tone of deep disapproval she said, 'Henry! I hadn't realised the place was so small! We shall have to extend, of course!'

'Whatever you say, my love. There'll be time for all sorts of plans later. Come! You must meet your niece. This is Katharine.'

As Katharine curtsied, Mrs Payne gave a little laugh

and said, '*Katharine?* Oh dear, we can't have that! That's my daughter's name. You will have to be Kate. *This* is Catherine!' She turned and beckoned her daughter forward. Catherine Payne was in white with more frills and ribbons than good taste would have thought necessary. But her face and figure could not be faulted. She was small, but perfectly proportioned, with large blue eyes, a rose and ivory complexion and guinea-gold curls clustered round her heart-shaped face. The Payne looks in enchantingly miniature form. She gave Katharine a delightful smile as she curtsied. Katharine feeling rather like an elephant beside Miss Payne's dainty grace, responded politely, and presented Miss Tillyard.

The Paynes gave the slightest of nods in Tilly's direction and swept into the entrance hall. 'Ah! Now something could be made of this!' exclaimed Mrs Payne, looking at the branching staircase and the white and gold coffered ceiling. 'It needs refurbishing, of course. It has been sadly neglected, but, yes, it has possibilities.' She turned to Katharine. 'I should like to see the bedchambers, Kate, before our belongings are brought in.'

'Of course. Shall I send for the housekeeper, ma'am?' Katharine asked coolly.

Mrs Payne replied with a smile, 'It is surely for *me* to send for the housekeeper, my dear? But it is an excellent idea.' She turned to a manservant who was waiting in the hall. 'You! Fellow! Fetch— What is the woman's name, Kate?'

'Mrs Jarnes, ma'am.'

'Fetch Jarnes!' The servant paused and looked at Katharine, who nodded.

'I expect she is upstairs, Charles,' she said quietly. 'Ask her to come down to meet her new mistress.'

Mrs Payne pursed her lips. 'As to "new mistress," we shall have to see,' she said. 'I hope I may be allowed to decide for myself what servants I hire. However, for the moment... I'd like you to come with us to look at the rooms, Kate. It would be easier to discuss the changes I shall make. After I have settled on bedchambers for my family, I suppose we shall have to find one for you. I understand from your uncle that we are all the family you now possess?'

'Yes,' Katherine replied. 'But...' She hesitated. She was not at all sure that she wanted to stay with Henry Payne and his wife, but it might seem discourteous to say so at this early stage.

Her aunt pursed her lips again. 'That is most unfortunate. We shall have to see what can be done. Your companion will be leaving, of course. *Her* room will definitely be required. What arrangements have you made for her departure?'

'Miss Tillyard is returning to her own home today, ma'am.'

'Good! Well, where are these rooms?'

Tilly went off to put her things together and Katharine was left to escort Mrs Payne round the house.

The following hour was one which Katharine would have been glad to forget. Herriards was not a large mansion; it was a comfortable, beautifully built family home. Succeeding generations had added their own touches to the house, but on the whole it was a harmonious collection of ideas and tastes. But it failed to meet with Mrs Payne's notions of what was due to her newly elevated status. She stared, criticised, planned to knock down walls, throw up screens, add doors or windows until Katharine was ready to scream. Nothing met with her approval until they came to Katharine's own rooms.

'Now this is a very pleasant suite,' she said as they entered, gazing round. Katharine was surprised and pleased. She had chosen the decoration schemes herself and the rooms were simply, but very prettily, furnished. She would not have thought they would appeal to Mrs Payne's taste.

'The prospect from the windows is extensive,' pronounced her aunt, 'and though the bedchamber is on the small side, the sitting room is quite large. Catherine will like these.'

'Catherine, ma'am?'

'Of course, they will need redecoration before they are fit for my daughter. The furnishing is sadly simple. But with curtains and a few extra draperies in the modern style, I fancy she will do very well here. Those bookcases would be taken out, of course, and room made for a larger dressing table and clothes chests.'

Katharine was stunned into silence, but Mrs Jarnes said, 'Beggin' your pardon, ma'am, these are Miss Katharine's rooms. This Miss Katharine.'

The cold blue eyes surveyed Mrs Jarnes. 'I think you mean they *were* Miss Kate's, Jarnes. Things have now changed. From now on, it is my daughter who will be known as ''Miss Catherine''. And she will have these rooms. Miss *Kate* will be accommodated elsewhere. The changeover will take place after the weekend.'

'But—'

Katharine intervened before the housekeeper could say any more. 'Mrs Payne is quite right, Mrs Jarnes. Herriards has new owners, who wish to make their own arrangements. We must fit in with their plans. As best we can.' She turned to her aunt and said firmly, 'These are the last rooms on this floor, Aunt Ellen, so I hope you will excuse me. I...I have promised Miss Tillyard that I will help her with her removal to Herriard Stoke.'

'Oh! Well, I suppose I shall have to,' her aunt said ungraciously. 'I had thought... Still, we have done quite a lot, and I suppose I am a little fatigued. Jarnes, I should like some tea. Bring it to the saloon in ten minutes, if you please.' She swept out, leaving Katharine and the housekeeper standing in the middle of the room. Mrs Jarnes shook her head.

'Don't say it, Jarnesy!' Katharine said. 'It won't help, and it may make matters worse. You must consider your own future.' Then, as the housekeeper turned reluctantly away, Katharine added under her breath, 'As I shall certainly have to consider mine.'

That evening at table Uncle Henry talked of the changes he intended to make on the estate. He talked glibly of yields and planning, of new methods and latest trends, but Katharine found him unconvincing. By dint of careful questions she found that her uncle had, in fact, had very little experience of running any kind of estate, and it seemed to her that his theme was exploitation, rather than development. The Paynes had apparently chosen to get rid of their own small inheritance some years before, and had since been living in style on the proceeds in Cheltenham. They were all full of ideas of what they intended to do with the new-found wealth and status which had come to them through Tom Payne's unexpected death.

'And that reminds me, Kate, my dear,' said her uncle. 'I intend to drive to Basingstoke tomorrow to see the lawyers. I noticed you had taken the phaeton out this afternoon to convey your governess to Herriard Stoke. I dare say it hadn't occurred to you to ask my permission. But in future I should like you to do so before you take any of the carriages out. That goes for the horses, too.'

'But the phaeton is mine, sir. For my own use. So are some of the horses.'

'That may have been true in the past, Kate. But as we keep saying, my dear, things have changed.'

'Not everything. The horses—'

'I will not be interrupted or contradicted at my own table, Kate! Not another word!'

'But—'

'Not one other word, Kate!' Uncle Henry still smiled, but the table fell silent. 'Once I have talked to the lawyers we shall see what can be done about your future. I will be as considerate as I can. But until then I do not wish to hear any discussion of the matter. Meanwhile, I hope you will do as I wish.' He looked round the table. 'We will now talk of something else.'

If I had a nobler nature, thought Katharine, I should make a better effort to prepare Uncle Henry for the shock which is waiting for him in Basingstoke, however richly he might deserve it. But, too heartsick and too weary to try, she listened in silence as Aunt Ellen talked of the bedchambers and how she proposed to allot them. And when, after debating which room could best be spared, her aunt finally decided to give her a small room on the upper floor, last used by a visiting maidservant, Katharine still said nothing. Neither the size nor the location of the room was of any consequence. She would not use it for long. To stay any length of time at Herriards under her uncle's regime was clearly out of the question.

Having come to this conclusion Katharine made up her mind to consult her guardians about a move as soon as possible. Indeed, she would have gone to see them the very next day if Uncle Henry had not already announced his intention of going into Basingstoke himself. But the thought of travelling to Basingstoke and back with her uncle was so unattractive that she decided to postpone her own visit till the day after. It seemed a harmless enough decision, but, if she had known what distress it would cause her in the weeks to come, she would have travelled in his company even if it had been twice as disagreeable.

At the time she congratulated herself on her foresight. The journey back from Basingstoke would have been highly uncomfortable. Uncle Henry was in a vile mood when he returned from his session with the lawyers who acted for the Payne estate. His horses showed signs of rough treatment as he drove up; he bellowed at the groom as he got down, and he roughly pushed aside the servant who opened the door and threw his hat and cane into the unfortunate man's face. Then he shut himself in the library and only reappeared when summoned to the dinner table.

Even though Katharine had a pretty good idea what had caused such ill humour in her uncle, she was

astonished at the change in him. His air of beaming,
self-confident benevolence had quite gone. Instead he
ate in silence, drinking heavily and beating an impatient tattoo on the table when his glass was empty.
Except for a brooding look in her direction from time
to time, he ignored the rest of the family. She looked
round. At the other end of the table her aunt, seemingly unaffected by her husband's behaviour, was deep
in conversation with her son and daughter, who were
seated on either side of her. Walter Payne, Uncle
Henry's son and heir, had only arrived that afternoon
and this was Katharine's first opportunity to study him.
Though he had given her a charming smile when his
mother had introduced them, had kissed her hand and
declared himself enchanted to meet her, his attention
had soon been caught by something else, and from
then on he had hardly spoken to her. She had the distinct impression that he had taken stock of his homeless Cousin Kate and dismissed her as unworthy of
further consideration.

Walter was tall, like his father, though less heavily
built, and he too had the Payne blue eyes, rich gold
curls and fresh complexion. Katharine felt strangely
puzzled as she looked at him. He was like, and yet not
like, Tom. He had something of the same looks, the
same readiness to laugh, the same charm, but, though
she couldn't quite put her finger on it, there was a
difference. Tom had been carelessly transparent, everything on show, nothing disguised or held back. He
might infuriate you, annoy you, upset you with his
lack of tact, but you always knew where you were with
Tom. Walter Payne's manner was altogether more
consciously charming, more carefully designed. For all

his apparent frankness, she had a feeling that there was more to him than he allowed the world to see.

She was startled out of her deliberations when Henry Payne suddenly roused himself and snapped, 'Walter! Why do you neglect your cousin in this cavalier fashion? She'll think you a boor!' As Katharine turned to look at him, surprised at his tone, he added with an attempt at geniality, 'We can't have Kate thinking you don't know how to behave, my boy.'

Father and son looked at one another in silence for a moment, then Walter shrugged his shoulders and said in a neutral tone, 'I'm sorry, sir. I wasn't aware I was misbehaving.' He turned to Katharine with a smile. 'Have I been rude, Cousin Kate? You must forgive me—I've been hearing all about Herriards from my sister and mother. They are full of plans for improvements to the house—though for my part I think it is perfect as it is. You will be sad indeed to leave it, I think.'

'Yes, I am,' said Katharine. 'I have lived here all my life. Anywhere else will seem strange at first.'

Catherine Payne turned at this. 'All your life? All the time?' Katharine nodded. 'But you must have been to London!'

'No, I've never been away from Herriards.'

Aunt Ellen's voice was heavy with disapproval as she asked, 'Do you mean to say that your grandfather made no arrangements for you to be introduced to Society? I am astonished.'

'I believe he had it in mind just before he was taken ill for the first time. There never seemed to be an opportunity after that.' Katharine spoke stiffly, resenting this criticism of her beloved grandfather.

'He should have made one! For look at the fix you are in now! At eighteen, as Miss Payne of Herriards, I daresay you might have made a very good sort of match. But at—what are you? Twenty-three?'

'Twenty-one, ma'am.'

'Really? Only twenty-one? I am surprised. But now that you are older, and Miss Payne of nowhere in particular, it will be much more difficult to find a suitable husband. I hope you will not look to me for help in the matter. It would be most inconvenient. We intend to launch Catherine this next year, and I shall need all my energies for that enterprise. Indeed, we hope for great things for her, don't we, my precious? I flatter myself that London will not often have seen such beauty as hers. There will be a great deal of expense, of course.'

Catherine Payne patted her blonde curls complacently. 'When Papa told us of your brother's death and that Herriards was consequently ours, we made such plans! Next year we are to take a house in London for the season, and I shall have a whole new wardrobe for my presentation! You cannot imagine how much I look forward to it—'

She jumped as her father's fist crashed on the table, and the storm finally broke.

'Hold your tongue! You don't know what you're talking about, miss! You none of you know what you're talking about!'

Catherine gazed at her father in hurt amazement. Then her eyes filled with tears and she turned to her mama. 'What's wrong?' she asked pathetically. 'What have I said? Why is Papa so cross? He promised we should go to London, didn't he? He promised!'

Mrs Payne said majestically, 'You are not to worry, Catherine. Your papa has guaranteed that you will be presented next year, and I shall see that he keeps his word, never fear.' She turned her attention to her husband. 'What is wrong, my love?'

Ignoring his wife, Henry Payne scowled at Katharine. 'Did it amuse you?' he asked heavily.

'What, Uncle?'

He got up and stood at the end of the table, glaring down at her. 'Don't pretend innocence with me, young lady! You allowed my poor wife to plan such changes here, you listened with a straight face while my poor little daughter talked of her dreams for her début, and all the time you knew that there wasn't the money to do half of it! How you must have been laughing!'

'What?' cried Mrs Payne. 'What are you saying, Henry?'

Henry Payne's outburst took Katharine's breath away for a moment. Then she said firmly, 'Sir, you are very mistaken. I knew of the situation, of course I did, but it was surely hardly my place to tell you of the terms of your inheritance. In fact, when I did make an attempt to say something at dinner last night, you forbade me to talk of it. But I assure you, I have never *laughed* at any of it. I don't believe I have felt like *laughing* since I heard that my brother had died and that I had…I had lost both him and my home.' Unable to continue, she got up and walked away to the windows. The gardens and terraces were bathed in the soft light of the dying sun. Herriards had never looked more beautiful. She told herself that she would survive this nightmare, she must. But she must get away from these people as soon as she could.

'Mr Payne, you will tell us, if you please, what you mean by all this!' said Mrs Payne. 'I insist! What is this talk of money?'

'Yes! Please tell us, Papa! *Please!*' Catherine's blue eyes once again filled with tears. 'Doesn't this place belong to us after all?'

'Herriards and the lands that belong to it are mine. The income from them is mine. But the lawyers here now tell me that the real wealth belonged to another branch of the family altogether. The Framptons. This girl's great-grandmother was an heiress, and her money, Frampton money, lies outside the entail. They say it has nothing to do with Herriards. It is all in a trust for your cousin here.'

'For Kate!' Aunt Ellen stared at Katharine in astonishment. 'What could she possibly want with it? No, I don't believe it—the lawyers must have made a mistake! You must question them further, Henry.'

'I'm afraid there's no mistake. My grandfather was free to leave the Frampton-Payne fortune where he wished,' said Katharine stonily, turning round again to face them.

Shock kept Aunt Ellen silent for almost a minute. Then she said blankly, 'So what are we to live on?'

Walter, who had been sitting very still throughout these exchanges, gave his father a significant glance as he got up and joined Katharine at the window. 'We must seem to you to be very mercenary,' he said. 'My father's words have obviously distressed you. But we have all had a great shock. Can you forgive us? I should imagine Herriards provides more than enough to live on, surely?'

'But not in style!' said his mother. 'Not the way we intended.'

Casting a glance at Katharine's set expression, Walter frowned at his mother and said, 'I am sure the situation is not as hopeless as it seems, Mama. We shall have to see what can be done. Meanwhile, I think my cousin has had enough of this conversation. She is looking very pale. Would you care to show me something of the garden, Kate?' He put Katharine's arm through his and led her firmly from the room, ignoring the rest of his family. Katharine, too weary to object, went with him without protest.

Chapter Three

The next day Katharine was furious to find when she went round to the stables that her Uncle Henry had already taken the phaeton out. She was forced to change her plans and, instead of driving to Basingstoke to consult her guardians, she decided to walk to Herriard Stoke to visit Tilly. The time would not be wasted. It would be useful to talk matters over with a friend before tackling Sir James and the General.

Tilly was delighted to see her, and ushered her through to the garden without ceremony. The cottage had been kept in good order during her absence and the little garden at the back was full of scent and colour. The two ladies sat under an apple tree and made themselves comfortable.

'Now, Katharine, you can tell me what is troubling you.'

She gave Tilly an account of the previous evening's discussion and ended by saying, 'One thing is certain. I could never live with my uncle and his family. I must see my guardians. I must get away.'

Tilly had never been one to beat about the bush. 'You haven't anywhere to go,' she said.

'Couldn't I stay here with you?'

Tilly smiled. 'There's nothing I would like better, but there really isn't room, my dear. Besides, your guardians would never hear of it.'

'I shall see them tomorrow! They must agree, they must! I refuse to stay with the Paynes!'

Katharine got up and walked around the garden. Miss Tillyard watched her with a worried frown. She said, 'If I were you I should wait a little before approaching General Armitage and Sir James. They will be more prepared to listen if you can speak calmly to them, show them that you are not being unreasonable. They must be persuaded that you have given living with your uncle a chance.'

'Tilly, what I fear most is that they would *never* be prepared to listen objectively. They are tired old men, and they have no notion of what they would do with me if I *didn't* stay with my uncle! What on earth my grandfather was thinking of to saddle me with such guardians I do not know!'

Though she privately agreed, Tilly did not say so. Instead she said persuasively, 'It is very early days yet. You haven't seen the Payne family at its best. People sometimes behave uncharacteristically when they have suffered a great disappointment. If Mr Payne had assumed that your grandfather's fortune, as well as Herriards, would be at his disposal, it would come as a great shock to them all to discover that this was not the case.'

'They have Herriards!' cried Katharine in tones of anguish. 'Why do they need any more?'

'Not everyone thinks of Herriards as you do. And *you* must stop thinking so much of it, my love. It is no longer your business. You must put it out of your mind and concentrate instead on what you are going to do with your own life. What can't be cured—'

'Must be endured. I know. And this is beyond curing.' There was a pause, then in a determinedly cheerful tone Katharine said, 'You're right, as usual, Tilly dear. It would be better to wait. I'll try to be patient. It's true that I can't do anything without my guardians' consent—my allowance is ridiculously small.'

'You should have had it increased when your grandfather died.'

'I know, I know! But while Tom was there, I had his authority to draw on funds from the estate, and I used them. I never thought—' Katharine stopped and swallowed. After a pause she went on, 'I was lazy, I suppose. I should have looked into it a long time ago.' She paused. 'Those old men still think of me as a child. And, worse still, a female child! It would be so much better if I had a man I could trust to represent me, someone they would respect...'

'What about your brother's friend, the one who wrote to you?'

'Lord Calthorpe?'

'Yes. He offered his help and it sounded as if he meant it. Why don't you write to him again? I should think he is exactly the sort of person the General and Sir James would listen to.'

'I think I will,' Katharine said slowly. 'You're right. Lord Calthorpe sounded like a man one could trust. I wonder if he is still in England? Tilly, you're a genius!

I'll write to Lord Calthorpe tonight! And this time I shall ask him to come and see me.'

Katharine was reminded of Tilly's words when she came downstairs the next morning. Uncle Henry seemed to have recovered from his displeasure of the previous day, and greeted her with a benign smile. He led her personally into the breakfast room, where her aunt was sitting. Neither Walter nor Catherine had yet appeared.

'My dear Kate,' her aunt said as she sat down, 'my dear Kate, what must you be thinking of us? I'm afraid we have not behaved as we ought. You will forgive us, won't you?'

'Of course,' Katharine murmured uncomfortably.

Her uncle cleared his throat and added, 'I hope you will overlook what I may have said last night, my dear. I'd had a hard day, d'y' see?' He gave her a look. 'You didn't take me seriously, I hope?' Katharine shook her head wordlessly, and he laughed and went on, 'Of course you didn't! I told Walter so. Kate's too sensible a girl, I told him, to be upset by a few hasty words. He was quite concerned about you.'

'The dear boy,' said Mrs Payne fondly. 'It has been very hard for us this past month, Kate. My health is not good, and when I am tired I, too, sometimes make mistakes. I dare say you thought me a little harsh and unfeeling when I arrived. It was all so confusing... But believe me, your rooms are yours for as long as you want them. I would not dream of turning you out of them.'

'You are very kind, ma'am,' said Katharine. 'But I intend to consult my guardians about my future. Miss

Tillyard and I have considered setting up house together.'

'You want to live with a *governess!*' exclaimed her uncle.

'As I said when you first arrived, Uncle, Miss Tillyard is a friend.'

'Oh, she may well be a very good sort of creature, but she is not exactly suitable company for a young lady of fortune! I don't imagine for one moment that your trustees would agree to such a plan.'

Aunt Ellen cried, 'No, indeed! It is an absurd idea!'

'I do not think so, ma'am,' said Katharine.

'Child, you do not realise what it would mean. Social ostracism! No, no, you would do much better to live with us, your family. It is only right!'

'Thank you, but I will see my guardians first, ma'am,' said Katharine firmly.

'Oh, don't be so obstinate, girl!' snapped Aunt Ellen, forgetting herself.

Giving his wife a warning look, Uncle Henry said gently, 'My love, discussing business with older gentlemen is no occupation for a young lady. I think you should leave it to me to deal with them.'

'No!' exclaimed Katharine. She made herself speak more calmly. 'Thank you, Uncle, but your intervention is not necessary. My guardians are elderly, but I have known them all my life.' Then, taking some liberty with the facts, she went on, 'In any case, I already have someone to act for me if it should be required.'

'Oh? Who is that?'

'A…a very good friend of Tom's. Lord Calthorpe. I have already written to him.' She did not say that the letter had not yet been despatched. It was at present in the hall, waiting to be taken to the receiving office in Basingstoke.

Her uncle eyed her thoughtfully. He said, 'Well, it all seems very odd. Your guardians received me very kindly yesterday.'

'Indeed, they seemed inclined to regard your uncle's plans with favour,' added Aunt Ellen with a satisfied smile.

Katharine felt a surge of anger but asked evenly, 'What plans are those, sir?'

'As your aunt said—that you should remain in our care for the foreseeable future. After that...well, we shall see, we shall see.'

Katharine rose. 'Your thought for me does you credit, Uncle Henry, but it is somewhat premature. I should prefer to settle my future for myself, directly with Sir James and General Armitage. By the way, exactly when did you see them?'

'Yesterday, my dear. I thought it only right to make myself known to them. And I took Walter along with me. We had a very pleasant half-hour with both Sir James and the General.'

'Since it was such a large party, I am surprised that you did not think to invite me to go with you, sir. Any discussions with my guardians surely concern me more directly than they do your son.'

'There you go again, Kate! When will you realise that it really isn't proper for a young lady to be so independent? You are no longer alone in the world. Your aunt and I are here to look after your interests.'

'Do you not rather mean ''my fortune'', Uncle Henry? Forgive me, but it seems to me that your concern for my safety is so much greater since you discovered the truth about the Herriard estate.'

Henry Payne smiled blandly. 'You're right, of course. But what is wrong in that? You are a considerable heiress, Kate. Would you rather you were left to the mercy of a selfish and self-seeking world? I think not.'

Aunt Ellen took one of Katharine's hands in hers. 'Our only concern, Kate, is to protect your interests. Poor child, you have no one else to look after you.'

'Indeed, ma'am, you underestimate me,' Katharine said, removing her hand. 'I have looked after myself, and this estate, for years. I need no protectors. And I wish most of all to make my own decisions about my future.'

Uncle Henry shook his head. 'Sir James said that you were wilful, that you had had your own way for far too long, and I can now see that he is right. But I fancy he will soon bring you round to our way of thinking. By all means see him, if you wish. It will make little difference.'

Katharine felt a shiver of apprehension. She said desperately, 'Sir James's notions are somewhat old-fashioned. But he has always been fond of me. I cannot believe he would force me to do anything which would make me unhappy. I must see him today. And I'll talk to General Armitage, too. Excuse me.'

Katharine ordered the phaeton and set off for Basingstoke as soon as she had changed her dress. Delay had already cost her the initiative. She would not wait another minute before talking to her guardians herself. She would not let them ignore her. To remain with the

Paynes was impossible, and she must make them see it.

In Basingstoke she had difficulty at first in seeing Sir James—his manservant said that his master was distinctly unwell, and unwilling to receive visitors. But Katharine knew her guardian of old. When faced with a problem of any kind, Sir James took refuge in illness. She insisted on being seen.

'I don't know why you have to disturb me, Katharine. You always were a headstrong child. What is it?' said Sir James testily.

Katharine explained her plan to leave Herriards and live somewhere else with Miss Tillyard as a companion.

'Why on earth do you want to do such a foolish thing?'

'I...I do not think that my uncle and I will deal very happily together,' said Katharine uncomfortably.

'What nonsense! Mr Payne seems an excellent fellow! And that son of his is as agreeable a young man as I've met in a long time!'

'Please believe me, sir! My uncle and I will never agree. Indeed, I refuse to stay at Herriards with them!'

'Refuse? Refuse? What do you mean, miss? Of course you won't refuse!'

'But I—'

'Don't say another word, Katharine! The trouble with you is that you've been allowed to go your own way for too long! I always thought you had too much say in the running of Herriards. That ain't work for a female. And now it has gone to your head.'

Katharine was incensed at the injustice of this remark. 'Taking charge of Herriards was not by my choice, sir. When my grandfather was ill and Tom was away there was no one else to do it!' she said hotly. Sir James glared at her, and she forced herself to speak more reasonably. 'But you are quite right. I am bound to feel injured when my uncle takes over the estate I thought would be...would be Tom's. So surely it would be wiser to let me go elsewhere?'

'Oh, no! You are not going to cozen me like that, girl! It's time you learned a bit of humility. Dammit, a chit of a girl like you ought to be *happy* to leave the running of Herriards to someone else. You should be thinking of dresses and dances, not trying to tell grown men what to do.'

'But I don't want to think of nothing more than dresses and dances!'

'It's time you did. And about marriage. If your grandfather had taught you to think more about that instead of running estates and the like, we wouldn't be in the fix we are now! However, your uncle has some very sensible ideas on that subject, too...but we'll speak of that another time.'

'What ideas has my uncle been suggesting? What right has he to suggest anything about my future? Please let me leave Herriards, Sir James. I—'

'No, not another word, Katharine. My mind is made up. The General and I may be two old bachelors, but what your uncle said made sense to us. He and his wife have children of their own—they understand young people, and from all accounts they are already very fond of you. We believe that they can give you exactly the sort of attention a young girl needs.'

When Katharine made a gesture of protest Sir James

went on firmly, 'You must put away this resentment and give them a chance.'

In despair Katharine said, 'Will you at least increase my allowance, Sir James?'

Sir James leaned back in his chair, put one hand to his brow and rang the bell on the table at his side with the other. 'No I shan't! Now, no more, please! My head is aching, and I'm sure one of my attacks is imminent. I should never have agreed to see you. I knew I should pay for the exertion.' He waved a vague hand at his ward. 'Come back another time, Katharine, when you are in a more reasonable frame of mind. Meanwhile, be grateful for your uncle's kindness. Ah, Roundell, see Miss Payne out, if you please. And then return immediately to attend to me. I must lie down. I don't feel at all the thing, not at all!'

Katharine left Sir James's house feeling angry and distinctly worried. Her uncle seemed to have worked his spell on one of her guardians at least. But, she told herself, General Armitage would have been harder to convince. She set off to see her second guardian full of determination to put her case to him as convincingly as she could. However, when she arrived at the General's house she suffered an even greater disappointment. He had left that morning for Bath and would be away for several weeks. Her heart sank. Henry Payne must have known about this, she thought bitterly, but he had said nothing to her. Once again her delay in coming to Basingstoke had cost her dear.

As Katharine returned to Herriards she was dismayed, but not yet defeated. It might take longer than she had planned, but she was determined to get her guardians' permission sooner or later. Sir James had always been something of a hypochondriac, and he was not fond of any disturbance. But she would ask to see him again as soon as she thought expedient. He couldn't refuse forever. And Bath was not the other side of the moon. She would write to the General straight away. Sooner or later she would escape from Herriards!

But even after summer had faded into autumn, and autumn was beginning to decline into the first signs of winter, Katharine had still not found a way of leaving.

October 1815

One dismal day in late October Katharine stood in her sitting room and frowned as she looked down at the garden below her window. It showed the signs of neglect which were beginning to be seen all round Herriards. She shut her eyes and gave the glass a thump with her fist. She must not give way to despair, she must not. But how long could she stay strong? Never before had she felt so helpless, so alone. There was still no prospect of escape, and now, to add to her worries, the plan hinted at by Sir James and her uncle was becoming all too clear. She was to marry Walter, thus at one stroke solving the problem of her future, and at the same time returning the Frampton fortune to the coffers of the Herriards estate. The prospect horrified her. Though she was certain that she would never, not even for one moment, consider such a match, everyone else in the house seemed to take it for granted.

Katharine was under constant pressure to spend time with Walter, to respond to his overtures, his offers of help and sympathy. In the early days, it was true, she had accepted his company, though it hadn't taken her long to realise that Walter's charm was all on the surface. Underneath he was essentially a cold man, seeking his own advantage in everything he did. But once she realised what the Paynes were planning, she had avoided Walter wherever possible. It wasn't easy. He was inordinately vain, and seemed to find it quite impossible to believe that Katharine was not attracted to him. For a time he had continued to exert his charm, teasing her for her shyness, suggesting that she was playing games with him. But recently he had begun to realise that she was serious in her refusals, and, though it hadn't put him off, his attitude had changed. He was becoming more persistent, while at the same time taking less trouble to disguise his true character. Katharine had found that the best way to avoid him was to keep to her rooms, and, apart from meals, she now spent very little time with the rest of the family. It all added to her sense of isolation.

There was a knock at the door, and it opened before she could say anything. Walter came into the room. She looked at him coldly. As usual he was immaculately dressed in clothes that were the acme of suitability. Today he was the country gentleman. His linen was, as always, spotless, his boots shone brilliantly, his buckskins were without stain or crease, his coat fitted like a glove. The guinea-gold hair was brushed with contrived carelessness over one brow, and his smile gleamed whitely as he sauntered in.

Katharine winced as a sudden vision of her brother Tom, coming into this very room a year ago, flashed across her mind. The contrast was painful. Tom had been out for a ride, his fair hair blown by the wind into a tousle of curls round a laughing, bronzed face. His buff breeches were spattered with mud, and his old green riding coat sat comfortably rather than elegantly across his broad shoulders. She had been annoyed with him, she remembered, had protested at his coming into the house in such a mess. With his usual insouciance he had only laughed the more, and in the end she had laughed too... They had seemed to spend most of their time together laughing...

Dear God, why wasn't Tom here to help her now? But Tom was dead, he had died at Waterloo, leaving her on her own to deal with the consequences—including the unwelcome attentions of her cousin Walter.

Katharine pulled herself together and said coolly, 'How many times do I have to tell you, Walter? Your father returned these rooms to me for my own private use. This is *my* room. And you are not welcome in it. Please leave! Now!'

'Demme, if you're not the most unfriendly girl I ever met, Kate,' he said with unimpaired good humour. 'As prickly as a bramble bush. How else can I talk to you if I don't come up here? You're never seen downstairs except at mealtimes. Come on, Kate! Be nice to your cousin. I'm starved for the sight of you.'

Katharine stiffened as he came further into the room, but she didn't move. Any sign of weakness would encourage him. She said stonily, 'I've told you. I like my own company.'

'That ain't very friendly, Kate.'

Katharine didn't answer, but turned back to the window. Walter came up behind her and put his arm round her waist. 'What's wrong with me, sweetheart?'

Katharine twisted out of his grasp and pushed him away. 'Stop fondling me, Walter. I don't like it, any more than I like you. I am not your sweetheart, and I wish you to go!'

Walter frowned and said, 'I wish I knew what the devil goes on in that mind of yours, Kate. Why are you always so hard on me? It's not as if there's anyone else—is there? If so, I don't know where you can have met him.' He studied her for a moment then shook his head. 'No, I'll swear that you haven't met anyone else…but there's something…' He moved closer and she stiffened.

'I've warned you, Walter. Stay away from me!'

Her cousin smiled. 'You look so fierce—like a little wild creature. The temptation to master you is almost irresistible. But there's no need to fight me, Kate. I'm on your side. I'd be your friend if you'd only let me be.'

'A real friend would help me to get away from this place and your wretched family!'

'I'll take you from here the minute you say the word, sweetheart! All you have to do is to marry me.'

'That is not a solution I would contemplate for one second. Now please get out of my room and leave me in peace!'

Walter regarded her thoughtfully. 'You have a great deal of spirit, Kate—I admire that. But you'll give in sooner or later, my dear. Apart from that old woman in the village, you have no friends that I can see. And, for all your fortune, you can't get your hands on very much cash. How will you ever escape? I shouldn't place your hopes on your guardians, if I were you. They aren't going to take you away from us. They'd have to find somewhere else for you to go, and Sir James isn't going to give himself that much trouble. Besides, they are delighted with my father—and with me. They think we are excellent fellows and quite right, too! We've worked hard to persuade them. No, Kate, face up to it. You'll have to give in in the end. Why not sooner rather than later? I'm sure I could make you happy.'

'You'll never have the chance! I'm as much of a fighter as Tom in my own weak, helpless, female way! I won't be beaten by such contemptible creatures as you and your father.'

'You poor deluded thing!' said Walter laughing softly. 'But I can wait. I'm looking forward to the fight. You won't be the first I've tamed.'

'Are you going, or shall I call one of the servants?'

Walter laughed again, his blue eyes alive with merriment. 'I'm going, my sweet. But I'll just take something on account…' Without warning he pulled Katharine towards him and bent her back against his arm. His fingers pulled her hair cruelly until she was forced to look up at him. He kissed her hard, then pushed her away, so that she stumbled against the window. All pretence of good humour quite gone, he said coldly, 'You'll have to learn something about me, Kate, my dear. I don't like being called a contemptible creature by a dab of a female. It's apt to make me rough. Don't do it again.' With that he turned and went out of the room. Katharine was left shaken and trembling by the window.

She stayed there staring out for some time. Walter's

attack had shocked her. Nothing remotely like it had ever happened to her before. Till now the men in her life might have been careless, had often forgotten that she belonged to the weaker sex—indeed, Katharine herself had frequently denied it!—but no one had ever before humiliated her in such a manner. In some ways she was very innocent for her age. At sixteen she had been forced to abandon a normal life in Society in order to look after her grandfather, who had become increasingly reclusive. In her few dealings with the outside world she had deliberately suppressed any femininity, preferring to treat the men she met in a businesslike manner. But now Walter's attack had made her aware of her vulnerability as a woman. And, for all her courage, Katharine began to feel the stirrings of fear.

For the first time she looked at her future realistically. Her uncle had made clear his desire—no, his *intention*—that his son should marry her. She could not forget the ruthless speed with which Henry Payne had acted immediately after his arrival. No sooner had he discovered that the Payne fortune was in Katharine's hands than he had persuaded her guardians to say she must stay at Herriards in his care. Even at that early stage he had taken Walter with him to visit them, Walter with his charm and his manly appearance, who was bound to make a favourable impression on them. At the moment Henry and his son were still hoping that Katharine's isolation from any other company, her loneliness, would make her vulnerable to Walter's powers of attraction. But when that failed she was fairly certain that other, less scrupulous, ways of per-

suasion would be found. And where could she turn
then?

Her distress grew. Fear mingled with feelings of
rage and frustration—not only with the living but,
worse than that, with the dead, too. She had loved her
brother and her grandfather, had grieved, and was still
grieving, for them, but between them they had left her
alone in the world, with no one to help her to fight
Henry Payne, or to cope with his son. Clouds of resentment were beginning to obscure her memories of
the two people she had loved best in the world. A
groan of despair escaped her. She *must* get out of the
house! She would go to Tilly. They *must* find some
way to save her from catastrophe.

It was a cold, grey day and the wind was tossing
the branches overhead. As she marched along the path
to Herriard Stoke, the weather seemed in keeping with
Katharine's mood. Her sense of injustice was growing
by the minute. She was only twenty-one, but she felt
that the cares of the world were bowing her down. Her
guardians were useless! Why on earth hadn't her
grandfather done as she had asked and replaced them
with younger men—his lawyer, perhaps, or his man
of business? General Armitage and Sir James Farrow
might well be the men of repute and honour he had
called them, but they were of little help in her present
predicament. Katharine kicked a branch which lay in
her path and gave an exclamation of angry frustration.
Tired old gentlemen, however honourable, were not
the ones to deal with a scheming, conniving villain
such as Henry Payne. Nor with his *worm* of a son!

Where in Heaven's name was she to find the help she needed?

As she came through the gate which led into the churchyard a sudden gust of wind caught her cloak and blew it up into the air. It was too much! Muttering, desperately trying to hold her hat in one hand, and anchor her cloak with the other, she ran full tilt into what felt like a wall. She staggered and sat down.

'I'm sorry! Ma'am, are you hurt? No, don't move, let me see if you are hurt first.' A tall figure squatted beside her and started to feel her legs. This was too much!

'Don't *touch* me, sir!' Katharine exclaimed fiercely. 'And don't try to help me get up, either! You've done enough damage already.'

To her annoyance the stranger ignored her words and, taking hold of her arm, helped her to rise. 'Let me escort you to your home, ma'am. I shan't be happy till I know you are not hurt.'

As soon as Katharine was on her feet she shook his hand off her arm and looked up angrily into his face. It was a good face, not exactly handsome, but definitely attractive. Just now it showed nothing but concern, but there was discipline and firmness in the jaw and mouth, and lines of laughter round the steady hazel eyes.

Katharine saw none of this. She said furiously, 'I told you! I'm perfectly able to manage, thank you! Will you kindly get out of my way?' Without looking at him again she started to walk away, brushing some leaves and mud from her cloak as she went. But Fate was not on Katharine's side. Her hat, without a hand to hold it, was attacked by another sudden gust of wind and was borne aloft, sailing away across the churchyard.

With a speed and dexterity which secretly impressed her, the unknown gentleman leapt after it and trapped it after a short chase. He returned and presented it to her with a bow. There was a distinct twinkle in his eye as he said, 'Forgive me for interfering yet again, ma'am. May I assist you to put it on?'

Katharine tied the strings of her cloak with a vicious tug, then more or less snatched the hat from the gentleman's hand. She was almost in tears. The fall had winded her more than she would admit even to herself. And now this…this *man* was laughing at her! 'I…I…' Her fingers were trembling as she fumbled with her hat.

'Allow me.' He took it from her, placed it carefully on her head and tied the strings under her chin. His touch was deft and quite impersonal. 'And now I shall accompany you to wherever it is you're going. Come!' He put his hand under her arm. She was appalled to find herself feeling helplessly feminine, experiencing an almost irresistible desire to lean on this stranger's arm and let him take control. If only she could just once place her burdens on such a man's shoulders… She stiffened. How could she be so weak? In her present situation she could not afford such idiocy. Strength came from independence.

She thrust him away from her again and said pugnaciously, 'Thank you for rescuing my hat. But I neither need nor want any more of your help. Goodbye, sir.' She marched along the path and turned into the street without a backward glance. But at Tilly's gate she turned and looked back. He was standing at the corner, presumably waiting to make sure she arrived safely at her destination. What a *busybody* he was! When he saw her looking he gave a slight bow, but Katharine ignored him and went in through Tilly's door.

Chapter Four

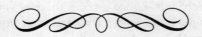

There was a small fire in Tilly's tiny grate. Katharine went over and warmed her hands, while her governess hung up her hat and cloak.

'What on earth have you been doing, Katharine? Your clothes are covered in mud!'

'I…I fell. In the churchyard. The wind caught me just as I came round the corner.'

'Did you trip?'

'No. I…I…er…bumped into someone and lost my balance. But I shall be fine in a moment. I'm a little cold, that's all.'

'You shall have a warm drink in an instant. Mrs Banks from the inn brought some of her raspberry cordial this morning. Sit there while I get it.' Tilly hurried to put a kettle on the hob and fetch the cordial and some beakers. Then she sat down in the chair on the other side of the fire and said, 'But what are you thinking of coming out on a day like this, my dear? I am delighted to see you, of course, but it's hardly a fit day for walking.'

'I had to get out, Tilly. It…it suddenly all seemed

too much.' To Katharine's shame her voice trembled and she was hard put not to cry.

'Oh, my dear child! Is it Walter, or his father?'

Katharine gazed at Tilly's concerned face and tried to pull herself together. 'It's hard to say. I don't know which of them is worse. I feel so…trapped. Oh, Tilly, I never thought…never thought I should long as I do to leave Herriards. I once loved it so.' Her voice broke.

Tilly sighed and said, 'I assume that you haven't heard from General Armitage?'

'No. He promised to come and see me when he returned from Bath but there has been no word. I assume he's still there.'

'But he's been away for three months now!'

'The trouble is, Tilly, that he doesn't see any need for urgency. Oh, what a fool I was! If I had known three months ago what a cunning man my uncle is, I would have made sure that the General heard what I had to say first.'

'You mustn't be too hard on yourself, Katharine. Tom's death was still too close. You weren't thinking very clearly.'

'Well, whatever the reason, it gave my uncle his chance. He impressed those two old men the way he impresses everyone outside the house. And now Sir James doesn't think it important to see me again, and the General thinks I'm unhappy simply because I haven't yet resigned myself to the new regime at Herriards.'

'I suppose that's natural…'

'Oh, yes! And so patronising! You'd think I was twelve, not twenty-one! Instead of coming to see what

was wrong, he recommended me to be a good girl and
do my best to learn to live with the changes.'

'That would be good advice, Katharine, in other circumstances. But as it is… My dear, why don't you try
again? Write to him once more! More strongly this
time.'

'What is the use? My cousin has pulled the wool
over that old man's eyes, in the same way that he has
deceived Sir James. Neither of my guardians will listen to me. I'm not to be taken seriously.'

'Sir James is ill. You can't blame him for not questioning your cousin's motives.'

'I don't blame *him!* I blame my grandfather for not
replacing them both with younger men! I blame my
brother for leaving me alone like this with no one to
turn to…' Katharine got up and walked about the tiny
room, twisting her hands. 'Day after day I watch
that…that greedy villain milking Herriards till there
will soon be nothing left. The fences go without repair,
roofs are leaking, fields are left unplanted… And yet
Henry Payne has only to smile, to flatter, to clap people on the back and tell a few stories, and everyone
in the county thinks he is a great fellow! I tell you,
Tilly, I am heartsick to see it all.'

'There, there, my love. There, there!' Tilly put her
arms round Katharine and led her back to her chair.
Then she sat her down and poured out some cordial.
'Drink that, and listen to me. General Armitage was
right in one respect. You *must* stop feeling personally
responsible for Herriards! I know it is hard, but, indeed, there is nothing you can do, Katharine! If you
go on in this way you will be ill! I am rather surprised
that you can't see this for yourself—since you grew

up you have always been such a sensible girl. But I suspect it is more than this, isn't it? Tell me!'

Katharine straightened up and tried to speak calmly. 'Uncle Henry is determined to push me into marriage to his son. He has my guardians' approval. And now Walter is... Walter is pushing his claims as well. He gets bolder by the day. I have absolutely no intention of giving way, but if you only knew what a strain it is! They are both so devious. I am so afraid that I shall have a brainstorm one day and wake up to find myself married to Walter after all. I have nightmares about it...' Katharine got up again as if she couldn't bear to be still. 'Worst of all—' She stopped, then went on, 'Worst of all, Grandpapa and Tom—' She broke off, then went on doggedly. 'I used to find consolation in remembering the happy times we had together, but now I can only feel resentment! Why have they left me to face all this alone? Oh, Tilly, I feel so wicked! So ungrateful! What am I to do?'

Tilly's face showed real anxiety. 'You must get away, my dear!'

'I can't! I haven't anything worth mentioning to live on! And, until I am twenty-five, I can't have my allowance increased without the consent of my guardians. That's another four years away.'

'It is a pity you never found anyone you could marry before now. To be so alone in the world is not pleasant.'

Katharine shook her head. 'I suppose before Grandfather was ill I might have met someone, when Tom and I used to visit the neighbours. But, compared with Tom, they all seemed so uninteresting! And my grandfather never allowed Tom to invite his friends to stay—he didn't approve of most of them.'

'Old Mr Payne,' said Tilly carefully, 'was the best of employers and a wonderful man. But he had a tendency to seek his own comfort rather than the best interests of others, especially when he was older.'

'You mean he didn't *wish* me to meet anyone I liked? Oh, no, Tilly! I am sure if I had found someone he would have been delighted. Oh, you're wrong! He loved me—I'm sure he wanted me to be happy. Later, of course, when he was ill... Well, it was different then. I didn't even want to leave him on his own. And in any case I never seemed to have the time for gadding about—with Tom away I was always too busy. So I lost touch with what friends we had...so many of them have died or moved away. And now...there's no one but you.'

Katharine came back to the fire and sat down. She took a sip of her cordial, then hugged the beaker close to her as if seeking comfort from its warmth. Tilly gazed at her in concern. Katherine's fingers were bone thin, and her face was pale and worn. It was difficult to believe that just four months ago she had been a lively young girl, full of energy and enterprise, running Herriards estate, looking forward to her brother's return, to the time when Tom should come home and take over. Now she looked years older, the spring had quite gone out of her step, and that wonderful smile, which had been so appealing in both the young Paynes, seemed to have vanished forever. The shock and distress of Tom's death and its consequences could have accounted for it during the first few months. But she should now be recovering, shedding the melancholy, which had enveloped her then. This growing resentment towards people she had adored was seriously worrying. Tilly cast about in her mind for something—anything—that might be done.

'Why don't you write to Lord Calthorpe again?' she said at last.

This suggestion roused Katharine, but not quite in the way Miss Tillyard had intended. 'Yes!' she said bitterly. 'There's another miserable specimen! So eager to write the moment Tom died. Such a charming letter, too! Saddened and grieved by Tom's death...di...da...di...da...such close friends, heard such a lot about me...would like to come to see me...entirely at my service... You yourself said what a charming letter it was. Someone to trust, we both thought. And what happened after that? Nothing! Now that I really need someone, charming Lord Calthorpe isn't available. And he must be back from France again by now! '

'You did say in your first letter that you needed time—'

'I did need time! But I wrote again later...'

'I remember. It was soon after Mr Payne and his family had arrived.'

'Yes. Even as early as that I thought that I needed someone. Someone who had known Tom, who might even help me to talk to my wretched guardians. So I wrote again. Uselessly. There wasn't a whisper from our noble friend.'

'Perhaps your letter went astray? You weren't sure of his address.'

The burst of energy had faded. 'It might have,' Katharine said listlessly. 'But I doubt it. I sent it to the

War Office address in London which Tom gave me to use. No, it's far more likely that Lord Calthorpe found life in London too amusing to bother. After all, his great friend died in June—a full month or more before. That's a *very* long time for a busy man to remember a great friend, don't you agree? Why should he feel obliged to leave his friends and come all this way to see a stranger? He probably assumed that my cousins were all the protection I needed.'

'I don't like to hear you speaking like this, Katharine. You are not usually so bitter. Besides, it's possible your brother never mentioned Mr Henry Payne and his family. Lord Calthorpe is probably unaware of the real situation.'

'I don't suppose he would care if he did! Don't let's talk of him any more, Tilly. He is just one more disappointment in a world that seems to be full of them. But if I ever meet him…' Katharine looked moodily at her drink, then finished it off. 'I must go back—it will soon be dark. I'm sorry to have been such a misery. I promise to be more cheerful next time. Goodbye, dearest friend!' Katharine bent over and kissed the little governess's cheek. Tilly held the girl's slender form to her for a moment, then let her go to walk her out to the gate.

'Think about writing to Lord Calthorpe again,' she said. 'And this time let me take the letter to the Receiving Office.'

Katharine stared at her. 'What are you suggesting?'

When Tilly stared back at her without saying a word, Katharine asked incredulously, 'You're surely not saying that Uncle Henry somehow stopped the letter?'

'I'm not suggesting anything. Except that you write again—and let me take it to the Receiving Office. Goodbye, my dear. Something will turn up, you'll see.'

As Tilly went back into her cottage she muttered to herself, 'Pray God it does! And soon!'

Meanwhile Katharine's stranger had walked back through the churchyard and into the church. Here he went into the Payne Chapel to the left of the chancel and stood gazing up at a new white marble plaque on the wall.

Sacred to the memory of
Thomas George Frampton Payne
1791–1815
Killed in action at the glorious battle of Waterloo
Only son of the late George Frampton Payne and
his wife Harriet
and beloved grandson of the late Thomas
Frampton Payne
of Herriards House
He won the affection of his fellow-officers
and the respect of his commanders
for his courage in action and his loyalty to his
friends
throughout campaigns fought in Portugal, Spain,
France and Belgium
Deeply mourned by his loving sister Katharine
who has lost the best of brothers and a very dear
companion.

Adam Calthorpe stood for some minutes before this silent tribute to Tom, laughing, devil-may-care Tom.

They had more than once saved each other on the field. And he had so often kept Tom out of trouble *off* the field. It seemed wrong that he should not have been there when Fate at last caught up with Tom Payne…

If she was married to you she'd be safe. Tom's words echoed in Adam's mind as he studied the simple tablet. He had not expected to be so moved at this memorial. So much had happened in the last months that memories of his life in the Army before Waterloo had been pushed to the back of his mind. But now he stood in the chapel, remembering so many campaigns, remembering the warmth of his friend's vivid personality, the ever-present laughter, the golden hair forever flopping over one eye, the reckless courage, the ready repentance when his impish sense of humour had taken him too far… And then the night of the Duchess of Richmond's ball, the night before the last great battle. Tom had been ablaze with excitement for most of the evening. But shortly before their ways had separated he had been, just for a few moments, uncharacteristically serious, worried about his sister's future… *If she was married to you she'd be safe.*

Adam stirred restlessly. That was the last time he had seen Tom. Ivo had given him the news two days later. The battle was almost over, the French in retreat when a shell from one of the last French guns to fire had killed Tom outright.

'I shall never forget the last I saw of him, Adam. You remember that look of his? The rest of us were fairly worn—it had been a long, hard fight. But Tom was charging up and down, urging his men on as if

he was fresh out of barracks. He was laughing! If ever
a man died doing what he loved most, that man was
Tom Payne.'

'You're right,' Adam had said sombrely. 'He was a
born soldier. And could have been a great one. I'm
sorry he's gone—I'll miss him.' After a moment's silence he went on, 'That sister of his is in trouble.
Tom's death will bring problems, as well as grief. I'll
write to her immediately.'

And he had. And he had written again. He had written four times in all. But apart from a polite acknowl-
edgement of his original letter, putting him off from
visiting her in the immediate future, he had not heard
a word from Miss Payne.

It had taken longer than he had thought it would to
get back to England. So many of the Duke's staff had
been killed or injured at Waterloo that Adam had been
required to accompany his Commander-in-Chief to
Paris. He had eventually managed to get away in September, and only then by pleading that his newly acquired estates in England urgently needed his attention. Since his return he had spent all his time on his
estate near Bath, working with his lawyers and agents
to sort out the tangle caused by his uncle's unexpected
death and his own long absence abroad.

But he had not forgotten his responsibility towards
Katharine Payne, and when there had been no reply to
his fourth letter he had voiced his anxieties to his
mother.

'It's clear, Adam! You must go to Hampshire at
once. The poor girl might be in *danger!*'

'Ma'am, don't let your imagination run away with
you! Katharine Payne is living in her old home, sur-

rounded by her cousins. How could she possibly be in danger? Old General Armitage seems happy enough about her.'

'General Armitage? What has he to say to anything?'

'He's one of Miss Payne's guardians.'

'Really? How did you know that?'

'Tom once mentioned him. So when I was in Bath on business recently I looked the old fellow up—he's taking the waters there. Since I was already acquainted with him, I thought it would do no harm to have a word about Miss Payne. His memory may not be what it was, but I would respect his opinion on most matters.'

'What did he say?'

'He is quite sure that Katharine Payne is being well-looked after, though she's naturally a bit down at the moment. She was always a touch strong-willed and he thinks that having to give up control of Herriards has upset her, as well. But he has no fears for her. He's met Henry Payne and likes him. He thought him a very sound chap, a sensible, kindly fellow, and well-respected in the neighbourhood, too. The son Walter made a very good impression on the old man, too. Though...' He paused.

'Well? What is it?'

'Tom didn't like Walter Payne. But there wasn't anything specific. There's nothing to suggest that these cousins, apparently perfectly respectable people, would keep Katharine Payne locked up incommunicado! Isn't it far more likely that she is happy enough not to need help from outside?'

'I still don't like it, Adam! Unless the girl is shock-

ingly ill-mannered she ought to write to reassure you,
at least!'

'Well, that's what worries me, too. Tom was careless, but he knew how to behave. I confess that I
should like to see for myself what is going on at Herriards. I don't at all mind paying them a visit, now
that most of Calthorpe's problems have been sorted
out. The difficulty is—'

'That you don't like the idea of forcing yourself on
a girl who would apparently rather not meet you? My
dear boy, you're being far too scrupulous! I don't
know why she should be so reluctant. You're a handsome enough fellow. Most girls would be delighted to
make your acquaintance. You're very eligible!'

Adam grinned. 'You wouldn't be biassed in my favour, would you, Ma?'

'Not at all!' Mrs Calthorpe reached up and kissed
her son. 'I was never so happy as when you returned
from the wars safe and sound, Adam. But you cannot
call me a doting parent. I just wish that you would
find a wife! I have an absurd wish to be a grandmother! It's time you married!'

'I assure you, Mama, I fully intend to!' He grew
serious. 'It's strange. The night before Waterloo Tom
suggested that I should marry his sister.'

'Just out of the blue? Gracious me! What a very
odd suggestion! You've never even met her, have
you?'

'No. But Tom was worried about her. I had told
him that I would look for a wife, you see, and he saw
it as a solution to his problem.'

'I should hope you can do better than to take an
unknown girl to wife merely to solve someone else's

problem, Adam!' said his mother somewhat tartly. 'Why did her brother have to ask among his friends to find her a husband? She must be an absolute antidote!'

'I don't think she can be. Tom was a handsome fellow—blond, blue eyes, regular features—and he always said that his sister was very like him. She's an heiress as well. I don't think finding her a husband would be difficult.' He considered for a moment. 'He was quite pressing. Poor Tom!'

Some business matter intervened, and their conversation had to be abandoned. But the next day his mother broached the subject again. 'I think I may have solved your problem, Adam.'

'Which particular problem is that, ma'am?' asked her son with a harassed look. Life in charge of a large country estate was not all enjoyment and ease.

'The Payne place is in Hampshire, is it not? Not far from Basingstoke? Well, I have some good friends near there who would be delighted if we paid them a visit. We could stay with the Quentins and still be in Dorking for Christmas.'

'Dorking?'

'I should like to spend Christmas in Bridge House, Adam. It's our old home. Calthorpe is beautiful, but it won't be a real home until it has a mistress. Your father brought me to Bridge House when I was a bride, and I've always loved it. Christmas there was always so…so cosy! Will you not spend Christmas with me there?'

'Of course I will! Are…are the Redshaws still our neighbours?'

'Oh, yes—and grander than ever! Ever since Julia

married Viscount Balmenny, John Redshaw has been extending the Court to match Balmenny Castle. You never saw so many turrets! But Julia hardly ever comes to visit her parents—she spends most of her time in London—or Ireland.'

Putting Julia Redshaw firmly out of his mind, Adam said, 'Spending Christmas at Bridge House is an excellent idea! And to visit the Quentins on the way is an even better one. If we were staying within reach of Herriards, it wouldn't be out of order for me to pay a visit. Miss Payne could hardly regard that as an imposition.'

'I shall write tonight. The Quentins will be so pleased—they have been urging me to visit them for a year or more.'

Everything had gone very easily after that. The day after Adam and his mother had arrived at the Quentins', the two ladies settled happily in Mrs Quentin's boudoir for a day of gossip about old times. But with a touch of embarrassment Mr Quentin excused himself to Adam. It was most unfortunate, but he was not free to entertain him that day. Adam assured him quite sincerely that he was perfectly happy to find his own amusement, and lost no time in riding over to Herriard Stoke. He left his groom in charge of the horses at the local inn, and walked to the church. Just a couple of miles away was Herriards, where Tom and his sister had grown up. And here was the last of Tom, this simple tablet on a church wall... *If she was married to you she'd be safe.*

It had been an absurd idea, born of Tom's sudden fear of leaving his sister alone in the world. But though

Adam had not made any commitment to marry the girl, he had promised to make sure she was looked after. His mother was right. Writing four letters and consulting General Armitage was not enough. He would call at Herriards in a day or two, and ask to see Miss Payne. He would ask his mother to come with him. That should avoid any awkwardness. Then, if the girl was happy and not in need of his help, he would consider his obligation to Tom fulfilled. That was what he would do.

Now it was time to collect his horse and get back to the Quentins. This had been just a lightning reconnaissance of the ground. Herriards was a good ten miles from the Quentins' place, and a proper visit would take the better part of a day. He made his way back to the inn to collect his horse and his groom. Before leaving he would have a pint of ale and a chat with Jem Banks, the landlord.

Banks was civil enough but rather taciturn. He couldn't say anything of the Paynes—since the old man had died the village hadn't seen that much of them. Miss Katharine's governess, though—Miss Tillyard—lived in the village.

'I think I saw her today,' Adam said. 'Does she live in the cottage next to the big white house?'

'The big white house... Oh, you mean the one belonging to Mr Cruikshank, the surgeon? Aye, that's the one. Miss Tillyard lives in the cottage next door to Mr Cruikshank.'

At dinner that evening he asked the Quentins about the Payne family.

'The Paynes?' Mrs Quentin said. 'Ah, yes, it was

very sad. That poor girl. We tried to visit, you know, after Tom Payne was killed, but Katharine didn't wish to see anyone, and I'm afraid we haven't bothered since. We don't hear a great deal about them now, Lord Calthorpe. Herriards is on the other side of Basingstoke, and we tend to mix with the folk on this side. We knew the old gentleman, of course—everyone in the county knew him. But since Mr Henry Payne has been in occupation we have seldom seen him. He seems an amiable enough man.'

'Young devils, the Paynes were, when they were children,' said Mr Quentin. 'They used to get up to all sorts of tricks! And Katharine was as bad as her brother. How they used to make us laugh! But since Tom went away…no, I don't think any of us has seen her. You were in action with Tom Payne, weren't you, Calthorpe? A pity he died. Great fellow. Would have been an asset to the county. Don't know about the new man or how he's managing. Entails are the very devil. I know Tom loved the Army, but…' He paused, unwilling perhaps to criticise. 'I hear you have just sold out yourself—do you miss Army life?'

For a while the talk was of the great battle which had been fought earlier in the year, the prospects for peace, the problems of owning land. Then Mrs Quentin said, 'Your mother tells me that you were in Herriard Stoke today. Did you not manage to gather some information about Katharine while you were there?'

'I only spoke to two people—the landlord at the inn, and a Miss Tillyard. In fact, I'm afraid I knocked Miss Tillyard over!'

The company demanded to know more, and Adam recounted the accident in the churchyard.

'But, Adam, I hope you saw that she was all right!'

'I tried to, Mama. I made sure that she wasn't seriously hurt, and then watched till she arrived safely at her cottage. Miss Tillyard wouldn't have thanked me if I had tried to do more. Indeed, she practically bit my head off when I rescued her hat.'

Amid laughter, Mrs Calthorpe said, 'This gets more and more bizarre! What happened to her hat?'

Again Adam explained.

'How ungrateful! She sounds rather a shrew, Lord Calthorpe.'

'A veritable tartar, ma'am!'

'If she had to keep the young Paynes in order, I'm not surprised!'

'She seemed a touch young to have done that...I wouldn't have said she was more than thirty. All the same, I hope I am not called upon to come to her rescue a second time! Once is quite enough!'

Chapter Five

But Adam had cause to remember his words two days later when he and his mother were approaching Herriards House. As they went Adam cast a critical eye over the condition of the drive. His recent experience at Calthorpe had shown him that the place had formerly been well managed, but had now been neglected for months. The drive itself was covered in places with dead weeds and grass, and the ground under a splendid avenue of elms on either side was obscured with a tangle of brambles and brushwood. Paths which had once been pleasant walks under the trees were overgrown. He shook his head. Henry Payne might well be the best of fellows, but he was not looking after his inheritance.

Something caught his eye—a flash of white on one of the paths. The woman he had encountered in the churchyard two days before was walking in some haste towards the drive. As he watched, a man who had obviously been following her came into sight and put a restraining hand on her arm. She shook it off impatiently whereupon the man pulled her round to face him, and snatched her into his arms. It looked as if the situation could become serious and Adam ordered the coachman to pull up. But even as he leapt out and started towards the couple the woman suddenly swung her arm in a wide arc and gave her companion a cracking punch on the nose.

'Leave me alone, Walter Payne! D'you hear me?'

Adam stopped where he was—this lady needed no rescue at the moment. Indeed, the man was in a worse way than she was. Blood was pouring from his nose and dripping down the front of his coat. He was making an effort to staunch it with a lawn handkerchief, but it still seeped through.

'Good God, what did you do that for?' said Walter Payne thickly. 'I wasn't meaning any harm! Look at this!' He gestured at the mess on his coat.

'It's your own fault!'

'My own fault? I was only trying to have a word with you, for God's sake! You've ruined my coat! I'll see you later about this.'

He went off in a rage, and the woman sank down on to the tree trunk nearby and put her face in her hands. Adam decided it was time to intervene. 'Are you all right, ma'am?' he asked gently.

She jumped up, startled. 'Oh! Oh, it's you again,' she said. 'What do you want now?'

'I asked if you were all right.'

'Why, yes, of course! I *enjoy* being mauled about by creatures like Walter Payne!' she said harshly. 'What do you think?'

'I think you have an impressive right hook, ma'am. Did he deserve such punishment?'

'Perhaps not,' she said. 'I didn't stop to debate it.

Perhaps I overreacted. But I was frightened... I dare say you thought it wasn't exactly ladylike...' Her voice wobbled and she put a hand to her brow. 'Oh Heavens, how I dislike men!'

Adam moved to her side. 'I'm sorry,' he said. 'Forgive me. But may I give you a piece of advice for the future? It is dangerous to hit a man when he is aroused. Another time you might not be so lucky.'

She regarded him with dislike. 'I've said before, sir. I neither want nor need your help, and least of all do I want your advice!'

Adam kept his calm. 'Very well,' he said equably. 'Consider it unsaid. Now, what can I do to make amends? Can I escort you somewhere?'

He had to admire her spirit. Pale and dishevelled though she was, she was not about to give an inch. 'No, thank you!' she said. 'I'll be all right now. He won't come back.'

'Adam? What is wrong?' Mrs Calthorpe had not seen what had happened, but was now leaning out of the window of the carriage.

'Stay inside the carriage, Mama!' he called. 'It's cold out here.' Then he turned to the 'governess'. 'You are still pale,' he said urgently. 'I really can't leave it like this. Can we not at least give you a lift to the house—?' Then, remembering too late that she had been dismissed, he corrected himself. 'Or to the village, if you prefer.' When she seemed to hesitate he added, 'You needn't be afraid, Miss Tillyard. My mother is with me, you would not be in any danger. I'm Calthorpe, by the way. Adam Calthorpe.'

She looked at him expressionlessly. After a mo-

mentary pause she said, 'Are you, indeed? Adam Calthorpe. Well, well! Er…who told you my name?'

'Someone in the village said you lived in the cottage
next to the doctor. I watched you go in there.' He
added, 'I wanted to make sure you were safe.'

'Really?' she murmured, almost to herself. 'Well,
better late than never, I suppose.' He was not sure he
had heard correctly, but then she continued, 'Thank
you, Lord Calthorpe, but I…I think I would rather
walk.' She looked at him once more, and gave him a
small smile. 'Goodbye, Lord Calthorpe. I wonder if
we shall meet a third time?'

Adam bowed and watched her walk away down the
path. What a strange woman she was! She was obviously a gentlewoman, and when she was not being
rude, her voice was most attractive. On the other hand,
she was also a first-class shrew, uncivil, ungrateful…he would even say ill bred. And then, her last
words had been spoken in a curiously semi-serious,
semi-mocking way. Adam was both intrigued and re-
pelled. What sort of governess was she?

'Adam, are you coming? In a moment I shall *die* of
cold and curiosity! Who was that girl? Why didn't you
offer her a lift to the house?'

Adam rejoined the carriage. 'I *think* it was a Miss
Tillyard, ma'am. And, if I am right, the last place she
would wish to be taken to would be Herriards—for
more reasons than one!'

When his mother demanded to know more he answered her as best he could, but Miss Tillyard remained an enigma to them both.

They drove up before the house in a few minutes.
Herriards was a beautiful old mansion, built just over

a hundred years before in the time of Queen Anne. It was not a large building, but handsomely proportioned with well-laid gardens surrounding it. Like the rest of the estate, it showed signs of recent neglect.

They were shown into the hall by a flustered house-keeper. 'If your lordship will wait here, I'll tell the master. Lord Calthorpe, was it?'

'And Mrs Calthorpe. Yes.'

'To see Miss Payne?'

'That is correct.'

A few minutes later a gentleman with a beaming smile on his face came through, holding out his hand. 'Come in, come in! I don't know why they kept you out here, Calthorpe! I am delighted to make your acquaintance. And Mrs Calthorpe, too. How delightful!' He shook their hands enthusiastically, but frowned when the housekeeper asked uncertainly,

'Er...shall I fetch Miss Katharine, sir?'

'That's not necessary,' said her master. 'You can fetch some more cups instead. Off with you!' He turned to Mrs Calthorpe. 'Come along, come along! It's warmer in the parlour.' He led them into a well-furnished room warmed by a large fire. Here they found the lady of the house sitting on the sofa next to the prettiest girl Adam had seen in a long time. Guinea-gold curls surrounded a delightfully pointed little face, long eyelashes lifted to reveal gentian-blue eyes before they fluttered modestly down again, the delicate rose in her cheeks echoed the deeper rose of a mouth shaped for kissing. Looking at this vision, Adam began to think that Tom's sister had a great deal to recommend her.

'Ellen, my love, may I present Mrs Calthorpe and

her son Lord Calthorpe?' The lady exchanged a look with her husband, then inclined her head graciously. She did not smile. In fact, she looked distinctly put out.

'And this is our Catherine. Miss Catherine Payne.' The diminutive Venus got up and gave a graceful curtsy, together with a smile which revealed pearl-like teeth. Adam was delighted. Katharine Payne was a prize indeed!

'Won't you sit down? Catherine, my dear, ring for some tea.' Mr Payne smiled benevolently at the company. 'My son Walter is somewhere about, Calthorpe. You might know him—he has spent some time in London.'

Adam smiled, but rather hoped Walter Payne would find it impossible to join them. He had no wish to be introduced to the fellow. Tea was brought in and the company talked desultorily. While Mr Payne chatted with Adam's mother, Adam spoke to Miss Payne. She listened to him with a charmingly modest air, just occasionally looking up at him through those long curling lashes. Tom's descriptions had led him to expect a rather more lively young lady, but Adam found little to criticise in this delightful creature. How fortunate it was that his mother had insisted on coming to Basingstoke! He gave his mother a smile and was surprised to see her frowning. What could possibly be wrong? But then just at that moment the door opened and a startled hush fell on the Payne family.

'Katharine! What are you doing here?' exclaimed Mrs Payne sharply after a brief pause. 'We never see you at this time of day! Is there something you want?'

As Adam rose to his feet, he was as startled as the

rest, for in the doorway stood a figure which was already familiar to him. The old cloak and stout shoes had been replaced with a simple round dress and slippers, the untidy hair was neatly, though not extravagantly dressed, but the young woman now closing the door was undeniably 'Miss Tillyard'. There was a slight pause while she turned and looked slowly round, her eyes resting on Adam.

'I heard you had company, ma'am. Asking to see Miss Payne. So I thought I would join you,' she said with a cool smile.

'Yes, yes, of course! In fact, I was…er…I was about to send for you, Katharine, my dear,' said Mrs Payne. 'Mrs Calthorpe, may I present Miss Katharine Payne?'

Adam's mother looked surprised. 'Miss Katharine Payne?' she said. She cast a glance at the girl sitting on the sofa. 'How…unusual. Two members of the same family with exactly the same name!' Looking round at the expressions of dismay on the faces of the Payne family, she added innocently, 'Does it not sometimes give rise to confusion?'

Mr Payne glanced sharply at her, but responded with a laugh, 'None, I assure you, ma'am,' he said. 'My daughter spells her name with "C", and is known as Catherine, whereas our dearest cousin Katharine is usually known as Kate.' He hesitated, then said to Adam, 'This is Tom's sister.'

Adam possessed considerable address—indeed, no one could have survived long on the Duke of Wellington's staff without it—but he was having a struggle to disguise his sharp disappointment. Tom's sister was not the enchantress on the sofa, but the shrew, the virago! The fact that she was not a governess did not altogether surprise him—somehow, the girl had not sounded like a governess—but that she was Tom's sister...! What had she said when they had parted in the drive? *I wonder if we shall meet a third time?* She had been laughing at him! Adam felt disappointment giving way to annoyance. Why the devil hadn't she told him who she was when he had given her his own name? What could possibly have been the reason? Pure malice? A desire to put him out of countenance when he learned the truth? It was almost as if she wished to take some sort of revenge—but for what? Confound it! The more he learned of this girl, the less he understood her!

With regret he looked once more at the girl on the sofa. Fate had truly played him a nasty trick. She had appeared to be everything he had hoped for. Pretty, compliant, dainty... She had fitted his own picture of Katharine Payne perfectly, and he had been well on the way to taking Tom's request quite seriously. But this was not Tom's sister!

He looked at the girl now advancing into the room. The contrast between the two Miss Paynes could not have been greater. How the devil could this tall, thin—no, *skinny*—dowdily dressed girl be the delightful creature Tom had described? Dull brown hair was a poor substitute for Tom's golden curls, and as for her eyes—not clear blue like those of her brother, and of the other Catherine—but a...a sort of mud colour! And he knew from personal experience that, far from being the fun-loving, tolerant girl he had been led to expect, she was a belligerent shrew!

However, his innate good manners did not desert

him. When he saw that no one else appeared to be anxious to offer Katharine Payne a seat, he gestured to his own, which was next to that of his mother. 'Miss Payne?'

She gave him a look, moved to the chair and sat down. 'Thank you, Lord Calthorpe. How kind of you. And how kind of you to respond to my letter…at last.'

Adam frowned and was about to ask what she meant, when Henry Payne interrupted him. 'Are you staying long in the neighbourhood, Calthorpe?'

Courtesy demanded that Adam reply. He turned away from Katharine and said, 'I'm not sure. My mother wishes to spend Christmas at our home in Surrey, so probably not more than a week or two.'

'I shall be glad to have a degree of comfort at last, Mr Payne,' said Mrs Calthorpe with a smile of apology at Adam. 'Calthorpe has been sadly neglected for years, and I have been helping my son in his efforts to restore it ever since he got back to England in September. But it is not yet the sort of place where one would wish to spend Christmas.'

'September?' said Katharine. 'I thought you would have been back in England sooner than that, Lord Calthorpe.'

'After Waterloo I was in Paris for nearly three months on the Duke of Wellington's staff, Miss Payne.'

His mother continued, 'You can imagine how much he has had to do to catch up! The house is still not in order even yet.' Mrs Calthorpe gave Katharine a rueful smile. 'So it isn't altogether surprising that this is the first time my son has been able to visit you. Has he not explained that?'

'He has not yet had an opportunity, ma'am.'

'But—' began Adam. He was interrupted again, somewhat arbitrarily, by Mrs Payne.

'Are you staying locally, Mrs Calthorpe?' she suddenly asked. 'Not that we know many of our neighbours as yet.'

Her husband broke in. 'Oh, come, my dear! I am sure we know at least a dozen families! All of them delightful company. Are you staying with the Faulkners, perhaps?' he said, turning to Adam. 'The Faulkners are a charming family, Calthorpe. He is Master of the local hunt, y'know. A very good fellow. Do you hunt?'

Adam's suspicions were aroused. It occurred to him that the Paynes seemed very anxious to prevent him from talking to Katharine Payne. In fact, their attitude had been curiously obstructive from the start. He answered politely, 'When I can. And no, we are not staying with the Faulkners, but with the Quentins, who live on the other side of Basingstoke. Mrs Quentin is an old friend of my mother's.' Then, before either of them could interrupt again, he went on, 'I hope you will excuse me, sir, but I should very much like a word with Miss Payne. I knew her brother very well. If she could bear it, I should like to have a private talk with her.'

After an infinitesimal pause his host said, 'By all means, my dear fellow, by all means! Go ahead!'

Adam turned to Katharine. 'Might I suggest a short walk? It is still quite light.'

Katharine said quickly, 'I should like that very much, Lord Calthorpe.'

'My dear child, it is far too cold—'

'Please excuse me, Uncle Henry. I intend to talk to Lord Calthorpe.' Henry Payne was obviously not particularly pleased, but there was little he could do in the face of such a very direct statement.

Katharine fetched her wrap and put on some boots, and she and Adam walked a short way down the drive.

'There are many things I should like to ask you, Miss Payne,' said Adam. 'Why you failed to tell me who you were when we last met is one of them. But we don't have much time. It is cold, and will soon be dark.'

'I see no reason to explain anything to you, sir. And I agree that we mustn't waste time. Now that you are here I...I have a favour to ask of you. I suppose I'm asking for your help, after all!'

Adam thought with a twinge of amusement that she didn't have the appearance of someone who was asking a favour. Her air was aggressive rather than ingratiating. He said, 'That's the third time you have made a comment which I don't quite understand!'

'Really?'

'You have three times implied that I have been somehow negligent. What did you mean?'

'I should have thought that was obvious. My brother died in June. It is now November,' she said shortly.

'But—'

'I know, I know! I put you off coming at first. Perhaps that annoyed you. Is that why you never wrote again? I...I would have expected you to have more understanding, Lord Calthorpe!'

'You are wrong. I was not annoyed, and I did understand.'

'Then why did you not answer when I wrote again?'

'Again?'

'I wrote to ask you very particularly to come. I hoped you would!'

'I have never had a second letter from you.'

She gave a snort of disbelief. 'Oh, come! There's no need for this, I am not a simpleton. You must have!'

Adam looked at her for a moment. Then he said coolly, 'Miss Payne, you have no reason to trust me, I know. But I was a good friend of your brother's. Tell me why you appear to have such a low opinion of me.'

She stared at him. Then she said slowly, 'I know I had no right to expect anything. But Tom thought the world of you. And you wrote such a…such a comforting letter after his death. At the time I didn't want to talk to anyone. But then…afterwards, when I really needed someone, you failed me.'

Adam was angry. 'How?'

'I asked you for your help last August, and since then this visit is the first I have heard from you. You don't think that is "negligent"—your word, I believe?'

'I assure you on my honour that I have never had a second letter from you.'

Katharine looked searchingly at him as if trying to read the truth from his face. Then she said reluctantly, 'I suppose it could have gone astray. I wasn't sure of your direction so I sent it to your headquarters in London.'

'It could have—but most mail sent there has reached me. But I'm puzzled—why do you say that you have never heard from me again? I have written four times!'

She stopped and stared at him. 'When?'

'At intervals spread over the months since Tom was killed.'

'*Four times!* I suppose you sent them here? To Herriards?'

'Of course. Where else?'

'How odd! How very odd!'

'Are you telling me that you've had none of my letters since the first one?'

'Not one.' They looked at one another in silence for a moment. Then Katharine said nervously, 'Could they have all been lost in the post…?' Her voice trailed off. There was an awkward silence. Then she said harshly, 'Tilly suggested I should write to you again and give her my letter to post. I refused to accept what she implied.'

Adam said gravely, 'Miss Payne, I'm afraid Miss Tillyard's suspicions were fully justified. Someone has been…intercepting your correspondence.' He glanced at Katharine Payne. She was whiter than ever. A new emotion joined the others he had felt towards this girl. He felt pity. He put his arm round her, half expecting the usual rejection. But instead she gave a sob and turned to hide her face against his coat. Almost without volition his other arm completed the circle of comfort, and, for a moment, they were held in a curious bond, which neither of them quite understood. Then she gave a muffled exclamation and threw his arm off.

'I've asked you before not to touch me!' she said belligerently.

He might have known she would react badly,

thought Adam. This was obviously a woman who didn't believe in the weakness of the weaker sex! After a pause he said calmly, 'You wanted my help, I believe. How can I oblige you?'

'I would like, if possible, to live elsewhere. My cousins are… I don't trust… What we have just found out…' Her voice wavered. She stopped, then began again more firmly, 'I do not find my cousins at all congenial.'

'I noticed that this afternoon,' Adam said gravely.

'You are laughing at me again! And I assure you it is no laughing matter.'

'No, truly, I am not. I am here to serve you. Tell me what it is you want.'

'Tom may have told you that I am not exactly poor, but perhaps he didn't make it clear that I have no control over any money until my twenty-fifth birthday. And that is still four years away.'

Adam looked at her in surprise. So she was only twenty-one! He would have said she was considerably older.

She went on, 'I need your help in persuading my guardians to increase my allowance from the estate my grandfather left me. If I had a little more, just enough to live modestly with my governess somewhere away from Herriards… And before you say anything, I have already written to General Armitage, to no effect. He approves of Henry Payne, you see, and thinks I am merely suffering from the vapours.'

'I saw the General in Bath before I came here. You're right. He thinks very highly of your cousin.'

'I suppose you do, too,' she said bitterly.

'Don't be absurd! Of course I don't! Not now. And as for Walter...'

'They are trying to force me to marry him. And my guardians are not averse to such an idea.'

He stopped and stared. 'You can't be serious! That would never do!'

'I'm relieved you agree,' she said with a touch of irony. 'To some, the idea of reuniting the Payne wealth with the Payne estate, regardless of feeling, might seem quite rational.'

'They can't *make* you marry anyone!'

'No, they can't. But the pressure is sometimes almost more than I can bear. Which is why...which is why I may have overreacted this afternoon. Walter is determined to marry me, and he never stops trying to...to persuade me. He is convinced that I will eventually give in. He knows that I have no one to help me, you see. Tilly has been the only person I could even talk to.'

'Ah! The real Miss Tillyard, I take it?'

'Tilly was my governess, and became a very good friend, especially after my grandfather died. Though she is powerless to help me, I don't know what I would have done without her to confide in.'

He thought for a moment then said, 'I know General Armitage. Who is your other guardian?'

'Sir James Farrow. He lives in Basingstoke, but he's ill. He doesn't receive visitors. Not me, at least. He, too, approves of Henry Payne.' Katharine Payne's voice cracked.

Adam suppressed his impulse to offer her a sympathetic arm. He was beginning to know Miss Katharine Payne and was pretty sure she wouldn't accept it. But he was concerned for her, all the same. Her eyes were huge in her pale face, every line of that thin body expressing tension. She had clearly been under an unbearable strain for months. He made up his mind. Even without his promise to Tom, he would have done all he could to rescue any woman from Henry Payne's tyranny. The man was clearly a villain. His boldness in suppressing their letters was astonishing, and his lack of scruple would be a continuing threat to Katharine. As for Walter...

After a moment's thought, he said, 'I wonder how ill Sir James really is? And if the Quentins know him?' He took Katharine's hand in his and held it reassuringly. 'I'll talk to them tonight and see Sir James as soon as I can. Try not to worry. We shall find something to do.'

For a moment Katharine Payne gripped his fingers so tightly that it was almost painful. She looked directly up at him, eyes wide open in appeal. They were beautiful eyes, he thought in surprise. Not mud-coloured at all, but the golden brown of sherry wine. Then she let go of his hand and said quietly,

'Thank you! You...you have no idea how much this means.'

It was as well that he had not expected effusive thanks or desperate pleas for speed. Not from this lady. Katharine Payne may be near the edge, but, as long as she remained in control of herself, she would regard desperate appeals or tears of gratitude as signs of weakness. Such determination to be strong was admirable, but not attractive in a woman, Adam thought.

'From what you have told me, your "escape", as you call it, will mean a lot to your cousin, as well.

Too much, perhaps. May I suggest that you keep our plans to yourself until they are complete?' He looked at her ironically. 'We don't want him worried before it is necessary. How often do you visit your governess?'

'Once or twice a week.'

'Can you call on her tomorrow afternoon? Is she discreet?'

'Absolutely.'

'Then I will leave news of any progress with her. We might even meet there.'

On their way back to the Quentins Adam and his mother discussed what they had seen and heard.

'Thank heavens we came, Adam! They are a *dreadful* family! Poor Katharine Payne!'

'Surely the daughter is charming? I rather liked her. In fact—'

His mother looked at him pityingly. 'My dear boy, I would have thought maturity would have given you more sense! Catherine Payne—how confusing those names are!—Catherine Payne, by whom I mean the blonde miss who sat by her mother, is a spoiled little minx. Another Julia Redshaw, if ever I saw one.'

Adam shook his head at his mother and smiled. 'Do you still condemn Julia for my unhappiness ten years ago? You mustn't be too hard on her, ma'am. I forgave her a long time ago. After all, she merely faced reality before I did. At the time I had nothing to offer her. Much as she loved me—'

'Loved you! No more than she loved all the other young men who buzzed around her like bees round a honey pot!'

'You are mistaken, Mama. I *know* that Julia loved me—she just didn't love me enough. But why are we discussing something that was over long ago?'

'Because Henry Payne's daughter is another such girl. However, you are quite right. We shall forget Julia Redshaw. What are you proposing to do about Katharine? Tom's Katharine.'

'I have promised to help. I shall certainly write tonight to General Armitage—he ought to be informed of our visit and what we have discovered. I'm sure he'll agree that Kate should leave Herriards.'

'But that will take weeks! The girl needs more urgent help than that.'

'I agree. I'll see Sir James Farrow, her other guardian, while we are here. He lives in Basingstoke. The Quentins probably know him.'

'And supposing you do convince these guardians? What then? Where will the girl go?'

'She proposes to set up house with her old governess.'

His mother turned round in her seat to stare at him. 'Are you out of your mind, Adam? You mustn't allow that!'

'Mama, Katharine Payne is a very determined young woman. I don't think anyone could stop her doing exactly what she had decided.'

'Nonsense! Of course you could! What is more, those guardians would never consent to her scheme— and I would agree with them! The girl is far too young to cut herself off from society in that way. She should be enjoying herself, going to balls, to parties, wearing pretty dresses, meeting eligible young men...'

'And how am I to arrange that?'

'Offer her a home yourself.'

Adam stared at her in astonishment. 'With the utmost respect, Mama, I would say that it is you who are out of your mind! How could I offer Katharine Payne a home—unless I married her? And now that I have met her, that is something I am not prepared to do, whatever Tom said. She's not the sort of woman I would ever wish to marry.'

'I expressed myself badly. I meant you could offer her a home with *me*. I should love Miss Payne to come to live with me at Bridge House.'

'The idea is absurd! I'm sorry for the girl, of course, but I'm not sure I like her very much.'

'Why not?'

'She is everything I find unattractive in a woman. Aggressive, strong-minded, ungraceful, ill mannered…'

Mrs Calthorpe shook her head. 'Oh, Adam, you are still so blind, for all your experience! I suppose you liked the other Miss Payne better?'

'Of course I did! Any man would.'

'I'm surprised. I suppose I must just hope that you'll learn before it's too late.'

'What on earth are you talking about?'

'Quality.' He looked blank and she went on, 'Nothing. It's just my nonsense. Now, how soon will Tom's Katharine be ready to join me at Bridge House? Could she be ready to travel with us when we leave here?'

'Wait, wait! I haven't said—'

'But I have! If you won't do it for Miss Payne, then do it for me. I should truly like her company. Oh, Adam, it could be so amusing! Katharine could spend the rest of the winter getting back her…her *joie de vivre,* and in the spring we would take a house in London for the season. I should love to do the season again, Adam!'

'I really don't think—'

Mrs Calthorpe gave a small sigh. 'You really are the most obstinate person of my acquaintance.'

'If you think that, then wait till you have more to do with Katharine Payne. She is far worse than I am.'

'She's had to fight to survive, Adam! No wonder she is determined. Look, if you won't do it for me, perhaps you should do it for Tom? How is his sister ever to be safe if she never meets anyone we can trust to look after her? You may as well give in—my mind is quite made up. Katharine shall stay with me, and I shall sponsor her presentation in Society next year. And you could join us.'

'Oh, no! I couldn't possibly spare the—'

'Of course you could spare the time! Calthorpe will be in better order by then, and you will need some amusement after all your labours. You mustn't let yourself grow *dull,* Adam! Next spring is the time for you to mix in Society yourself. How else will you find a wife?'

'I don't think…'

'Though why you don't wish to marry Miss Payne is beyond me. She is the only sister of your friend, well bred, an heiress, pretty—'

'Pretty!'

'Perhaps not. Pretty isn't the word.'

'Of course it isn't!'

'I should have said beautiful. At least, she will be, once she is herself again.'

Adam regarded his mother with exasperation.

'Mama, I wonder sometimes whether you know what you're saying. How can you call Miss Payne beautiful?' His mother would have answered, but Adam went on, 'And if she were the queen of beauty herself I *still* wouldn't marry her!'

'Why not?'

'I've told you. She's a strong-minded shrew! She has a tongue as sharp as a sabre. I'd die the death of a thousand cuts before we had been married a year!' Remembering Walter Payne's bleeding nose, he added, 'And she is not afraid to use physical violence, either.'

Mrs Calthorpe burst out laughing. 'You poor defenceless lambkin! Has she attacked you?'

'Not yet,' said Adam. 'But she probably would. And it's all very well for you to laugh, but it isn't easy for a gentleman to deal with a lady who doesn't behave like one!'

'The girl is cracking under the strain of living with Henry Payne's family. Nothing she did at the moment would surprise me. But, Adam, she would soon change once she was free of those cousins of hers.'

Adam raised a sceptical eyebrow.

His mother went on, 'Well then, I shan't try to persuade you any more. But if you don't wish to marry her yourself, you ought to see to it that she meets suitable alternatives. And she won't do that cooped up with her governess in a cottage in the country.'

Her son was silent for a moment. There was some truth in what his mother said. Moreover, she seemed to have taken a liking to Katharine Payne—the girl would be company for her during the winter while he was busy at Calthorpe. He said at last, 'I must speak to Sir James. And then we shall see if it can be arranged.'

'Henry Payne won't let her go without a fight,' warned Mrs Calthorpe.

'If I have the support of her guardians, I can soon settle Henry Payne. But what if Katharine doesn't wish to live with you, Mama?'

'I assure you, my son, after Henry Payne and his delightful family, she would be glad to live with anyone. As you know, I can be very persuasive when I choose. In any case, what normal girl would refuse the prospect of a season in London?'

Chapter Six

Armed with an introduction from the Quentins, Adam called on Sir James Farrow the next day. Sir James, dressed in a brocade dressing gown and velvet-tasselled cap, received him in a stiflingly warm study. Next to his chair was a revolving bookcase full of books and papers. A decanter of wine and a glass, a dish of nuts and biscuits, a bowl of fruit and a plate and silver knife were arranged on the small table on his other side.

'Come in, come in and shut the door, Calthorpe! I can't abide draughts, they're not good for me. Sit down where I can see you and tell me about Waterloo! They say it was pretty close. Is that right? What was your regiment? Help yourself to a glass of wine.'

Adam obediently helped himself and sat down on the other side of the fire. 'I was in the same regiment as Tom Payne.'

'The Fighting 52nd, eh? Colborne's lot. They did well, I hear.' He paused. 'Were you with Tom when he was killed?'

'No, I wasn't with the regiment at that point. I'd

been seconded to the Duke's staff and was doing liaison work on that last day with the Prussians at the other end of the battlefield.'

For a while Adam answered the old man's eager questions about Wellington and the changes of fortune at Waterloo. Then, after a while, he paused. Sir James sat up a little.

'Talked yourself dry, have you? Have another glass of wine!'

'Thank you, Sir James, I still have some. But I would really like to talk of Tom Payne. You knew the family well, I gather.'

'Ah, yes! His grandfather was a great friend of mine. The boy was called after him—Thomas Frampton Payne. Sad business, his death. Very sad! What did you want to say about him?'

'Tom had a sister.'

'Did he? I never knew that! Fancy old Tom Payne not telling me that! Wrong side of the blanket, was she?'

'I mean the grandson had a sister. Katharine.'

'Oh…oh! Well, I know that, my boy! You don't have to tell me that! Her guardian, ain't I?'

Adam patiently worked his way through a series of explanations to the point where he could raise the question of Katharine's future.

'Want to marry her, do you? I thought she was to marry that cousin of hers. What was the fellow's name, now…? Walter! That's it! Sensible thing to do. As Henry Payne said, gets the money back where it belongs. You can't run an estate like that on nothing. Eh? What does a female know about it? Pretty little thing, Katharine, but when all's said and done, she's a female, ain't she?'

Adam reflected that Katharine's Uncle Henry had done his job well. He had used exactly the sort of argument which would appeal to the old man, and as a result Sir James was obviously inclined to look favourably on a match between his ward and Henry's son. It took all the guile and negotiating skills Adam had acquired during ten years in the Army to persuade the old man to agree at least to hear Katharine's views on the matter.

'You'll bring her along yourself, will you? Can't stand dealing with females on m'own. Never could. Why I never married. Come the day after tomorrow.'

'Thank you, sir.' It occurred to Adam that some reinforcement might be advisable. 'Er...Miss Payne would perhaps like some lady to accompany her?'

'Not that governess female! Can't abide her.'

'May I bring my mother, who is with me in Basingstoke? She is an old friend of Mrs Quentin's, you know.'

'Ah! The only sensible woman I ever knew, Quentin's wife. Very well. Bring your mother, my boy. Why not?'

Adam's plans nearly foundered at their birth. Katharine raised strong objections to the changes he was proposing to make to her future.

'I told you what I wanted!' she said. 'To live quietly with Tilly. Your mother is very kind, but I have no wish to live in a big city, to be presented to a crowd of strangers, to make conversation with people with whom I have nothing in common. I shan't know what

to wear, what to say, I don't know the latest dances…
I shall feel totally out of place. The idea is absurd! I
won't even consider it.'

Adam held on to his calm. 'You really are the most
unexpected female I have ever met! Most young
women would be delighted at the prospect of having
a season in London. Your own cousin Catherine, for
example, would give anything to be in your shoes.'

'Oh, yes, Catherine would—but she is a feather-
brain.'

'She is a very pretty one.'

Katharine looked at him, then uncannily echoed his
own thoughts. 'And would be a huge success. What a
pity I am not more like her—that's what you are no
doubt thinking! Well, with a little luck, you will be
able to indulge your admiration for her as much as
you wish next season. She fully intends to be in London then. So why do you need me there? I assure you
that I would much rather be in my own house in
Tilly's company.'

'Thank you,' Adam said ironically. 'You really
shouldn't flatter me so.'

Katharine had the grace to look ashamed. 'I didn't
mean it quite like that,' she said. 'It's just that…' She
hesitated, then burst out, 'I'm sure you mean well, but
I have managed my own life for so long. I resent being
told what I am to do!'

'I had noticed,' murmured Adam. 'But I quite
thought you had asked for my help?'

'I did! But I wanted you to arrange for me to live
with Tilly! Not to go gallivanting about the town! I
tell you, I won't do it!'

'Katharine Payne!' said Adam in a voice his junior

officers would have recognised. 'Do you or do you not wish to leave your uncle's house?'

'Well, of course I do! It's just—'

'Then for once in your life you will do as you are told!'

'But—'

'No buts! If you wish me to persuade Sir James to change his present plans for your future—which, if you remember, favour a marriage to Walter Payne—then you will remain silent and leave all negotiations to me. Understood?'

Katharine gazed at him mutinously. 'He's *my* guardian.'

'And you have so far been conspicuously unsuccessful in dealing with him. Look, it's not altogether your fault. Sir James doesn't like women, and he doesn't like exertion. Left to himself, he won't take kindly to what *he* sees as the rebellion of a spoilt female, nor will he make the slightest effort to find a more agreeable alternative for you. But if we can present him with a ready-made plan which fits in with his notions of what is proper, and moreover one which makes no demands on him, he will listen. It's your only hope, Katharine. Choose now—Herriards, or Bridge House and London.'

'It has to be Bridge House. But I don't like it!'

'You ungrateful brat! You don't deserve my mother's offer!'

When Adam vented his exasperation to Mrs Calthorpe she was unsympathetic. 'You must have handled the matter very clumsily, Adam. There isn't a girl alive who would not wish to visit London in the season at least once in her life.'

'So I told her. Her cousin Catherine—'

'You surely didn't mention her, did you?'

'Yes. Why not?'

'*Why not?* You have to ask me why not?' said his mother in exasperation.

'I merely said that her cousin would love to have such a chance,' said Adam defensively. 'I thought it might persuade our Miss Payne to change her mind. But that was when she announced that she would prefer Tilly's company to mine!'

His mother looked at him in amazement. 'Adam, you have managed to be the positive embodiment of tact for years, but Tom's poor sister seems to have a strangely adverse effect on you. Why on earth did you bring Catherine Payne into it? Your Katharine may not have been very polite, but I really cannot blame her for what she said! You deserved it. But believe me, your Katharine would without doubt like to go to London, though she would never admit it—not in her present state.'

'Please, Mama! She is not "my" Katharine!'

'Well, how am I to distinguish between the two girls? It is a ridiculous situation!'

'You could call her "Tom's Katharine", or at a pinch she could be "our" Katharine. Or better still we could call her Kate. But she is not my Katharine! Please!' His mother put her head on one side and regarded him quizzically.

'She really has upset you, hasn't she?'

'Not at all. But I know you. Now tell me what has persuaded you that Kate wants to come to London in spite of all her words to the contrary. I have to confess you have lost me.'

'Consider for a moment, my dear! In the space of a few months she has lost everything which made her feel secure—her grandfather, her brother, her home... even her fortune has proved to be not an asset, but a source of stress. Her guardians have ignored her, and for months she thought you had deserted her, too... She has had to learn to fight her own battles with little prospect of help from outside. Is it any wonder that she is exhausted? Your obvious admiration of her cousin Catherine must have been the last straw.'

Adam looked uncomfortable, as his mother went on, 'Kate is not conventionally pretty. The other Catherine's attractions are so much more obvious, and, what is more, that little minx has learned to make the most of them. Tom's sister was brought up by two male relatives and a governess. She has never been encouraged to spend much time on her appearance, and, if she thinks about them at all, she probably rates her looks rather low. It isn't surprising that she is nervous when faced with the prospect of submitting herself for inspection by Society. Perhaps you don't know how critical the *ton* can be.'

'Nervous? Kate Payne?'

'Yes,' said his mother firmly. 'Whatever you may think, Kate Payne's confidence is at the moment non-existent. I am convinced that all the things you disapprove of, Adam, her rudeness, her aggression, her desire for independence, they are all a form of defence. But you needn't worry. Once she has been in my care for a month or two you will be astounded at how she will change.'

'It can only be for the better,' muttered Adam.

His mother decided to ignore him. But, she thought ruefully, the next few months would prove quite interesting if Katharine Payne agreed to come and stay, and Adam persisted in this disapproval of her.

Adam was still not completely sure how Katharine would behave in the all-important interview with Sir James, so he arranged for them all to meet at Tilly's beforehand. Mrs Calthorpe had been given the task of persuading Katharine to look more favourably on the idea of being presented next season. She even pointed out that six or seven months were not a lifetime. If Katharine were of the same mind after experiencing life in London, she could still, supposing her guardians would consent, look for her house to share with Tilly.

'But pray do not mention that today, Kate! Today we all have to concentrate on getting Sir James to allow you to accept my invitation. If he has the slightest notion that you might revert to your original scheme, he might well refuse to listen to anything further.'

'I really don't see why he would object—Tilly is eminently respectable.'

'Kate, believe me, I know what I am talking about. It won't work! To be frank, I should be very surprised if any guardians worthy of the name would ever consent to such a scheme. In their eyes it would certainly mean virtual isolation from your proper position in society, and they would regard it as their duty to your grandfather to see that it doesn't happen. In fact, the very possibility might cause them to insist on your returning to your uncle.'

This gave Katharine pause. Then Tilly added her voice to the debate. The governess told her plainly that Lord Calthorpe was acting beyond the call of duty, and that Tom would have been astounded and very angry if she refused Mrs Calthorpe's invitation.

'I don't understand you, Katharine. For months you have thought of nothing but escape from Herriards, and now, when such a golden opportunity is presented, you hesitate, merely because it isn't quite the rescue you wanted. Not the retreat we planned, but an adventure into a new world—a world that should have been yours years ago. Yes, it needs courage, but you have never wanted for courage in the past. I shall think you a coward, if you do not do as Lord Calthorpe suggests. Learn to enjoy life as you were meant to, my dear!'

When they reached Sir James's house, Adam presented his suggestion for Katharine's future, claiming that he was fulfilling the promise made to Tom at their last meeting.

'Tom said that, did he? Asked you to look after his sister? He should have been here to look after her himself, the young scamp! But you may be right, Calthorpe, you may be right. You've shown sense in your career, you probably know what you're doing otherwise,' Sir James said at last. He turned to Mrs Calthorpe. 'What do you think, ma'am? You know the world as I do not. What do you say?'

'You can hardly expect me to give you a completely unbiassed view, Sir James. I would regard it as a great kindness on your part if you would grant me Katharine's company. But, since you ask...' She hesitated.

'Well? What is it?'

'Katharine has spent all her life at Herriards. I mean no offence, but have you considered how the world might regard it, if you agreed too readily to Mr Payne's plan for her to marry his son?'

Sir James sat up a little. 'How is that, ma'am?' he asked, a trifle coldly.

Mrs Calthorpe was undisturbed. She went on calmly, 'The temptation to bring a fortune back into the Herriards estate must be strong, especially to Mr Payne, and his wish for his son to marry into the Payne fortune might seem very reasonable. Though it is odd that such a thought had not occurred to Katharine's grandfather. Was it because he did not approve of his cousins? One cannot tell. But how will the world regard it? Living retired as you do, it may not have occurred to you that young ladies of Katharine's birth and wealth are generally expected to be presented to Society before marriage. Sir James, Katharine really ought not to be married off before she has seen anything of the world.'

'Ha! I never thought of that! You're quite right, ma'am, quite right! But we can't do it!'

'Why not, Sir James?'

'You see a sick man before you, Mrs Calthorpe,' said Sir James, sinking back into his chair. 'And I dare swear old Armitage's state is not much better, for all his cures in Bath. How could either of us junket about arranging chaperons and dressmakers and milliners, and I don't know what else besides?' He took a sip of wine, and settled himself more comfortably. 'It can't be done!'

Katharine began eagerly, 'In that case—' but Mrs Calthorpe's voice drowned hers.

'If that is the only difficulty,' she said cheerfully, 'then it is easily overcome! There's nothing I should like better than to introduce Kate to Society. And we women, you know, positively enjoy visiting mantua makers and buying gloves, shawls and all the rest. There is no problem there, I assure you.' She paused. 'Er…Kate will need to have her allowance considerably increased…'

'Strange,' said Sir James shaking his head. 'There's no accounting for female taste. Still, if you mean what you say, ma'am, that you're prepared to stand the racket of it all, you needn't worry about the cost. Send the bills to my man of business. He'll deal with them. And I dare say your son here will take an interest in her welfare, too, eh? Well, well, well!' He smiled benignly at his ward. 'I hope you're grateful for all the trouble I'm taking over you, miss!'

Katharine opened her mouth. 'But you've not heard my—'

'She is indeed, Sir James. Quite speechless with gratitude,' said Mrs Calthorpe firmly.

'All I wanted—' Katharine began again.

'Was to have your permission to travel with us when we leave for Dorking in a day or two's time. She is such a dutiful child,' said Mrs Calthorpe with an admonitory look at Katharine and a sweet smile for Sir James.

Since the 'dutiful child' was beginning to look prepared to argue, Adam decided it was time to take their leave. Pleased to have solved the problem of Katharine with so little trouble, Sir James readily agreed that she should leave Herriards when the Calthorpes set off for Dorking in a few days' time. This was all subject to General Armitage's agreement, of course, but there was no doubt that he would give it.

There was only one small flaw, as far as Adam could see. Sir James seemed to think that Adam had a deeper personal interest in his ward. And though there was nothing he could put his finger on, Mrs Calthorpe appeared to have fostered this belief. For some unaccountable reason she seemed to find Katharine far more attractive than her son did. Adam decided that he must be on his guard against whatever plans his mother was brewing. She had a knack of getting her own way before anyone noticed what she was up to. But in this she would be defeated—Katharine Payne possessed none of the qualities he was looking for in a wife. Not even her fortune was enough to tempt him!

Katharine did not seem to have noticed any of this—she was too preoccupied to question anything. But just before the carriage reached Tilly's cottage the Calthorpes realised that she was still fighting.

'I shouldn't have agreed so easily,' she said, turning to Mrs Calthorpe with a worried frown. 'What will Tilly do? How can I leave her to fend for herself?'

'It seems to me very likely that once Miss Tillyard knows that you are safe and well she will be perfectly happy in her little cottage. Dorking is not a hundred miles away, you know. But ask her yourself. If she is anxious to keep a closer eye on you, I am very willing to offer her a room in Bridge House while you are with us.'

Katharine sighed and sank back. 'You are so kind,'

she said in a slightly depressed tone. 'How will I ever repay you?'

'I'll find a way,' said Mrs Calthorpe, with a twinkle. 'Give me time.'

They all agreed that Katharine's departure had to be sprung on Henry Payne without warning. If he knew of her plans in advance, he would certainly set up some reason to delay her. Surprise was their best strategy. So it was arranged that Katharine would pack a small bag for herself, and that Adam and his mother would simply pick her up on their way from Basingstoke to Dorking. A carrier would be sent later in the day to collect the remainder of Katharine's possessions under the supervision of Miss Tillyard, and she would see that it was sent on.

On being asked what she herself wanted to do, she had kissed Katharine affectionately and said, 'I would prefer to stay where I am for the moment, Katharine, dear. Let us see what comes of your London excursion. Perhaps I shall change my mind after that. Meanwhile I shall be quite happy here. There's so much to do.'

The day for departure came about a week later. Adam arrived at Herriards in the morning and asked to see Mr Payne. At first Henry was all affability, but when he learned that Adam was there to take Katharine away with him, he denied at first that Katharine was in, then he said she was ill.

'And even if she were not indisposed, Lord Calthorpe, I could not in honesty consent to a mad scheme like this. What? Allow you, on the spur of the moment like this, to…to whisk my little cousin away from the only home she has ever known? To remove her from the company of those who regard themselves as her guardians and friends? No, no! I know my duty better than that. Katharine is a considerable heiress, an innocent in the ways of society. She needs protection from those who might seek to exploit her.'

'Am I to suppose you count me among such people?' asked Adam. His voice was quiet, but something in it caused Henry Payne to take a step back and hastily disclaim any such suggestion.

'No, no! You misunderstood me, Lord Calthorpe. I am sure you seek to act from the best of motives—your friendship for her brother, for example. But whatever sort of friend you were to Tom Payne, it is not at all necessary for you to concern yourself with his sister, sir! She is not, as you might have thought, alone in the world. I am, after all, her guardian.'

'You surprise me,' said Adam politely. 'I understood that Sir James Farrow and General Armitage were responsible for Miss Payne?'

Henry Payne gave him a malevolent look, then pulled himself together and gave Adam a smile of forgiveness. 'I should have said that they regard me as one,' he said. 'Her real guardians are elderly—they know they can trust me to look after her as if she was my own daughter, and have been happy to delegate their responsibilities to me. Lord Calthorpe, I'm afraid that on behalf of Katharine's guardians, I must decline your very kind invitation. I cannot allow her to go with you.'

Adam had had the forethought to arm himself with

a letter from Sir James. He now handed it over in silence.

'What is this?' Henry Payne read it through twice. When he looked up the expression on his face was ugly, his mask of benevolence quite gone. 'What are you trying to do, Calthorpe?' he muttered. 'The money, that's behind this, isn't it? Payne money—*my* money, if I had my rights! You're going to carry the heiress off and marry her yourself, is that it?'

'You would naturally think so,' drawled Adam, allowing the distaste he felt for the man to show through. 'However, that is not my purpose. I am merely escorting the ladies to Dorking. My mother, who is in the carriage outside, has simply invited Miss Payne to pay her a prolonged visit—an invitation which your cousin has accepted. It is very possible that my mother will do as the Payne trustees wish, and bring Miss Payne out next year.'

Henry Payne snarled his opinion of this idea. Adam raised his brows.

'Really? I am disappointed in you, Payne. One might have thought that you and Mrs Payne, as Katharine's self-styled ''guardians'', would be delighted to see her introduced to Society at such little cost of time and trouble to yourselves. Fortunately there is no need for debate—it is already settled. Discussing it further would be a waste of time. Now, where is Miss Payne? She assured me she would be ready... Ah! Here she is.'

'My cousin doesn't need to be introduced to Society or to anyone else!' Henry Payne said between his teeth. 'She's going to marry Walter. She's going to

marry him any day now! I won't let you take her, do
you hear?'

'You must know that is not true, Uncle Henry,' said
Katharine as she came into the hall. She was carrying
a small valise and was dressed for travelling. She
looked pale, but steadfast. 'I think Lord Calthorpe has
explained the situation. We must not keep his
mother—and his horses—waiting any longer.' Adam
watched in some admiration as she said, without the
slightest trace of irony in her voice, 'I must thank you
for giving me a home for the last few months. And
please convey my best wishes for their future to the
rest of your family. I'm afraid I haven't been able to
speak to them—they are still in their rooms. A carrier
will call for the rest of my things later today.' She
looked at Adam, who took her valise, gave the briefest
of bows to Henry Payne and escorted her to his carriage.

Henry Payne came to the door. 'You haven't heard
the last of this!' he shouted, his face contorted with
rage. 'Abduction, that's what it is!'

The groom was standing at the door of the carriage.
Mrs Calthorpe was at its window, waiting to welcome
her. But Katharine stopped and turned. 'The only abduction I have ever feared,' she said, the tremble in
her voice revealing the depth of her feeling, 'was that
threatened by you and your son. Goodbye, sir!'

She entered the carriage, followed by Adam. The
groom closed the door and got up behind. The coachman gave his orders, the horses moved slowly off, and
Katharine's journey to a new life had begun.

Chapter Seven

It was a distance of forty miles or so to Dorking, and now in winter the hours of daylight were limited. Adam had taken the precaution of reserving rooms for them at the Bush in Farnham, which was about half-way, and it was as well, for darkness was already falling as the carriage drove up the main street of the pleasant little town. Katharine had hoped to see the castle, which was the ancient seat of the Bishops of Winchester, but she saw little more than a tantalising glimpse up a broad street to the left just before they reached the inn.

A hearty welcome awaited them at the Bush. They were quickly taken to their rooms and maidservants scurried round to make them warm and comfortable. Both ladies were glad of a few minutes' rest after the somewhat fraught circumstances of their departure from Herriards, followed by a journey of twenty miles on a cold winter's day. But then they tidied themselves up and came downstairs for the evening meal. Winter was not a time when many people travelled, and though Farnham was on the main road to Winchester, the inn was not full. However, there was a great deal of noise and bustle about the place—a celebration of sorts appeared to be going on in the main taproom—and Adam and his ladies were glad to be served in a private parlour.

The food was good and plentiful, but Katharine found she had little appetite. She felt drained, both emotionally and physically. Reaction had set in after months of tension. Adam saw how it was with her—he had observed the same symptoms in his junior officers after a particularly vicious bout of fighting. He gave her a glass of wine and told her to drink it all.

'And, if you will take my advice, you will go to bed as soon as you have finished it,' he said. 'Tomorrow will be a different story. You'll see.'

Katharine was too worn out to object. She made her excuses and went slowly upstairs, leaving Adam and his mother to finish their meal together.

But once alone in her room she felt restless, unable to relax. Though she was exhausted, the thought of undressing and settling into bed simply did not appeal. She dismissed the maid and sat by the window. She was missing Tom more than ever. Nothing could bring back those days of sunshine and laughter at Herriards when they had both been children. But today, when she had left behind everything they had shared, the old life had never seemed so dear.

Impatiently she stood up. This was no way to go about it! Katharine Payne was no watering pot, no weakling to mourn what she couldn't any longer have! She must start on a new life, with new friends and new interests. Herriards was no longer a haven of happy dreams. It was a place of fear, of nightmare, even. She should be thanking her lucky stars that she had escaped at last. And perhaps thanking Adam Calthorpe, too.

The thought of Adam Calthorpe gave her pause. Something of an enigma, his lordship. Did he never lose his temper? Though she had been impossibly rude to him, he had maintained his calm. Though Henry Payne had insulted him, Lord Calthorpe had remained a gentleman. He must be a fighter—he wouldn't otherwise have had such a long and successful career in the Army. But she had seen no evidence of it, apart from a certain officer-like arrogance which set her teeth on edge. But he was otherwise so impartial, so patient, so...cool! How unlike his mother he was! She was all impulse and warmth, and Katharine already liked Mrs Calthorpe a great deal. But not the son! What a contrast he was to Tom—laughing, mischievous, reckless Tom! Her heart sank as she realised that she was back with thoughts of Tom again...

This would not do! She was never going to be able to rest. She looked desperately out of the window. The moon was full, silvering the streets and houses opposite. The castle would look magical in this light... Katharine made up her mind. She snatched up her cloak and, without questioning whether she was being wise, slipped down the stairs and out through the side door. The street that led to the castle was only a step or two away. She would see if a little lunar magic would calm her, make it possible for her to sleep.

The castle was just as she had imagined—spectacular in the moonlight, the essence of fairy tales, the embodiment of dreams. Katharine stood at the bottom of the street in rapt contemplation. But she was given a rude awakening. A pair of arms grabbed her around the waist and brandy-soaked fumes breathed over her.

'Well, well! What've we here, then, eh? Lookin' f'r company, sweetheart?'

The voice was that of a gentleman, but the gentleman in question was more than half drunk. He must have been part of the crowd in the tap room.

'You are making a mistake—'

'No need to b' coy, girl! What else would you be doing loose on the town like this? C'm here!' He pulled her closer. Katharine managed to wrest herself free of his embrace, and, deciding that discretion was the better part of valour, started to run back towards the inn. Unfortunately, the young buck had a companion, equally well to the wind. He caught her as she turned and half-carried her back to his friend, laughing at her efforts to escape. Katharine was in a panic. She forgot discretion and hit out wildly, fists bunched the way Tom had taught her. She caught one of them full in the face. Shock and pain made him angry, and, instead of letting her go, he stopped laughing and retaliated. Katharine could do nothing to stop them. One hit her straight away, then held her while the other prepared to take his revenge. Katharine strained desperately against the cruel arms holding her. She closed her eyes... Then she heard a voice she hardly recognised saying furiously, 'Leave her alone, you scum!' and she was suddenly free as the fellow holding her fell back, and measured his length on the cobbles.

A powerful arm skimmed past her ear and Katharine heard the crunch as a fist met its target. Her second attacker went staggering back, holding his jaw. If she had been less frightened she would have felt sorry for the man. She looked round. Lord Calthorpe was standing behind her, legs apart, rubbing his knuckles threateningly. The moonlight had turned his face into a mask of steel.

'Are you all right?'

She nodded, whereupon he looked round, ready to turn his attention on her attackers again. They had, wisely perhaps, vanished.

'Do you need help to get back to the inn?'

Katharine shook her head, still unable to speak. They went back to the inn and up to her room in silence.

Then she said in a subdued voice, 'Goodnight, sir.'

'Oh, no, Miss Katharine Payne! You don't get off as lightly as that!' Lord Calthorpe pushed Katharine into the room and shut the door.

'What…what are you doing?' she asked nervously.

'You needn't be afraid I have designs on your virtue!' he said in a scathing voice. 'I merely want privacy to ask you what the *devil* you thought you were doing? Were you actually *looking* for adventure? Is that why you left us early?'

Katharine fired up. 'Of course not! How dare you suggest such a th—'

'That's as well. You would have found more than you bargained for, believe me! *And* you chose to disregard the excellent piece of advice I've already given you!'

'Which bit was that?' asked Katharine mutinously.

'Not to hit a man when he's attacking you. Scream for help, run away, but don't respond in kind! You're bound to lose.'

She pulled the rags of her dignity together and an-

swered him with spirit. 'I...I assure you, sir, I was far
from looking for any kind of adventure. I...I merely
went for a walk! I wanted to see the cas—'

'A *walk!*' Words seemed to fail Lord Calthorpe, but
not, thought Katharine miserably, for long. He proceeded to express with fluency and feeling his contempt for her intelligence, for her complete lack of any
sense of self-preservation, and finally for her want of
any consideration for his mother, not to mention himself.

'You are meant to be in our care, Miss Payne, but
how can we protect such a want-wit? How on earth is
my mother to cope with such stupidity?'

Katharine was angry and ashamed. She hated to admit it, but the man was right. She had been stupid.
She wondered briefly whether he would disown her
and send her back to Hampshire, and said forlornly,
'You need say no more, Lord Calthorpe. I was foolish.
I see that now. I suppose I am not used to towns—
though that is no excuse. I...I am ashamed. And grateful to you for rescuing me.'

Lord Calthorpe looked at her closely. 'This doesn't
sound like you! Are you sure you are all right? Let
me see!' He took her chin in his hand and turned it to
the light of the candle. 'There's a nasty bruise there.
Why didn't you say you were hurt? My God, I should
have hit those brutes harder!'

'I don't think you could have,' Katharine said, trying to smile. She winced as the bruise on her cheek
made itself felt.

'Sit down, here by the light!' His voice was peremptory, but his hands were gentle. She allowed him

to examine her face. 'Just the one bruise on your cheek. What about the rest of you?'

'They didn't have time to do any real harm. You appeared almost as soon as they did. There's nothing amiss, other than the bruise here.'

'Thank God for that! You've been luckier than you deserve.'

'I know,' she said, trying not to sound resentful at his tone.

He gave her a look. 'You have courage, Kate Payne, I'll give you that, but you're reckless, like your brother. I can see we're going to have to teach you some sense. But enough said. That cheek must hurt like the devil. I'll get something for it.'

He disappeared, but returned as discreetly as he had gone, with a small bottle. 'Arnica,' he said. 'It will deal with the worst of it. And I've brought some drops. My mother uses them occasionally when she can't sleep.'

'I don't think—'

'Don't argue, Miss Payne! Just do as I tell you. I'll bathe that bruise, and then wait while you take the drops. There'll be time to undress after I've gone.'

'Well, that's a relief,' Katharine said rebelliously. 'I was afraid you were going to deal with everything.'

He smiled. 'I see that your spirits are improving. Shall I send a maid to help you? Or shall I undo the necessary hooks before I go?'

'I'll have the maid, if you don't mind,' said Katharine hastily.

'Good! Then drink this…' He poured one or two of the drops into a glass of water and handed it to her. She hesitated, but he looked at her calmly until she downed them. 'And now I'll find a maid. Goodnight, Miss Payne.'

The maid came, not without a slightly puzzled air, but Katharine was too tired to notice. In spite of her bruised cheek she smiled as she fell asleep. She had been mistaken. When roused, Adam Calthorpe was not at all cool... And that punch had been as good as she had ever witnessed—even Tom couldn't have done better.

The next morning Mrs Calthorpe exclaimed at Katharine's cheek, which was now purple. 'You may well have a black eye!' she cried. 'My dear girl, how did you do it?'

Scarlet mixed with the purple in Katharine's face. She hesitated.

Adam came to her rescue. 'Perhaps Miss Payne knocked her head against the post,' he said. 'I very nearly did myself—the beams in our rooms are very low. Did you do it last night?' Katharine nodded. 'Then though it looks ugly—it does, though you must forgive my saying so—it is a good sign that it has discoloured so quickly. A day or two and it will have disappeared completely. No black eye. How did you sleep, Mama?'

'Oh, there was so much to-ing and fro-ing that I took my drops before I got into bed. You know I always sleep very soundly after I have those. You needn't look like that, Adam! I hardly ever take them now. Indeed, I'm not even sure where I put them last night. They weren't on my bedside table this morning.'

'Perhaps you put them on the washstand?'

'Perhaps. But, Adam, you were not very sympathetic with Kate. She is not one of your soldiers, you know, but just a frail girl. Look at her—a breath of wind would blow her away. Are you fit to travel on, my dear? We could easily wait a day here. We might even visit the castle.'

'I think Miss Payne has seen enough of Farnham for the moment, ma'am. She would probably like to get to Dorking. I certainly should.'

And Katharine was, for the first time in their acquaintance, in complete agreement with Adam.

They arrived at Bridge House just as the sun was bathing it in a late afternoon glow. Katharine found it altogether delightful. It was built of brick, in a soft rose colour, and was surrounded by a park, which sloped down to the river. At this season few of the trees had any leaves, but Katharine could see that they had been planted by an artist. A small channel had been diverted from the river to create a lake, and as the carriage drove along its edge towards the house, Katharine was entranced to see moorhens and coots, ducks and swans, all busy about their affairs on the reed-fringed water. Nearer the house shrubs and flowerbeds enclosed a terraced lawn, dotted with specimen trees. There was little of grandeur or formality in the disposition of the house and grounds, but much that paid tribute to the owners' thought and taste.

'You like it, Kate?' said Mrs Calthorpe with a pleased expression.

'It is beautiful! Oh, I can well sympathise with your wish to spend Christmas here at Bridge House! Indeed,

I cannot imagine how you could spend as long as you have away from it!'

'I confess I am glad to be back. I have great hopes for Calthorpe, Adam's house near Bath, once it is occupied and given the attention it deserves, but my brother-in-law never spent a penny more than he had to on the place, and as a result it is somewhat bleak. Adam has already worked miracles in the grounds. And when he has a wife they will work together inside the house. That is what Adam's father and I did here, and I think it turned out well.'

Adam was not listening. His attention had been caught by a herd of deer which had appeared to the left of the house.

'That damned agent of yours, Mama!' he said. 'He can't be supervising the men properly—those deer ought not to be able to get so near the house. The ditches must have filled up. What the devil does Frenton think we pay him for?'

Katharine leant comfortably back again against the cushions and eyed him covertly. Even though his words were strong, he still spoke judicially, without undue heat. Perhaps last night had been uncharacteristic after all, and this was his usual mode—calm, even-tempered, unruffled. Together with his air of confident authority it was rather irritating... What sort of husband would he make? Of course, he was immensely eligible; even she, ignorant as she was of the world, could see that. Rich, titled, well bred, a Hero of Waterloo... And far from being the bewhiskered older man she had pictured when she received his letter, he was really quite handsome. He could undoubtedly take his pick of the young ladies who would appear next season, looking for a husband. Lord Calthorpe might be a touch too sure of himself for her taste, but there were probably any number of girls who would be impressed by his habit of command. And his manners were unquestionably impeccable. Apart from his outburst last night he had always been unfailingly courteous in her experience. Yes, he would be a protective and considerate husband. But fun to be with? Exciting? Romantic? Passionate? She thought not. Unlike Tom, Adam Calthorpe would never rush headlong into an adventure of any sort, and she could not imagine that he would ever lose his head over a woman.

What sort of wife would he look for? Certainly not one who expected fun, excitement or passionate romance. The future Lady Calthorpe would probably be blonde with blue eyes, and be chosen for her suitability and propriety; the sort who would defer to her husband, even in the management of her house and children. She would have impeccable manners, too. She would never employ rough tricks taught her by her brother, scorn tears as a form of weakness, refuse to surrender one jot of her right to form her own opinions, resent interference with her decisions... She would never fall headlong—and unsuitably—in love, either. Katharine sat up with a jerk. Where on earth had that thought come from? How in Heaven's name had she come to connect herself with falling headlong in love? A fine thing that would be—especially with a cool fish like Adam Calthorpe.

'What startled you, Kate?'

'Startled? Er...I wasn't startled, ma'am. The...the deer look so pretty I sat up to see them better.'

Mrs Calthorpe raised an eyebrow, but made no comment.

Adam said, 'Admire them while you can. They'll be back where they belong tomorrow.'

Katharine found it very easy to settle in at Bridge House. The release from stress seemed to give her boundless energy, and she was soon well acquainted with the house and grounds. She spent quite a little time with Mrs Calthorpe, delighting in that lady's gift for scatty conversation, which always seemed to end up making sense. They grew close, and before long Mrs Calthorpe was treating Katharine more like a daughter than a guest, calling her Kate, inspecting her wardrobe, declaring it unfit and taking her to buy new and prettier dresses. Little was seen of Mrs Calthorpe's son. He seemed to be very busy putting the affairs of Bridge House in order. But he did find time to send for Katharine's phaeton and horses, including the powerful stallion which had been Tom's.

'He's a splendid brute,' said Adam. 'But I'm not sure what we are going to do with him.'

'Why, ride him, of course!' Katharine said in amazement. 'I always exercised him when Tom left him behind at Herriards.'

'You won't do so here, however,' said Adam firmly. 'The horse is simply not suitable for a lady.'

'Oh?' said Katharine with a dangerous lift to her chin. 'Then perhaps you do not think me a lady, sir? For I assure you, Sholto is entirely suitable for me, and I intend to ride him. As I have for the last four years.'

Adam looked unconvinced. 'Tom never had a great

deal of sense, but I cannot imagine he would allow his sister to risk her life on a brute like that.'

Kate laughed. 'The only reason Tom kept Sholto for himself when we went out together was that he knew I could beat him on any other horse. You needn't worry about me. Sholto won't get the better of me—I know his tricks.'

'All the same, you will please me by not taking him out while you are here. I'll get one of the grooms to exercise him when I can't do it myself.'

Mrs Calthorpe sighed. She was beginning to know her young guest quite well, and directing her what to do or not do was not the best way to manage her. She had not changed her mind about Katharine Payne. She still thought that the girl would make her son just the sort of wife he needed, though whether he would ever come to recognise that fact she was not so sure. He was still hopelessly prejudiced about the girl, and it was true that Katharine did not show herself to advantage in his company. Adam's calm assumption of authority seemed to rouse the worst in her.

But Mrs Calthorpe was a woman who saw below the surface. Katharine Payne had spirit and character, and underneath the cool facade was a loving, passionate heart. The man who captured that heart would be fortunate indeed. However, the girl still had a lot to learn. Her life till now had been far from ideal as a preparation for success in polite Society. Dancing and deportment, dress and social customs could be taught relatively easily in the months before next April. But persuading Katharine to adopt the attitude of a debutante would be far more difficult. The girl had been neglected, left to run her own life for far too long.

Forced by circumstances into managing her grandfather and the Herriards estate, she was now more accustomed to giving orders, rather than taking them. Adam was equally used to giving orders and expecting them to be obeyed. It was inevitable that the two should frequently clash—and they did!

But to Mrs Calthorpe's relief, Kate seemed in this instance, at least, to have no desire to argue. She merely gave Adam a straight look, and then turned to Mrs Calthorpe to ask about engaging a dancing master.

Life was comparatively peaceful in the weeks leading up to Christmas. Adam took the opportunity of going into London to see one or two of his old friends from Army days, and the two ladies spent their time supervising preparations for the feast, and decorating Bridge House.

'I cannot say how delighted I am that you are here, Kate,' Mrs Calthorpe said as they were busy winding garlands of green round the banisters in the hall. 'I seem to have spent so many Christmasses on my own, and now I am to have both you and Adam with me.'

'I am very happy to be here, ma'am,' said Katharine. 'And especially grateful that you rescued me from a Christmas spent at Herriards. Even if my aunt and uncle had been the pleasantest people imaginable I would still have felt unhappy there. There are so many associations with Tom.'

'You were very close.'

'Very,' said Katharine in the detached manner she adopted when talking of Tom. 'My mother was always an invalid, and after she died my father travelled a great deal. So Tom and I were left at Herriards with my grandfather and each other for company. I was several years younger than Tom and a girl. I suppose many brothers would have ignored me, but not Tom. He treated me very much as a younger brother, and we did everything together.' She paused in her work. 'We loved each other, but we quarrelled a lot. I suppose we were quite competitive in a way. Tom always wanted to win, and so did I. Grandfather used to laugh at us.'

'Did you never have an older person to look after you? Someone to teach you the ways of the world?'

'I had Miss Tillyard. And after my father died and Tom went to Eton, Grandfather engaged a chaperon for me. But she didn't last a month. Grandfather was irritated by what he called her finicking ways. He was always reluctant to have strangers in the house, especially after he became ill.'

'You never went into society?'

'There never seemed to be time. I was usually needed at home. And even when he was in good health my grandfather never cared for making calls.' Katharine gave her hostess a challenging look. 'I didn't mind. I never had much to say to the young people we knew. And I never met anyone whose company I liked better than Tom's.'

Mrs Calthorpe nodded and appeared to concentrate on arranging a particularly difficult piece of greenery. But she was angry. Kate had had so little support from the men in her life. Old Mr Payne had ignored his granddaughter's needs and thought only of his own comfort and convenience. He hadn't bothered to change Kate's guardians, though he must have known

himself that they were too old for the task. Nor had
he taken the trouble to provide Kate with a proper
chaperon, a gentlewoman who would prepare her for
Society. Miss Tillyard was no doubt an excellent governess and had been a good friend, but she was not a
suitable person for such a task as that.

And though Tom Payne had been her son's friend,
Mrs Calthorpe was of the opinion that he had been as
selfish as his grandfather. He should have been running the estate during his grandfather's illness, not
burdening his sister with it. And much more than
that—knowing what would happen if he was killed,
he should never have risked his life in that last campaign.

Well, thought Mrs Calthorpe, she had spent some
weary years since Adam had left home and her husband had died. She had often wondered what she
should do with her life. And now, thanks to Adam's
promise to Tom Payne, she had found something
which was proving to be both enjoyable and reward-
ing. She could offer Katharine Payne some of the care
and attention which she had so far lacked. The child
would probably not welcome it at first—she had no
idea what had been missing. But it would not be Mrs
Calthorpe's fault if her protégée were not one of next
season's outstanding successes! And there was always
the hope that somewhere along the way her son would
learn to value the girl as highly as his mother did.

Three days before Christmas Adam arrived back
from London with an armful of interesting parcels. He
brought with him as well an invitation from their
neighbours to an evening party on Christmas Eve.

'I met Sir John in Bond Street, and he was most pressing, Mama. I hope I did right to accept the invitation?'

'Oh! How kind of him,' said Mrs Calthorpe somewhat flatly. When she saw her son's surprise at her tone, she visibly pulled herself together and spoke with more enthusiasm. 'My dear boy, of course you were right! You could hardly refuse. And I am glad for Kate's sake that we have somewhere to visit. She has hardly been out of the house since she arrived, except for a few shopping expeditions to Guildford. And her daily rides, of course, but one can hardly count those. Kate, my dear, you must wear one of your new dresses. The Redshaws like a touch of formality—especially since their daughter married into the aristocracy. Who else is to be there, do you know, Adam? Is…is Julia with her parents at the moment?'

'I believe so. Together with her husband. There will probably be quite a large party.'

Katharine looked nervous. She said, 'I…I cannot imagine your friends really want my company, ma'am. You and your son will have so much to discuss with them and I shall only be in the way. Pray make my excuses to Lady Redshaw.'

'What nonsense is this? Of course you must come,' Adam said briskly. 'I told Sir John you were staying with us—he will expect to see you.'

'Then he will have to wait!' said Kate defiantly. 'I am not yet ready to face strangers! I did warn you before I ever came that I do not like company!'

'Oh, Kate, my dear, pray do not disappoint me!' Mrs Calthorpe gave Adam a warning glance and went over to take Kate's hand. 'I was so looking forward to seeing you in your new dress—the one with the bronze velvet ribbons. And this would be the best possible occasion to practise the little tricks of manners and deportment we have been discussing, you know. Your first practice. You need not concern yourself about the Redshaws. They are really not important, except in their own eyes. They are never seen in London.' Then, as Katharine still looked hesitant, she said, 'Is it Adam? Has he frightened you off?'

Katharine's response was instant. 'Frightened me off? Of course not! What an idea! It was just…it was just… Well, then, if you think you would like me to come, then I shall,' she said somewhat desperately.

'Good! That's settled, then. I suppose there's hardly time to have some of this made up,' said Adam, fetching the parcels and putting them down in front of his mother. 'Besides, it sounds as if Miss Payne already has something to wear.'

'Adam! What have you brought us?' cried his mother, starting to unwrap the first one. She gave a cry of delight as she held up a length of silvery grey silk. 'It must be French!'

'I asked Ivo to bring over a selection of silks for you both from Paris. I hope you like them.'

'They are beautiful!' She held up a swathe of pale golden taffeta. 'Look, Kate! This would be perfect for you!'

'For me?' said Katharine. She looked at Adam in surprise. 'You asked your friend to bring some for me?'

'Don't look so amazed, Miss Payne. Tom must often have done the same.'

'No, never,' said Katharine, touching the delicate

material hesitantly. 'I don't think it ever occurred to him.' She looked up. 'Did you really mean this for me, Lord Calthorpe?'

'Of course!'

Mrs Calthorpe laughed at Katharine's stunned expression. 'I'm afraid you'll have to revise your opinion of my son, Kate! He has some good about him, after all!'

Katharine blushed. 'You make me sound so ungrateful, ma'am. Indeed, Lord Calthorpe is always very...kind. But this is quite unexpected.' She fingered the material. Then she came over to Adam and held out her hand. 'I don't think I have ever had a present that pleased me more. I'm not sure what to say...'

Adam took her hand in his, looked at her gravely, then lifted her hand and kissed it. 'Don't say anything—but have it made up, and wear the dress for our first outing in London.' He turned to his mother. 'I think Ivo put some lace for you in one of the other parcels, Mama.'

'Adam! You are very good. Let me see!'

The evening that followed was one of complete harmony. Katharine saw a new side to Adam as he entertained them with news of his friends in London and Paris. Tom's sense of fun had been strong but robustly simple, making no great demands on one's intelligence. But Adam Calthorpe's humour was a revelation to her. He had a dry, keen wit, and a strong sense of the absurd, and Katharine found herself stimulated and amused. His account of the Duke's reactions to the excessive formality of the newly reinstated French court had her laughing for the first time in months. This was Adam Calthorpe at his most charming, and

Katharine went to bed that night more in charity with her arrogant rescuer than she would have thought possible.

Adam had also been surprised. Katharine Payne had for once dropped the slightly belligerent air she adopted in his presence, and there had been signs of a different, more appealing personality. Laughter transformed her, and for the first time in their acquaintance he had seen something of Tom's natural, unaffected charm in her. Though she was still far from his ideal, he was more prepared to believe that she might have some success in London, after all.

Sadly, this happy state of affairs did not last even for twenty-four hours.

Chapter Eight

Katharine felt more cheerful than she had for months as she came out of the house for her ride the next morning. The sun was dazzling on the frost-covered lawns and she paused at the top of the steps to look at the view. It was incredibly beautiful, but cold! She took a couple of steps, then paused again. There was ice on the steps—the ground would be hard. Was she wise to take Sholto out? While Adam had been away she had ridden her brother's stallion every day, and, though she hated to admit it, once or twice recently it had taken all her skill to keep him under control. The downland in this part of the world was more demanding than the flat, soft acres of Hampshire, and though her riding ability was not in doubt, her strength had been more than once severely tested. Perhaps today she should leave it to the stable lads to exercise him?

Halfway to the stables she found Adam Calthorpe waiting for her. He was dressed for riding, but there was no sign of groom or horses.

'Good morning!' she called. 'Are you riding with me this morning? Where are the horses?'

'The horses are back in their stables. I've already been out with them. I have something to discuss with you.'

Katharine stiffened. This was not last night's charmer speaking. This was Lord Calthorpe, the officer in charge. 'What is it?' she asked coolly.

'Why have you been ignoring my wish that you should not ride your brother's horse? I understand that you have been taking him out quite regularly.'

'And why should I not?' asked Katharine, bristling. 'Sholto is now mine and whether I ride him or not is my concern, not yours!'

'Wrong, Miss Payne! While you are a guest in my mother's house, I regard you as very much my concern. We did not rescue you from your uncle's clutches only to have you break your neck on a horse which is manifestly unsuitable for a woman to ride—and certainly not in conditions like these. I cannot permit it.'

Katharine said angrily, 'Permit? What do you mean by *permit?* I shall ride the horse whenever I choose!'

Adam was unaffected by this defiance. He said calmly but firmly, 'I'm afraid you can't. There are several other horses in the stables which you may ride with my good will. But I have given instructions that Sholto is to be exercised by me, or one of the grooms—no one else.'

'How *dare* you!'

'Come, let us not be melodramatic!' said Adam with a touch of impatience. 'If you were not so headstrong, you would admit that I am right. I had him out myself this morning, and I simply cannot believe that you haven't had trouble with him. Once or twice it was all I could do myself to control the brute.'

When Katharine remained silent he went on, 'Can you honestly say that you have never had doubts when riding Sholto? Or are you too pig-headed to admit it?'

'No, I... I—' Katharine stopped short as she tried to keep a rein on her temper. She was too honest to deny what Adam Calthorpe had said, but detested having matters taken out of her hands in such an arbitrary fashion, and most unwilling to give in without a fight. 'I am not pig-headed!' she said.

'No? It looks remarkably like it to me. Does my mother know that you've been riding Sholto?'

'No.'

'Do you think she would approve?'

'No, I know she wouldn't. She has said he is too much for me. But she is wrong! And you had no right—'

He interrupted her. 'Miss Payne, could you not simply agree to my request—'

'Request? Is that what it is? It sounds rather more like an order to me.'

Adam took a breath and prayed for patience. 'I will try to put it differently,' he said. Then, speaking with exaggerated care, he went on, 'My dear Miss Payne, I know that my mother would be extremely anxious if she knew that you were still riding Sholto. It would relieve my mind enormously if you would promise not to ride him again. You need not worry about the horse. I shall make sure he is properly exercised.'

Katharine, feeling that she had been somehow out-manoeuvred, scowled and said ungraciously, 'Since you put it like that, and for your mother's sake—very well!'

'Good!' said Adam, starting back to the stables.

'But only till the weather is milder.'

Adam, who had been congratulating himself on his victory, turned round in surprised anger to give Katharine Payne the benefit of his tongue, but she had curtsied and gone before he could find the right words. He stood there impotently for a moment, then, unwilling to pursue her, he continued on his way to the stables. But he wondered as he went what had possessed him to take in Tom Payne's sister. She was a menace, a positive menace, with all of Tom's lack of subordination and none of his charm! And he, who had always prided himself on keeping cool in the most difficult or provocative circumstances imaginable, who had been famous throughout the Army for his patience and tact, had very nearly descended to her level! He could not remember when he had last felt so angry.

When they next met Mrs Calthorpe noticed at once that Adam was most unusually curt with Katharine, and that Katharine had again adopted a belligerent air towards her son. Mrs Calthorpe was very disappointed. She had been much encouraged by the improvement in relations the previous evening, and this change in the atmosphere did not augur well for the visit to the Redshaws, which was to take place the next day. Mrs Calthorpe had her own reasons for hoping for harmony on that occasion, so, when later in the day Adam excused himself and went out, she decided to do something about it. The two ladies were sitting in Mrs Calthorpe's little parlour—a favourite place on cold winter days, and a perfect setting for confidences.

'Kate, my dear, what is wrong? You and Adam are clearly at daggers' drawn again. And I had such hopes for you both last night. What has happened?'

Katharine had had time to think things over. Perhaps she had been a touch stubborn—though 'pig-headed' was a term she thought more suited to Adam, rather than herself! His ban on riding Sholto was really quite reasonable, but the arbitrary manner in which he had presented it had roused a devil of opposition in her. She said as much to Mrs Calthorpe.

'I must confess that I am highly relieved at your decision not to ride Sholto, though I am sorry if Adam's manner offended you—he doesn't always remember that he is no longer in the Army. I can understand *your* resentment, Kate. But why is *he* in such a mood? I haven't seen him as put out as this for years. He is normally the most even-tempered of creatures.'

'That is easily explained, ma'am. I dared to disagree with him!'

'It must have been more than that. He isn't usually so touchy. I have to say that I am disappointed in you both. I was so hoping we should all three present a united front to the Redshaws.'

'The Redshaws? Why?' asked Katharine, astonished.

Mrs Calthorpe paused. 'I think I shall tell you. But it is in confidence, mind.'

'I can be very discreet, ma'am.'

'Well, years ago, before he joined the Army, Adam once fell headlong in love.'

'*Your son!* Headlong in love? I can't believe it!'

'I suppose it does seem unlikely now. But at twenty he was the most idealistic, romantic creature you could imagine. He fell in love with Julia Redshaw, and, after leading him on for months, she rejected him.'

'This was your neighbour's daughter—the present Lady Balmenny?' Mrs Calthorpe nodded. 'I see. How did he take it?' asked Katharine, still struggling with the thought of Adam Calthorpe as a lovelorn young man.

'Badly. He went away and joined the Army. We saw nothing of him for years.'

'But he has surely recovered now.'

'Oh, yes. At least…he is a very different person now. I doubt that he would ever be as foolish as he was then.'

'Then, forgive me, but why are you so concerned?'

'Because though Adam is no longer passionately in love with Julia Redshaw, he still has a fondness for her. And she…'

'Yes?'

'I never shared Adam's admiration of Julia. She was, and still is, I believe, a heartless minx. There, I've said it. I dare say you're shocked. It isn't at all the sort of thing one ought to say about our neighbour's daughter.'

'I still don't quite understand why you are so worried, ma'am.'

'Think, Kate! Julia Redshaw was determined to marry into a fortune, and she did—she married an elderly aristocrat, whose assets are his wealth and position, rather than any personal charms. Now the wealth and position are no longer a novelty and Julia is bored with her husband. She has a reputation for flirting with any personable young man who comes near her. How will she behave when Adam comes back into her life? She was quite attracted to him when he was a tongue-tied student, fresh from Oxford, but now? A handsome, distinguished, self-assured man? I can't see Julia resisting that challenge!'

'Oh, come!' said Katharine, smiling. 'I may have reservations about your son's attitude to me, ma'am, but I am absolutely certain that, whatever a lady's charms, he would never allow himself to be tempted in the way you fear.'

'You haven't seen Julia Redshaw!' said Mrs Calthorpe.

There was a short pause. Then Katharine said, 'But if that is the case, how could I help?'

'You could help quite a lot. But there is one major difficulty.'

'What is that?'

'I think you are, at the moment, more likely to avoid Adam's company than to seek it, isn't that so?'

'Quite!'

'Could I possibly persuade you to change your attitude—even if it is just for tomorrow evening? Could you stay as close to him as you can?'

'Why on earth…?'

Mrs Calthorpe took a breath and said rapidly, 'I want to discourage Julia from trying to attract Adam again. I'd like her to believe that Adam is interested in you—that's why you are staying with us.'

Katharine was shocked into rudeness. 'That's absurd!' she cried. 'Oh, forgive me, ma'am, but I couldn't do it! I couldn't pretend anything like that!'

'You wouldn't have to pretend very much,' said

Mrs Calthorpe with a pleading look. 'All you need do is to stay by Adam, and manage to give him an occasional smile or friendly look. That is all the pretence I ask. You must admit that all he gets at the moment is a series of basilisk stares, which is not what is wanted! You may leave the rest to me.'

Katharine looked at Mrs Calthorpe with suspicion. 'And what does the rest consist of, ma'am?'

'Oh, hints, and glances. They will be enough,' said Mrs Calthorpe airily. Then she grew serious. 'Katharine, help me in this! I know Julia Redshaw. She is beautiful, clever and unscrupulous. Adam thinks she is everything he has always admired in a woman, and she will be careful to foster the illusion, to enmesh him again merely for her own amusement. Like you, I am quite certain that my son would never allow himself to be embroiled in anything scandalous, but he could be made deeply unhappy again. I don't want to run that risk. And, apart from forgetting your present quarrel with Adam—just for one evening—your behaviour really needn't be very different.'

'What—to pretend that I am…I am…interested in your son? That sounds like a big difference to me!'

'Kate, dear, you have a natural reserve about you. It is obvious to everyone that you are not someone who would ever wear her heart on her sleeve. Apart from disguising your present antagonism toward Adam you could behave quite normally. Let the world suspect that there is more feeling than there is. I am sure you could do that!'

'Well, if that is all, I suppose I could try,' said Katharine reluctantly. She gave Mrs Calthorpe a sudden grin. 'But I cannot answer for Lord Calthorpe's co-operation. He is not very fond of me at the moment, I think!'

'I will deal with Adam. Thank you, my dear.'

But by the time Katharine began to dress for the party the next evening she was bitterly regretting her promise to Mrs Calthorpe. Though she would never have admitted to anyone just how nervous she was about it, the visit to the Redshaws promised to have all the elements of a nightmare. She had never mixed a great deal in company, and to date her appearances in public could be counted on the fingers of one hand—every one of them with Tom there to support her. He had even taught her a few rudimentary dance steps, but there had been little time to practise them, and she had always felt stiff and awkward when dancing with anyone else. The thought of facing all these strangers without Tom terrified her.

And, worse still, Adam's mother had given her a task for which she felt hopelessly inadequate. How could she possibly hold Adam's attention in competition with a woman who, from all accounts, was both beautiful and sophisticated? Katharine stared at herself in the mirror and saw plain Katharine Payne, brown-haired, brown-eyed, compared so often unfavourably with her handsome brother. 'You've twice the character and only half the looks, Kate!' her grandfather had once said with regret. 'Why couldn't it have been the other way round?'

And even her short-lived chaperon had regarded her in despair. 'Katharine, you should take more pains with your appearance. You cannot afford to neglect it if you wish to be a success.' Then she had sighed, 'It's such a pity! Matters would be so much easier if you only had your brother's blue eyes and blond curls...' Such comments and others like them had never worried her—the way she looked had never been very important to her. But tonight... She frowned at the dress she had thought so pretty—a simple slip of white with bronze ribbons as its only decoration. Dull, that's what she was. Very dull.

Mrs Calthorpe's heart sank when she saw Katharine coming downstairs to join them. Far from looking affectionate, Kate scowled as she greeted Adam at the bottom of the stairs, and Adam's response was hardly any more pleasant.

'That dress suits you perfectly, Kate, my dear!' said Mrs Calthorpe warmly, suspecting that Katharine's expression was the result of nerves, not ill-feeling.

'Thank you. I'm sure you mean well.' Katharine's tone was curt, and Mrs Calthorpe saw Adam look sharply at her and start to frown at what he regarded as rudeness to his mother.

'Help Kate with her cloak, Adam,' Mrs Calthorpe said hastily.

She could not have suggested anything more suited to her plans. For, as Adam arranged the cloak, his hands rested on Katharine's shoulders for a moment, and he was astonished to find that she was shivering. He was touched. The girl might look perfectly self-possessed, but she was in a panic! He watched as she tried to tie the ribbons with fingers that trembled.

'Let me do that,' he said gently. Their hands met— hers were icy. He forgot his earlier anger and wanted only to reassure her. 'Do you remember the first time

I helped you to tie some ribbons?' he asked conversationally as he pulled the ribbons into a bow. 'It was the first time we met. You were quite ready to bite my head off, and I thought you a Gorgon. But then I discovered you were Tom's sister.' He put his hands back on her shoulders. 'You don't look like your brother, Kate, but last night when you were laughing I could see Tom in you.' He held her until she looked up at him. Katharine's eyes were huge. He noticed once again what a curious and beautiful colour they were—the amber-gold of the wines of Spain. Then he smiled ruefully. 'We really shouldn't fight. I promised your brother that I would make sure you were safe. Don't condemn me for taking that promise seriously.'

She dropped her eyes, cleared her throat and said slowly, 'I'll try not to. You were right about Sholto. And I know you mean well. I'm just not used to obeying orders.'

'Is that what they sound like? I'm sorry. Let's make a bargain. I will try to sound less peremptory, if you will make an effort to meet me halfway when I am doing my best to look after you. Agreed?' He put his finger under her chin and made her look at him again.

If Adam Calthorpe was always as nice as this when making his requests, thought Katharine, she might well agree without demur to anything he suggested. She smiled back at him and nodded.

'Good! That's settled,' said Mrs Calthorpe, who had been listening to this exchange with delight. As Katharine went out before them to the carriage Mrs Calthorpe said in a low voice, 'We shouldn't have insisted on her coming with us, Adam. It's too soon. The child is terrified of company, and she misses Tom.'

'I realise that now. But don't worry, Mama. I'll look after her.'

Well satisfied, Adam's mother preceded Adam to the carriage and they set off.

The ballroom of Redshaw Hall was at the back of the house, and Katharine looked curiously about her as they walked through the marble-columned hall and along what seemed like miles of tapestry-lined passage. The Hall was an imposing mansion, she thought, but not a comfortable home like Herriards or Bridge House.

They were met at the door of the ballroom by a major-domo who announced them in a resounding voice. The party was well under way with crowds of people milling round the room. But they had hardly gone a few steps when they were halted by an exquisitely diminutive figure.

'Adam!' called this vision. 'Adam Calthorpe, as I live and breathe! How *nice* to see you after all these years!'

'Lady Balmenny.' Adam bowed.

'What nonsense is this? I thought we were *friends*— you must call me Julia, as you did in the old days.'

Smiling, Adam said, 'You remember my mother, I think?'

'Oh, of *course*,' cried Lady Balmenny. 'How are you, Mrs Calthorpe? So *nice* you could come... Adam, we must have a long chat. I cannot *wait* to ask you about the Duke. Is he as bad as they say?'

'Julia, I don't think you know Miss Payne,' said Mrs Calthorpe firmly. 'May I introduce her?'

Julia stared at Katharine. 'How d'y' do, Miss Payne.

I heard Mrs Calthorpe had a friend staying with her. You must meet my parents. Do come with me.' She led the way through the crowded room across to an alcove to where a small group of people were sitting. Julia presented them to Sir John and Lady Redshaw, but then wasted no time in dragging Adam off to dance with her.

The Redshaws showed no surprise at their daughter's extraordinary behaviour, but greeted Mrs Calthorpe very kindly and expressed their pleasure in meeting Katharine.

'Is this your first visit to Surrey, Miss Payne?' asked Lady Redshaw.

'Yes, and I find it very attractive, even in winter.'

'Are you planning to stay long?'

'I'm…I'm not sure…'

'What Kate means is that she will be presented next season, and then…' Mrs Calthorpe allowed her eyes to rest on her son for a moment. 'We shall see….'

'Oh?' said Lady Redshaw, regarding Katharine with increased interest.

'I cannot say more as yet,' Mrs Calthorpe went on with a significant smile. 'Kate's guardians wish her to have her season first. But when that is over…'

Katharine blushed and looked reproachfully at Mrs Calthorpe, who gave her a fond smile and went on, 'The dear child would rather die than admit it, but she is at the stage when she feels lost without Adam,' she said. 'And he feels just the same. Look, he and Julia are coming back already. What did I say?'

Katharine began to feel annoyed. This was going too far! An occasional smile at Adam was all very well, but to be portrayed as a pair of lovelorn fools was too much! She was within a hair of denying it all when Adam and Julia returned.

'I now know *all* about you, Miss Payne,' cried Julia. 'Adam has been telling me of his friendship with your brother, and I am *deeply* impressed. It is *so* like Adam to take on the responsibility of looking after you. He is sometimes *too* good! But *do* say you will let me help him!'

'Good heavens, Julia! How do you think you can help?' said Mrs Calthorpe.

'Well, to take a share in teaching Miss Payne the ways of Society. Adam tells me that she has been brought up in the *depths* of Hampshire and knows *nothing* of the world. I should be *delighted* to guide her. *Do* let me help!' she said, turning to Katharine with a smile. Gentian-blue eyes surveyed Katharine's hair and dress. 'Adam couldn't *possibly* advise you on how to make the *best* of oneself, and what to *wear,* and so on, and I could. My friends tell me I have a gift with even the most *unpromising* material—' Julia put her hand to her mouth. 'Oh, do forgive me, Miss Payne! My wretched tongue! I didn't mean that the way it sounded. Oh, what must you think of me?'

'I think Adam has been spinning you stories, Lady Balmenny. I am by no means as helpless as he suggests,' said Katharine with a sparkle in her eye.

Adam looked slightly embarrassed, but protested, 'Believe me, Kate, I didn't suggest anything of the sort. I merely told Lady Balmenny that my mother had agreed to bring you out next season, and that you would spend the winter preparing for it. Your offer is generous, Julia, but it really isn't necessary. I am sure my mother will provide any help and advice Kate might need.'

Julia sighed and looked hurt. 'You think I've been tactless, and you are quite right. I shouldn't have said anything. But when I see something wrong, I can't *bear* not to put it right! I only meant to help, Adam.'

'I am sure you did and it does you credit,' Adam said with an indulgent smile. 'But it was hard enough to persuade Kate to accept even my mother's help. You have no idea what an independent creature she is.'

'Are you, Miss Payne? I do so *admire* you for it. But then you are *tall!* A tiny creature such as myself would merely look *ridiculous,* striding about, insisting on doing everything for myself.' Julia smiled bewitchingly at Adam. 'I have to rely on my menfolk.'

'And where *is* your husband, Julia?' asked Mrs Calthorpe briskly. 'I should love to meet him. Is he not here?'

'Julia, you and I will take Mrs Calthorpe to find Bernard,' said Lady Redshaw. 'He is probably over there by the buffet. Lord Calthorpe will look after Miss Payne, I am sure.' With a kindly smile at Katharine, Lady Redshaw gathered Julia and Adam's mother up and swept them off towards the other end of the room. Adam looked at Katharine.

'You're very quiet, Kate.'

'Am I? The conversation seemed to be flowing quite nicely without me.'

'It's amazing! Julia is still a most bewitching creature! I knew her years ago—in fact, at one time I was very fond of her. And now she has been married eight or nine years, but she doesn't seem to have changed a bit.'

'Really?' said Katharine, and, remembering Mrs Calthorpe's views on Julia Redshaw, she thought that was probably perfectly true.

'I hope you weren't offended by her words. I am sure she didn't mean to upset you—she is very good-hearted.'

'I did wonder what you had said to her...'

'Nothing you would have objected to! I told her of Tom. I said you missed him. And that is true, isn't it?'

'Yes,' sighed Katharine. 'I miss him a lot—especially on occasions like these. Mind you, we quarrelled nearly all the time. He was a most exasperating fellow...'

'He was, wasn't he?' Adam grinned. 'He was a first-class officer, but you'd be surprised at how often I felt like wringing Tom Payne's neck. But then he would look at you...'

'How well I know that look! His puppy-dog look. You would end up laughing with him, or feeling guilty for being so unreasonably annoyed!'

'And then you would finally risk your own reputation in order to save him...'

'Or make up all sorts of excuses to Grandfather for him and be punished yourself...!'

They looked at one another and burst out laughing. 'I am so glad someone else knew him as well as I did!' Katharine said impulsively.

Adam regarded her. Katharine Payne was a different creature altogether when she laughed. Her assertive, rather aggressive air disappeared, revealing a younger, warmer, and in some strange way more vulnerable woman. Which was the real Katharine Payne? It was irritating—even after nearly two months he was still as undecided about her as on that day in November when he had first seen her!

'Come!' he said suddenly. 'We shall dance.'

The laughter died, and she frowned. 'Thank you, but I don't wish to dance,' she said abruptly.

'Nonsense! That is why we're here. Come!' He took her arm.

'I said I don't wish to dance!' she whispered fiercely, and turned her back on him. At the other end of the room Julia Redshaw was staring at her. Katharine remembered her promise to Mrs Calthorpe, swallowed her temper and turned back. She gave Adam the most bewitching smile she could manage. It was not to be compared with Lady Balmenny's, of course, but it was the best she could do.

'You're sounding just a touch peremptory, Adam,' she said sweetly. 'I thought we agreed earlier that you would try not to give orders?'

'And you promised to meet me halfway,' he said.

'That's not—' Katharine stopped short. She had nearly forgotten again. Giving him a charmingly rueful look, she said, 'Oh, Adam, I see I shall have to confess the awful truth. I can't.'

'Can't what?'

'I have never learned how to dance properly! Tom taught me one or two steps, but that is all. It's one of the many things your mother was going to see to. We've already arranged for a dancing master to come after Christmas.' She came closer and put her hand on his sleeve. Adam looked surprised, but to her relief he didn't seem to object. With a look of appeal she went

on, 'But don't force me to make an exhibition of myself here and now—especially after telling your friend
that I didn't need her help. Please don't make me!'

Adam put his hand over hers. 'My dear girl, of
course I won't! I'm not a monster. We'll join the others at the buffet.'

'Oh…er…couldn't we sit somewhere else? I would
dearly love to hear some stories about Tom.'

'A much better idea! I'll get one of the servants to
bring some refreshments to that table over here. Come,
Kate!' He took her hand and led her over to the table
in a small alcove, and saw her seated. 'Stay there,' he
said with a charming smile. 'I'll be back in a moment.'

Really, thought Katharine, that was quite easy. Perhaps I have something to learn from Lady Balmenny
after all. But I'm not sure I could keep it up for long.
We tall women are too independent! And too honest!

Adam kept Katharine entertained with his tales of
life with Tom for a good half-hour, and then escorted
her over to his mother. They were introduced in their
turn to Lord Balmenny. After a few minutes' conversation, Julia once again took Adam off to introduce
him to some of her friends, and Katharine was left
with Julia's husband. Lady Redshaw and Mrs Calthorpe were deep in conversation a little distance
away.

'You a friend of Calthorpe's, Miss Payne?' asked
Viscount Balmenny, his eyes on the figures circling
the floor.

'My brother was, sir. I would say that I am rather
a friend of Lord Calthorpe's mother.'

'That's not what I hear,' said the Viscount, turning

to look at her. His eye closed in a wink. 'Still, if that's the story you want to spread, I shan't interfere. As long as m'wife knows the truth.'

'I'm not sure what you mean, Lord Balmenny,' faltered Katharine.

'Don't suppose y'do. Y'needn't concern y'self about it.' He turned back to the table and poured himself a glass of wine. 'I'll drink to your success and happiness, Miss Payne. Success and happiness.' He drank deep, then called to one of the waiters. 'You! Fellow! Give the lady a glass of champagne.'

'I don't think—'

'Yes, y'do, Miss Payne. How else can y'drink to *my* happiness?' He spoke in an ironic tone, but there was more than a touch of pain in his eyes. Katharine found that she liked Julia's husband.

'I'll do that with pleasure,' she said.

The evening came to an end before midnight. A number of the guests wanted to attend the midnight service at the church nearby. But later that night, when Julia was preparing for bed, Lady Redshaw came into her daughter's bedroom. She took the hairbrush from the maid and dismissed her. As she brushed Julia's hair she said casually, 'Did you know that Adam Calthorpe is as good as engaged to Miss Payne?'

Julia turned to look at her mother. 'I don't believe it!' she said sharply. 'Who told you? The girl herself?'

'No, Adam's mother.'

'I see.' Julia was silent for a moment. Then she shook her head. 'It doesn't matter. The girl is a nonentity, a dull, ungraceful beanstalk. She will never hold him.'

'Adam Calthorpe is not a boy any longer. I believe he is a man who will keep his word, whatever happens. But you should not concern yourself with him, Julia.' There was a warning note in Lady Redshaw's voice.

'What do you mean?'

'Bernard is no fool. And your exploits are starting to annoy him.'

Julia smiled scornfully. 'I can manage Bernard, Mama. And I fancy I can manage Adam Calthorpe, too.'

Lady Redshaw shook her head. 'I think you underestimate your husband. And I strongly doubt that you would find Adam Calthorpe as easy a conquest as you did ten years ago. I beg you not to try it, Julia.'

'Dearest Mama, you have just made it impossible for me to refuse the challenge! Do you seriously believe that Adam Calthorpe would resist me if I set out to capture him? You should have more faith in me!'

Chapter Nine

Katharine Payne had been given food for thought by the evening with the Redshaws. Till now her attitude towards the opposite sex had been regulated by her dealings with her grandfather, her brother, her guardians and those she had met in running Herriards. Her grandfather had demanded respect and obedience, and had spoiled her. Though she had loved her brother deeply, her relationship with him had been keenly competitive, each of them striving to outdo the other. Her guardians were elderly gentlemen, remote creatures whom she found a source of irritation, but had been forced to obey. And, up to the moment her uncle had arrived, her position at Herriards had been one of authority, in which she gave orders and expected them to be carried out.

Not one of these relationships had prepared her for social exchanges with eligible young men. Moreover, unlike most girls of her age, she had had very little instruction or experience in the manners and modes of polite society. As a result of all this, the most inexperienced débutante knew more about the arts of attraction than Katharine Payne.

Up to now this had never troubled her. She was not vain—the fact that Tom was so much better looking than she was had never disturbed her—and her personal appearance had never been a matter of importance in dealing with elderly gentlemen, her brother or her servants. But Katharine was no doormat, and she had not enjoyed being treated like one by Julia Redshaw. Her love of challenges and her lively spirit, which had almost disappeared in the dreadful months following Tom's death, had gradually been returning. And Julia Redshaw's obvious scorn was a spur which finally completed the process.

At the Redshaws, she had seen the liberties a beautiful, unscrupulous woman could take with an otherwise intelligent man. From the top of her burnished curls to the toes of her dainty slippers, Julia Redshaw's appearance and behaviour were designed to charm the gentlemen. And, to Katharine's amazement, Adam Calthorpe had been charmed, had seen only the surface beauty, not the lack of manners, the malice, the selfishness which lay beneath. It was a lesson worth remembering. Though she had no desire to be like Julia Redshaw, Katharine decided that she would profit from what she had observed.

Katharine's enterprise and energy now found a new outlet. The attention to detail, the determination to succeed, which had gone into making Herriards so successful, were now engaged in pursuit of a different goal. Katharine Payne, with Mrs Calthorpe's enthusiastic co-operation, would not become just another average débutante, one of many who appeared every year on the London scene. She was determined to make her mark. She might never be as beautiful as the lovely Viscountess Balmenny, but her person would be as exquisitely cared for, her dresses would be as elegant and her dancing as graceful. And she would put the lesson she had learned at the Redshaws to the best possible use.

Life was very busy in the weeks following Christmas. Katharine paid a short visit to London in the company of Adam and Mrs Calthorpe to set in motion the arrangements for their stay during the season. Adam spent his time finding a suitable house to lease, while Mrs Calthorpe took Katharine round on a preliminary tour of the dressmakers, milliners, and purveyors of shoes, slippers, shawls, fans and all the rest of the necessities for an aspirant to the highest society. They were also visited at their hotel by a number of ladies' maids, for Mrs Calthorpe was insistent that Katharine should have the attentions of an expert dresser. The wages demanded by these persons seemed astronomical to countrified Katharine, but Mrs Calthorpe assured her that they were perfectly normal.

'A good maid is very important, Kate. You have great potential, but I should be less than honest if I denied that your appearance badly needs the sort of care and attention that an experienced maid can provide. We must engage someone straight away, and then persuade her to spend the next couple of months in the depths of Surrey—something not all of them would be willing to agree to. You may have to pay over the odds for the best, but I assure you she will be worth every penny.'

In the end they were fortunate to find Miss Kendrick who had just left the service of Lady Abernethy, one of London's most fashionable women. Lady Abernethy was about to go to Vienna with her husband, and though she had begged her maid to accompany her, Miss Kendrick had regretfully declined the honour. She preferred, she said, to stay in England. The interview went very well, though Katharine thought one could be pardoned for thinking that she was the one being interviewed, not the prospective maid! Miss Kendrick graciously agreed to join them as soon as she was free.

Well satisfied with their endeavours, the ladies returned to Bridge House, where Katharine embarked on various courses of instruction. The dancing master took her through the basic steps of the dance, exclaiming all the while how badly she had previously been taught! 'No, no, no, Mees Payne! Not gallop, not like ze 'orse! Leap like ze bird, like ze feazher! Lightly! *Comme ça!*' And Katharine, remembering Tom's dancing, was forced to agree that it had indeed been 'like ze 'orse' and tried to do better.

Mrs Calthorpe spent a great deal of time with her. The friendship between Adam's mother and her young guest grew with every day that passed, and some of the time was spent in cosy gossip and reminiscence. But at least an hour a day was spent in serious discussion of the structure and habits of London's polite world. Katharine was soon familiar with the ramifications and politics of the great families who formed the major part of Society; she learned how she should address these august personages, and the different degrees of respect to be shown in her curtsies. More than that, Mrs Calthorpe had been a beauty in her day, and was well able to advise Katharine how to deal with compliments or, worse, impertinence.

'Not that I shall need such skills, ma'am,' Katharine said one day, rather dispiritedly. She had just come through a disastrous dancing lesson. Also, Adam had stayed behind in London, and Bridge House seemed surprisingly dull without him.

'What nonsense! It's time you woke up to the fact, Kate, that you are—or could be—an exceptionally striking female! You are not so commonplace, I hope, as to be wishing for blue eyes and golden curls?'

'I suppose not. But it is surely easier to be graceful if you are small. Leaping "like ze feazher" is quite difficult when you are as tall as I am.'

Mrs Calthorpe looked annoyed. 'I see I shall have to have a word with Monsieur Edouard. This isn't the right way to teach you. Kate, you have such a natural dignity! You walk like a queen! There is not the slightest necessity for you to leap about like a feather—if a feather *could* leap, which I doubt.'

'But the dance step—'

'Adam will be back tomorrow evening. You can discuss this with him.'

Katharine felt a lift of excitement, but she said sedately enough, 'Why Adam, ma'am? How can he help?'

'Kate! Surely you noticed? Or were you too annoyed with Julia Redshaw? Adam is a superb dancer! If he would be willing to take you in hand, you would have no problems at all. You would be dancing "like ze feazher" in no time. I shall speak to him. Indeed, you may well have two partners, for Adam is bringing a friend of his back with him. Lord Trenchard is on his way to the west country and will stay the night here. It is most annoying that that maid has not yet arrived! We could have impressed Adam with your elegant new appearance...and Lord Trenchard, of course.'

Katharine laughed at her. 'Your son will never be impressed with me, ma'am, whatever arts we employ! He remembers our first meeting too well. But perhaps I could have captured Lord Trenchard? What a pity it is not to be! Without my London maid I am still plain, unadorned Kate.'

'If the stories I've heard are true that is perhaps as well, my dear! Ivo Trenchard is the world's worst flirt.'

'Tom liked him.'

'Tom wasn't a bored society beauty looking for amusement.'

'Neither am I.'

Mrs Calthorpe laughed. 'That's true! Life is far too interesting for both of us.'

The weather had improved, so the next afternoon they took a walk down to the stables. The horses were in the paddock nearby, Sholto dominating the rest.

'I'm so glad you agreed not to ride that brute, Kate. He is far too big and powerful for you.'

'But you will admit he is a beautiful creature, ma'am. He has such spirit as well as strength. There isn't another to match him, not even in Adam's stable.' She sighed. 'But you are right, of course, and so is Adam. Sholto is a man's horse. He was bought for my brother, not me. I suppose I really wanted to ride him to keep a link with Tom, but I must admit he was often almost too much for me.' She turned to Mrs Calthorpe. 'How would it be if I gave Sholto to your son? He and Tom were very good friends, and Adam has done a great deal for me. Would he like it, do you think?'

'This is a new Katharine Payne!' exclaimed Mrs Calthorpe. 'I thought you disliked Adam!'

'Oh, I do!' Katharine said with emphasis. 'Quite a lot of the time…and especially when he starts telling me what to do. But I will admit it to you and to no one else—Adam is sometimes right!'

'Good heavens, Kate! Are you quite well?'

'I haven't felt so alive for months, ma'am! And I have you and your son to thank for that!'

'Nonsense! We have done very little. It was merely a matter of time.'

'I cannot imagine that I would feel like this if I were still at Herriards.'

'Perhaps not.' They walked in silence towards the house. 'I think Adam would be delighted with Sholto—if you are sure you wish to part with the horse.'

Katharine sighed. 'Yes, I am sure. I'll find another horse to suit me some time. But for the moment…' She pulled a face at Mrs Calthorpe. 'For the moment I must concentrate on other accomplishments. Like dancing.'

Mrs Calthorpe started to laugh. 'How was this morning's lesson? Is Monsieur Edouard still trying to teach you to "leap like ze feazher"?'

'No, this morning he gave up the steps of the dance, and demonstrated "ze grand curtsy". I was not exactly impressed. He looked like Madame du Barry wearing breeches. Then I had to try, and by the time we had finished he was in despair again.'

As they walked up the steps to the terrace outside the long windows of the saloon, Mrs Calthorpe was still laughing. Katharine stopped and said severely, 'It is no laughing matter! The poor man was practically in tears!' She put her hands to her head in a dramatic gesture, then threw them up in the air. '*Mademoiselle, mademoiselle,* why ees eet zat ze English womens is so stiff? You must move not like ze drilling soldier, but like ze waves of ze sea. *Comme ça!*' Katharine took a wide step, flung her arms out to the side, then swayed down to the ground in an impressive sweep. She looked up at Mrs Calthorpe and raised an eyebrow. '*Comme ça?*'

Mrs Calthorpe could hardly talk for laughter. 'Kate, that is absurd!' she gasped. 'Even the King couldn't expect such an obeisance! Get up, do!'

Katharine jumped up, her face sparkling with mischief. 'You don't like it? Did it not flow enough like "ze waves of ze sea"?'

'You ridiculous child! I ought to be annoyed with you for being so disrespectful to poor Monsieur Edouard—' A movement by one of the windows caught her eye. She stopped, then cried, 'Oh! Oh, Adam! What are you doing here? Kate, Kate, look! Adam has arrived!' She flew over to her son, who had stepped through the window door and was observing them both in amusement. Behind him was another, extremely handsome gentleman. He, too, was smiling as he regarded Katharine.

Adam kissed his mother, then greeted Katharine.

'Where are you thinking of making your début, Kate? At the theatre in Drury Lane?'

Katharine blushed. 'You weren't supposed to see that,' she said.

'No, indeed!' said Mrs Calthorpe. 'You weren't supposed to be here till this evening. This is a delightful surprise. Lord Trenchard, welcome. I am very pleased to see you again.'

Ivo Trenchard greeted Mrs Calthorpe with genuine warmth, then looked at Katharine.

'I don't believe you know Miss Payne, do you?' said Adam's mother. 'Kate, may I introduce Captain Lord Trenchard?'

'Miss Payne, I am delighted to know you at last,' said Ivo Trenchard, taking her hand and kissing it. 'Tom spoke so often about you. You are just as he described you.'

Adam raised an eyebrow. Ivo was at his tricks again. Kate might be looking a lot happier than she had in October, but she was still far from being the charmer her brother had described!

'Really, sir? Dare I ask how that was?' Kate asked with a look of mock apprehension.

'You would accuse me of flattering you, Miss Payne...'

Adam felt a spurt of irritation. He hoped Ivo was not about to start one of his flirtations with Kate! He would have to put a stop to it if it were so. Kate wasn't like the ladies of Spain and Brussels, she didn't know the rules.

'Do let's go in,' said Mrs Calthorpe. 'Now that the sun is lower it is getting cold again. We've been down to the stables, Adam.'

'Ah! Good! But you won't have seen the latest addition—she has just arrived. Could you bear to walk back again, Mama? I'd like you to see her. You too, Kate!'

Lord Trenchard clearly knew what was afoot, for he nodded to Adam and tactfully excused himself, explaining that he needed to see to some of his things. The two ladies followed Adam to the stable yard. In the centre of the yard, held firmly between two grooms, was a handsome bay mare.

'What a beauty!' cried Katharine, enraptured. 'Oh, Adam, where did you find such a lovely creature?'

'She may look well enough,' said Mrs Calthorpe doubtfully. 'But she seems a touch fiery to me.' She kept her distance as she examined the mare. The animal was restive and the grooms were having quite a job to hold her. 'I must say, Adam, that it's not a horse I should like to ride! In fact…in fact, she reminds me of Sholto. She's smaller, of course, but she looks just as wilful, just as full of energy and spirits.' She turned to her son. 'What are you going to do with her? I wouldn't have said that you needed another mount. And in any case, Katharine— No, let her tell you herself.'

'What is this, Kate?' Adam frowned. 'Have you been riding Sholto again?'

'I have not!' said Katharine.

'What? Even though the weather is milder?'

'Don't provoke the girl, Adam. Far from riding that great brute, she has been concentrating hard on her dancing.'

'Dancing? Is that what I saw?' He laughed when he saw Katharine bristling. 'Peace, Kate! We shall talk of the dancing later. Meanwhile, what were you going to tell me?'

'I...I have come to see that you were right. Sholto isn't really a suitable horse for me...' adding, with a touch of her old belligerence '...though that isn't to say that I can't manage him!'

Adam waited without comment. Katharine went on, 'So, if you wish it, I would like to give Sholto to you, Adam. I...I think Tom would approve.'

There was a short silence. Then Adam cleared his throat and said, 'That is breathtakingly generous of you, Kate. There is nothing I would like more as a remembrance of Tom. Thank you. I accept.' He took her hand and kissed it. 'But—' He smiled.

'Do hurry, Adam. I'm getting very cold!' said Mrs Calthorpe. 'I want to know what you are going to do with that mare now that Kate has given you Sholto.'

'I am going to do what I intended from the start—' Adam started to laugh again. 'I bought the mare for Kate! I thought she might enjoy riding her.'

'You bought the mare for me!' Katharine's eyes were shining. 'For me? Do you really mean it?'

'Of course.'

'But that horse is almost as dangerous as the stallion!' exclaimed Mrs Calthorpe. 'Just look at it! Kate will be killed! What were you thinking of, Adam?'

'There's no need to be anxious, Mama! That mare may be spirited, but she's not at all vicious. I've had her through her paces, and I assure you that, once she knows who is master, she is wonderfully responsive. Kate is too good a rider to be in danger.'

Adam was talking to his mother but his eyes were on Katharine, who had left them. She had taken something from one of the grooms and was now totally absorbed in the mare, feeding her a titbit, talking to her, stroking her, speaking to her all the while in a low voice.

He went on, 'Do you really think Kate Payne would be content with a steady, safe ride? You should know her better! She's like her brother in that respect—not content without a challenge. Sholto was too much of one, and I cannot tell you how relieved I am that she has seen it for herself. But she must have some adventure left in her life, something for her to enjoy.'

'I should have thought that learning the necessary social graces for entering London Society was enough of an adventure for anyone!'

'That's just it! The life ahead is bound to be difficult for her, but hardly enjoyable. We both know that Kate isn't likely to be one of the season's successes, in spite of her wealth—'

His mother raised an eyebrow. 'You're rather blunt. And a bit too pessimistic. She may surprise you.'

'Oh, come! I know you like Kate—'

'And you don't?'

Adam paused. 'I like her a lot better than I did. But she can still be irritatingly obstinate. And while I've no doubt you will do your best with her, she isn't likely to take the town by storm, is she? If only she had been more like Tom in looks...'

'Adam, I won't let you say another word! I am surprised at you. You may have had a huge success in your Army career, but it hasn't done much for your judgement of women!'

'Mama—!'

Katharine had finished her chat with her new acquisition and was coming back to them. Mrs Calthorpe said quietly and urgently, 'But whatever your opinion, help us, Adam. Help to make Kate as much of a success as we can. Do it for Tom's sake, if not for hers.'

'Of course, I will, though I still think…' He stopped. Katharine was too close. 'What is your opinion of the horse, Kate?'

'She's beautiful,' Katharine said. 'I shall call her Cintra. Tom once said what a beautiful place it was.'

'He was right. It's a good name for the mare.'

'Thank you, Adam. But it's cold and she ought to be indoors. Has she been fed and watered?'

Her tone was businesslike, almost cool, but Adam was not put off as he might have been earlier in their acquaintance. He had noticed before that, when Katharine Payne was most moved, her manner was most detached.

Ivo Trenchard had been almost as close to Tom as Adam himself had been. So that night, over an after-dinner glass of port, the talk naturally turned to Tom and from there to Tom's sister and Mrs Calthorpe's plans for her début. To Adam's amazement Ivo Trenchard, a true connoisseur of women, was inclined to agree with Mrs Calthorpe. He thought it quite possible that Katharine would be a success.

'But, Ivo!' Adam protested. 'You saw her this afternoon! She looks more like a…a governess than a débutante! In fact, that's what I thought she was when I first met her.'

'Well, I thought she looked remarkably like Tom— and he was a handsome enough fellow.'

'What the devil are you talking about? Tom was blond!'

'She hasn't the colouring, perhaps. But that smile…absolutely his. Very charming.' Ivo smiled as he remembered it. 'Completely captivating.'

'*Captivating?* How much port have you had?'

'Not enough,' said Ivo promptly, and helped himself to some more. 'Why are you so critical of the girl? I've seen you charmed by ladies a lot less pretty. There was one in Ciudad, I remember…'

'Yes, but she had other talents…'

'Well, what about Comtesse Whatshername's daughter? The one in Toulouse.'

'I hardly spoke to the girl! Her cousin was a charmer, though. A pity about the fiancé. Do you remember the night we…?'

From that point Katharine Payne was forgotten. The talk turned to past experiences, not all of them respectable.

Unfortunately Ivo had to continue his journey the very next day. He expressed his regret and took his leave of Mrs Calthorpe, with whom he was clearly a favourite. She pressed him to visit them when they would all be in London.

'I shan't be able to keep away, ma'am!' he said. 'I can't wait to witness Miss Payne's triumph!'

He told Katharine that he didn't need to wish her a successful début—that was assured. 'But I hope you will reserve at least one dance for me at the first ball we both attend.'

'I shall no doubt be grateful for at least one partner,

Lord Trenchard. But I have to confess that my dancing is not yet up to standard.'

'It will be, it will be! Get Adam to teach you—he was the best dancer on the Duke's staff. Twinkle-toes Calthorpe, we called him.' He laughed and dodged Adam's arm. 'Enjoy your new mare, Miss Payne. The next time I am in Surrey I shall hope to see her in action.'

Adam accompanied him to the carriage. 'Good luck on your mission, Ivo.'

'Thanks. I have no great hopes that my father will agree to see me, but I have to try. Meanwhile, don't you underestimate Tom's sister. She's worth some effort, Adam. Tom was right to be so proud of her. *Adios!*'

Adam walked thoughtfully back to the house. Was Katharine Payne as attractive as Ivo and his mother seemed to think? Had he been too strongly influenced by that first meeting in October? He had discovered later that she had been going through a very bad time for months—no woman would be at her best after such a prolonged strain. Perhaps he was prejudiced. He made up his mind to try to take a fresh look at her, to attempt to see her with his mother's eyes.

But when he found Katharine, her face and manner were most unlikely to improve anyone's opinion of her—rather the reverse. She was standing in the centre of the room face to face with a little man, who was gesticulating wildly, trying to make himself heard. Katharine herself was scowling fearsomely as she overrode him.

'You are unreasonable, sir! I can't remember everything at once! Waves and feathers don't know the difference between left and right, and no more do I when I am trying to imitate them. Which is, as we both know, a hopeless task! I wonder you continue to try!'

'What is this?' asked Adam.

'Milor' Calthorpe, ze case, it ees 'opeless! I 'ave taught many young ladies ze art of dancing, most of zem much younger, of course, but Mees Payne is impossible to teach. Impossible!'

'Indeed?'

But Monsieur Edouard was too angry to take heed of the warning tone in Adam's voice. He went on, 'She turns left when she should turn to ze right, and right when she should turn to ze left! And she argues! All ze time!'

Katharine's protests had ended when Adam had come in. She stood silent, head in the air, too proud to defend herself.

Adam said coldly, 'Monsieur Edouard, we seem to have made a mistake in engaging you. You have failed lamentably to appreciate Miss Payne's particular needs. You will be paid for the full course of lessons, but pray do not come again.' The dancing master started to expostulate but Adam said curtly, 'Thank you. That will do.'

When Monsieur Edouard had left the room Adam said softly, 'Come here, Kate.'

She looked at him mutely, but made no move. He smiled and said again, 'Come here!'

Still scowling, Katharine walked stiffly towards him.

'What has that fool done to you?'

'Don't blame him,' she said bitterly. 'I'm just not made for dancing.'

'I don't believe that for one moment. But I can believe that you're not quite made for teaching—not his sort of teaching, anyway.'

'Your mother was told he was the best dancing master in Dorking. Where shall we find anyone better?'

'I have no doubt we shall find someone when you are more…amenable to instruction. Meanwhile—'

'"Amenable to instruction"? What an unreasonable thing to say! I have tried as hard as I can to learn from that…that little popinjay!'

'Exactly. That is why you can't learn from him—you despise him. I suspect you despise the whole art of dancing as well. Am I right?'

'It all seems such a pointless exercise! I don't like jumping about all over the room, being pushed here and pulled there, with no rhyme or reason behind it! And all I've learned from Monsieur Edouard is how to fall over my own feet while this is going on!'

'Oh, my intractable Kate!' said Adam, laughing at this sad picture. 'Poor Monsieur Edouard. Teaching you must have given him nightmares!'

Katharine walked away from him and stood looking out of the window. 'Laugh away!' she said bitterly. 'But don't ask me to join in. I know that dancing is an important accomplishment, whatever my opinion of it. And I so hoped…I had such ambitions… Well, never mind.' She leaned her forehead wearily against the window.

Adam came over and stood close behind her. He said gently, 'Forget about the important accomplishment, Kate. Learn to enjoy it. Dancing isn't just noise and confusion, you know. It can give pleasure in so many ways.'

'How?'

'Well, there's the music—you like music, I know you do. I've heard you play. Then there is pattern, design, not confusion. Each dance has its own pattern, and surely there is satisfaction in seeing the pattern worked out to its proper end? And there are the steps. There are really very few of them—you could learn them in an hour, if you wanted to. But...'

He took her by the shoulders and turned her round to face him. 'But that's not where the difficulty lies, is it? You resist dancing because it means physical contact, and I think you've had very little experience of that. You're afraid of it.' He paused, but when she didn't speak he went on, 'There's no need to be.'

She kept her head down, refusing to meet his eyes, but slow colour covered her cheeks, as he slid his arms down to her elbows and pulled her closer.

'Do you think I mean you harm?' he asked.

She looked up, startled. 'Of course not!'

'Then why are your fists clenched?' He took one of her hands, uncurled the fingers and held it against his chest. 'Trust me, Kate. I want nothing but your good, believe me.'

'I do believe that. You've been very kind.'

'Then don't pull away. Let yourself lean against me. Relax.' He put his free arm round her, so that she was loosely held against him.

The scene in the churchyard at Herriard Stoke flashed into Katharine's mind. Even before she had known who he was, she had felt the same strange desire to let herself be guided by this man, to let his arms enfold her…but she mustn't…!

'You're tightening up again,' Adam said. 'Just when you were doing so well. What is it?'

'I…I have never…I have learned never to depend on anyone.'

'Now that I know more of your history I don't find it surprising. But that doesn't mean that you have to push people away.'

Held by his arm, her hand resting on his chest, Katharine considered this. 'You're saying I can't dance because I can't relax? But I can't think how to do that.'

'Don't try to think! Stay here like this, just for a moment.' The room was silent, shadowed except for a strip of pale sunshine through one of the long windows. Beneath her hand Katharine could feel Adam's heart beating steadily. Slowly the tension seeped away and, perhaps for the first time in her life, she felt at ease in close contact with someone else.

After a moment Adam said softly, 'You know, there's a new dance now called the waltz. It's danced all over Europe, and it's even beginning to be seen in England. The couples stand almost as close as this to each other. Shall I teach it to you?'

She stiffened again.

'Don't, Kate! There's no need. Put your left hand on my shoulder. Good! Keep your head up! Now follow my steps. Count in threes. Very slowly. Like this. One, two-three, one, two-three…'

He took her slowly round the room, his left hand still clasping her right, the other at her waist. His touch was light but firm and, after a stumble or two, she began to follow more easily. His pace gradually quickened, but she found that she could still follow, the hand at her waist always guiding, telling her which way to turn, when to slow down, when to move more quickly. The steady, rhythmical counting entered her bloodstream and she found herself swaying, dipping with the turns. It was like magic, like champagne, she was floating…

They came to a stop. Adam said, 'Kate…that was wonderful!' He put both arms round her, then bent his head and kissed her. The kiss may not have been passionate, but it was none the less real. To Katharine who, with the exception of Walter's onslaught, had never been kissed by any man other than her brother and grandfather, it was a revelation. That a kiss could be so warm, so comforting, and at the same time so spellbinding… She had difficulty in holding on to her reason, to stop herself from putting her arms round Adam's neck, from holding on forever to a moment of such enchantment…

Chapter Ten

The kiss came to an end and Adam briefly hugged her, putting his cheek next to hers. 'Dear Kate!' he said, his voice full of affection and warmth.

It was like a splash of cold water and it brought Katharine to her senses. 'Dear Kate!' No excitement, no desperately whispered 'Darling Kate', 'Sweetheart Kate', 'Kate, the love of my life'! Just an affectionate 'Dear Kate'—the sort of thing you called your mother, or your aunt, or your sister. That was how he regarded her, of course. A sister, as Tom had arranged. More than ever thankful that she had not succumbed to that mad moment of temptation, Katharine managed to smile as she released herself from his grasp.

'That…that was like no dance I have ever attempted,' she said shakily. 'The ending was…was… quite unique!'

Adam gave a shout of laughter. 'Oh, please, Kate! You needn't worry yourself. The waltz is daring enough, but a kiss normally plays no part in it! That was my own compliment to a wonderful dancer. Were you angry?'

'Not at all. Why should I be?'

'Good! Though I should really be scolding you, not paying compliments.'

'Why?' she asked in surprise.

'You are a fraud!'

'W...What?'

'Pretending you are unteachable, can't move, don't know the steps. Poor Monsieur Edouard—you really had him fooled!'

'What on earth are you talking about? I never pretended anything—I can't dance!'

Adam took her hand again and kissed it. 'You are as natural a dancer as I have met! The sense of rhythm, the instinct for movement... What do you mean by deceiving us all?'

Adam's touch had sent a frisson up her spine. Removing her hand, she pulled herself together and said calmly, 'I don't know what you are talking about, Adam! Th...that wasn't dancing! Not the sort I've come across, anyway.'

'The waltz is very different from the old dances, I agree. But that isn't what matters. Kate, the way you danced with me just now proves that you have the rhythm and grace to make you a first-class dancer! I cannot think why that fool of a dancing master couldn't see that!'

'I think you're underestimating the part *you* played in my performance just then,' she said. 'What was it Lord Trenchard called you? "Twinkle—"'

He put his hand over her mouth. 'Don't even think of saying it! And don't believe for one moment that anyone ever called me that. Ivo Trenchard's sense of humour got the better of him. He was making it up.

But don't lose sight of what I was trying to tell you, either. Edouard was the very worst sort of instructor for you. All you need to learn are a few special steps and four or five figures—there aren't many of them. And that is all. Any country dance is made up of a selection of these put together. I can teach you myself in the week I have left.'

'You're…you're going away?'

'If I am to have eight or nine weeks during the season in London, I must spend some time on Calthorpe beforehand. The place is still in need of a lot of attention. But don't look so worried—a week is more than enough to start you on the right track. The rest is merely practice. We'll arrange for some visits to Guildford or Reigate, where they have some Public Assembly Rooms. You can try your wings in relative obscurity there.'

Adam was as good as his word. He engaged a fiddler from one of the villages nearby and for an hour each afternoon he was a relentless taskmaster. Katharine learned to walk the patterns of the dances until she knew them by heart. He taught her to glide, to skip, to lift and fall to the music. When he found her dropping her head to watch her feet, he put a scarf round her eyes, and made her dance blindfold. The room resounded with cries of, 'Head up, Kate! Up, I say!' and 'You can't see your feet anyway, so don't look!' and 'Dammit, lift your head, girl! That's better! Beautiful!'

It wasn't all work. They rode every day, and Adam showed Kate the favourite places of his boyhood. She had never known such enjoyable companionship, not

even with Tom. There was no sense of rivalry, no need
to guard against any reckless tricks which would
plunge them into danger. Adam was no coward, he
rode right up to Sholto's capabilities, which were considerable, but she felt safer with him than she ever had
with Tom. The kiss was never repeated and, though
Katharine felt a curious ache in her heart whenever
she thought of it, she was glad. Adam was growing
fond of her, she could tell that from his manner, but
it was clear that he regarded her as a sort of sister.
Nothing more. And so, though it had taken something
of a struggle, she had her feelings firmly under control
again. But another kiss, however harmless, could easily undermine all her efforts.

At the end of the week Adam took his mother and
Katharine to the Assembly Rooms in Guildford, where
Katharine felt she acquitted herself reasonably well
with a variety of partners. She found herself enjoying
the occasion, and during the evening several young
gentlemen reappeared to ask her to dance with them
a second time. However, during the supper interval,
Adam, who seemed to be slightly out of humour, dis-
abused her of this conceit. He pointed out that her
partners had not exactly been in a position to judge
her, being so lacking in grace themselves, and added
that she had looked down at her feet twice in the figure
of eight, and missed two entries.

'I still think that I acquitted myself quite creditably,'
said Katharine with a touch of her old belligerent tone.

'Quite creditably! Is that what you want? In that
case, accept my congratulations. But it wouldn't be
enough, for me!'

'Adam!' his mother protested. 'You are too hard! This is Kate's first venture into public. You mustn't put her off at the start. Remember how nervous she was when we first arrived. It isn't at all surprising that she forgot one or two details. She needs cherishing, not criticism. Why haven't you danced with her yourself?'

'He's ashamed to be seen with me, ma'am,' said Katharine with a malicious look at Adam. 'He has his reputation to think of.' She turned to Adam and asked innocently, 'What was that you were called? "Tw—"'

Adam pulled her to her feet. 'The supper interval is over, I believe, Miss Payne!' he said with a threatening smile. 'May I have the honour of this dance? Excuse us, Mama.'

He hauled her to the floor without waiting but, as he gazed at her laughing face while they waited to begin, his ill humour faded.

'You are a minx, Kate,' he said. 'And one day you will get your desserts. But for now we shall converse in the manner expected at a ball. What do you think of the orchestra?'

As they wound their way faultlessly up through the set and back again, Adam was surprised at Katharine's vivacity and charm. He found himself thinking that, if only she had had Tom's looks, she could have been a great success. But her colouring was against her. And, perhaps because of her height, she still had that irritating air of independence. Where were the dimples, the air of helpless femininity, the innocently coquettish glances which appealed to so many men, himself included? No, whatever Ivo and his mother thought, he himself could still not see how Katharine Payne could possibly be the success they predicted.

But, when the music stopped, he found himself strangely reluctant to release her. The time had passed so quickly, he felt they had not finished what they had been saying, though he was not sure what that was. It was very odd! He had spent many a duller half-hour, even among the cream of European society. And, as they walked back to join his mother, the memory of the first time they had danced together in the saloon at Bridge House flashed unbidden into his mind. She had felt so right in his arms, so responsive. And that kiss at the end... It had been extraordinarily sweet! He looked down at the girl walking so calmly beside him and decided to ask her to dance with him again later on. The waltz, perhaps...

In the event, he did not manage to engage Kate for the rest of the evening. She was never free. Katharine Payne seemed to be surprisingly popular with the young men of Guildford.

The next day two things happened. Adam left for Calthorpe, and they finally had news of Miss Kendrick's arrival. Katharine was glad of the second, for she had felt somewhat low ever since she had looked out of her bedroom window early in the morning and seen Adam setting off. Theirs had not been what you would call a friendly parting. Adam had been somewhat silent the night before, and, for someone who was leaving at the crack of dawn, remarkably reluctant to let the evening come to an end. When they got back to Bridge House he suggested that they should have a

chat before retiring. He had one or two things to sort
out with them, he said, before leaving the next day.

But the chat turned out to reveal Adam at what
Katharine considered to be his worst. He issued orders,
thinly disguised as advice, to both of them. In essence,
Katharine was to take care when riding the mare, she
was always to have a groom with her, and she was to
avoid one or two places, which he named, where the
going was not always safe.

'Would you prefer me to ride only in the paddock,
sir?' Katharine asked with suspicious meekness. 'And
perhaps it might be safer if the grooms used a leading
rein on Cintra—though, even if *I* were to tolerate it, I
doubt *she* would!'

'It's all very well to laugh, Kate, but—'

'I assure you I am not laughing!' said Katharine
coldly. 'I think I know enough to ride sensibly, however.'

'That is arrant nonsense and you know it! You can
be every bit as reckless as your brother when the mood
takes you! And, as I think I said before, I didn't rescue
you from your uncle merely to have you break your
neck while in our care!'

Mrs Calthorpe decided to intervene. 'Adam, I think
you may trust Kate. She knows how it would worry
me if she took risks while you are away. Isn't that so,
Kate, dear?'

Katharine scowled at Adam, but nodded and Mrs
Calthorpe relaxed.

But then, when her son proceeded to give her sug-
gestions for Katharine's further progress, Mrs Calthorpe herself became irritated. 'Really, Adam, you
must think I am in my dotage! We shall go to as many

Assemblies as I think fit, and as Kate wishes! And of *course* I shall chaperon Kate to them all—why on earth should you think I wouldn't? Furthermore, you really have no need to ask me to keep a careful eye on her partners—any chaperon would do that quite as a matter of course. What *has* got into you?'

Adam, realising that his two companions, far from being grateful for his advice, were both bridling, sought to make amends. 'I'm sorry, Mama,' he said. 'I suppose I feel responsible for the success of our campaign. We have all worked so hard—I should hate to ruin it for want of a little foresight.'

Katharine stood up. 'Lord Calthorpe!' she said. 'Pray do not think me ungrateful for your help thus far. You have been…have been most…most…kind. But I am not a ''campaign''! Nor am I one of the men in your command, to be told what to do and what not to do! Unlikely though it may seem to you, I think your mother and I will manage very well while you are away. May I suggest that you concentrate your mind on Calthorpe, and leave the success or otherwise of my début to such poor skills as your mother and I possess?'

Adam did not take this with his customary even temper. He bowed coldly and said with a most unusual bite in his voice, 'In that case, Miss Payne, I have no more to say. Except that my only wish has always been to see you launched into society as easily as possible. And that I hope to find you in a more amenable frame of mind when I see you next.'

They wished each other a frosty goodnight, and Katharine went to her bedchamber. But she could not sleep. She was suffering from such a turmoil of feel-

ings that sleep was impossible. She told herself that
Adam Calthorpe was a domineering, insensitive block,
and she was mad to feel as she did about him! But
after a while memories of the times when he had
shown a great deal of understanding began to haunt
her, and she decided that she had been monstrously
ungrateful. She was filled with remorse and wondered
whether to go downstairs and apologise. She even
reached the first landing, but then Mrs Calthorpe's
voice floated up to her.

'I have to say that I have some sympathy with
Kate,' she said. 'You can sound very arbitrary, Adam,
and she is not a girl who reacts well to orders.'

'I don't know why you always defend Madame Independence, ma'am! To my mind, Katharine Payne
should learn to accept perfectly well-meant advice
with more grace. The sooner the better! Her guardians
were quite right! She has had her own way for far too
long!'

'Adam! You are not usually so unjust! What *is* the
matter with you?'

Katharine didn't wait to hear any more. She went
back towards her room, fuming. Madame Independence, indeed! Who did Adam Calthorpe think he
was? What right had he to forbid her to ride any horse
she chose? But he *had* forbidden her. Sholto first, and
now Cintra! What a tyrant he was—telling her where
to go for her rides, how often to go to the Assemblies,
with whom to dance... If she gave in to him now she
would be condemned to be a spineless puppet, she,
Katharine Payne of Herriards, who had until recently
managed her life quite successfully with very little
help from anyone else. It was not to be thought of!

She entered the room, undressed and went to bed. Eventually she slept, but her last illogical thought was a wish, quite a desperate one, that Adam Calthorpe could see her more as a desirable woman, and less as one of his many responsibilities.

Miss Kendrick arrived two days later, and before the week was out had established herself as a force in the household. When asked what she wished to be called, Miss Kendrick said, 'Her ladyship always called me "Kendrick", miss.' After a pause she added, 'Below stairs I shall, of course, be known as "Miss Kendrick".'

She seldom smiled and a mere look from Miss Kendrick could strike fear into the hearts of the other maids. Even Wigborough, Mrs Calthorpe's long-established butler, addressed her with more deference than was his wont with the rest of the female servants, and she had a way of saying, 'Certainly, ma'am!' which frequently caused Mrs Calthorpe to re-examine her orders feverishly for unnoticed errors. But she was outstandingly good at her job. Fortunately for Katharine, it had been many years since Miss Kendrick had prepared a young lady for her début, and she rather liked the idea. She made no bones about the fact that she regarded Katharine a challenge, but nor did she expect to fail.

'Lady Abernethy was only moderately presentable when she first engaged me,' she said calmly. 'But, in the end, I believe she was one of London's most admired ladies of fashion.'

'Miss has excellent bone structure,' she said on another occasion, 'and her colouring is unusual enough to be interesting.'

'Interesting?' Katharine had exclaimed. 'Really?'

'We have quite a lot to work on, of course,' Miss Kendrick had added. 'Miss has neglected her appearance for too long. But I am optimistic about the result.' She was even inclined to look favourably on Katharine's height. 'Miss is tall, but that is by no means a disadvantage,' she pronounced. 'Present modes favour the tall figure.' She gave Katharine a severe look. 'As long as the lady in question carries herself well. Not one of my ladies has *ever* slouched.' Katharine didn't doubt it. Fear of Miss Kendrick would be more effective than a whole library of books carried on the head!

Throughout the weeks that followed Katharine's face, figure, deportment and dress were subjected to Miss Kendrick's iron discipline. Katharine had never thought much about what she wore, had never concerned herself about styles which flattered, or colours which complemented her own colouring. But now one disapproving look from her maid could send favourite dresses to languish at the back of the cupboard forever, and other gowns, in shades she had never thought of wearing, took their place. Fortunately they both agreed that simplicity was more Katharine's style than the feathers, frills, and ribbons depicted in the fashion magazines. But Katharine soon learned that Miss Kendrick's 'simplicity' owed a lot more to art than was apparent to the casual eye.

Mrs Calthorpe was delighted. She went around the house with the look of a cat that has found a whole bowl of cream, though in her letters to Adam she

merely reported that Miss Kendrick was excellent at
her task, and that Katharine was working hard at her
dancing. She also took care to inform him that Katharine was well chaperoned whenever they went to the
Assembly Rooms, and that it was just as well—Miss
Payne was proving to be very popular. She added that
she wouldn't be surprised if Katharine made an excellent match before the London season was halfway
through. But though Mrs Calthorpe was a fond mother,
her motive in giving her son these assurances was not
to make him feel happier. It had not escaped her that
Adam was becoming more personally interested than
he realised in her protégée, that he had been not as
pleased as one might have expected at Katharine's
success with the young men of Guildford. Adam's
mother saw no harm in giving him even more to think
about.

Katharine's marriage prospects were being discussed a mere forty miles away, too. Henry Payne and
his family were also preparing to go to London,
though not in such splendour as they had planned.
Herriards was a comfortable property, but without the
income from the Frampton-Payne inheritance, it would
not run to expensive luxuries.

'I hope you realise that we are all depending on you,
Walter,' said his father one day in March. 'The only
way to bring the Frampton fortune back to Herriards
is for you to marry that confounded girl. You missed
your chance once, and you mustn't miss it again. I
don't know why she took against you—you're a personable enough fellow, and when you put yourself out
the women usually seem to like you. But you'd better

make sure you don't fail with her in London. Your cousin Kate is no beauty—she won't find it easy to attract the gentlemen on her own account. It'll be the money which will draw them. All you have to do is to persuade her that you're different from the rest, that you "love her for herself alone".'

'I'll try, Pa,' said Walter, pulling a face. 'But don't underestimate the task. She can be damned difficult.'

'Walter! You are not to let your dislike of the girl stand in your way! You surely don't need reminding that *we need her money!* Unless you know of another heiress you might persuade to marry you?'

'No, I don't. And I have to admit—there's a certain charm attached to the thought of getting that girl in my power. She wouldn't be so high and mighty for long.'

'You'll have to win her first.'

'Aye, there's the difficulty. What about the Calthorpe fellow?'

'He won't present a problem. From what I saw, he didn't like the girl much more than you did. I'd be willing to wager that it was his mother who pushed him into taking her away from here. She probably regrets it now. No, Calthorpe's swimming in lard himself, he doesn't need the Frampton money. He won't be interested in her. Look, Walter, you have to remember that you have one great advantage—you can offer your cousin Herriards. She was besotted about this place, God knows why. Tell her how much the people here miss her, remind her that in time she would be mistress here again. Play that tune, and she might well fall into your arms. But marry her you must. And soon.'

The two men sat in gloomy silence, contemplating the sheaf of bills and accounts on the table. After a while Walter said idly, 'I just wonder...'

'What?'

'Well, do we know what happens to that money if Kate Payne were never to marry?'

'She gets control of it when she is twenty-five. She can leave it wherever she likes then. For heaven's sake, don't waste time on speculation, boy! You can't afford to. If Kate marries someone else, or reaches the age of twenty-five without marrying, the money will be gone forever as far as we are concerned. You *have* to marry her, Walter.'

'And...if something happened to her before she is twenty-five?'

'I'm not sure, but I believe it reverts to the Herriards estate.'

'Does it really?' Walter got up and walked about the room. 'Well, well!'

'You're grasping at straws! As far as I know your cousin is in perfect health! She isn't going to fade away and die just to save you from having to marry her! Pull yourself together, Walter! Stop fantasising and concentrate on what is possible!'

Walter stopped pacing, and looked at his father enigmatically. Then he shrugged his shoulders and appeared to abandon whatever he had been thinking. He said, 'You're right, Pa. Kate has had time to get over her spleen at the loss of Herriards. And by now she must be over Tom's death, too. She'll probably be much more amenable. Don't worry. I'll get her.'

All was now ready for the Calthorpe household to move to London. The house just off Berkeley Square was ready to receive them, a few of the servants, together with numerous additional domestic comforts, were already installed there, and everything needed for the wardrobe of two fashionable ladies was finished and waiting to be packed. It only needed Adam's presence for the changeover to take place. Some business in Bath had caused him an unexpected delay, but he was now expected hourly. In the event, his arrival took them by surprise. Katharine had been out with Cintra and she returned to find Adam waiting for her at the stables. She quite forgot the cloud under which they had parted, and gave him a dazzling smile.

'You seem to make a habit of surprising us,' she said gaily as he helped her to dismount. 'Though I cannot say this time that you were earlier than expected. Have you seen your mother?'

'Not yet,' he replied, smiling at her in turn. 'I left the carriage to follow on, and rode the last bit of the way, in order to be here sooner. When I saw you and Cintra on the other side of the river I waited for you here. Shall we go in?'

They strolled up to the house. 'How are you and Mama? You at least are looking well.' She replied suitably and enquired after his journey and the progress of the work at Calthorpe.

It was all very companionable and easy, yet Katharine was a trifle put out. She had planned Adam's first sight of her, and it wasn't meant to take place in the stables after she had had a demanding ride. Her hair was all over the place, she was prepared to swear that her cheeks were red with her exertions, and her old riding habit was not nearly as flattering as any of her new gowns. It was a far cry from the newly elegant Miss Payne with which she had hoped to astonish him!

Adam, on the other hand, was feeling very pleased. Perhaps Ivo Trenchard had not been so far out, after all! Kate's smile was indeed captivating, and, in spite of her height and the absence of any dimples, she had a great deal of charm. He had been quite taken with her when he had first seen her just now—cheeks flushed, hair loose... The riding habit was old, of course, but it somehow suited her. Perhaps it was because he was used to seeing it on her. He had missed Kate at Calthorpe, had frequently thought of her riding with him on the Downs dressed in that same habit. He had recalled their conversations, her delight in the world about them, her determination to keep up with him, however hard the going... Adam found himself hoping quite passionately that she would not be disappointed in the new world she was about to enter. What if his mother and he had not between them prepared her well enough? He did not like to think of that smile growing dimmed, of Kate becoming once again the unhappy creature he had met last October... He mustn't let it happen!

They went into the house, where his mother greeted him with enthusiasm. Katharine excused herself and disappeared.

'And what do you think of Kate?'

'I told her—she is looking remarkably well, though not much changed. Is the new maid any good?'

Mrs Calthorpe began to laugh. 'My dear boy, never let Miss Kendrick hear you say so! And, in any case, what do you mean? Kate has been transformed!'

'Oh, really, that is going too far! The girl is happier,

certainly, and that adds a charm to. her looks which was lacking before. But transformed? Surely not!'

His mother regarded him thoughtfully. 'You don't think so? Well, perhaps I am wrong. We shall see.'

Dinner was late that evening, after the last-minute preparations for their departure the next morning were complete. Adam was waiting at the bottom of the stairs when Kate came down, his mother having deliberately delayed her own descent to give him time to appreciate the new Kate Payne. At first he did not recognise her. For the moment before he came to his senses he found himself asking who this slender creature descending the stairs so gracefully could possibly be. Head held high, one hand holding the train of her golden silk dress, she had reached the bottom step before he had found his voice.

'Kate!' he exclaimed.

'Well, Adam? Do you like the dress? It was your Christmas present, you know.'

Stammering like the newest subaltern, Adam said, 'Y…yes, of course I do! It suits you very well.'

She gave him a cool sideways look. 'You sound doubtful?'

'No, no, I assure you! I was merely taken somewhat aback. You look so different.'

'I should hope so,' she said. 'But why do I still have the impression that you don't approve? Isn't it what you wanted?'

'It is! Of course it is! The dress is lovely. And…and your hair is very nice, too. I think.'

'I beg your pardon?' she said, beginning to sound annoyed.

'It's just that...it doesn't... It's all so elegant—it doesn't look like you at all! Oh, God, that's not what I meant to say—' Adam stopped in confusion.

Since Katharine was starting to look as if she would like to give Adam a most inelegant box on the ears, Mrs Calthorpe decided it was time she joined them. 'It is very strange,' she said, giving Katharine a wicked smile. 'Numerous acquaintances over the years have complimented me on my son's exquisitely polished manners. I believe the Duke himself has said as much. What has happened to them tonight, my dear?'

Adam pulled himself together and gave his mother a rueful smile. 'You are quite right, Mama. Forgive me, Kate! I was indeed overcome by your transformation! You look superb! I can see that I shall have a busy time keeping your suitors at bay.' He bowed formally to each of them in turn. 'Shall we go in to dinner, ladies?'

Mrs Calthorpe noticed with delight that, though Adam's eyes were frequently on Katharine, the girl did not allow this to put her off. Her company manners and conversation were exactly as Mrs Calthorpe had taught her, and if Adam's mother had ever entertained any doubt about Kate's suitability to be her son's wife it would have been dismissed that night.

Adam himself soon recovered all his famous aplomb, and the dinner table resounded with laughter and good humour. They talked of their plans for their stay in London. The dates for the various parties and outings which Mrs Calthorpe had planned were already fixed, of course, including one for the ball which Katharine's guardians had asked her to arrange. But they made plans for other occasions, and Mrs Calthorpe reeled off a list of people she wished Katharine to meet.

'That reminds me,' said Adam. 'I saw Ivo when I was in Somerset. He seemed quite eager to receive an invitation to your ball.'

'He is at the head of the list,' said Mrs Calthorpe. 'Dear Ivo! He is such a valuable guest at a party or ball. He loves dancing and is always extremely popular.'

'Until he makes off with the ambassador's wife, or some such lark,' said Adam caustically.

Later that night, after Katharine had gone to bed, Mrs Calthorpe tackled Adam about his behaviour.

'The dear child has worked so hard, Adam. I think she was a little disappointed that you did not immediately show more approval. And I have to say that you had me a little puzzled as well.'

'I'm not sure how to explain, Mama. There's no doubt that you and Miss Whatever-her-name-is have worked wonders. Between you—'

'And with Kate's help!' interposed his mother.

'And with Kate's help, you have produced a young lady of fashion who is bound to rouse a certain amount of admiration—'

His mother interrupted again. 'A great deal of admiration,' she said gently.

'Whatever you say. But…it isn't Kate. I found the girl I saw this afternoon down at the stables far more appealing than the elegant creature at the table tonight.'

Mrs Calthorpe paused. Then she said, 'Adam, what

was your aim in bringing Kate away from that uncle of hers?'

'I...I wanted to rescue her from a life of misery. I had promised Tom, and I could do no less.'

'Not to marry her yourself, I think?'

'Good heavens, no!'

'Well, then, what are you worried about? Kate doesn't have to appeal to you. If she is to find a suitable husband, she needs to be successfully launched into Society. The young lady at the table tonight will find that far easier than the girl you met this afternoon. You know what the polite world is like. Our job is to prepare her as fully as we can, to introduce her to the right people and then to try to make sure that she chooses a husband wisely. Your responsibility to Tom's sister will then be at an end.'

She looked sideways at her son. He was hunched over his glass of wine, looking anything but pleased at this description of the task ahead. She smiled. She didn't like it any more than he did, but then...she had an idea that Adam's responsibility for Katharine Payne would not come to an end with the London season!

Chapter Eleven

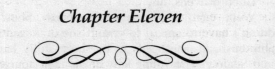

Their journey the following day was accomplished without delay or incident, and soon, after three weeks in London, Katharine felt as if she had lived there all her life. She quickly adapted to London hours, rising late and going to bed in the early hours, and in no time at all she knew the latest *on dit,* which were the most stylish shops, and where the most fashionable coffee houses were to be found. And the capital soon got used to the sight of Miss Payne dancing at Almack's, riding through the park, driving out to Kew, or visiting Vauxhall, together with all the other activities which made up the life of the polite world during the season.

Society agreed that Miss Payne was not quite in the accepted mode. She was neither divinely fair, nor ravishingly dark, her eyes were not celestial blue, but an unusual brown and, though her figure was good, she was taller than the ideal. She did not appear to set herself out to charm, but behaved in an open, natural manner. All of which made it quite astonishing that she was on the way to becoming one of the season's successes. Certainly the sight of her slender form weaving its way gracefully through London's ball-rooms aroused a great deal of admiration. To evoke Miss Payne's dazzling smile was an object of importance with many an otherwise sensible young man. And numbers of eligible bachelors were impressed by the discovery that she sometimes preferred an interesting conversation to listening to extravagant compliments.

In short, by the time the Balmennys appeared in London, Katharine Payne was on the way to having the success her heart had desired. Adam was beginning to realise that he had been wrong and his mother and Ivo Trenchard right. And, as time passed, he got used to the new Kate Payne, and began to see her with the world's eyes. The shabby governess of Herriard Stoke churchyard was gone forever, replaced by an elegantly fashionable young lady with exquisite manners. Kate the virago was lost, buried inside a light-hearted, light-footed creature who danced and smiled her way into the hearts of Society. Adam was fascinated with the change, but was occasionally irritated by his own perversity in regretting the disappearance of the belligerent shrew and wishing he could see her just once more.

Mindful of his responsibility he kept a watchful eye on her, but took care not to appear to be too close. The world must regard Katharine as his mother's protégé, not as any kind of future bride for himself. In this respect he and his mother were at odds, he knew. But better acquaintance with Kate had not given him any reason to change his mind. He had grown to like her, but she possessed neither the sort of looks he admired, nor the qualities he was seeking. Life with Katharine Payne would never be easy—for one thing, she argued too much. And Adam was still looking for the kind of wife he had pictured back at the ball on the eve of Waterloo—gentle, calm and undemanding, someone for whom he would have a mild affection without the turmoil of passionate love. If she happened to be a blue-eyed blonde so much the better.

Another newcomer to the London scene would seem to be ideal. Kate's cousin, Miss Catherine Payne, enchantingly fair, with eyes the colour of summer skies, and a delicately submissive air, had already impressed him at Herriards, and she was now also in London for the season. And because of a curious set of circumstances he found himself quite frequently in her company.

Henry Payne and his family had arrived not long after the Calthorpes. Their paths did not cross at first, for they tended to move in different circles. But, ironically enough, it wasn't long before Society was divided into two camps, each claiming that the success of the season would be a Miss Payne. The smaller, more discerning, group declared that Miss Kate Payne was the cream of the débutantes. They refused to allow that her lack of more conventional beauty in any way detracted from her charms. The larger group, while granting that Miss Katharine Payne was very charming, swore that London had seldom seen as beautiful a creature as her cousin, Mr Henry Payne's daughter, the lovely Miss Catherine Payne. Rivalry between the factions increased, and society hostesses, eager to add interest to the endless round of balls and soirées, tried to make sure that both girls were present at their events as often as possible.

Katharine was thus forced to see far more of her cousins than she wished. To avoid them would encourage just the sort of gossip she disliked. Society already found it slightly odd that she was being sponsored in London by Mrs Calthorpe, rather than by Mr Henry Payne and his wife. If it was seen that she was reluctant even to talk to her cousins, society would soon start to speculate on the rift in the Payne family. Even less did Katharine want to encourage any thought of rivalry between herself and the family beauty, Catherine. So she hid her distrust of them, chatted to Catherine, danced with Walter, and listened with apparent attention to her uncle and aunt. And of course, Adam saw quite a lot of them too.

Walter was delighted. Matters could not have turned out better. After his failure to attract her in Hampshire, it was most unlikely that Kate Payne would have spent a second longer in his company than she had to. But now fate, and Society, had taken a hand, and it was up to him to take advantage of it. He took care to escort his sister to every occasion where Kate was likely to be present. Once there, he made sure he reserved at least one dance with his cousin before she could legitimately claim that her card was full. And during the dances he exerted himself as never before to remedy the damage done to his cause at Herriards.

At first Katharine froze him out whenever he became personal. But Walter was a fast learner and he soon knew how to hold her interest by giving her tit-bits of information about the people she had known at Herriards. He had always been an excellent improvisor and his accounts of how he had defied his father to defend the interests of the poor in the community were quite convincing. After a month or so, Walter began to feel that he was making some headway, that in a while Kate Payne would listen more favourably to his suit. And about time, too! Very few women had resisted him for this long before.

Into this intriguing situation came Lady Balmenny, beautiful, spoilt, trapped in a boring marriage and looking for amusement.

The day after she arrived, she appeared at the Marchmonts' ball halfway through the evening. It was one of the season's most prestigious events and the rooms were full. Julia wandered slowly through the throng, waving her fan languidly, apparently enjoying the scene. But she was searching all the while for one face among the crowd, and she finally saw it. Adam Calthorpe was dancing.

She turned to the person next to her, who happened to be an old friend. Hetta Jerrard was one of London's most notorious gossips. 'Who is that delightful girl?' Julia asked. 'The tall one dancing over there.'

'You mean the one with Lord Calthorpe, Julia?'

'I suppose I do. Yes.'

'That, my dear, is one of the latest stars. A Miss Katharine Payne. Charming, isn't she? Some say she is *the* star. But I myself prefer her cousin. She is infinitely prettier. You must meet her, Julia.'

Julia nearly dropped her fan. 'Wait! Katharine Payne! You said Katharine Payne? That girl dancing with Lord Calthorpe is *Katharine Payne!* I don't believe it! Is she staying with the Calthorpes?'

'Yes. Mrs Calthorpe is sponsoring her. We are led
to believe that there isn't any other reason for Lord
Calthorpe's interest in her. But one does wonder...
they seem very close.'

Julia looked at the pair on the floor. They were
laughing as they rejoined the set. 'That's nonsense,'
she said sharply. 'It's easily explained—she's the sister of one of Lord Calthorpe's friends, who was killed
at Waterloo. Adam made him some ridiculous promise
about looking after the girl. That is all.'

'It can't quite be all, my dear. Katharine Payne is
not alone in the world. She has some perfectly good
cousins, who are also in London for the season. Why
aren't *they* looking after her?' Lady Hetta sent a significant look in the direction of the dancers. 'Perhaps
Lord Calthorpe's interest is more than just an obligation to a friend?'

'What nonsense you talk, Hetta! The girl isn't at all
his style.'

'That's true,' said Lady Hetta with regret. 'He appears to be far more taken with her cousin.'

'What cousin?'

Hetta Jerrard started to smile. This was going better.
Julia sounded quite annoyed. 'Another Miss Payne,
Julia dear. Another Catherine Payne! And a real dia-
mond. The two girls may be cousins, but they are not
at all alike—one is tall and the other tiny. In fact...'

'Well?' said Julia impatiently.

'The other Miss Payne bears a remarkable resem-
blance to you—as you were years ago. You might almost be mother and daughter!'

Julia took a moment to recover, then snapped, 'You
were never very good at arithmetic, Hetta. I dare say

there's a bare seven or eight years between the chit and me. And what do you mean—as I was years ago? I look exactly the same now as I did before I married Balmenny. Everyone says so.'

'Well, they would, wouldn't they? But perhaps it would be better if you didn't meet the second Miss Payne, Julia. In fact, I would stay away from her altogether if you can. Comparisons can be very disconcerting, don't you think?'

'I don't know what you're talking about. Excuse me, I see that the set is ending. I must go and congratulate Katharine Payne on her début.'

Hetta Jerrard watched eagerly as her friend made her way through to Adam Calthorpe and his partner. She would eat her best hat if Julia's interest was in Miss Katharine Payne. Not when handsome, charming Lord Calthorpe was standing right next to the girl.

'Miss Payne!' called Julia. 'Miss Payne, don't go away! Remember me? You came to Redshaw Hall on Christmas Eve—' She turned and gave a start. 'Why, Adam! It's you! This is an unexpected pleasure. Still looking after Katharine, I see.' She smiled at him archly. 'When do you take time off for your *own* enjoyment, Adam?'

'Julia! When did you arrive in London?'

Julia fell into step with them as they walked towards the supper room. 'Last night. What a *journey* we had! The packet tossed us about till I thought we should *die!* And then the roads were *impossible!*'

'But here you are tonight, looking as beautiful as ever.'

'Oh, never say so! I am a *hag,* a positive hag!' said Lady Balmenny, looking deeply pleased.

Katharine was annoyed. She had not been taken in by Julia's apparent surprise at seeing Adam. The woman had probably come over with the express design of talking to him. And though Julia's barbed remark seemed to have passed him by, it had not been lost on her. Refusing to allow Julia to leave her out of the conversation, she said now, 'Have you come direct from Ireland, Lady Balmenny?'

'What? Oh, yes. Balmenny left everything so late that there wasn't time to stop for any length of time on the way. We spent but four days driving from Holyhead.' Her wonderful eyes turned back to Adam. 'I really wanted to be here much sooner,' she said wistfully.

Katharine persisted. 'Is Lord Balmenny here tonight?'

'I don't think so.' There was a slight snap in Julia's voice. 'He said he was going to rest this evening.' She threw out her hands and said, 'But you know me, Adam. I was *starved* for some company. Ireland is a *desert*. However, I have to say that I recognise very few people here tonight. I feel very alone.'

They had reached the supper room. 'In that case, why don't you join us for supper?' said Adam. Katharine gazed at him in disbelief. Even while they were walking the short distance from the ballroom, at least a dozen people had nodded to Julia! But the invitation had been made and it was impossible to get out of it. Katharine sighed. She had been looking forward to this supper with Adam. He seemed to spend so little time with her nowadays. And though she frequently reminded herself of his arrogant, domineering ways, of how often he had annoyed her, she had not yet found anyone else whose company she enjoyed more. Try as she might to stop herself, Adam's face was the one she first looked for, Adam's voice the one she wanted to hear…

And now, the rare prospect of a delightful supper party *à deux* with him had been ruined by this…this relic of the past! She was willing to wager that, if matters were left to Julia Redshaw, the *à deux* supper would consist of Lord Calthorpe and herself, and Katharine would be pushed to the fringe. But that was not going to happen. She could not get rid of Julia, but she could enlarge the party—perhaps not altogether to Lady Balmenny's taste. It wasn't to hers either, but in matters of war… Walter Payne was passing their table with his sister on his arm.

'Walter! Catherine! Do come and join us,' she called.

Walter could hardly believe his ears, but he didn't hesitate. 'This is very nice,' he said as he approached. 'Good evening, Kate. Calthorpe.' He nodded and regarded Julia.

'Lady Balmenny, may I present my cousins, Catherine and Walter Payne?'

Introductions over, Katharine ignored a glance of outrage from Adam and sat back. She wasn't particularly happy, but she found the situation intriguing. Adam, she knew, couldn't stand Walter, but he had a very soft spot for Walter's sister. And now, looking at Catherine and Lady Balmenny as they sat together, she could see why. Julia Redshaw had been the love of his life ten years earlier, and Catherine Payne must be almost the image of Julia at seventeen. Even now they were very alike, but Catherine's beauty still had the dew on it, a rose which was delicately unfurling. Julia was a strikingly beautiful woman, but her looks were just beginning to owe less to nature and more to art. The comparison was cruel.

Conversation flourished, in spite of the tensions round the table. Julia did her best to dominate Adam's attention, but was not altogether successful—largely because Adam's innate good manners wouldn't allow the rest of the party to be excluded. When Adam was talking to Catherine or Kate Payne, Julia turned her attention to Walter, who was, after all, a very handsome young man. He responded gallantly, for Lady Balmenny was an illustrious member of the highest circles, and he found her overtures most flattering. However, it annoyed Julia to note that the true focus of Walter's attention was always his cousin Katharine, and as soon as he could he turned to talk to her again. Catherine Payne contributed little, merely gazing shyly at Adam and blushing whenever he addressed her.

Katharine found this most irritating. How did the girl manage it? she asked herself. She sits there, saying nothing worth listening to and blushing to order, and Adam looks at her with a warmth in his eyes which I have never seen directed towards me... Just when Katharine was regretting her impulsive invitation, and beginning to long for the end of the supper interval, a diversion occurred.

'Adam! I've found you at last! And Miss Payne, too.' It was Ivo Trenchard. 'I see you have a spare place at the table—you weren't by some miracle saving it for me, were you?' He smiled engagingly at the rest of the company.

All three ladies were delighted to make the numbers even with such a handsome and distinguished addition to the party. More introductions were performed and Ivo sat down next to Katharine. 'I've been hearing so much about the ravishing Miss Payne, that I was very much afraid I would never get near you. You haven't forgotten your promise to dance with me, I hope?'

'No, indeed,' said Katharine warmly. 'You were my first supporter, sir, I don't forget such things.'

'Wonderful! Do you dance the waltz? And, if so, would you delight me by saying you will dance it with me? I believe it follows the next set of country dances.'

'I would love to dance the waltz with you, Lord Trenchard,' said Katharine, casting a glance at Adam. He was frowning slightly, but at his friend, not at her.

'Adam! *You* must dance the waltz with *me!*' cried Lady Balmenny. She turned to the company. 'I was such a *child* when I knew Adam last that we would *never* have been able to waltz together. Indeed, I don't believe I knew how! Miss Payne, you must have made *lots* of progress since last Christmas, if you can manage the waltz. When Mama last wrote, you appeared not to be having a great deal of success with your dancing. I understand that Monsieur Edouard gave up in *despair!*'

'Ah, but since then I have had the best of teachers, Lady Balmenny,' said Katharine demurely.

'What? Better than Monsieur Edouard? Who was that, pray? We always considered Monsieur Edouard *outstandingly* good, even with the most *inept*. Who was this wonder?'

Ivo had been regarding Lady Balmenny with appreciation. He said now, 'My dear ma'am, do not ask! Mrs Calthorpe produced him, just at the right time.'

'But what was he called?'

'Er... He had a very curious name,' said Lord Trenchard with a grin. 'Twinkletoes... Twinkletoes... What was the rest?'

'Smith!' said Katharine promptly. 'Twinkletoes Smith. An excellent fellow. But I understand he has retired from the art of giving instruction. At least, I hope he has.'

Lord Trenchard gazed at Katharine in laughing admiration. 'Why did I wait so long before returning to London? You're even better than your brother said!' he exclaimed.

'What *are* they talking about, Adam?' asked Lady Balmenny, looking bewildered.

'Don't waste time trying to understand them, Julia. Lord Trenchard often talks nonsense and he has infected Kate,' said Adam, with a glare at his former fellow officer.

The sound of music came from the ballroom. Walter, thinking it was time he made a mark, stood up and reminded Katharine that she had promised him the set of dances after the interval. Adam had already asked Catherine Payne. With a look on his face which Adam had seen countless times in ballrooms all over Europe, Ivo Trenchard bowed to Lady Balmenny.

'May I have the pleasure of dancing this set with one of the most beautiful ladies in London?' he asked. Julia looked at him sharply. Had there been a touch of cynicism in Lord Trenchard's tone? But then he smiled, as he took her by the hand and led her to the ballroom, and she was reassured.

* * *

Walter had been much encouraged by Katharine's spontaneous invitation to join her at supper. Now, dancing the long set of country dances with her, he allowed himself to become more personal again. He spoke more boldly of his hopes for the future, of how much she really meant to him...

Katharine hardly heard him. Whenever the dance permitted she watched Adam's tall figure out of the corner of her eye. As he danced with her cousin Catherine, his face, which in repose was normally rather severe, was softened by an indulgent smile. Her heart twisted. It seemed to Katharine that she had been watching that smile for weeks, while Adam talked, danced or walked with her cousin Catherine. He seemed to handle the girl as gently as he would a piece of the delicate porcelain she so much resembled. Was this what Adam wanted? Someone to cherish, to protect? Was he about to ask Catherine Payne to marry him, thinking he would find in her, not an equal, but someone who would let him make the decisions, without argument or protest? Or was she merely a reflection of his lost love—a younger, available, substitute for Julia Redshaw?

For all the smiles Katharine directed at Walter as she made her way up the set with him, her heart was heavy. Julia would never have made Adam happy, and nor would Catherine. Catherine might be young, but she was just as selfish, and, in spite of her submissive appearance, just as determined to have her own way as the lovely Lady Balmenny. They neither of them regarded men as partners, as possible friends, but as trophies, to be coaxed with smiles and threatened with tears into giving them whatever they wanted at the time.

What a waste it would be! Life with Adam Calthorpe could be wonderful! What a strong, loving, tender husband he would make for the right woman! He might be a touch autocratic, and his self-control was such that Katharine couldn't imagine him ever falling desperately in love again. But there was no one in the world that she, Kate Payne, would rather marry…

Her heart missed a beat and she came to a sudden halt. *No one she would rather marry?* Was she really in love with Adam Calthorpe! Yes! It seemed to her that she had always really been in love with him, ever since the beginning, ever since he had knocked her over in the churchyard. Though she had only just realised it, she had fallen in love with him then, and had loved him ever since!

'Kate? Kate! Are you unwell?'

Katharine came to with a start. Walter was looking at her in concern. The set round them was in some confusion.

'I…I'm sorry,' she said. 'Please excuse me… No, no, I am perfectly well—pray carry on.'

Fortunately the set came to an end shortly after and they returned to the table in the supper room. Walter, still full of concern, went away to fetch Katherine a drink of water, and Adam came to sit by her almost immediately.

'What was the trouble?' he asked.

'Nothing!' For the life of her she could not speak naturally. She knew her tone was too detached, almost rude, but the revelation on the ballroom floor had been too great a shock.

'You're ill!'

'No! No, I'm not ill.' She gave a little laugh. 'I must have missed my entry, Adam. For some reason I was totally confused. I'm glad you were not my partner. You would have been less understanding than Walter.' He started to argue, but she put out her hand. 'Please don't make any more fuss. I am perfectly well. And I don't want to miss my waltz with Lord Trenchard.'

He looked sternly at her. 'I don't like it,' he said severely.

The Kate which the world never saw wanted to cry, 'Please, please, Adam, don't look at me like that! Look at me as you look at my cousin, tenderly, warmly. Take my hand as you take hers, as if it might break in your grasp... Tell me you care for me...!'

But what Katharine Payne rather coldly said was, 'Don't be tiresome, Adam! Ivo Trenchard is one of your oldest friends. You've always told me what an excellent dancer he is. He'll see that I manage.'

'That's not what I was worried about—' He could say no more. Walter Payne was coming back with the water, and at the same time Ivo Trenchard returned to the table with a laughing Lady Balmenny. His skilled compliments seemed to have restored her good humour.

She said as they sat down, 'So. Your Signor Twinkletoes doesn't seem to have taught you *everything*, Miss Payne. What confusion you brought to your set! And in such a *simple* dance, too.'

'Miss Payne was ill,' said Walter, putting a solicitous hand on Kate's shoulder.

Adam's gaze rested on it for a moment, then he said coldly, 'Payne, I expect your sister will be looking for you. I took her back to your friends in the small saloon.'

Walter looked as if he wished to demur, whereupon Adam added very firmly, 'I promised her I would send you to her.' Walter could hardly disagree without challenging Adam, so he shrugged his shoulders, gave Katharine a warm smile, bowed to the rest, and left.

Adam said to the others, 'I think Kate needs a breath of fresh air. Excuse us. We'll be back in a moment. Kate?' He held out his arm and Katharine, still in something of a daze, took it. They went through the hall into the small garden which lay behind the Marchmonts' house.

Here Adam stopped and turned to Katharine. 'I should have thought you had seen enough of that fellow, Kate.'

'By "fellow" you mean Walter Payne, I suppose? Unfortunately he is my cousin. I think tongues would wag if I refused to recognise him. Besides, I really think he has changed. He says he is sorry for his behaviour at Herriards.'

'Leopards don't change their spots. I've known a good few like Payne in my time. They're not to be trusted. Don't spend so much time with him.'

Katharine exclaimed, 'I wish you would not always try to dictate to me, Adam! What business is it of yours what I do? I don't need your permission to talk to my cousin. It nearly always concerns Herriards and the people down there.'

'Don't you think this nostalgia for Herriards is a mistake?' said Adam coldly. 'You might remember that it is no longer your affair. Or are you now regretting your decision to leave there?'

His coldness, his indifference, cut Katharine to the quick. Without stopping to consider, she said defiantly, 'I could go back there any time I liked! Walter said so.'

Adam's frown grew. 'Don't be such a fool! You would never stand it! While your Uncle Henry is in charge, Herriards would be the last place you would wish to live!'

Some perverse demon caused Katharine to carry on. 'But afterwards? If I were mistress there? I dare say I could be if I wanted to, you know.'

She had succeeded in surprising him. He said at last, 'You mean you might marry Walter? You? I refuse to believe it! What a waste of all our efforts that would be!'

So much for my hopes, thought Katharine. I'd just represent a waste of effort! That's all.

Sounds of music came through the windows. 'We'd better return,' she said wearily. 'This breath of fresh air doesn't seem to be doing either of us much good.'

They returned to the ballroom in silence. The waltz was just about to begin. Ivo Trenchard swept Katharine up and they launched straight away into the swirl of figures circling the room. Adam watched them grimly. He didn't believe for one minute that Katharine Payne had the slightest intention of returning to Herriards! She had only said it to provoke him. It must be that! What a perverse creature she was!

'Adam!' Julia was standing a yard away, tapping her foot angrily. He pulled himself together.

'Please forgive me, Julia! Someone caught me as I came through the hall and I was held up. Shall we dance?'

Julia Redshaw was having quite a difficult time. She was not accustomed to being kept waiting. In fact, the whole evening was turning out to be far less agreeable than she had thought. It had been a blow to find that her throne as London's queen of hearts was being threatened by a chit of seventeen! Several misguided friends had raved about Catherine Payne, had even thought they were complimenting her when they said the girl was so like Julia at her age. And when she had glanced into the small saloon—just to see if Adam and the other Payne girl were there—she had been annoyed to see Catherine Payne surrounded by a bevy of gentlemen, among whom were several of her former lovers, gentlemen who not long ago had sworn undying devotion to her, Julia Redshaw! She could get them back, of course, any moment she chose! But it was irritating, all the same.

Then there was the question of Adam. He seemed quite unnecessarily concerned with the other Katharine Payne, his friend's sister! What a burden that girl was to him! His mother was behind it, of course. Mrs Calthorpe had never liked Julia, and she was using the girl as a shield to keep her son from falling in love all over again with his childhood sweetheart. Well, Mrs Calthorpe would fail! The Adam of today was a prize worth having and Julia fully intended to conquer him again. She was sure it wouldn't have been difficult except for the presence of those wretched girls—Walter Payne's sister, who looked so like her, and Tom Payne's sister who was just always there!

These thoughts and others like them caused Julia to sound more ill-tempered than was her custom in public when she answered Adam's question.

'And where is Miss Kate Payne now? Better, I hope?' she snapped.

Chapter Twelve

Julia looked quite shrewish, thought Adam. A genuine shrew, as opposed to the shrew he had found in the churchyard, a shrew who was really a girl at her wits' end, trying to cope with the loss of everything she loved and hitting out at the world... His heart gave a thump. What if Kate wasn't teasing? What if she really did consider Herriards worth a marriage to Walter Payne? No! That mustn't happen. She *mustn't* go back to Herriards! He would have to stop it somehow...

'Well?' said Julia impatiently. 'Have you managed to get rid of her?'

Adam looked at Julia again and said coolly, 'She's dancing with Lord Trenchard. Over there. See? Shall we join in?'

He had been offended at her tone. Julia took a breath and told herself to be careful. The Adam of ten years before would have fallen over himself to explain, to make excuses, done anything to win back her smiles. The Adam of today was a distinguished man of the world. He was less easy to deal with—though, she had to admit, infinitely more interesting. But a crowded ballroom was not the place to deal with him.

'Adam, I don't feel like dancing. We've had so little time to talk. Will you take me, too, into the garden for a breath of fresh air?' She smiled sweetly and a little sadly at him. There was a touch of moisture in her deep blue eyes.

Adam bowed and said, 'Of course. If you think it is wise?'

'Balmenny isn't here,' she said, taking his arm. It wasn't quite what Adam had meant, but, though he frowned, he accompanied her into the garden.

Once outside Julia said softly, 'Forgive me if I sounded impatient before. It's just that…I dreamed so often of meeting you again. When I heard you were going to be in Surrey at Christmas I was determined to be there, too. Balmenny doesn't like travelling in winter, but I made him bring me to visit my parents. And we met again on Christmas Eve. It was just like old times, didn't you feel it, too?'

'Hardly. In old times we had to meet in secret,' said Adam drily.

'Oh, yes—and it was so romantic! Oh, those summer days! We were so in love… I didn't forget you, Adam. After you left England I was quite desolate, you know. And then I heard of your success, and of all those balls and parties you would be attending, and I longed to be there with you. How I envied those foreign ladies who were your partners. You once said that I was just as high as your heart. Were there many who made you feel the same?'

Adam looked down at her. 'I forget,' he said easily. 'It all seems so long ago. I remember the fighting better. But, Julia—surely you didn't pine for long? I thought I heard that you married Balmenny that same year?'

'Oh, Balmenny!' she said pettishly. 'Don't let us talk of him! I wish I had never met him!'

Adam took a step back and examined her, letting his eyes wander over her dress of silk and lace, and the clusters of diamonds at her throat and in her hair. 'He's been very good to you,' he said a little cynically.

'He's dull! And old! Adam! Please, don't be unkind! Surely you haven't forgotten how much we loved one another! Confess! I don't believe you have. I've watched you with Catherine Payne, and you look at her as if you're looking at a ghost. As if you were seeing me. Isn't that true? Everyone says how like me she is.'

'It is certainly true that she is very like you.'

'Tell me that I'm right. That when you're with her, you don't see *her* at all. You only see *me*. Isn't that so? You imagine that we are together again.' She drew a little nearer. 'But why make do with the imitation? I'm here! I'm real! And, Adam—I now have so much more to offer...'

Adam's face was in shadow. Disconcerted by his silence she went on, her voice full of pathos, 'You can't have forgotten how much you loved me!'

Adam hesitated. Then he said, 'That was a long time ago, Julia. We've both changed since then.'

'It isn't so long! And I won't let you say we've changed! Please, Adam, can't we at least be...friends again?' She gave a small sob. 'I'm so lonely. My marriage was a mistake. And I'm not hard and independent like that other girl—the one you've been saddled with. Katharine Payne. I need someone to fight my battles for me. I need help. I need love.'

Julia moved even closer. Her tiny hands were against Adam's chest. She raised her face to look at him, her beauty unaffected by the tears now rolling down her cheeks...

Adam had a sudden vision of Kate standing back, angrily refusing to accept sympathy from anyone. He remembered the detached tone she adopted when most moved, her refusal to parade her emotions. And as he regarded Julia now he was surprised to feel nothing but a slight distaste. He took a step back and said as gently as he could, 'I don't believe I am the right person for that, my dear. And Kate is not as invulnerable as you think. Kate needs me more than you do. You see, she has no husband to guard her interests.'

Julia looked at him in disbelief. He had rejected her! The tears stopped and a tide of colour swept over her cheeks. Her tone was venomous as she echoed his words. '"*Kate needs me more than you do!*" That lump of a girl? Needing help? Of course she hasn't a husband! Who would marry *her?* How dare you compare her with me! But don't worry! I understand what you really wanted to say. Adam Calthorpe is too much of a gentleman, too *noble* to make love to a married woman—isn't that it? My God! You always were a prig, Adam Calthorpe! I wonder why I ever tolerated you. Well, that's all over. I don't care which of the Paynes you marry. Marry the simpering miss if you wish—you won't find *her* as innocent as you think! But it's my belief you'll end up with the overgrown beanpole! That's what your mother intends! As for me, I wish you joy of neither!'

She ran to the door which led into the hall, but remembered to stop for a minute or two while she carefully dabbed the marks of tears from her face. Then she shook out her fan, took a breath and walked into the house, smiling right and left at her acquaintance, waving her fan gracefully, as beautiful and as charming as ever.

Adam watched her go with nothing but relief. The old dream had been shattered. For the first time he had seen Julia Redshaw as his mother saw her, and he marvelled at his former blindness. What an escape he had had all those years ago! But it wasn't long before his thoughts turned again to Katharine, and he followed Julia inside. The waltz was still in train, and she and Ivo Trenchard were dipping and turning with the rest. What the devil had Julia meant? Kate was no lump, no beanpole, she moved like a queen! Hardly knowing it, he walked down the room, watching the pair from a distance. Kate seemed to have recovered her spirits. She was laughing up into Ivo's face, saying something which made him laugh in turn. It worried Adam. Someone ought to warn her. Ivo was the best of fellows, but not one to be trusted as far as the ladies were concerned. He left a trail of broken hearts wherever he went. True, they usually belonged to ladies who should have known better—Ivo seldom spent his time on débutantes. In fact, this was the first time Adam had seen him do so. One might have thought that Ivo's friendship with Tom would protect Kate, but it apparently didn't...

There they went again, Ivo pulling Kate closer to avoid a collision with another couple! Adam had a sudden memory of Kate dancing with him in the saloon at Bridge House, how she had seemed to float in his arms. He had kissed her...

This really wasn't good enough! Something had to be done about Katharine Payne! She was too inexperienced, too green to be out alone! First it was Walter, and now here was Ivo! They could say anything they liked to the girl and she believed them! Well, it wasn't going to continue. Tom had extracted a promise from him to look after his sister. He had even wanted Adam to marry the girl! And if that was the only way Kate Payne would be safe, then it ought to be considered at least!

The following day Katharine was out visiting some friends and Adam and his mother were alone. A previous engagement had prevented Mrs Calthorpe from attending the Marchmont ball and she wanted to hear all about it. At the end of Adam's carefully edited account of the people who had been there and who had danced with whom, Mrs Calthorpe put her head on one side and asked, 'And what happened, my dear?'

'I've told you.'

'No, I mean what happened to make you so uneasy?'

Adam started to deny that he was uneasy, then he stopped and thought. His mother waited in silence.

'It's Kate,' her son said finally. 'I'm not sure she is always very wise.'

Mrs Calthorpe looked serious. 'I knew I should have gone with her last night. It was my duty to do so. I should have made my apologies to the Carterets and accompanied her. But tell me what happened? I can't believe she behaved badly.'

'No, no, no! Nothing like that. You needn't reproach yourself. And you couldn't possibly have disappointed your other friends. Kate was perfectly safe and perfectly well-behaved.' He stopped and thought. 'Except with me. She seems to enjoy provoking me. I don't know why—she is always charming with everyone else.'

'Could it be that you provoke her?'

'If offering perfectly good advice can be called provoking, I suppose I do. She refused to listen to it, of course.'

'You can sound a little peremptory, my dear. Kate is a girl of spirit.'

'Too much so for her own good! It made me uneasy about the future.'

With a touch of anxiety Mrs Calthorpe asked, 'She hasn't found someone else—?' She stopped short and then began again. 'She hasn't found someone in whom she is interested, has she?'

'That's just it! Ivo Trenchard was in one of his frivolous moods, and Kate seemed quite taken with him. They spent half the evening laughing and making jokes... And then he danced the waltz with her.... I must confess I was surprised at him. I hope he isn't setting up one of his flirtations with Kate, Mama!'

'That's a relief. I was worried for a moment. There's no harm in Ivo, Adam! I am quite sure Kate would come to no mischief with him. You can be easy on that score.'

'But Kate doesn't know the rules—she could be hurt!'

'Is that all that makes you anxious?' Mrs Calthorpe was clearly not anxious herself.

'No. Walter Payne is working hard to persuade Kate that he is a reformed character. I think she almost believes him.'

'Oh, dear! Now that is a far more serious matter, I admit. But Kate is surely too intelligent to be in any danger from him?'

'One would think so. But he tempts her with talk of Herriards, and of course she is more than ready to listen. It meant a lot to her. Does she still pine for the place, do you know?'

'She never mentions it.'

'That means nothing,' Adam said gloomily. 'The more Kate feels, the less likely she is to talk about it.'

'It might mean that she is enjoying herself too much, that she has too many other things to talk about, you know. Don't be too depressed, Adam.'

'But Payne tempts her with Herriards! He tells her she can return there at any time, that she could one day be mistress of it! What if she is persuaded?'

Mrs Calthorpe, who had her own suspicions what Kate's real feelings were, said, 'Most unlikely. But what can you do about it if she is?'

'We must stop her! Look, Mama, I should be betraying my promise to Tom if I let her go back to that place! Especially if it meant marriage to that tricky character.' He walked restlessly about the room. 'That girl is more trouble than she is worth!'

'You don't mean that, Adam.'

'It would all have been much simpler if I had married her when Tom asked me. There wouldn't be any of this nonsense then! And Ivo wouldn't be a risk, either.'

'Well, why don't you?'

'What? Marry Kate after all?'

'It would seem to be the only solution.'

'You'd like that, I know,' Adam said, with a rueful smile.

'Yes, I would. I like Kate. I think she would make you an excellent wife. But I don't want her made unhappy. It wouldn't be any use if you were still hankering after Julia Redshaw or that ninny that looks so like her, Kate's cousin.' There was a question in her voice.

Adam said decisively, 'There's no question of that. Julia is in the past and will stay there. Catherine Payne is lovely to look at, but after ten minutes in her company I'm bored.' He moved restlessly. 'When I was in the Army I had such a clear idea of the sort of wife I wanted, but now… To tell the truth, Mama, I haven't found anyone that fits.'

'That's a pity,' said his mother with a satisfied smile.

'So we come back to Kate. She can be very provoking, but I like her better than I did. We should quarrel, of course. I can't think marriage to me would tame her. But we usually come about in the end. And she is never boring. Yes, I'm of the opinion that marriage to me would be the best solution.' He came back to his mother. 'I'll speak to her today.'

'Be careful, Adam! Kate is not an ordinary girl. She won't fall over with gratitude just because such a handsome, lordly creature as yourself has asked her to

marry him. Don't take too much for granted.' Adam
bent over and kissed his mother.

'You make me sound such a coxcomb! I don't take
anything for granted—not with Kate Payne. But, as
far as I can tell, there isn't yet anyone else. And on
the whole she is fairly open to reason. I think she likes
me, and she is certainly very fond of you. Have no
fear, Mama—I think I can persuade her.'

Later that day three things happened. The first was
that Walter Payne was riding in the park when he saw
Lady Balmenny being driven along in her elegant barouche. He felt he had made a good impression on the
lady the night before, and since he was a man who
was always ready to improve his stock in the eyes of
the world, he rode up to enquire of the Viscountess
how she was. Julia was not deceived by his attention.
She was still resentful of his interest in Katharine
Payne. But it didn't do any harm for the world to see
that Julia Redshaw could still hold a handsome young
man in conversation, and they talked for several
minutes.

Just before they parted company, Julia said sweetly,
'I do hope you are going to wish your cousin happy,
Mr Payne.'

Walter looked puzzled. 'I'm afraid I don't perfectly
understand you. Why should I wish her happy?'

'Oh, am I betraying a secret? I shall say no more.'

'No, please! Tell me!'

'Well, Lord Calthorpe and I are old friends, you
know. He confides in me. And from something that
was said last night, it seems that he is intending to ask
your cousin Katharine to marry him. I gather it was a

choice between your sister and your cousin, and your cousin won. Intriguing, is it not? I hope your sister is not too disappointed. Goodbye, Mr Payne.' And, well satisfied with that little piece of revenge, Julia drove off. She had no idea which girl Adam Calthorpe would choose. But Walter Payne's hopes had been dashed for a little while, at least!

The next thing that happened was that Adam caught Kate as she came in from her visits and asked her to join him in the library in a few minutes. He sounded rather serious, and Kate wondered what she had done. She hurried upstairs and tidied herself, then came down and entered the library. Adam was standing in front of the fireplace looking grave.

'Sit down, Kate.'

Somewhat nervously Kate sat in one of the chairs nearby.

Adam cleared his throat. 'Kate, am I right in supposing that you have not yet found anyone you would like for a husband?'

Now there's a difficult question to answer, thought Katharine. What should I say? That I discovered last night that *you* are the only man I could bear to marry? No, I don't think I want to tell you that, Adam. After a slight hesitation she replied, 'Why do you ask?'

'You may confide in me, you know. Though if you have a liking for Ivo Trenchard I ought to warn you—'

'I like Lord Trenchard very much, but I would never think of him as a possible husband.'

'Good. Good! And...what about Walter Payne?'

'Walter Payne? Why on earth should you suddenly think that I want to marry Walter Payne?'

'It might be because you almost said as much last night,' said Adam, slightly nettled at her tone.

'I did? Well, I didn't mean it.' When Adam looked unconvinced she said firmly, 'Of course I didn't, Adam! You should know me better than that! It was just because you were being more than usually dictatorial and I resented it. I wouldn't marry Walter Payne—'

'Not for Herriards?'

A shadow passed over her face, but she said firmly, 'Not even for Herriards.'

Adam started to lose his temper. 'Do you mean to say that I have been worrying quite unnecessarily? That you told me you were tempted to marry Payne, merely for *amusement?*'

'You needn't sound so annoyed. You deserved it. And I didn't think you would take me seriously, anyway. Not for long.'

'You really are the most provoking girl it has been my misfortune to meet!' he exclaimed angrily. 'To think that I worried half the night about you! I was even going to ask you to marry me!'

Katharine went pale. 'Ask me...to...to marry you!'

'Yes, dammit!'

'And...and...now?' she said breathlessly.

'It's not necessary now!'

'N...not necessary?' Shock and disappointment had almost taken Katharine's breath away. She paused, swallowed, then said, 'What a strange word to choose—necessary.' Her voice rose as she went on, 'Of *course* it isn't necessary! Why should you think it was?'

'I wanted to prevent you from making a mistake. To protect you, as I promised Tom I would.'

'Protect me? From what?'

Adam was feeling distinctly off balance. The decision to ask Kate to marry him had been taken almost in a spirit of sacrifice. Now that he had discovered that she was in no danger from either Ivo or Walter Payne, he ought to be feeling relief. But it wasn't so. He seemed overnight to have become accustomed to the thought of Kate as his wife. It was disconcerting, not comforting, to find that he needn't marry her after all.

'I was worried when Ivo started to flirt with you— I was afraid you might take him seriously.'

'And why shouldn't I? Had it occurred to you that he might mean what he said? Do you find it so unlikely?'

'What did he say?' demanded Adam. 'By God, if he has—'

'Stop being so possessive, Adam! I've told you— I'm not interested in Lord Trenchard, any more than he is interested in me. Except as a friend who knew Tom.'

'I'm not possessive! What have I to be possessive about?'

'Exactly!' said Katharine with a snap. 'So why were you worried?'

'Because I consider I have a responsibility towards you! And then when you started saying you would marry Payne—'

'I did not, I did not!'

'Well, I thought you had! So I decided the best thing would be if I married you myself. It's not perhaps what either of us would have planned, but I thought it would work.'

Katharine got up. 'How very *noble* of you,' she said sarcastically. 'You can have no idea how *obliged* I am to have someone who was prepared to sacrifice *so much,* just to protect *me!*' Her tone carried little indication of obligation—indeed, it was positively vitriolic. She went on, 'But what a narrow escape you've had, Adam!'

'I don't think of it as an escape. In fact, I'd—'

Katharine swept on, growing angrier by the minute. 'Oh, I don't mean from the necessity of marrying me. I meant from loss of face! For, if you had brought yourself to the point of *actually* asking me to marry you, I'm afraid I would have had to decline the offer, however overwhelmingly generous you might have thought it!'

'Why on earth would you do that?' asked Adam in genuine astonishment. 'You've said there's no one else. Didn't you?'

'If and when I do marry, it will be because someone wants me for myself! Not because of some *stupid…senseless…*promise made to my dead brother!'

Adam, offended at the scorn in these last words, said icily, 'If I remember correctly, ma'am, you did not regard my actions in rescuing you from your uncle's clutches as either stupid or senseless!'

After a brief pause Katharine managed to calm down enough to say, 'No. I was and am grateful to you for that. But you may now regard all obligation to my brother at an end. You have done enough.'

Adam was not sure exactly what he did want, but it was not this. 'It *isn't* enough,' he exclaimed. 'You can't dismiss the matter like this. Tom wanted me to do more than look after you—he asked me to marry you.'

Katharine found this more humiliating than all the rest put together. 'How thoughtful of him! How very kind!' she said bitterly. 'After leaving me to cope with Grandfather, and with Herriards for years, he finally delegates his responsibilities to his commanding officer. As if I were a…a puppet or…or a doll, to be disposed of at will. You must have been highly embarrassed, sir! Dare I ask how you responded?'

'I…I said I would see that you were safe,' said Adam uncomfortably.

'But you didn't wish to offer marriage. Of course you didn't!'

'Dammit, I hadn't even seen you!'

'And when you did? Ah, yes! I remember now. You thought my cousin was Tom's sister. I remember you looked quite besotted!'

'Beso— I was not besotted!'

'How disappointing it must have been to discover that it was the plain Miss Payne who was to be your bride! I'm not surprised it has taken all this time for you to bring yourself to the sticking point!'

'I wasn't going to marry you! Not at first. I thought it would be enough if I made sure you were safe… That's why I saw your guardian. That's why I rescued you from Henry Payne.'

'But it was your mother who pushed you into bringing me to London. Wasn't it? And you were prepared to make the final sacrifice. Noble Major Calthorpe, rushing to rescue this innocent girl from the enemy, and prepared even to marry her! Thank you, but I don't want your empty gallantry!'

Adam was incensed. 'By God, Kate, you *are* the shrew I first thought you! Empty gallantry, is it?' He pulled her towards him and kissed her hard. She fought to escape, wriggling in his grip, stamping on his toes and kicking him in the shins, but her delicate sandals made little impact and she only succeeded in hurting her feet. He laughed at her efforts and kissed her again, more lingeringly. Kate's struggles lessened and died. She was in a daze. How had she ever believed Adam incapable of passion? These kisses were a world away from the kiss at the end of the waltz in Bridge House. Under no circumstances could they be called brotherly and, though she resisted them, they roused in her a desperate longing to respond. She had never before been in greater danger of losing control. The discipline she had exercised for so many difficult years, refusing to give way to her emotions, refusing to let the world see what she felt, was in danger of melting away in the magic, the heat of this moment. For the first time in her life Katharine experienced overwhelming desire.

Adam held her away from him and laughed again. 'You'll marry me,' he said with satisfaction.

For a moment she was still, gazing into Adam's laughing face. Then shame and anger overcame her at this final betrayal and she swung her arm to give him a ringing slap on the cheek. He bit back an exclamation and grabbed her arms. 'You little termagant!' he said. 'I've told you before that it's dangerous to hit a man when he's aroused.'

Katharine glared back at him unafraid. 'What am I

supposed to do?' she hissed. 'Lie back and allow you to rape me? Who can I call on for help? My uncle? Walter Payne?'

'*Rape* you! Kate!'

'Let me go!' she said frantically. 'I won't marry you any more than I would marry my cousin. You're the same, both of you! Animals.'

Adam stood back and stared at her, shocked. He was pale except for the scarlet mark on his cheek. 'How could you think...? And yet...I suppose it was natural...' Then he turned and walked to the window. 'I am...deeply sorry for what occurred just now, Kate,' he said, his back to her. 'I...I don't quite know what happened. I didn't realise...'

Katharine gazed at his back. She would not give in to tears, she would not! Now, more than ever before, she had to be strong. She must suppress the desire to go over to him, to beg him to ignore what she had just said, to beg him to love her, to tell him that she would marry him whatever his reasons for asking her. That she had enough love for both of them...

But some instinct which was wiser than her rioting emotions told her that this was not the way to happiness. Unless Adam Calthorpe fell in love with her she could not marry him. She would be happier alone.

He turned back. 'I hadn't realised how strongly you felt about me,' he said. 'I knew you were often angry at me, of course. But I believed...I believed we were friends. Sometimes. So I thought.... But it's obvious you dislike me too much even to contemplate marrying me. Don't look like that, Kate. I won't bother you again. But before I go...promise me you will be on your guard with Walter Payne. He is a villain.' Adam gave a twisted smile. 'Much worse than me. You mustn't trust him, Kate. And now, if you will excuse me...'

He bowed and went out of the room.

Katharine, left to herself, sat like a stone. She would not cry! Adam Calthorpe was not worth it. No man was worth it! How could he believe that she disliked him? How could he be so blind? Stupid, stupid man! As if she could even *look* at Walter Payne after getting to know Adam Calthorpe! And now he had gone, believing she disliked him. Oh, why had she been so cruel to him? He might be blind, but he had done so much for her...more than he realised. He had caused her to fall in love for the first time in her life, with a man who merely wanted to be sure she was safe!

Why was it that all the men she loved only succeeded in hurting her?

At that point the day's third event—one which was to have a profound effect on the weeks that followed—took place. The footman came in to say that a Mr Payne wished to see her. Katharine was still hastily denying him access when Walter Payne came striding in.

'I'm sorry. But I had to see you!' he said.

Katharine hesitated, then gave a nod to the footman, who left the room. 'What can I do for you?' she asked.

'Tell me it isn't true! Tell me that you're not going to marry Calthorpe!'

For the second time that day Katharine's breath was taken away. Her inner turmoil was masked with anger. 'Whatever do you mean by bursting in here and asking such an impertinent question?' she exclaimed. 'I think the world has gone mad!'

'I demand that you tell me!'

'I shall do no such thing! What right do you think you have to demand anything of me?' said Katharine even more angrily.

'Because I love you! Because I want you to marry *me!* Because you have encouraged me to think that you would!'

'I encouraged you?' asked Katharine, fighting off an attack of hysterical laughter. 'Whenever did I encourage you, sir?'

'Don't try to pretend. It won't do! Last night, when we were dancing together we talked of Herriards. You said you would like to be mistress of it one day. That must mean that you wish to marry me, after all. Don't deny it, Katharine!'

Katharine began to regret bitterly her behaviour at the ball. It had seemed so harmless at the time, but it was having such disastrous consequences! 'I'm sorry if I gave you the wrong impression, Walter,' she said carefully. 'But I assure you—'

'But you must marry me! You must! You don't realise what it means—'

'I will not, sir!' Katharine's hysteria was even more imminent. Fighting off two importunate suitors in one afternoon was more than her nerves would stand! But this one was less of a gentleman. Walter took hold of her without warning or provocation, but panic gave Katharine strength. She pushed him away and fled behind the table out of his reach. He pursued her, desperate with frustration and rage, calling her names, telling her she must love him and threatening dire pun-

ishment all at the same time. At last she managed to
dodge round to the fireplace and take hold of the bell
pull.

'If you lay a finger on me I will call the servants
and have you thrown out,' she said fiercely. 'I made
you no promises, Walter Payne. I listened to your stories of Herriards, though I only half believed most of
them. And I may have tried to be pleasant to you and
the rest of your family. But even that was sometimes
more than I could stomach. As for marrying you...
You?' Katharine stopped as fury almost choked her.
'Heaven knows I have no particular cause to admire
the male of the species, but *you* are beyond contempt!
I would never even *consider* marrying a worm like
you! Now leave this house! I wish never to speak to
you again!'

Walter's face was suffused with rage. A vain man,
he could hardly bear the biting scorn in Katharine's
voice, and, even worse, the collapse of all his hopes.
'I'll go,' he snarled. 'And I won't bother you again.
But I'll find other ways to solve my difficulties. You'll
pay for this, Katharine Payne.' He went out, slamming
the door behind him.

Chapter Thirteen

Katharine sank back on to her chair. Her knees were
trembling and she was perilously close to crying. She
sat there for some time, trying to get calm, the
thoughts churning in her head. None of them concerned Walter. The interview with him had been unpleasant, but neither Walter nor his family could affect
her very deeply, and his threats had not seriously disturbed her. The cause of her distress was not with him.

For the scene with Adam was still vividly in her
mind. Apart from the occasional sign of irritation he
had always before been so cool in her presence. She
had always found the very qualities which had made
him such a successful Army commander—a strong
sense of duty, a cool head and an iron will—at the
same time admirable and irritating. And she realised
now that, during that last scene with him, consciously
or unconsciously, she had been goading Adam
throughout until his self-control had finally snapped.
What sort of a girl was she? And what had she gained?
She already knew that Adam Calthorpe would never
be ready to risk all for love. For honour, for a promise

made to a dead man, to protect the weak—for all of these Adam Calthorpe would fight to the death. But not for love. That had gone with Julia Redshaw.

However, Katharine had begun to hope that Adam might one day ask her to be his wife because he wanted to, because he liked her for herself. So, when he made it so clear that he would marry her simply to satisfy his obligation to Tom, simply to save her from making idiotic mistakes, never because he wanted to, she had been left with a desire to hurt him, to make him angry. As she had. And what had been the result? Adam was convinced that she disliked him, and she…? She had been left not only with the sadness of love which was not returned, but also with an aching desire for more of Adam's kisses, more of Adam's embraces—a desire which was most unlikely ever to be satisfied.

The tears could not be held back. They rolled slowly down her cheeks, and because she fought them ugly red blotches appeared on her face. She couldn't even cry as beautifully as that wretched woman!

'Kate! Oh, my dear child, what is it?' Mrs Calthorpe had slipped into the room unnoticed.

'Nothing!' said Katharine, frantically scrubbing her face with her sleeve.

'Don't be ridiculous! Look at you! I've never seen you in such a state. Come with me. We can't have you sitting here in the library looking like that. Adam went out some time ago, but he might be back at any moment. We'll go to my dressing room.'

Once installed in the little room which she had made into her private chamber, Mrs Calthorpe bathed Katharine's face and gave her a clean handkerchief.

She ordered some tea to be sent up and told the servant they were not to be disturbed.

'Now,' she said. 'Was it Walter Payne? I was on my way down to see you when he arrived. So I waited. And just when I was thinking you might need support, I heard him leave. Was he...importunate?' Katharine was still coping with sobs and couldn't answer, but she shook her head.

Mrs Calthorpe said with sudden anxiety, 'You haven't said you will marry him, have you?'

'No, no!'

There was a silence. Then Mrs Calthorpe said slowly, 'It was Adam, wasn't it? What did Adam say to you?'

The tears broke out afresh. 'He...he didn't ask me to marry him!' sobbed Katharine.

Mrs Calthorpe looked completely bewildered. 'I don't understand,' she said. 'He fully intended to. What stopped him?'

'He s...s...aid it wasn't necessary!'

Mrs Calthorpe waited till Katharine was calmer again, then said, 'Kate, I'm sorry to press you, but...did he explain what he meant? Dear child, I think you had better tell me the whole. For when Adam left me he was fully determined to make you an offer.'

Katharine now had better control of herself. She said, 'I don't know why Adam thought I would really want to marry Walter Payne. And even less why he brought Lord Trenchard into it. I told him that I liked Lord Trenchard, but was never in any danger from him... And then I said that I had never had any intention whatever of marrying Walter. That was when

Adam became quite angry.' She stopped and looked slightly guilty.

Mrs Calthorpe waited until Katharine went on, 'You see, last night Adam had annoyed me and I wanted to worry him. I...I pretended to be more tempted by Walter's offer than I was... I think it did worry him.'

'Yes, I think it did, too!'

'I thought he knew me better than that! But it seems that I had made him really anxious. So when I told him today that I had never had any intention of marrying Walter, he grew angry and called me the most provoking girl he had ever met. That was when he said that he had been going to ask me to marry him.' She paused, then said forlornly, 'But then he said that it wasn't necessary any longer.'

'I wouldn't have believed that a son of mine could be so stupid! What did you say to that?'

'I got angry, too, and said that that was just as well, for if he had asked me I would have refused him!'

Mrs Calthorpe bit her lip. There was a slight quiver in her voice as she said, 'So the situation is this... My son nearly asked you to marry him, but didn't, and you would have refused him, but didn't have the chance. Is that right?' When Katharine nodded she continued, 'And that is why he has gone out in the worst temper I have seen him in for years, and you have been crying your eyes out?'

Katharine looked down. 'It's not as simple as that,' she said unhappily. 'I made Adam really angry after that. Something I said... He...he...'

'Adam kissed you?'

'Yes. Because he wanted to punish me, I think.'

'My dear girl, I have never subscribed to the ridiculous idea that men kiss us to punish us! They wouldn't do it if they didn't enjoy it! And Adam is not the sort of man—at least I don't think he is—who would hurt someone for pleasure. Don't deceive yourself—if Adam kissed you it was because he wanted to. May I ask—did you respond?'

'Not more than I could help,' said Katharine earnestly.

Mrs Calthorpe nodded. 'I remember the feeling,' she said sympathetically.

'But then he laughed at me! He was so...so sure of himself! He was so sure I would marry him after all.'

'The stupid fellow,' exclaimed Mrs Calthorpe. 'Really, I could lose patience with my son! What did you do?'

'I slapped him.'

'Quite right! He deserved it. Did he kiss you again?'

'No.'

'That's a pity!'

'And now he thinks I dislike him,' wailed Katharine, bursting into tears again.

'I can see that he might,' agreed Adam's mother. 'My dear, forgive me if I seem impertinent, but am I right in thinking that you do, in fact, love my son?'

Katharine nodded her head. 'I didn't realise it myself till last night,' she said miserably.

'Well, it is my opinion that he is very likely in love with you.'

'Oh, no! I am not at all the kind of woman he admires. I know that. He likes my cousin. Or...or Lady Balmenny.'

'I think you are wrong. He is no longer in love with Julia, certainly. And I think he is just beginning to realise that he needs to look for something more than a pretty face. But he is sometimes so blind... Now, may I suggest that you put yourself in Kendrick's hands? Get her to make you pretty again, and wear one of your new dresses for dinner tonight. You mustn't let Adam think you are unhappy.'

The new dress suited Katharine very well and Kendrick's ministrations removed all traces of the afternoon's distress. But Adam was not in to dinner to see her. He left a message to tell his mother that he would be out for the evening. And from then on they saw rather less of him, as he appeared to lose interest in the social scene. His mother noted, however, that he always seemed to know where she and Katharine were going each night, and that he often appeared wherever it was for a while before leaving again, apparently in pursuit of his own pleasures. And she knew that the servants all had strict instructions to accompany either of the ladies whenever they went out. Adam had not abandoned his obligations.

The supper parties, the balls, the evenings at Almack's continued as the London season entered its last few weeks. Katharine had at first enjoyed life in town more than she had expected, but she was now heartily sick of it. She smiled, conversed, danced as charmingly as ever, but without Adam's attention the evenings had lost their zest. Even when he escorted them he avoided her company, and when he was forced to dance with her his touch, like his conversation, remained impersonal. The Adam who had tried to dominate, who had quarrelled with her, taught her to dance, forbidden her to ride Sholto, bought her Cintra instead, that Adam had vanished and in his place was Major Calthorpe, the complete officer and gentleman, a perfect member of the Duke of Wellington's staff. It was sometimes almost more than she could bear. As the weather grew warmer and the streets dustier Katharine began to long for the fresh air and cool breezes of the countryside. She grew pale and listless, and that special smile of hers, the one which transformed her into a beauty, was seen less and less often.

Mrs Calthorpe looked on in concern. She had tried several times to talk to her son, but he was as courteously unresponsive as she had ever known him. Using the expertise gained in the Duke's service, he fended off all her careful attempts to discover the state of his mind with an easy switch in the conversation, or some skilful diversion of her attention. She suspected that he was every bit as unhappy as Katharine, but could never get near enough to him to find out.

In fact, Adam was more miserable than he had ever been in his life—even including the dreadful months after Julia Redshaw had rejected him. His youthful despair then had given way surprisingly quickly to enjoyment of his new life, and the new lands and people he was getting to know. But now nothing seemed worth the effort. He went through the motions of life in London, and pretended an interest he did not feel in the people round him. It seemed to him as he watched Katharine Payne that she continued to charm everyone around her as much as ever. Sooner or later she would find among her many admirers someone to love, someone who wouldn't annoy her, who might even be willing to let her have her own way as often as she wanted it. And the poor idiot would be completely wrong for her! Why the devil couldn't she have accepted his own offer of friendship and care? He and Kate would have had a good life together, he was sure of that.

Whenever he remembered the scene in the library he was filled with regret. He had been a fool—so certain that Kate would accept his offer of marriage in the spirit it was meant. Perhaps if he had taken more trouble to explain... Had managed to keep his temper... But then he hadn't realised himself until it was too late just how important Kate was to him. Though his behaviour at the end had been unforgivable, he couldn't forget how sweet it had been to hold Kate in his arms, to feel her slender body pressed close to his, and, when he had sensed a response in her, he had suddenly felt like a king! He had laughed in sheer happiness at the thought of marrying her... How wrong he had been! She hadn't felt the same. She had felt ashamed, had believed he was laughing at her. It wasn't surprising that she disliked him. And now here he was, tied to a London which was like a desert, waiting for the season to end and his release. He could go then to Calthorpe and work this misery out of his system.

Katharine had been in regular correspondence with Tilly ever since she had left Herriards. A little while ago she had been worried to receive a shakily written letter from her governess in which Tilly said she had a cold, but making light of it and assuring Katharine that she would soon be her normal healthy self. When Katharine didn't hear for some time after she sent a note to Tilly's neighbour, Mr Cruikshank, the surgeon, with an anxious enquiry about her friend. The reply was not reassuring. Tilly seemed to be unable to shake her illness off.

Katharine went to Mrs Calthorpe straight away and showed her the letter.

'I expect you would like to see for yourself how Miss Tillyard does, Kate. I'm sure something could be arranged.'

'As soon as possible,' said Katharine gratefully. 'But I can't ask you to leave London in the middle of the season. I can go alone.'

'Of course you can't! Sir James would never forgive me!'

'But there really isn't room for more than one visitor in Tilly's little cottage, ma'am! And no suitable accommodation in the village for you. I wouldn't dream of going anywhere near Herriards, even though the Paynes are here in London.'

'Not so, my dear! They left London yesterday but not for Herriards—for Bedfordshire. Catherine and her family have accepted Lord Acheson's kind invitation to stay with him at Souldrop. I rather think your cousin is about to announce her engagement to a most eligible *parti*.'

'I didn't know Lord Acheson had a son!'

'He hasn't. The *parti* in question is the noble lord himself.'

'But my cousin is only seventeen and he's forty if he is a day!'

'And rather rich,' added Mrs Calthorpe dryly.

'Poor Catherine!'

'Not at all—from what I have heard, she is delighted. But it means that your uncle and his family are all to be in Bedfordshire throughout July and Au-

gust. You would be quite safe in your old home, if
you wished to stay there.'

Katharine instantly rejected the idea. 'No! I
wouldn't dream of going back! Never!' she said,
sounding almost desperate. 'I'll stay with Tilly.'

Mrs Calthorpe smiled sympathetically. 'I quite understand. We must think of something else.' She
thought for a moment. 'How would it be if I stayed
with the Quentins once again? It isn't so far away. I
could come over whenever you needed me, and I'm
sure they would be pleased to see me—I had a letter
from Marjorie Quentin just the other day repeating her
invitation.'

'What would your son say to this?'

'Ah, yes! Adam. I think he could quite easily be
persuaded to agree. I have the impression that he is
no longer enjoying life in London—any more than you
are!'

'You…you think Adam is unhappy?'

'Yes, I do. But don't ask me more, because I
couldn't tell you. When he wishes, Adam is even more
successful than you at disguising his feelings.'

As a result of these plans Katharine spoke to Adam
at some length for the first time since their argument.
She naturally wished to leave London immediately,
and tried hard to persuade the Calthorpes to let her go
without them.

'I should be perfectly safe,' she said desperately.
'And Tilly needs me now, not next week!'

'If all goes well, we can leave quite soon,' Adam
said decisively. 'I've already sent to the Quentins to
tell them of our plans, and the groom will go on to

Herriard Stoke to find out the present state of Miss Tillyard's health. You surely don't wish to arrive on Tilly's doorstep before anyone knows you are coming?'

'Adam is right, Kate dear. You mustn't travel alone to Hampshire. What would Sir James do if something happened to you?'

'I think you know very well what Sir James would do! He'd express his sorrow for a minute or two, grumble about the extra work my death would cause him for the next half-hour, then take to his bed.'

'There's something I've been intending to ask you,' said Adam slowly. 'Would you mind telling me the terms of the Frampton-Payne trust? For instance, what would happen to it if you *should* die?'

'Adam!'

'I'm not asking out of idle curiosity, Mama!'

Katharine said reluctantly, 'In that event, if I haven't married, it returns to the Herriards estate.'

There was a curious silence. Then Mrs Calthorpe said briskly, 'This is a gloomy subject and, moreover, it is not one that will ever need to be discussed. Kate is not going to die, she is going to marry and be very happy. Now, Adam, stop asking unnecessary questions and tell us how soon we can travel.'

'I should think before the end of the week. I have one or two things to see to, and we shall then be off.'

Adam did not tell them that one of the things he was determined to do was to find out exactly when and where Henry Payne and his family were planning to be, in particular Henry's son, Walter. But it seemed perfectly safe. The Paynes were all quite certainly staying with Lord Acheson at Souldrop Court, a full seventy miles from Tilly's cottage. They would stay there at least six weeks, and it would be late August at the earliest before they would return to Hampshire. There was no risk that Katharine would meet them at Herriard Stoke. Not for some time, at least.

The one matter which was not discussed was what Katharine would do when she eventually left Herriard Stoke again, though it was a question which had occurred to all three of them. It was as if they were all waiting to see what the future would bring, for events to run their course.

All arrangements were complete even before the day Adam had promised. Letters were sent and acknowledged, the London house shut up and the keys returned to the agent, the luggage packed, and Miss Kendrick given two months' paid leave. There would be no place for her in Herriard Stoke, and Mrs Calthorpe had her own maid to go with her to the Quentins. Katharine was reluctant to dismiss Miss Kendrick altogether. She hoped that her own future would be clearer after two months, and she could decide then whether there was a role for Miss Kendrick in it.

The Calthorpe party left London for Basingstoke early on Thursday morning. It was a bright, sunny day and they had an easy journey, the two ladies in the carriage and Adam riding alongside. All the same, though she put on a brave face, Katharine's spirits were low. Tilly's illness, her own uncertain future, and, most of all, the change in the man accompanying them made it impossible to stay cheerful. Adam Calthorpe seemed to have withdrawn into himself. An invisible barrier surrounded him that Katharine found impossible to cross, however much she wished she could. He remained courteous, helpful, concerned for her comfort, but the easy, natural companionship, which had become a feature of their acquaintance, had disappeared. Adam Calthorpe was not in any way an enemy, but he was no longer a friend.

They arrived at the Quentins in the early afternoon. Mrs Quentin insisted on serving them a delicious meal before Katharine could leave again. But at last she set off in the middle of the afternoon on the last stage of her journey. Adam accompanied her.

'Really!' she had protested. 'I don't need your escort, Adam. It isn't far, and I'm sure your men are trustworthy!'

'I would rather come with you, all the same,' he had replied, still in that coolly courteous voice. 'I am sorry if you find the situation difficult if I do, but we don't know what is waiting for you in Herriard Stoke. You cannot go alone, and my mother is too tired to come with us. But I assure you I will not bother you more than I have to. I'm afraid I must ride with you inside the carriage, if you don't mind.'

Katharine wasn't sure whether to be delighted or appalled at the thought of sitting next to Adam for a journey of an hour or more. She hesitated, the colour rising in her cheeks, before saying in a restricted tone, 'Of course not.' His expression grew even more remote.

Promising to see her very soon, Mrs Calthorpe kissed Katharine and hoped that she had good news at the other end of her journey. 'Remember, my love, that you can send for me at any time! Adam and I will be here for you whenever you want us.' Then she whispered, 'And try to be kind to my poor son.'

Katharine pulled a face and whispered back, 'I doubt he'll allow me! But I'll try.'

They drove in silence for a while, then Adam seemed to make up his mind. He sat up and said, 'I wonder if we might talk a little about your future?'

Katharine's heart missed a beat. 'Of course!' she said as calmly as she could.

'Since you don't as yet seem to have formed any attachment—' He stopped and asked, 'Am I right to assume so?'

Katharine had difficulty in finding her voice. 'Yes,' she whispered.

Adam showed neither approval or disapproval. He simply nodded and went on, 'And since you have also rejected the solution I put forward a week or two ago—'

'Adam, I—'

'Please! The last thing I want is to cause you embarrassment. I don't intend to go further into that. But…since that is so, would you like me to talk to Sir James while I am here?'

'To say what?'

'To support your original plan of setting up house with Miss Tillyard. You are obviously very attached to her, and, from what her neighbour says, Miss Tillyard will find it difficult to live by herself much longer. You could provide her with a more comfortable home, and servants to look after her. Now that you have established yourself in the eyes of Society, I think it would no longer damage your social position.

You could…you could look for somewhere with some life in it, where you might make new…friends. You would be wrong to cut yourself off from the possibility of a future marriage. I would suggest that you remove from Hampshire, however.'

To hear Adam talking of her future in this impersonal manner was painful in the extreme. The plan, which had seemed so desirable just a few months before, now seemed sterile. But what else was there for her? It was most unlikely that she would ever marry, and it seemed that Tilly needed her. More than anyone else did. But she was reluctant to shut the door completely. She said, 'Can we wait a day or two, Adam? I must first see how Tilly is. But I agree with you. Whatever I decide, I don't wish to stay anywhere near Herriards.'

'Agreement at last!' said Adam with a wry smile.

'I have never wished to disagree with you,' Katharine said in a low voice.

'Haven't you? I'm disappointed. I found it one of your most refreshing characteristics.'

'How can you say that? You always seemed impatient when I did.'

'Perhaps. But I still enjoyed it.'

Katharine hardly dared to breathe. Adam was at last talking almost normally once again. He sat back against the squabs of the carriage and mused, almost as if he was talking to himself, working things out as he went.

'You see, I spent almost ten years in the Army, and, except for the first year or two, nearly always in a position of command. I hope I had a good relationship with the men under me, but they didn't answer back.

Or, if they did, I soon saw to it that they stopped. I never thought of myself as a tyrant, merely as someone who worked out the best strategy and saw that it was carried out. I gave the orders. And then I met you.' He looked at her. 'I didn't like you at first, you know.'

'Any more than I liked you,' said Katharine.

'I know. But I changed my mind.'

'So did I.'

'Did you? Did you, Kate? Never wholly, I think.'

'You made it so clear that I was not the sort of woman you admired. My cousin—'

'Kate, you've seen Julia Redshaw. I am aware that you don't like her, but, just for one moment, forget the way she acts, just think of the way she looks. She was and is still exquisitely beautiful—can you not agree?'

'Perfectly.'

'Your cousin is just like her. At twenty I idolised Julia Redshaw. To me she was the epitome of female beauty. For years I judged all other women by her. And though I no longer loved her, I still thought I would one day marry someone who looked something like her. I knew exactly what I sought—Julia's looks, small, perhaps a little clinging, delightfully dependent on me, in need of my protection... After all the years of dirt and noise and warfare, I wanted a peaceful life. I wanted someone who wouldn't argue...and then I met you.'

'Why did you take so much trouble with me?'

'I had given my word to Tom.'

'I don't think that is the whole story at all. You saw

I was desperate. If Tilly had been in the same straits you would have done the same for her.'

'Some of it. But not all. You became a thorn in my flesh, an ever-present source of irritation, someone I had to do something about before I was driven mad. You became, not Tom's responsibility, but mine.'

'I didn't want to be anyone's responsibility!'

'I know. That was what made it all so intriguing. I had intended to look for a beautiful, delicate clinging vine, and what did I find? A girl who is fiercely independent, a girl who has a spirit like Sholto's, and is as tricky to handle.'

'You don't handle—'

'Shh! I haven't finished.' Adam settled himself more comfortably and went on, 'The lady of my choice was to be a soothing influence in the home, full of patience and forbearance, an example to our children. And what was I presented with? A girl who plays tricks, who would rather fight than give in, who becomes belligerent when she is nervous, or thinks she might be in the wrong, who is even prepared to use her fists when she is angry enough.'

'I wonder you spent any time at all on such a virago,' said Katharine sourly.

'Ah, but this same girl has such courage! Such a determination not to evoke anyone's sympathy by a parade of feeling when she is hurt. I have met many courageous men in my time, but she is as courageous as any of them, and as loyal. She is intelligent, too. And when she smiles she can charm the world. Do you want me to go on?'

'Why are you saying these things?'

'I'm trying to explain why I've made so many mistakes. How it is that I have made you dislike me so?'

'I don't dislike you.'

'Not even...after the way I treated you when we were together in the library.'

'It was partly my own fault. You're right. I do play tricks, I do get belligerent. I must take some of the blame for what happened. Adam, if you only knew how I've reproached myself for the way I goaded you, gave you and Walter Payne an entirely false impression on the night of Lady Marchmont's ball. So much evil came of it.'

'I know what I did. What did Payne do?'

'He came that same day, just after...after you had gone. He asked me to marry him, said I had encouraged him.' She turned to the man beside her. 'That was not so, Adam! But I had invited him to join us at the table...'

'Why did you?'

'Oh, I wanted company. Lord Trenchard hadn't yet appeared and...and you and Julia Redshaw seemed to want a tête-à-tête.'

'I remember feeling annoyed with Julia. And later I saw for the first time what she was really like. But go on. Payne thought you had encouraged him and was disappointed when his hopes were dashed...'

'He wasn't just disappointed. He was beside himself. He...he raved like a madman.'

'What did he say?' Adam, who had been leaning back, now sat up sharply. 'What did he say?' he repeated urgently.

'I really don't remember. I was still...still upset. He threatened me, I think. Nothing specific. He said some-

thing about making new plans. Something like that…
I really can't remember.'

'Kate, if Walter Payne ever comes near you, you
must send for me, do you understand? No independence, no thinking you can deal with him alone.'

'Very well.' She paused, then said hesitantly, 'Will
you be there, Adam?'

'Whether you want me or not.'

They were entering Herriard Stoke. Speaking rapidly Adam said, 'Kate, you say you don't dislike me.
If that is indeed so, won't you at least consider my
proposal? I still think we could have a happy life together. You need a home, and I need a wife. And we
have neither of us found anyone else we should wish
to marry. It isn't a question of necessity or otherwise.
I'm asking you to marry me.'

Chapter Fourteen

Katharine was torn. It was far from a declaration of love, but Adam had come closer in the last hour to showing genuine admiration for her. Was it enough? She looked at him, her doubts and anxieties clearly revealed.

Adam shook his head. 'I'm a fool! Of course you're upset at the moment. This isn't the time to make important decisions, and I shouldn't have asked you. But may I hope that while you're here you'll consider what I've just said?'

'I...I will, Adam. And I am very happy that we are...friends again.'

'Friends?' he said with a smile. The carriage was drawing up at Tilly's gate. Adam took her hand and kissed it, then leapt out. He helped her out of the carriage and they went up the path together. Tilly's little maidservant showed them in.

Tilly was lying on a day bed, but her eyes were bright and she had colour in her cheeks. Katharine went over and hugged her, then plied her with questions about her health.

'I'm better for seeing you, Katharine. And Lord Calthorpe, too! Good evening, sir. How kind you are!'

The next half-hour was engaged in bringing Katharine's luggage in from the chaise, and discussing plans for the next few days. Tilly had clearly been more seriously ill than Katharine had realised, but it looked as if she might at last be on the mend.

Adam went next door to spend a few minutes with the surgeon, who assured him that Miss Tillyard was no longer in any danger, but would benefit from company. He finished by saying, 'That servant of hers is a good, sensible little girl, but Miss Tillyard sometimes gets bored with her chatter, and that's when she gets up and tries to do too much. Miss Payne will keep her in order. It's very pleasant to see her again. I'm afraid things here aren't quite the same as they were when her grandfather was alive.'

When Adam returned they had some of Tilly's favourite cordial, then it was time for him to go.

Katharine went to the gate with him. 'After we had met for the first time, I looked back from here and saw you waiting at the corner,' she said. 'I thought you overbearing even then.'

'And later I went back to the Quentins and described how I had met a shrew.'

'We make a fine pair,' Katharine said, smiling ruefully.

'I think we do,' Adam replied, looking serious. He took her hand in his. 'Let go of the past, Kate. Think of the future.'

Katharine sighed. 'I know you're right. Whatever happens, Tilly and I will leave Herriard Stoke when she is well enough, and we shan't come back. I shall use the time I'm here now to visit all the places I knew with Tom—and bid them a final farewell.'

'Ah! I almost forgot. Cintra and her groom will arrive tomorrow. I've arranged for her to be stabled at the inn down the road. But...' He seemed to be at a loss. 'I hardly dare say this! You'll take care, won't you?'

Katharine's face lit up with laughter. 'You needn't look so worried, Adam. I promise not to snap at you any more when you try to look after me. But, in any case, I know this place and its people like the back of my hand. I won't come to any harm round Herriards.'

Adam was driven off, and Katharine went back into the cottage. She was still smiling.

'You're looking cheerful, Katharine.'

'Tilly, Lord Calthorpe has taken the trouble to have Cintra delivered to Herriard Stoke for me to use while I'm here. Isn't that thoughtful?'

'I think he's a very thoughtful man. You seem to be on better terms with him than when I last saw you together?'

'It varies, it varies!' Katharine found herself unwilling to discuss her relationship with Adam Calthorpe, even with Tilly. She was still confused about it herself. 'We seem to be friends at the moment. Now, how shall we set about making you absolutely well again?'

In the days that followed Katharine looked after Tilly and caught up with the news of the district. It wasn't all good. The Paynes had till now had a reputation for looking after their own, but Henry Payne was failing to live up to it. The good impression he had created on his arrival had been dissipated by broken promises and blatant neglect of his obligations. He was no longer as popular in the area as he had been, even among the gentry. Katharine could only commiserate and try to comfort. She was powerless to help.

After two days Adam brought Mrs Calthorpe over to see Tilly. They came laden with gifts and good wishes and stayed for several hours. Adam made no attempt to have private conversation with Katharine. It would have been difficult in any case, but she felt it was more than that. He was deliberately giving her time to think things through, and she was grateful. Just occasionally she had to chide herself for being idiotic enough to daydream, foolishly imagining a day when Adam would appear and demand her answer, swear undying devotion, tell her that he was desperate, he could wait no longer for her reply... Of course, that would never, never happen. Adam *liked* her, they were *friends*. Not lovers.

Cintra was regularly exercised, but at first Katharine did not go very far, because she did not like to leave Tilly alone for too long at a time. But then, as Tilly progressed, she took to riding further afield, doing as she had said she would, bidding the scenes of her childhood farewell. Now, after a year of freedom from the stress his death had caused her, she could remember Tom with a love free of resentment, could look back on their adventures and games in and around Herriards with fond amusement.

She returned regularly to their favourite haunt—the remnants of the old castle which had been the first dwelling of the Paynes of Herriards. She and Tom had been whipped more than once for climbing among its ruins, for the masonry was unstable, and the ground was dangerously uneven. Her grandfather had had its old well partially filled up and covered over after twelve-year-old Tom had climbed down and found himself stuck. It had taken a team of farm hands several hours to bring him out, and there had been moments when rescue had seemed impossible. Tom had boasted of it afterwards. He claimed he could have saved himself by climbing up the series of rungs on the side, which had once formed part of the ladder that went all the way down. But it was as well he hadn't tried. The rungs were rusted and brittle. It wouldn't have taken much for them to give way, and Tom would have fallen all the way to the bottom.

They had both kept clear of the place for a long time afterwards. And now, Katharine tied Cintra to a tree well clear of the castle, and herself walked with caution along the paths through the ruins. Dangerous it might be, but the place was beautiful. The air was full of herby fragrances, birds and small animals of all kinds had their homes in the ruined chimney stacks, in the scrub, in the thick ivy which covered the walls left standing, and summer flowers were beginning to appear in the overgrown heaps of stone. She sat here, remembering the past, thinking of the future, trying to come to terms with the reality of her relationship with Adam. And after a while she reached a decision. She would marry him. Life with him had so much to offer. She must learn to be happy with what there was, and not to dream of having the moon.

Meanwhile Catherine Payne, up in Bedfordshire with the rest of her family, was being fêted, complimented and admired to her heart's content. Lord Acheson was a gregarious character and, moreover, he wished to show off his latest acquisition, his future bride—lovely, young and fresh as a rose. So the house party at Souldrop Court was a large one, and numbers of visitors came and went. Some of the guests envied Catherine the match, for Lord Acheson was a very rich man. Very few dared to express doubts about its suitability, for he was also a bad-tempered one.

Henry Payne and his wife basked in their daughter's reflected glory, and enjoyed the luxury of life at Souldrop. For a while at least they could forget their financial embarrassments and join in the many entertainments offered by their prospective son-in-law. Only Walter was finding it less than enjoyable. His sister's success made his own failure the more obvious. In private his father lost no opportunity to rail at him, to remind him of his boastful promise to marry Katharine Payne and her fortune.

'But why do I expect anything of you, Walter? You always were a great talker, but a poor doer! You're a fine fellow with the housemaids and farm girls from what I've heard, but you don't seem to be such a success where it matters! I warn you, if you don't do something about this money, I shall be sunk! And you along with me! We've spent far more than we ought in impressing Acheson. What do you suppose he'll do when his betrothed's father is declared bankrupt? I can't see that bag of conceit sticking to Catherine when the family is in disgrace, can you?'

Walter, still smarting at Katharine's contemptuous rejection, had not yet told his father how hopeless his case was. He said with as much bravado as he could muster, 'Don't worry, Pa! I'll see that Kate comes round. Something will come of it yet.'

'I'll be glad to see some evidence of that! Perhaps you'd better get back to town. You're wasting your time here when Kate Payne is in London! For God's sake go and do what you said you would!'

Or more, said Walter to himself. He was in a dangerously vindictive state, furious with himself, furious with his father, but chiefly furious with Katharine Payne. He would go to London, he would find her, he would make her listen...or... He had said she would pay for his humiliation, and it was time to see that she did!

But at dinner that night, one of the guests newly arrived from London mentioned that the capital was remarkably thin of decent company and listed several families who had recently left.

With a significant glance at Walter, Henry Payne said, 'However, I suppose my niece is still in town? She is staying with the Calthorpes.'

'They left last week, the three of them! I was surprised—we all were. One day they were there, and practically the next they were gone! I wonder what can have caused such haste—do you know, sir? Not a family crisis, I hope?'

'Not as far as I know. Strange. I find that worrying. Walter, I think you had better look into it. I could not be easy if I thought dear little Kate was in trouble and we were doing nothing about it.'

Walter left the next morning and made straight for Dorking. This was where the Calthorpes had taken

Katharine before Christmas, and he had decided it was the most likely place to which they would return. But Bridge House proved to be closed, the only activity being round the farm buildings and the stables. Questioning the stable hand only produced a scratching of the head.

'Has your mistress gone to Lord Calthorpe's estate near Bath, perhaps?' asked Walter impatiently.

'I don't rightly know, sir... But wait a minute! Jem,' he shouted to a lad nearby. 'Where were they to take Miss Payne's mare?'

'Quite a distance. Somewhere near Basingstoke, I think. Would it be Herod...Stone? Stoke? Something like that.'

'Thank you. I think I know where you mean.'

'But his lordship's horse didn't go there,' said the lad, anxious to be helpful. 'I think his lordship and the mistress are staying at friends of theirs. It's nearer still to Basingstoke.'

'Thank you, again,' said Walter slowly. He threw the lad a few coins and rode off. What he had just learned was deeply interesting! Katharine Payne was at Herriards, was she? Taking advantage of his family's absence, no doubt. And Calthorpe and his interfering hag of a mother were not with her! How very interesting! Herriards had been shut up and most of the servants sent away while his family were in London. It looked as if he might have that girl all to himself... Walter continued on his journey, almost cheerfully.

He was disappointed therefore to find that Katharine was not, after all, at Herriards, but staying with her old governess in the village nearby. But he didn't give up his hopes of catching her. He kept his own presence quiet by staying in one of the deserted outbuildings, and paying one of the farm girls to fetch him food and drink. He was pleased to see that he hadn't lost his touch with farm girls, at least! The girl, a friend of Miss Tillyard's Meg, quite innocently informed him of Katharine's habits, prattling away, in response to some clever questioning, about Master Tom and Miss Kate and their games in the past, wondering at Miss Kate's present wish to visit her old haunts, and asking if it meant Miss Kate was soon to leave them forever. Walter listened, reassured her and sent her on her way. He soon picked up Kate's trail, and by following her, always at a safe distance, discovered that she was particularly attached to the old castle and often to be found there. Now here was an opportunity! The castle was some distance from any other buildings, and it was so dangerous that the local people avoided it. Surely he could approach Katharine here, and make her listen to reason—or force her to consent! He might even enjoy that. Walter laid his plans and waited.

And eventually he was rewarded. After only a couple of days of lying in wait Walter heard Kate arrive, tie her horse up to one of the trees at the edge of the clearing, and walk slowly into the castle precinct. She sat on the edge of the old well, lost in thought. Walter took his chance.

'Good afternoon, Kate!'

Katharine swung round, startled. 'Walter! What are you doing here?'

'I live here now. Had you forgotten? No, don't get

up! You look charming there.' He smiled at her engagingly.

'What do you want?'

'I said, don't get up! Why are you so suspicious of me?'

Katharine clutched her riding crop more firmly. 'I suppose because the last time we met, we didn't part on the best of terms. And now I must go—I feel I'm trespassing.'

'Trespassing? That's a harsh word. I'm sure no one would hold it against you, Kate. What is it that brings you here? A touch of nostalgia?'

Katharine looked at him suspiciously. Walter was being too friendly. 'I'm...I'm saying goodbye,' she said, trying to edge round him.

He stood firmly in her way. 'Why should you do that? When you'll be living here.'

'I won't. You were right. I've decided to marry Lord Calthorpe.'

'That isn't so, Kate, my dear,' he said, still calmly, still with that hatefully false smile on his face. 'You're going to marry me! *Me,* do you hear!'

'Let me pass!' He shook his head, and put his hand on her arm.

'Kate, listen to me! I'm ready to make a bargain with you. And I'm afraid you won't be going anywhere until you've heard what it is.'

'Take your hand off me first.'

Walter took his hand away and held it up. 'You see? You've no need to be frightened. I'm harmless, really.'

'I'm not frightened, Walter.'

'Well, you should be!' he said with sudden viciousness. The change in his manner was so abrupt that

Katharine was shocked. This was more like the Walter she knew, but there was such an added venom in his tone that she began to think he might be a little mad.

She said cautiously, 'Well? What is this bargain, Walter?'

'I've seen you and Calthorpe together. You're not in love with him any more than he is with you. I don't know why you want to marry him. It's not as if you need his money, and he certainly doesn't need yours!' His voice rose. 'But *I* do! I need the Payne money. So does my father. We'll go bankrupt without it. And it's *our* money! Ours by *right!*' He almost shouted the last words at her.

Katharine moved back nervously. Walter saw it, and made a visible effort to speak more calmly again. 'If marriage is all you want,' he said, trying to smile, 'you can marry me and have Herriards, too. My father won't last forever, and I'll see to it that you are not bothered with either of my parents.'

When Katharine began to shake her head, Walter said quickly, 'You needn't be bothered by me, either. As a husband, I mean. All I want is for you to marry me. I swear I'll leave you alone afterwards. If that is what you want.'

For the life of her she could not control a gesture of distaste. Walter saw it and his expression changed. He suddenly became a very dangerous man.

She swallowed and said placatingly, 'Walter, I need to think over what you've said. I understand about the Payne money. I agree, it isn't really fair. And Herriards is a tempting prize, believe me. Give me some time. Let me go back to Tilly's and I promise I'll consider—'

'What sort of a fool do you take me for? I saw the way you looked at me just now. You don't want to think things over, you want to get away! Well, I'm not having any of your tricks! I'm not letting you go! I want an answer! Now! And if I have to take you by force right here on the spot to make sure of you, I'll do it! Do you understand?' He took hold of her arm again and pulled her roughly towards him.

Katharine raised her riding crop and struck him across the mouth.

Walter was consumed with white-hot anger. He grabbed a piece of wood which was lying on the ground next to him and struck her hard on the head. She gave a little gasp and dropped to the ground like a stone.

Walter stared at her in horror. Katharine lay quite still, and her face was colourless, except for a scarlet trickle of blood down the side. What had he done? The thought of getting rid of Katharine Payne was not new, but this reality was terrifying! Frantically he knelt down beside her and pulled open her riding habit, but there was no sign of life. He had killed her! For a moment he was overcome with remorse and fright, but then the instinct for self-preservation took control. He looked around. Except for her horse cropping the grass by the edge of the trees, the woods were silent. No one was about. By the time Katharine was missed there would only be a couple of hours' daylight left—three at the most. It would be morning before anyone could possibly search properly. If he concealed the body well enough, they wouldn't find her for hours. He could be miles away before it was discovered. No one would suspect him—no one in the village knew he had ever been at Herriards. The girl from the farm knew, but he would see to it that she didn't talk.

Walter looked at the figure on the ground and panic rose in him again. Oh, God! What had he done? What would happen to him if anyone found out that he was a murderer? He must hide the body, put it out of sight, quickly, quickly! Where? Walter gazed round wildly. The well! He dragged the cover away, hauled Katharine's limp form up on to the parapet, then tipped it over. He didn't wait to hear it land, but picked up the whip and ran to the horse in the trees. His own horse was back at Herriards, where he had left it deliberately in order to lie in wait for Katharine unobserved. Hers would do to take him away from here. He would turn it loose later. That was all that mattered, to get away! He untied the horse and mounted it, kicked his heels hard into its flanks and gave it a slash with Kate's whip...

Cintra, all her instincts at war with the terror emanating from this stranger, and thrown into a panic by his rough treatment, reared up violently, then took off in a mad dash to rid herself of the unwelcome burden. Walter was powerless to stop her. He held on desperately for a minute or two, but then was knocked flying by an overhanging branch, and was thrown into the undergrowth, where he lay half-hidden. He didn't move. He would never move again. His neck was broken.

Instinct eventually took Cintra back to the stables, where she created chaos as the groom tried to catch her. The alarm was raised, one of the lads ran round to Tilly's cottage, and Lord Calthorpe was sent for straight away. But it was too late in the day to wait till he arrived before taking any action. It would be almost three hours before he could possibly be at Herriard Stoke, leaving little daylight for a search. All the inhabitants of the village knew Miss Kate, and they were all anxious to do what they could. Jem Banks, the landlord of the inn, organised search parties and they were sent off along all the bridle paths, over the fields, along the lanes. With no result. Unfortunately, they were all working on the assumption that Cintra had thrown Kate, and that she was lying injured somewhere near a path or road of some kind. It never entered their minds to go into the castle grounds. Nobody would ever take a horse there, and very few would venture there themselves.

Adam arrived far sooner than anyone had a right to expect, but even so the daylight was just beginning to fade. He questioned the men as they returned, asked Tilly for anything Kate might have said about her plans for the afternoon, went to have a look at Cintra, and demanded an explanation from the groom as to why the man had not accompanied Miss Payne on her ride. The servant was worried and distressed and it took him a minute or two to tell a coherent story.

'Miss Kate told me she wasn't going for a ride this afternoon,' he said. 'She hasn't been what you might call riding out properly for a few days now. She's been exploring more. She said she didn't need me. In fact, she said she didn't want me!' he said aggrievedly.

Adam was too fair a man to blame the groom. He knew how insistent Kate could be. 'Tell me where she used to go on these explorations,' he said brusquely. 'No! Don't bother! You don't know the district.'

He went back to Tilly. 'What has Kate been doing these past days? The groom says she hasn't taken him because she didn't need him. Where would she go?' he asked.

'Adam, she's been saying goodbye. She's been to all the old places where Tom and she used to play. They're not usually very far away... The castle! She might have gone to the castle! She's been there more than once.'

Jem Banks had accompanied Adam back to Tilly's. He shook his head. 'She wouldn't go there!' he protested. 'It's dangerous!'

'We're going to look all the same,' said Adam peremptorily. 'You say you've looked everywhere else.'

They gathered together some lanthorns and sticks and rode in the direction of Payne Castle. It was gloomy under the trees, and the men were distinctly uneasy. It didn't help when one of the horses shied and nearly threw his rider. They stopped.

'What's that?' exclaimed one of the men. He pointed to a figure lying in the undergrowth a short distance away. Adam leapt off his horse and ran over to it.

'It's a man!' he shouted. 'And he's dead—his neck is broken.' He rolled the body over. 'Oh, my God!'

'It's Walter Payne!' said someone. 'What's he doin' 'ere?'

'You mean what was he doing here,' said Adam grimly. 'And my guess is nothing good. Come on! We'll deal with this on our way back.'

They left the body lying where it was, and picked their way cautiously through the trees to the castle.

'You'd best not take your 'orse any further, your lordship,' said Jem Banks. 'The ground is mortal bad for 'orses.'

They dismounted and advanced into the clearing. It was very nearly dark. 'Kate!' shouted Adam. 'Kate!' He turned. 'All of you! Shout!'

They shouted and waited, but when the echoes died the place was silent.

Adam took a step forward. 'I'm going to look round,' he said.

'My lord, it isn't safe!' Jem protested. 'You'd end up with a broken neck yourself! This is a dangerous place even in daylight. It's impossible in the dark. We'll have to come back tomorrow morning. Unless Miss Kate is found somewhere else before that.'

Adam said, 'She's here. Somewhere. I know it.' He thought for a moment. 'I'll stay here,' he said. 'I...I can't leave.'

'It's madness!'

'I'll stay here,' Adam repeated. 'I won't do anything foolish. I just...I just don't want to leave. Understood?' He looked at Jem's disapproving face. 'She might be lying unconscious somewhere round here. And if she comes to during the night and manages to call, I'll hear her. I don't want anyone else to stay— you can come back tomorrow.'

'Er...what about Mr Payne, my lord?'

'Who? Oh, yes. We must do something about him. From the way he was lying it looks very much as if he has been thrown. But where's the horse? You'd

better ask someone to look into that. I can't do anything about it at the moment.'

'Would he have been riding Miss Kate's mare? She
turned up without a rider.'

'In that case, what has happened to Miss Kate?'

The men shook their heads and looked grave. Adam
said, 'It's all such a confounded *mystery!* But I am
still certain that she is somewhere here...' His eyes
searched the darkness ahead. The men waited. Adam
turned and said, 'What are you waiting for?'

'Mr Payne, my lord. What to do about him.'

'Oh, yes. Yes. I'd be obliged if two or three of you
could deal with him. He should be taken to Herriards.
Is anyone there?'

'A caretaker, that's all. The Paynes took one or two
of the old staff to London, and let the rest go for the
summer.' There were some murmurs. This was obviously a matter for resentment.

'Well, something has to be done with him. And a
message must be sent to his family. What a mess this
is! Look, take him to Herriards and help the caretaker
to find somewhere suitable to lay him. Inform Mr
Cruikshank. I'll see to the rest later, when...when...I
have time. Good night.'

'Very good. We'll be here tomorrow first light.'

'And bring some equipment with you—ropes, that
sort of thing. We might need them.'

'You're sure you'll be all right, my lord?'

'Quite certain. Goodnight.'

Adam was left to himself. He took Sholto to a
nearby stream and rubbed him down with some grass.
The stallion wouldn't suffer from staying out on such
a warm night. Then he came back into the clearing

and surveyed the scene. The men were right—searching the ruins tonight was impossible. But it was equally impossible that he should leave this place. Not while he was so convinced that he would find Kate here. The night was warm and he was used to camping out. He wouldn't come to any harm. He sat down on a fallen boulder.

What had happened today? What had Walter Payne been doing in Herriard Stoke? Adam was sure it had something to do with Kate, and his heart was heavy. Walter had probably known where Kate was now, but he wasn't going to tell anyone. He was silenced forever. When would they find Kate? What in God's name had happened to her? Unable to sit still, Adam got up and shouted again.

'Kate! Kate! Where are you?' He waited, but there was no answering cry. He slammed one hand into the other in a gesture of frustration and despair. What would he do if Kate...if Kate... No! It was impossible! Kate couldn't be dead! She couldn't be! Not when she meant so much. He gazed around again. The moon was rising, casting slanting shadows of silver over the ruins of the castle. Black and silver everywhere. No colour, no life. He threw himself down again, his head bowed, resting his elbows on his knees, gazing down at his loosely clasped hands. To lose Kate was unthinkable. She was the other half of himself, his companion, his friend... He looked up, startled, at the moon. Kate was more than all of these! Kate was the love of his life! The centre of his existence. He sat staring at the moon like a lunatic as this thought gradually filled his consciousness. Then he closed his eyes. What a stupidly complacent fool he had been! Thinking his desire to marry Kate was merely for her good, merely to protect her. He, who had always prided himself on his clearsightedness, on the power of his reason. How could he have believed it? Why had he not identified his own feelings sooner? He wanted to marry Kate because no other woman would do! He jumped up impatiently. 'Kate!' he called, louder than ever, his voice echoing through the ruins. 'Ka-a-a-ate!'

Katharine blinked as reflected moonlight fell on her face. Where was she? Wherever it was it was not very comfortable... She gasped as she tried to move. White hot pain lanced up her arm. She felt sick...dizzy... faint...

When she next noticed anything she saw that it was dark. The moonlight had gone. She must have been asleep, though how that was possible with a head like hers was difficult to see. It was pounding. What had woken her? Had she heard something? There it was again! *'Kate!'* She tried to shout back, but the sound wouldn't come. She couldn't speak! She became agitated, tried to shift her arm, and this time the pain was even greater. Kate fainted again.

The next time she came to, she was shivering. It was cold and dark here...walls all around... She was down a hole! With her good hand she felt behind her. Stones. Metal. How was this *possible?* She was down the well at the castle! Frightened, she called as loudly as she could. 'Adam! Help me!' It came out as a mere whisper. Katharine slumped in despair. No one would ever hear that! She was chilled to the bone...she was going to die! She would never see Adam again, never be able to tell him that she loved him...never marry

him...live with him...love him... But then she set her
jaw and roused herself. She was not going to die! She
must live, must get out of this dreadful prison! How
on earth had she got here in the first place? She must
concentrate, but it was difficult with this hammer beating in her head... Half-dozing, half-waking, she
pieced together the events of the day before. Walter's
face swam before her eyes, contorted with rage, a red
slash running diagonally across his mouth. She had hit
him with her riding crop... Why? He had attacked
her... Then what had happened? But memory
wouldn't come back... She gave a silent little whim-
per. She couldn't remember...

When Katharine next opened her eyes she felt a
little more wide awake. The piece of sky she could
see was less dark. This was better! Daylight was coming again. Surely someone would come to look for
her? She struggled to stand up, sweat pouring down
her face as her head throbbed and her arm was a sear-
ing pain. But pain was forgotten as she heard Adam's
voice shouting.

'Kate! Kate! Where are you?'

'I'm here, Adam. I'm here! Help me! Oh, Adam,
help me! I'm down the well!'

More voices. Adam talking again. 'Be quiet! I
thought I heard something, but it got lost in your talk.
Listen!'

Katharine's knees could hardly hold her. She clung
on to an iron support with her good hand. 'I'm here!'
she screamed. 'Help me! Adam, help me!'

Chapter Fifteen

The patch of daylight disappeared as heads leant over the parapet of the well. A chorus of exclamations, 'She's there!', 'Look!', 'It's Miss Kate!', 'She's standing!', 'God be praised!' and then Adam's voice again.

'Move away! Let's have some daylight. Get the ropes!' Then, leaning over, he called, 'Kate, how badly are you hurt?'

Kate took a deep breath. It was really extraordinarily difficult to do the simplest things—to talk, for example. That scream had taken her last bit of strength.

'Come on, Kate! I need to know, so that we can get you out safely.'

How practical he is, thought Katharine hazily. How very *rational*, not to waste time on exclamations of relief or gratitude. Even the men were more enthusiastic! Come on, Kate! Answer him! She took another breath. 'I think…I must have broken…my arm. Nothing…else.' She started to feel faint again, and held on fiercely to her support.

'Good!' Adam wiped the sweat from his brow with his sleeve. Without comment one of the men passed

him a drink. He nodded his thanks, drank some of it
and felt better. 'I'll go down,' he said, taking his coat
off. 'Put the rope round me for a standby, but I think
I can climb down.'

Jem Banks, looking at Adam's pale face, said, 'One
of the others could—'

'Save your breath! I'm fetching Miss Payne up.
But—thank you. You'll have plenty to do, Jem. Hard
work. Do you know how it's done—pulling two people up by rope? Or do you want me to demonstrate?'

'I can do it, my lord. You leave that to me. Now,
are you ready?'

'I think so.' He leant over the parapet. 'Kate, listen
to me!'

'I'm…listening, Adam.' Her voice seemed weaker.

He said urgently, 'Hold on! One more minute and
I'll be with you. Just make sure you're to one side.
Can you do that? I don't want to crash into you.'

'I think so.'

'Right!'

Adam nodded at the men who were now preparing
the ropes, and climbed over the side. The well was not
in fact very deep—it had been partially filled in—and
the remnants of the iron ladder gave him a few foot-
holds. He had done many a more difficult descent in
his Army career. But never before in circumstances
like these. Kate was weakening—he had heard it in
her voice. She might well be more badly injured than
she knew—or had admitted. Shock would have taken
its toll, too… How could he manage to get her out
without making things worse for her? If Kate was really badly injured…

Adam swore silently and told himself to concentrate. It wouldn't do Kate any good if he gave way to his fears. He made his way down slowly, carefully, till, looking down, he could see her face just below his feet.

'Now for the most difficult bit,' he said. He edged his way past her, and with a sense of enormous relief felt his feet touch the base. 'My good girl!' he said approvingly as she held herself back to let him pass. But he was a long way from happy. Kate's knuckles were white where she was clinging to the bar. Her other arm was hanging uselessly at her side. Her face was dirty, but underneath it was chalk white—except for a dark blue bruise on her temple. There was some dried blood on her cheek...

Adam took a deep breath. Now was not the time to hug Kate tightly, to give way to his overwhelming relief. First he had to check her for any other broken bones before he moved her, and then Kate had to be taken out of this hell-hole as quickly and as safely as possible. Gently he felt her all over. No other breaks as far as he could tell. He looked at her again. She was, if possible, even whiter. Her lips were trembling, and though she had winced as he had touched her, she hadn't said anything. Kate was really at the end of her tether. Adam allowed himself the luxury of a short, swift, featherlight kiss.

'You'll soon be safe, Kate!' he whispered. 'I've got you now. And I shall never let you go again.' He wasn't sure that she had even heard him. Her head was falling forward, and the hand holding the bar was slipping... Adam worked as quickly as he could in the restricted space. He used a strap one of the men had given him to bind the broken arm close to her body, and at this point Kate passed out completely. He caught her as she fell and held her wrapped in his arms for a moment, consoling himself with the thought that it was just as well she was unconscious—she would not enjoy the next few minutes. Then he wound the ropes round the two of them and shouted to the men to pull them up. Slowly, painfully the double burden was raised to the surface. Willing hands, surprisingly gentle for such big men, lifted Kate over the parapet and put her down on the grass. Adam climbed out after her. He covered her carefully with his coat, then stood, breathing fast, waiting to get his strength back. The men were already replacing the cover on the well, and winding up the ropes. Then Adam lifted Kate into his arms and walked to where the horses were tethered. He asked one of the men to hold her for a moment, then mounted and took her back. Sholto moved restlessly, but calmed down again when Adam spoke. Kate's eyelids fluttered open for a moment. A smile appeared on her worn face.

'Adam!' she said contentedly. 'Adam!'

The little procession made its way slowly back to the village. Some of the men had ridden on ahead to warn Tilly and the surgeon of their arrival, and by the time they reached Tilly's cottage, a bed had been prepared for Katharine, and Mr Cruikshank was waiting. The broken bone was soon set and the surgeon thought there was no reason for it not to heal perfectly well. He was more concerned about the bruise on her head, and the fact that she had spent the night in a state of shock in such uncomfortable circumstances.

After that moment of lucidity Kate had lapsed into

semi-consciousness. As the day wore on she grew quieter and stiller. When Mrs Calthorpe arrived Adam was at Kate's bedside, looking himself like death, but fiercely rejecting all offers of help.

'Adam, be reasonable,' his mother said. 'Go and get some sleep. Kate doesn't even know you're here! I'll look after her for the moment. Mr Cruikshank will find a nurse tomorrow if he thinks one is necessary.'

'What are we going to do?'

'Mr Cruikshank has offered us rooms in his house. If you will go and get some sleep now while I keep watch, then you can sit with Kate this evening. Miss Tillyard is not yet well enough to do much, but she will fill in. She can fetch one of us if there's any change. Do as I say, my dear! You'll do Kate no good at all if you collapse, too! Be reasonable.'

Adam reluctantly gave way. In his time he had given so much good advice to others to be reasonable, to be patient, not to worry... How totally worthless it all seemed now!

However, he did manage a couple of hours' rest and returned to Kate's room refreshed and ready to deal with whatever was necessary. His mother greeted him at the door with relief.

'She's very restless. I can't keep her quiet, Adam. I've given her some drops, but they don't seem to have done much good, and the surgeon says we mustn't give her any more until he calls again. I'm so glad you're back. She's asking for you all the time, though I'm not sure she knows what she's saying.'

Adam went to the bed.

Kate's arm prevented her from moving a great deal,

but she was twisting her head from side to side, murmuring impatiently, moaning, then calling out in a cracked voice, 'Adam! Help me, Adam! You said you'd be there! Where are you?'

'I'm here,' said Adam calmly. He sat down close to the bed and took Kate's good hand in his. 'I'm here, Kate. You can rest now.'

The sound of his voice seemed to calm her for a moment. Then she began again, turning her head restlessly. 'Adam, don't go away from me! Don't go!'

He reassured her once more, and she was quiet, but only briefly. The cracked voice soon began again.

'You look at her so fondly, Adam. I'd like you to look at me like that... Why can't you look at me like that? Such a loving smile... You don't love me, that's why, isn't it? Adam! You like me, that's all.' The hand in his moved convulsively. 'It will be enough, Adam, I'll make sure it's enough. But please, please don't leave me! Please don't go away!'

To hear strong, independent Katharine crying out such an urgent need of anyone almost overset both her watchers. Adam's mother had tears in her eyes.

'I knew she loved you. I didn't realise how much. You mustn't let her down, Adam.'

He shook his head. 'I won't let her down. You go and get some rest. I'll stay here for now.' He turned back to the figure in the bed, talking to her softly, reassuringly until she was quiet again.

The daylight slowly faded. Tilly came in with a lamp which she placed on a table shaded from the bed. She stayed for a short while, then went back to rest. Her maidservant came in with a tray for Adam and fresh barley water for Katharine. Later on Mrs Calthorpe came back and, after taking a look at Katharine, insisted that Adam go out for some air.

'You say she's been quiet for some time? I actually think she's asleep. That's a good sign. Come back in half an hour.'

As soon as Adam appeared outside in the street he was swamped with enquiries about Katharine. He said what he could to reassure them, and thanked them all once again for their help.

'It was a bad day for us when Master Tom was killed, your lordship,' said one grizzled farmer, heavily. 'Herriards will never be the same without Miss Kate.'

Adam nodded. His world would never be the same without Miss Kate, either.

When he returned to the sick room his mother assured him that Katharine had not stirred. 'Don't look so worried, my dear! I truly think she is on the mend. The surgeon called in and gave her some more drops, so she is sleepy again, but he was very hopeful. We are to see that she drinks plenty of the barley water. You can sit with her here, if that is what you want. I'll rest on the couch.'

Mrs Calthorpe made herself comfortable on the couch by the window, and Adam sat down by the bed again. Kate's colour was better, and she was breathing more peacefully. The room was quiet, as the world settled down for the night. He sat lost in thought by Katharine's bedside, thinking of Tom, of how the death of one young man could make such a difference to so many lives, wondering what would happen to Herriards and its people now that Henry Payne's heir was dead, even feeling some pity for Walter's family. But most of all he was content to sit by Katharine and feel profoundly grateful that she had survived.

Katharine's hand stirred. Adam got up and bent over her. Her eyes opened.

'Are you thirsty?' he whispered. She nodded drowsily, and he took the glass of barley water and supported her while she sipped. When he started to withdraw his arm she gave a little moan of protest.

'Don't go!' she whispered. 'Stay with me. I need you here, Adam. I think I'll always need you. I don't think I can face life without you.'

He was deeply moved. 'I've told you. I won't go away,' he said softly, putting the glass back on the table and settling her more comfortably on his arm. 'But you mustn't talk.'

She smiled at him sleepily. 'I want to! I have to tell you. All I could think of during the night…was that…I wouldn't be able to tell you if I…if I died down there…I love you, Adam. I was wrong to say I wouldn't marry you. I love you so much that it doesn't matter…' Her voice faded away.

'What doesn't matter?'

'That you don't love me the way I wanted you to love me. The way you loved Julia.'

'I *do* love you, Kate!'

'I know you do, really. And it would be stupid of me to want more, wouldn't it? I love you enough for both of us. It's enough that we would be together. But…but don't ever leave me—I couldn't bear that. I couldn't bear it, Adam…' Tears rolled slowly down her cheeks and she moved restlessly.

'Kate, you're sick, you need to sleep. I shan't leave you, I promise. I promise you, I'll never leave you. But rest now. We'll talk when you're better. Go back to sleep, my darling.' Adam settled her down on her pillows, wiped her tears and kissed her lingeringly on the cheek. She gave a little sigh of contentment and fell asleep again.

Adam got up and stretched himself. His arm was stiff, but that was of no importance. It really looked as if Kate was almost herself again. But what *was* Kate's self? He felt as if he had never really known her. He studied the sleeping form in the bed. She had always been so careful to conceal the vulnerable, passionate woman that was the real Katharine Payne. Did she even know herself that such a Kate existed? His own discovery of how much, how comprehensively, he loved her, had been so recent, that he hadn't had time to think about her feelings towards him. The last ten minutes had been a revelation. Detached, independent Kate had wept, had pleaded, had revealed her soul to him. Kate loved him almost as much as he loved her! He looked back at the bed. My darling, he thought, I will never feel prouder or more humble than I do at this moment. I adore you! And I will never, as long as I have breath in my body, knowingly hurt or disappoint you!

Mrs Calthorpe stirred. 'I'm sorry, Adam. I must have fallen asleep. Has there been any change?'

'A slight one, I think,' he said, trying not to smile. 'Kate seems much better, Mama. She's sleeping very peacefully. I think we're almost out of the wood.'

His mother regarded him closely. 'Adam, I haven't

seen you look like this since you were a little boy, and
your father gave you your first pony. Remember? You
were ecstatic with delight.' She came and kissed him.
'I think something *has* changed. And I think you and
Kate are going to be very happy.'

Adam hugged her. 'I think we shall be, Mama. You
were right about Kate Payne, all the time. She is the
one for me. The only one. But how did you know?'

'I just *did!*' said Mrs Calthorpe.

But the next day it looked as if all was not to be
such plain sailing.

Katharine slept the night through and in the morning
was, except for her arm and the bruise on the head,
almost her old self. Mr Cruikshank said she could get
up for a few hours, and sit in the garden. Adam came
to see her as soon as she was dressed and proposed
carrying her downstairs.

'I'm sure that isn't necessary,' she said coolly. 'I
can walk perfectly well.'

He looked at her warily. This was the Kate he had
known in the churchyard last year. Kate the shrew. A
slow bubble of amusement grew inside him, till he
thought it would burst out into delighted laughter. But
he was careful to let no sign of this appear in his face.
Kate was suffering from reaction. The emotional
scenes of the day before had horrified her. He should
have known this would happen!

He said calmly, 'In that case, let me go ahead of
you down the stairs. It would be a pity if you damaged
the arm further. Come!'

She walked unsteadily across the room, stopped at

the door and leaned against the post. Then she said, 'I think I'll stay here. It will be too hot in the garden.'

'Kate, my darling shrew, my sweet virago, let me carry you downstairs! To please me. I badly want to talk to you, and I can't here.'

'You talked enough last night,' she said.

'I rather thought you did, too.'

'I was ill. I didn't know what I was saying.'

'Didn't you? Didn't you, Kate?' He held her eye.

After a moment she looked away. 'Perhaps I did. But you needn't pay any attention to it,' she said in her old detached manner.

'Oh, no, you can't use that tone with me—not any more. I've seen the real Kate Payne.'

Katharine looked at him with desperation in her eyes. 'Can't you forget what I said last night, Adam? It's so humiliating!'

'Let me take you downstairs. There's something I want to say to you. We shan't be disturbed. Mama has taken Miss Tillyard for a drive in the country.'

'What do you want to say?'

'I'll tell you in the garden.'

She gave a little gesture of resignation and allowed him to pick her up and carry her downstairs.

In the garden she sat under the apple tree, gazing at her fingers, refusing to meet Adam's eyes. He took her hand.

'Don't shut me out, Kate. Don't ever shut me out.'

'What do you mean?'

'I mean,' he said deliberately, 'that it would hurt me, more than I have ever been hurt before, if you were to deny me the girl I saw last night. Let the rest of the world be happy to know the Katharine Payne it

saw in Bridge House, and in the London ballrooms.
But you mustn't deprive me of the real Kate Payne. I
fell in love with her before I really knew she existed,
but now that I've seen her, I will never be content
with less. I love you, Katharine. Never doubt that. Passionately and forever.'

'You...you said you wanted us to marry because I
needed a home and you needed a wife.'

'I was mad! I need *you!* No other woman will do.
And making a home with you, living at Calthorpe,
building our future together, is everything I want. Can
you forgive me for being so blind before?'

'I suppose you *did* call me your darling,' she said
slowly.

'I thought you were asleep!'

She smiled. 'I heard that,' she said. 'So perhaps you
do mean what you said. Perhaps it's not just because
you feel sorry for me—'

'*Sorry* for you! Are you mad? Just wait till you're
stronger. I'll show you what I feel for you!'

'It's only my *arm*, Adam...' Kate gave him a sideways look. He found he couldn't stop the laughter. It
came out, joyful, jubilant, triumphant. When Kate began to look offended, he drew her from her seat, put
his arm carefully round her good shoulder, and pulled
her slowly to him. The kiss that followed began
gently—almost a brotherly kiss, thought Katharine,
disappointed. But then she decided she had been too
quick to judge. The kiss grew in depth, in feeling, in
passion. The sensation was like nothing she had ever
before experienced. She was whirling round like a leaf
in a storm, floating like thistledown, the blood coursed
through her veins with a singing joy, yet all the time

she felt safe, held close, held in a lover's arms. When he released her she had to hold on to him—she would otherwise have fallen. He held her with trembling hands for a while. Through her own tumultuous heartbeats she could feel his. They were just as uneven.

'I'm so sorry,' he said. 'I meant to treat you so carefully… And then…you're like wine, Katharine! Champagne! You go to my head. I could have hurt you! I shouldn't have—'

'No! Don't say that! It wasn't weakness. If I held on to you it wasn't because I was ill, Adam. And you mustn't say you shouldn't have kissed me like that. I…I liked it. I want more! Indeed, I think I could become addicted!'

Adam shook his head. 'I shouldn't have done it, all the same. This isn't the time or the place for such things. Talking of which…'

He sat her down again. 'Now we've sorted ourselves out—'

'Is that what you call it?' murmured Katharine. 'I've seldom felt more unsorted, myself.'

Adam ignored this interruption. 'I'll tell you what I really brought you down here to say. And I'm not afraid you'll misunderstand me. Not now. I want you to marry me—'

'Well, I should hope so!'

'Be quiet and let me finish! I want us to marry almost immediately. Apart from a very natural desire to have you to myself, I want to see you absolutely safe. Let's have no more nonsense about the Frampton inheritance. Until you're married you will be in danger.'

'I don't think Walter will try any more tricks,

Adam. He will be so shocked to hear I am still alive that he wouldn't dare.'

'Do you remember what happened in the castle grounds?'

'Walter came. He wanted to talk, he said. He said he was going to marry me whether I liked it or not. I tried to get away... Then he attacked me.'

'Did he hurt you?'

'Not then. I...I hit him. With my crop. There was blood on his face.'

'What happened next?'

She frowned. 'I'm not sure. I think he hit me with something heavy... And when I woke up I was in the well.'

Adam hesitated. 'He was a villain. Thank God we found you in time.' He grasped her hands firmly in his. 'But, Kate, I have to tell you this. Walter got his desserts. He's dead.'

'Dead! How? You didn't—'

'No. He was dead when we found him. He'd been thrown.'

'How could he have been thrown? He didn't have a horse with him! I'd have seen it.'

'Where was Cintra?'

'I tethered her under the trees. I didn't want to risk taking her into the castle grounds.'

'That's how Walter died. He tried to get away on Cintra. He was probably in a panic.'

'And Cintra threw him? I think she might if he treated her badly.'

Adam nodded his head slowly. 'That was probably the way of it.'

'I can't help feeling sorry for him, Adam. That

wretched inheritance! If only he hadn't been so obsessed by it...'

They sat in silence for a moment. Then he said, 'I still want to marry you as soon as possible.'

She gave him a glance. 'It's not *necessary* now, is it?'

'More than ever! And you will marry me here in Herriard Stoke, as soon as you are well enough! It will be a quiet wedding, of course. Your cousin's death, to say the least—'

'Are you ordering me what to do, Adam?'

'Yes!'

'In that case, and for this once, I submit. I think it's a wonderful idea!'

'Good. I'll put things in motion straight away. I must get in touch with Ivo, too. I'd like him to be there.'

'I'm so glad.'

'Why?'

'Why not? He's your friend. I like him. He dances the waltz *so* well. And he talks so charmingly, too,' said Katharine with an innocent look.

Adam took her chin in his hand. He said with a mock-threatening look, 'If I ever see you flirting with *any*one, best friend or anyone else, I shall run him through with my sabre, then cut out his heart. Do you understand?'

'Perfectly! And if I ever see you looking besotted at Julia Redsh—'

'I was not besotted! I have never been besotted in my life!' He stopped short. 'I *am* besotted,' he said in tones of disgust. 'I'm besotted with my future wife!'

Epilogue

July 1817

One year later, more or less to the day, Lord Calthorpe came into his lady's bedchamber with a letter in his hand. Lady Calthorpe was sitting up looking slightly wan.

'Are you feeling more the thing, my love?' he asked, bending over to kiss her.

She caught his hand. 'I expect I will soon,' she said. 'Give me another quarter of an hour. Is the letter from your mother? It's not to say she can't come this month, is it? I hope not! I can't wait to show her all the things we've done at Calthorpe since she was last here.'

'My darling girl, I can't imagine what could possibly arise to keep my mother away!'

'Good! It's time we told her that she's to be a grandmother in six months' time, as well.' Katharine looked worried. 'She won't mind, will she?'

'Not in the slightest. That's why she was so anxious to have me married! She wants grandchildren.'

'Oh? And I thought it was because she liked me,' said Katharine mournfully.

Adam kissed the fingers twined round his hand. 'She adores you,' he said. 'But not as much as I do.'

After a short interval Katharine said, 'Tell me who sent the letter.'

'Ivo. He's going down to visit his father at Sudiham, and he would like to call in on his way.'

'That's very good news! When?'

'Tomorrow fortnight. Do you agree?'

'Of course! But I don't think I'll try the waltz with him this time!'

Lord Trenchard arrived to the warmest of welcomes from both the Calthorpes. Katharine had felt at ease with him from the start, even though she had never had the slightest desire to flirt with him. Adam, of course, still counted him among his closest friends.

After dinner that night Ivo gave them the latest news from town. Towards the end he said carefully, 'I hear Henry Payne is back at Herriards, but I doubt he'll hold on to it for long. Rumour has it that he is trying to break the entail. Have you heard anything about it?'

'We haven't been away from Calthorpe since we first came down here last year. We haven't heard a thing. What is being said, if anything, about Walter?'

'There were rumours, of course. But nothing substantial. Nothing the scandalmongers could get their teeth into. Acheson married Catherine Payne, in spite of her father's difficulties. And now the world doesn't know whom to pity more—the bad-tempered husband or his flighty wife.' They all laughed. Ivo went on with a comic look, 'Talking of which, Balmenny has kept his lady firmly at home in Ireland. London hasn't seen her this season. I think he's trying to set up a family before it's too late.'

'Wise man!' said Adam idly, filling his guest's glass. Then he sat back. 'So, Ivo, what brings you to Somerset? Your father?'

'First, yes. I'll spend some time with him. Since we became reconciled he seems to need to see me quite often. He's getting old, Adam. I'm sorry now for the years we spent apart. Still, there's nothing I can do about that—it's water under the bridge...' He paused. 'I saw Colonel Ancroft in town, by the way. He has sold out of the Army, and has leased a house in Mount Street. He lives there alone. To tell the truth, I thought he looked a little lost. Has he no family?'

'It's a long story, Ivo,' Adam said. His tone indicated that he wasn't about to say any more.

'And not a story for publication, I take it?'

'Well, not mine to tell, at least,' agreed Adam a touch apologetically. 'It would be good to see the Colonel, though. Kate, sweetheart, would you mind if I invited him down? I'd like you to meet him.'

'Er...it'll have to be soon, won't it?' asked Ivo with a wicked look. 'Or is he to be the godfather? I was rather hoping that would be my assignment.'

'Be quiet, Ivo!' said Katharine, blushing.

Adam raised his eyebrows. 'What? Burden our child with a rake for a godfather?'

'I'll reform! I'll take the cloth! I'll do whatever you say! What do you wish me to do?'

'Nothing so drastic. But we'll talk of it nearer Christmas,' said Adam with a grin. 'I expect when the time comes we'll consider it. Will you be ready to report for duty?'

'Try to stop me!'

'Ivo, it sounded almost as if you had another reason to be down here,' Katharine said, thinking it time to change the subject. Though her husband laughed at her, she was childishly superstitious about tempting fate.

'Well, there is another reason—'

'A lady! A lady! Tell us!' cried Katharine gleefully.

'Not exactly a lady, Kate. A girl. Or better still, half-boy, half-girl.'

'What? This doesn't sound like your normal quarry, Ivo!'

'Oh, I'm not pursuing her. She's far too young. She pursued me. With a pistol. She was a jolly fine shot, too.'

Katharine looked at him in disbelief. 'You're making this up!'

'I swear I'm not.'

'My dear chap, why are you planning to seek her out again?' asked Adam. 'I should have thought you would want to steer well clear. So why?'

'I'm curious. I want to see what happened to her... It's an intriguing situation...would you like to know more about her?'

The Calthorpes demanded to know the whole story immediately.

'I don't know the *whole* story. I suspect it hasn't yet come to an end.' Ivo sipped his wine, thought a moment, then began.

'It all started when I was on leave in the spring of '15. I tried to visit my father, to make my peace with him before rejoining the regiment, but he refused to see me. So, since I was at something of a loss, I decided to stay with my aunt who lived not far away...'

The night was warm and, after their guest had gone to his room, Lord and Lady Calthorpe took a walk in the garden.

'What do you think of Ivo's story?' asked Adam.

'I think that this may be the best thing that has ever happened to him,' Katharine said slowly.

'What on earth do you mean?'

'He may not be very complimentary about the girl. But she intrigues him. And you know, Adam, Ivo would never be happy with your conventional débutante. She would bore him in no time. Yes, I predict some interesting times ahead for your friend.'

'You may be right,' said Adam, losing interest as he turned to take Kate in his arms. 'But there are more interesting times ahead for us, my love. My very... dearest...love.'

They kissed. Ivo caught sight of them from his window, and felt, just for a moment, that there was something he had not yet found... Something that could be wonderful.

*   *   *   *   *

The Society Catch

by

Louise Allen

Louise Allen has been immersing herself in history, real and fictional, for as long as she can remember, and finds landscapes and places evoke powerful images of the past. Louise lives in Bedfordshire and works as a property manager, but spends as much time as possible with her husband at the cottage they are renovating on the north Norfolk coast, or travelling abroad. Venice, Burgundy and the Greek islands are favourite atmospheric destinations. Please visit Louise's website – www.louiseallenregency.co.uk – for the latest news!

Also available next month – Louise Allen's fabulous new Regency romance, ***The Notorious Mr Hurst***.

Chapter One

The encounter that led directly to Colonel Gregory being disinherited by his father and to Miss Joanna Fulgrave running away from home in disgrace took place at the Duchess of Bridlington's dress ball on the sixth of June.

It was a very splendid occasion. As her Grace fully intended, it succeeded in both marking the approaching end of the Season and ensuring that any other function held between then and the dispersal of the *ton* from town seemed sadly flat in comparison.

Joanna progressed as gracefully to the receiving line outside the ballroom at Bridlington House as the necessity to halt on every step and to guard her skirts from being trodden upon allowed. Beside her Mrs Fulgrave mounted the famous double staircase with equal patience. The Fulgrave ladies had ample opportunity to exchange smiles and bows with friends and acquaintances, caught up as they all were in the slow-moving crush.

As always, mothers of less satisfactory débutantes observed her progress, and in undertones reminded

their daughters to observe Miss Fulgrave's impeccable deportment, her exquisitely correct appearance
and her perfectly modulated and charming manner.

If Joanna had not combined these enviable virtues
with a natural warmth and friendliness, the young
ladies so addressed would have long since begun to
dislike her heartily. As it was, they forgave her for
her perfections while their mothers poured balm upon
each other's wounds with reminders that this was
Miss Fulgrave's second Season now drawing to a
close and she was still unattached.

That was a matter very much upon her fond
mama's mind. No one, Mrs Fulgrave knew, could
hope for a more dutiful, lovely, conformable daughter
as Joanna. Yet not one, but seven, eligible gentlemen
had presented themselves to Mr Fulgrave, were permitted to pay their addresses to Joanna and went
away, their pretensions dismissed kindly but firmly.
In every case Miss Joanna was unable, or unwilling,
to provide her harassed parent with any explanation,
other than to say she did not think the gentleman
would suit.

However, that very morning Joanna had refused to
receive the son of her mama's dearest school friend,
a gentleman of such excellent endowments of birth,
fortune and looks that her father had rapidly moved
from astonishment to incredulous displeasure and Joanna discovered the limits of parental tolerance at last.

'How can you say you will refuse Rufus?' her
mother had demanded. 'What can I say to Elizabeth
when she discovers you have spurned her son out of
hand?'

'I hardly know him,' Joanna had said placatingly, only to meet with a snort from her parent. '*You* hardly know him: why, you said yourself that you had not met his mama for over ten years.'

'You met Rufus Carstairs when you were six.'

'He pulled my pigtails and took my ball.'

'When he was ten! Really Joanna, to turn down the Earl of Clifton because of some childish squabble is beyond everything foolish.'

Joanna had bitten her lip, her eyes downcast as she searched for some acceptable excuse. To tell the truth, the reason why she would have turned down anyone from a Duke to the richest nabob, was quite out of the question, but she was hesitant to wound her mama with the specific reason why she would not have considered Rufus Carstairs in any case.

'Well?'

'I do not like him, Mama, really I do not. There is something in his eyes when he looks at me...' Her voice trailed off. Those penetrating blue eyes were the only clue to something burning inside the polite, elegant exterior that filled her with a profound mistrust. 'It is as though I have no clothes on,' she finally blurted out.

'Joanna! Of all the improper things...I can only hope that your natural innocence has led you to mistake the perfectly understandable ardour of a young man in love for something which I sincerely trust you know nothing about!' Mrs Fulgrave had broken off to compose herself. 'Has he said anything to put you to the blush? No. Has he acted in any improper manner? No, I thought not. This is another of your whims and your papa and I are reaching the end of our patience with you.'

Pausing yet again on the stairs, Joanna closed her eyes momentarily at the memory of her mother's voice, normally so calm and indulgent. 'You could not hope for a more eligible or flattering offer. I suggest you think very seriously indeed about your position. If you think that your papa can afford to support you in an endless round of dances and parties and new dresses while you amuse yourself toying with the affections of decent young men, you are much mistaken.'

'Mama, I am not toying with Lord Clifton's affections,' she had protested. 'I hardly know him—he cannot love me! I have not seen him since we were children...' But her mama had swept out, throwing back over her shoulder the observation that it was fortunate that the earl would not be able to attend the ball that evening and risk a rebuff before Joanna had a chance to come to her senses.

They climbed another two steps and came to a halt again. Mrs Fulgrave exchanged bows with Lady Bulstrode, taking the opportunity to study her daughter's calm profile. What a countess she would make, if only she would come to her senses!

Long straight black hair coiled at the back of her head and held by pearl-headed pins; elegantly arched brows, which only she knew were the result of painful work with the tweezers; wide hazel eyes, which magically changed from brown to green in extremes of unhappiness or joy, and a tall, slender figure. Mrs Fulgrave could never decide whether Joanna's white shoulders or her pretty bosom were the best features of her figure, but both were a joy to her *modiste*.

Madame de Montaigne, as the *modiste* in question styled herself, had excelled with tonight's gown. An underskirt of a pale almond green was covered by a creamy gauze with the hem thickly worked with *faux* pearls. The bodice crossed in front in a mass of intricate pleating, which was carried through to the full puffed sleeves, and the back dipped to a deep V-shape, which showed off Joanna's white skin to perfection. Her papa had presented her with pearl earrings, necklace and bracelets for her recent twentieth birthday and those completed an ensemble that, in Mrs Fulgrave's eyes, combined simple elegance with the restraint necessary for an unmarried lady.

It was no wonder that the earl, who could hope to engage the interest of any young lady who took his fancy, should be so taken with the daughter of his mother's old friend. He had seen her again for the first time as adults on his return from a continental tour where he had been acquiring classical statuary for what was already becoming known as a superb art collection. Joanna might not be a brilliant match, but she was well bred, well connected, adequately dowered and lovely enough to turn any man's head.

Joanna herself was engaged, not in wondering how her gown compared with anyone else's, nor in dwelling on that morning's unpleasantness, but in discreetly scanning the throng on both wings of the staircase for one particular man. She had no idea whether he would be there tonight, or even if he was in the country, yet she hoped that he would be, as she had at every function she had attended since her come-out more than two years ago.

The man Joanna was looking for was her future husband, Colonel Giles Gregory, and for his sake she had spent almost three years preparing herself to be the ideal wife for a career soldier. A career soldier, moreover, who would one day become a general, would be elevated far above his own father's barony and would doubtless, like the Duke of Wellington, become a diplomat and statesman of renown.

She had fallen in love with Giles Gregory when she was only seventeen and just out of the school-room. She was already causing her anxious mother to worry that when she came out she would prove to be a flirt and a handful. Unlike her calm, biddable sister Grace, who had become engaged to Sir Frederick Willington in her first Season, Joanna showed every inclination to throw herself into any scrape that presented itself.

Then their cousin Hebe had arrived from Malta to plunge the family headlong into her incredible and improbable romance with the Earl of Tasborough. As the earl was in deep mourning and had just inherited his title and estates, yet insisted that his Hebe marry him within three weeks, preparations were hurried and unconventional. As groomsman, the earl's friend Major Gregory found himself thrown into the role of go-between and supporter of the Fulgrave family as they coped with the marriage preparations.

Much of his time had been taken up amusing young William Fulgrave, freeing William's mama from at least one concern as she made her preparations. Army-mad William had plagued the tall major for stories and neither appeared to take much notice of sister Joanna, who would quietly come into the room in her brother's turbulent wake and listen silently from a corner.

Joanna moved up a few more steps, her eyes on the black-clad shoulders of the gentleman in front of her, her mind back in the tranquil front room of the house in Charles Street. The sedate parlour had become full of vivid and exciting pictures as Giles held William spellbound with his stories of life on campaign. She had soon realised that, whatever William's blandishments, his hero never talked about himself but always about his soldiers or his friends. Insidiously the qualities that meant that his men would follow their major into hell and back, and then go again if he asked, drew Joanna deeper and deeper into love with him.

She understood very clearly that she was too young and that he would not even think of the gauche schoolroom miss that she was now in any other light than as a little sister. But she would be out that Season and then she could begin to learn. And there was so much to learn if she was going to be the perfect wife that Giles deserved. And the wife she knew with blind faith he would recognise as perfect the moment he saw her again.

Almost overnight Mrs Fulgrave's younger daughter became biddable, attentive and well behaved. From plucking her dark brows into submission to mastering the precise depth of a curtsy to a duchess or a rural dean, Joanna applied herself. Her parents were too delighted in the transformation in their harum-scarum child to question what had provoked this miracle, and no probing questions disturbed Joanna's single-minded quest for perfection.

And month after month the army kept Major, then Colonel, Gregory abroad. Joanna never gave up her calm expectation that they would meet again soon, although every day, as soon as her father put down his *Times*, she would scan the announcements with care, searching anxiously for the one thing that would have shattered her world. It never occurred to her that Giles might be wounded, let alone killed, for she believed that no such fate would intervene in his pre-destined path to greatness. But there was another danger always present and each morning Joanna breathed again when the announcement of Colonel Gregory's engagement to some eligible lady failed to appear.

Mother and daughter finally reached the top of the stairs and Joanna sought diligently for something appropriate to say to the duchess. It would be important as the wife of a senior officer to say the right things to all manner of people. The Duchess of Bridlington, Joanna recalled, liked to be in the forefront of fashion, setting it, not following. She eyed the unusual floral decorations thoughtfully.

'Mrs Fulgrave, Miss Fulgrave.' Her Grace was gracious. She liked pretty girls who would enjoy themselves, flirt with the men and make her parties a success, and Miss Fulgrave, although not a flirt, was certainly a pretty girl who was never above being pleased with her company. 'A dreadful squeeze, is it not, my dear?' She smiled at Joanna.

'Not at all, your Grace.' Joanna smiled back, dropping a perfectly judged curtsy. 'It was delightful to have the opportunity to admire the floral decorations

as we came up the stairs. How wonderful those palms
and pineapples look, and how original: why, I have
never seen anything like it.'

'Dear child,' the duchess responded, patting her
cheek, highly pleased at the compliment. Her garden-
ers had grumbled about stripping out the succession
houses, but she had insisted and indeed the exotic
look had succeeded to admiration.

Joanna and Mrs Fulgrave passed on into the ballroom, its pillared, mirrored walls already reverberat-
ing with the hum of conversation, the laughter of nervous débutantes and the faint sounds of the orchestra
playing light airs before the dancing began.

As she always did, Joanna began to scan the room,
her heart almost stopping at the sight of each red coat
before passing on. She must not let her anxiety show,
she knew. An officer's wife must be calm and not
reveal her feelings whatever the circumstances. A
small knot of officers was surveyed and dismissed and
then, suddenly, half a head above those surrounding
him, was a man with hair the colour of dark honey.
A man whose scarlet coat sat across broad shoulders
strapped with muscle and whose crimson sash crossed
a chest decorated with medal ribbons on the left
breast.

'*Giles!*' Joanna had no idea she spoke aloud, and
indeed her voice was only a whisper. It was he, and
three years of waiting, of loving, of hard work and
passionate belief were at an end.

He was making his way slowly up the opposite side
of the dance floor, stopping to talk to friends here and
there, bowing to young ladies and now and again, she
could see, asking for a dance. Joanna's hand closed

hard over her unfilled dance card, which dangled from her wrist on its satin ribbon. As it did so a voice beside her said, 'Miss Fulgrave! May I beg the honour of the first waltz?'

It was a round-faced young man with red hair. Joanna smiled but shook her head. 'I am so sorry, Lord Sutton, I will not be waltzing this evening. Would you excuse me? I have to speak to someone at the other end of the room.'

She began to move slowly but purposefully through the crowd, her eyes on Giles's head, trying to catch a glimpse of his face. Why was he in London? She had seen no mention of it in the *Gazette*. Anxiously she studied the tall figure. Her heart was pounding frantically and she did not know that all the colour had ebbed from her face. She felt no doubts: this was her destiny. This was Giles's destiny.

He had almost reached the head of the room now. Joanna fended off three more requests for dances. Her entire card had to be free for whenever Giles wanted to dance. Or would they just sit and talk? Would he recognise her immediately or would she have to contrive an introduction?

She was almost there. She calmed her breathing. It was essential that his first impression was entirely favourable. She could see his face clearly now. He was very tanned, white lines showing round his eyes where laughter had creased the skin. He looked harder, fitter, even more exciting than she remembered him. Ten more steps…

Giles Gregory turned his head as though someone had spoken to him, hesitated and stepped back.

Joanna saw him push aside the curtain that was partly draped over an archway and enter the room beyond.

The crowd was thick at that end of the room where circulating guests from both directions met and spoke before moving on their way. She was held up by the crush and it took her perhaps three minutes to reach the same archway.

When she finally lifted the curtain she found herself alone in a little lobby and looked around, confused for a moment. Then she heard his voice, unmistakably Giles's voice. Deep, lazily amused, caressing her senses like warm honey over a spoon. She stepped forward and saw into the next room where Giles was standing…smiling down into the upturned face of the exquisite young lady clasped in his arms.

'So you will talk to Papa, Giles darling? Promise?' she was saying, her blue eyes wide on his face.

'Yes, Suzy, my angel, I promise I will talk to him tomorrow.' Giles's voice was indulgent, warm, loving. Joanna's hand grasped the curtain without her realising it; her eyes, her every sense, were fixed on the couple in the candlelit chamber.

'Oh, Giles, I do love you.' The young lady suddenly laughed up at him and Joanna's numbed mind realised who she was. Lady Suzanne Hall was the loveliest, the most eligible, the wealthiest débutante of that Season. Niece of her Grace the Duchess of Bridlington, eldest and most indulged daughter of the Marquis of Olney, blonde, petite, spirited and the most outrageous flirt, she had a fortune that turned heads, but, even penniless, she would have drawn men after her like iron filings to a magnet.

Why does she want Giles? Joanna screamed inwardly. *He is mine!*

'Oh, it is such an age since I have seen you! Do you truly love me, Giles, my darling?' Suzanne said, her arms entwined round his neck, his hands linked behind her tiny waist.

'You know I do, Suzy,' he replied, smiling down at her. 'You are my first, my only, my special love.' And then he bent his head and kissed her.

The world went black, yet Joanna found she was still on her feet, clutching the curtain. Vision closed in until all she could see was a tiny image of the entwined lovers as though spied down the wrong end of a telescope. Blindly she turned and walked out. By some miracle she was still on her feet although she could see nothing now: it was as though she had fainted, yet retained every sense but sight.

Outside the archway she remembered there had been chairs, fragile affairs of gilt wood. Joanna put out a hand and found one, thankfully unoccupied. She sat, clasped her hands in her lap and managed to smile brightly. Would anyone notice?

Gradually sight returned, although her head spun. No one was sitting next to her, no one had noticed. She tried to make sense of what had happened. Giles was here, and Giles was in love with Lady Suzanne.

She had read—for she read everything that she could find on military matters—that it was possible to receive a mortal wound and yet feel no pain, to continue for some time until suddenly one dropped dead of it. Shock, the doctors called it, a far more serious and deadly thing than the everyday shocks of ordinary life. Perhaps that was what she was feeling: shock.

Joanna was conscious of a swirl of bluebell skirts by her shoulder and Lady Suzanne appeared, hesitated for a moment and plunged into the throng. Her voice came back clearly. 'Freddie! I would love to waltz with you, but I have not got a single dance on my card left. No, I am not teasing you, look…'

Joanna found she could not manage to keep the smile on her lips. Her hands began to tremble and she clasped them together in her lap. Any minute now someone was going to notice her and start to fuss. She *had* to get herself under control.

'Madam, are you unwell?' The deep voice came from close beside her. Joanna started violently, dropping her fan, and instantly Colonel Gregory was on one knee before her. 'Here, I do not think it is damaged.'

She began to stammer a word of thanks, then their eyes met and he exclaimed, 'But it is Miss Joanna Fulgrave, is it not?' Joanna nodded mutely, taking the fan from his outstretched fingers, using exaggerated care not to touch him. 'May I sit down?' Taking her silence for assent, he took the chair next to her, his big frame absurdly out of place on the fragile-looking object.

'Thank you, Colonel.' She had managed a coherent sentence, but it was not enough to convince him that all was well with her. Joanna fixed her gaze on her clasped hands, yet she utterly aware of him beside her, his body turned to her, his eyes on her face.

'You are not well, Miss Fulgrave. May I fetch someone to you? Is your mother here, perhaps?'

'I need no one, I thank you,' she managed to whisper. 'I am quite well, Colonel.'

'I beg leave to differ, Miss Fulgrave. You are as white as a sheet.'

'I...I have had an unexpected and unwelcome encounter, that is all.' Her voice sounded a little stronger, and emboldened she added, 'It was a shock: I will be better presently, Colonel.' *Please leave me,* she prayed, *please go before I break down and turn sobbing into your arms in front of all these people.*

Giles Gregory was on his feet, but not in answer to her silent pleas. 'Has a gentleman here offered you some insult?' he asked, keeping his voice low and his body between her and the throng around the dance floor.

'Oh, no, nothing like that,' Joanna assured him. She forced herself to look up. The grey eyes with their intriguing black flecks regarded her seriously, and, she realised, with some disbelief at her protestations.

'I will fetch you something to drink Miss Fulgrave; I will not be long, just try and rest quietly.'

Joanna sat back in the chair, wishing she had the strength to get up and hide herself away, but her legs felt as though they were made out of *blanc manger*. Her mind would not let her think about the disaster that had befallen her; she tried to make herself realise what had happened, but somehow she just could not concentrate.

'Here. Now, sip this and do not try to talk.' He was back already, two glasses in his hands. How had he managed to get through the press of people? she wondered hazily, not having observed the Colonel striding straight across the dance floor between the couples performing a boulanger to accost the footmen who were setting out the champagne glasses.

The liquid fizzed down her throat, making her cough. She had expected orgeat or lemonade and had taken far too deep a draught.

'I would have given you brandy, but I do not have a hip flask on me. Go on, drink it, Miss Fulgrave. You have obviously had a shock, even if you are not prepared to tell me about it. The wine will help calm your nerves.' He sat down again, turning the chair slightly so his broad shoulders shielded her. He watched her face and apparently was reassured by what he saw.

'That is better. Now, let us talk of other things. How are your parents? Well, I trust? And your sister is married by now, I expect?' He seemed happy to continue in the face of her silent nods. 'And William—how old is he? Twelve, I should imagine. And still army mad?'

'No.' Joanna managed a wan smile. 'Not any longer. He is resolved to become a natural philosopher.'

Giles Gregory's eyebrows rose, but he did not seem offended that his disciple had abandoned his military enthusiasms. 'Indeed? Well, I do recall he always had an unfortunate frog or snail in his pocket.'

'That is nothing to the things he keeps in his room.' Joanna began to relax. It was like having the old Major Gregory back again: she could not feel self-conscious with him and the last few minutes seemed increasingly unreal. She took another long sip of champagne. 'And he conducts experiments which cause Mama to worry that the house will burn down.

Papa even takes him to occasional lectures if they are not too late in the evening.'

'And your father is not anxious about this choice of career?'

'I think he is resigned.' Despite herself Joanna smiled, fondly recalling her father's expression at the sight of the kitchen when Cook had indignantly summoned him to view the results of Master William's experiment with the kettle, some yards of piping and a heavy weight. She took another sip and realised her glass was empty.

Giles removed it from her hand and gave her his untouched glass. 'Very small glasses, Miss Fulgrave,' he murmured.

'Have you heard from the Earl of Tasborough lately?' she asked. It must be the shock still, for she was feeling even more light-headed, although the awful numbness was receding to be replaced by a sense of unreality. She was having this conversation with Giles as though the past three years had not been and as though she had not just seen him kissing Lady Suzanne and declaring his love for her.

'Not for a week or so. My correspondence is probably chasing me around the continent.' He looked at her sharply. 'Why do you ask? Is Hebe well?'

'Oh, yes,' Joanna hastened to reassure him. 'You know she is…er…in an—'

'Interesting condition?' the Colonel finished for her. 'Yes, I did know. I had a letter from Alex some months ago, unbearably pleased with himself over the prospect of another little Beresford to join Hugh in the nursery. I will visit them this week, I hope.'

Joanna drank some more champagne to cover her

confusion at his frank reference to Hebe's pregnancy.
Mama always managed to ignore entirely the fact that
ladies of her acquaintance were expecting. Joanna had
wondered if everyone secretly felt as she did, that it
was ridiculous to pretend in the face of ever-
expanding waistlines that nothing was occurring. The
Colonel obviously shared her opinion. 'You are home
on leave, then?'

'Yes.' He frowned. 'It is a long time since I was
in England.'

'Almost a year, and then it was only for a week or
two, was it not?' Joanna supplied, then realised from
his expression that this revealed remarkable knowledge about his activities. 'I think Lord Tasborough
said something to that effect,' she added, crossing her
fingers.

'I am a little concerned about my father. My
mother's letters have expressed anxiety about his
health, so when the chance arose to come home I took
it.' He hesitated, 'I have many decisions to make on
this furlough: one at least will entail a vast change to
my life.'

His marriage, Joanna thought bleakly. That would
certainly be a vast change to a man who had lived a
single life up to the age of thirty, and a life moreover
which had sent him around the continent with only
himself to worry about.

'Shall I take your glass?' Joanna realised with surprise that the second champagne glass was empty.
Goodness, what a fuss people made about it! She had
only ever had a sip or two before and Mama was
always warning about the dangers of it, but now she
had drunk two entire glasses, and was really feeling

much better. She gave Giles the glass, aware that he was studying her face.

'You seem a little restored, Miss Fulgrave. Would you care to dance? There is a waltz next if I am not mistaken.'

Joanna took a shaky breath. Mama did not like her to waltz at large balls and permitted it only reluctantly at Almack's or smaller dancing parties. But the temptation of being in Giles's arms, perhaps for the first and only time, was too much.

'Yes, please, Colonel Gregory. I would very much like to waltz.'

Chapter Two

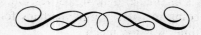

Joanna let Giles take her hand and lead her out on to the dance floor, trying not to remember what had just happened, forcing herself not to think about how she would feel when this dance was over and he was gone. Time must stand still: this was all there was.

She let her hand rest lightly on his shoulder and shut her eyes briefly as his fingers touched her waist. This was another memory to be added to the precious store of recollections of Giles, the most vivid being the fleeting kiss which she had snatched in the flurry of farewells when Hebe and her new husband had driven off after the wedding. Everyone had been kissing the bride and groom: what more natural in the confusion than that she should accidentally kiss the groomsman? Giles had laughed at her blushes and returned the kiss with a swift pressure of his lips on hers: Joanna could still close her eyes and conjure up the exact sensation, the scent of Russian leather cologne…

'Miss Fulgrave?'

'Oh, I am sorry! I was daydreaming, thinking about

my steps,' she improvised hurriedly to cover up her complete abstraction. She must not waste a moment in his arms by thinking of the past: only this moment mattered.

The music struck up and they were dancing, dancing, Joanna realised, as if they had been practising together for years. Giles Gregory was a tall man, but her height made them well-matched partners and his strength and co-ordination meant that their bodies moved together with an easy elegance which took her breath away.

'You dance very well, Miss Fulgrave,' he remarked, looking down and meeting browny-green, sparkling eyes. He had thought her much improved on the bouncing schoolroom miss he remembered; in fact, he had hardly recognised her at first sight, but now with the colour back in her face and animation enhancing those unusual eyes, he realised that he had a very lovely young woman in his arms. Who or what had so overset her? he wondered, conscious of a chivalrous urge to land whoever it was a facer for his pains.

'Thank you, Colonel, but I think I must owe that to you. Do you have the opportunity to attend many dances whilst you are with the army?' Joanna realised she must take every opportunity to converse, as while they were talking she could be expected to look into his face. She tried to garner every impression, commit each detail to memory: the darkness of his lashes, the small mole just in front of his left ear, the way his mouth quirked when he was amused, that scent of Russian Leather again…

He swept her round a tight corner, catching her in close to avoid another couple who were making erratic progress down the floor. Joanna was very aware of the heat of his body as she was suddenly pressed against him, then they were dancing once more with the conventional distance between them.

'Dances?' He had been considering her question. 'Surprisingly, yes. We take whatever opportunities present themselves, and as not a few officers have their wives with them whenever circumstances allow—and certainly when we were wintering in Portugal—there is often an impromptu ball.'

'And the Duke encourages such activities, I believe?' Joanna asked. As they whirled through another ambitious turn she caught a glimpse of her mama's face, a look of surprise upon it. She felt wonderfully light-headed. *This* was reality, the music would never stop. Giles would never leave her.

'Yes. Wellington enjoys a party and he thinks it does us good,' Giles smiled reminiscently.

'*His family*, he calls his officers, does he not?'

'You know a lot about old Nosey, Miss Fulgrave. Are you another of his ardent admirers? I have never known such a man—unless it were that fellow Byron—for attracting the adulation of the ladies. None of the rest of us ever stood a chance of the lightest flirtation while Wellington was around.'

'Why, no, not in that way, for I have never seen him.' Better not to think of Giles wanting to flirt. 'But he is a fine tactician, is he not?'

She saw she had taken Giles aback, for he gave her a quizzical look. 'Indeed, yes, but that is a question I would have expected from Master William, not from a young lady.'

'I take an interest, that is all,' she said lightly, wishing she dared ask about his life with his regiment, but knowing she could never keep the conversation impersonal.

And then, with a flourish of strings, the music came to an end, Giles released her and they were clapping politely and walking off the floor. Joanna felt as though the places where his hands had touched her must be branded on her skin, it felt so sensitive. Her hands began to tremble again.

'Miss Fulgrave, might I hope that the next dance is free on your card?' It was Freddie Sutton looking hopeful. 'And now that I know you have changed your mind about waltzing tonight, may I also hope for one a little later?'

'Miss Fulgrave.' Giles Gregory was bowing to her, nodding to Freddie. 'Sutton.' He smiled at her, and she read a look of reassurance in his eyes and guessed that she must be looking better. 'Thank you for the dance.'

Then he was gone, swallowed up in the crowd. She looked after him, catching a glimpse of the back of his head and slowly realising that with the ending of that dance the entire purpose for which she had been living for the past three years, and her every hope for the future, had crumbled into dust.

'Thank you, Lord Sutton.' She turned back to him, her smile glittering. 'I would love to dance the next waltz with you, but just now what I would really like is a glass of champagne.'

To the chagrin and rising dismay of her mama, to
the censure of the flock of chaperons and to the horrified and jealous admiration of her friends, Joanna
proceeded to stand up for every waltz and most of
the other dances as well. She did refuse some, but
only to drink three more glasses of champagne, to be
escorted into supper by Lord Maxton, a hardened rake
and fortune hunter, and to crown the evening by being
discovered by the Dowager Countess of Wigham
alone with Mr Paul Hadrell on the terrace.

'I felt I must tell you at once,' that formidable matron informed an appalled Mrs Fulgrave, who had
been looking anxiously for her daughter for the past
fifteen minutes. 'I could not believe my eyes at first,'
she continued, barely managing to conceal her enjoyment at having found the paragon of deportment engaged in such an activity with one of the worst male
flirts in town. 'I am sure I do not have to tell *you*,
Mrs Fulgrave, that Mr Hadrell is the last man I would
want a daughter of mine to be alone with!'

This final observation was addressed to Mrs Fulgrave's retreating back, for Joanna's harassed mother
lost no time in hurrying to the doors that led to the
terrace. It had never occurred to her for a moment
that Joanna might be out there, but there indeed she
was, leaning against the balustrade in the moonlight,
laughing up at the saturnine Mr Hadrell, who was
standing far too close and, even as Mrs Fulgrave approached, was leaning down to—

'Joanna!' Her errant daughter moved away from
her beau with her usual grace and no appearance of
guilt. He, however, took one look at her chaperon's

expression and took himself off with a bow and an insouciant,

'Your servant, Miss Fulgrave. Mrs Fulgrave, ma'am!'

'Joanna!' Emily Fulgrave repeated, in the voice of a woman who could not believe what she was seeing. 'What is the meaning of this? You have been flirting, waltzing—and, to crown it all, I find you out here with such a man! And to make things even worse, I was told where I could find you, and with whom, by Lady Wigham.'

Joanna shrugged, a pretty movement of her white shoulders. 'I was bored.'

'*Bored!*' Mrs Fulgrave peered at her in the half-light. 'Are you sickening for something, Joanna? First your obstinacy this morning, now this…'

'Sickening? Oh, yes, I expect I am, but there's no cure for it,' she said lightly. She did indeed feel very odd. The aching pain of Giles's loss was there somewhere, deep down where she did not have to look at it yet, but on top of the pain was a rather queasy sense of excitement, the beginnings of a dreadful headache and the feeling that absolutely nothing would ever matter again.

Her mother took her arm in a less than sympathetic grip and began to walk firmly towards the door. 'We are going home this minute.'

'I cannot, Mama,' Joanna said. 'I am dancing the next waltz with—'

'No one. Home, my girl,' Emily said grimly, 'and straight to bed.'

*   *   *

The dreadful headache was there, waiting for her the next morning when she awoke, as was the hideous emptiness where all her plans had once been. It was as though the walls of a house had vanished, leaving the furniture standing around pointlessly in space.

Joanna rubbed her aching head, realising shakily that she must be suffering from the after-effects of too much champagne. How much had she drunk? Hazily she counted five glasses. Could she have possibly drunk that much? She could recall being marched firmly from the ball with her mama's excuses to their friends ringing in her ears. 'The heat, I am afraid, it has brought on such a migraine.' But the carriage ride home was a blur, with only the faintest memory of being lectured, scolded and sent upstairs the moment they arrived home.

Oh, her head hurt so! Where was Mary with her morning chocolate? The door opened to reveal her mama, a tea cup in her hand.

'So you are awake, are you?' she observed grimly as her heavy-eyed daughter struggled to sit up against the pillows. 'I have brought you some tea, I thought it might be better for you than chocolate.' She put the cup into Joanna's hands and went to fling the curtains wide, ignoring the yelp of anguish from the bed as the light flooded into the room. 'Well, what have you got to say for yourself, Joanna?'

'Have you said anything to Papa?' Joanna drank the tea gratefully. Her mouth felt like the soles of her shoes and her stomach revolted at the faint smell of breakfast cooking that the opening door had allowed into the room. Surely she could not have a hangover?

'No,' Emily conceded. 'Your papa is very busy at the moment and I do not want to add another worry for him on top of your refusal yesterday to receive dear Rufus. Unless, that is, I do not receive a satisfactory explanation for last night.'

'Champagne, Mama,' Joanna said reluctantly. 'I had no idea it was so strong.' She eyed her fulminating parent and added, 'It tasted so innocuous.'

'*Champagne!* No wonder you were behaving in such a manner. Have I not warned you time and again to drink nothing except orgeat and lemonade?'

'Yes, Mama. I am sorry, Mama.' *I am sorry I drank so much*, her new, rebellious inner voice said. *I will know better next time, just a glass or two for that lovely fizzing feeling...*

'I had thought,' Emily continued, 'of forbidding you any further parties until we go down to Brighton for the summer, but I am reluctant to cause more talk by having you vanish from the scene, especially as I know the earl will be in town for at least another fortnight. Fortunately there are only minor entertainments for the rest of the month. I hope the headache you undoubtedly have will be a lesson to you, my girl.'

She got up and walked to the door. 'I must say, Joanna, this has proved greatly disappointing to me. I had been so proud of you. I can only hope it is a momentary aberration. As for Rufus Carstairs, I will have to tell him you are indisposed and will not be able to receive him for a day or two.'

On that ominous announcement the door closed firmly behind her and Joanna curled up in a tight ball

of misery and had a good weep. Finally she emerged,
feeling chastened and ashamed of herself. It was very
good of Mama not to punish her for what had happened, she fully appreciated that. And dissipation
only made one feel ill, it appeared. Perhaps she
should return to normal, if only to prevent her mother
ever speaking to her in that hurt tone of voice again.

It was all hopeless, of course: she was twenty years
old and as good as on the shelf. How could she bear
to marry another man when she would always be in
love with Giles? Still, spinsters had to behave with
modesty and decorum, so she might as well continue
like that and become used to it.

This pious resolve lasted precisely two days; in
fact, until the rout party at Mrs Jameson's and her
next encounter with the Earl of Clifton. Mrs Jameson's parties were always popular although, as she
admitted to Mrs Fulgrave when the ladies were standing talking halfway through the evening, it did seem
rather flat after the Duchess's grand ball. Emily, who
could still not think of the ball without a shudder,
agreed but pointed out that anything on such a scale
must induce a sense of let-down afterwards.

Her daughter was certainly feeling that sensation,
for the combination of being on her best behaviour,
and knowing that many of those present this evening
had observed her behaving in quite the opposite way,
was oppressive. She tried hard not to imagine that
people were talking about her behind her back, but
could not convince herself. It became much worse

when she realised that Lady Suzanne Hall was amongst the young ladies present.

Joanna had never had more than a passing acquaintanceship with Suzanne, who was at the centre of a group of her friends, all talking and giggling together. Knowing that she was going to regret it, but quite unable to resist, Joanna strolled across and attached herself to a neighbouring group so she could hear what was being said behind her.

There was a lot of giggling, several gasps of surprise and then one young lady said, 'Colonel Gregory? Why, Suzy, you cunning thing! What does your papa say?'

'As it is Giles, why, what could he say? He has always been against it, but darling Giles is *so* persuasive.'

'Oh, you lucky thing! I saw him at the Duchess's ball and I thought he was so dashing and handsome…'

Joanna moved abruptly away. So, he had asked Lord Olney for Suzanne's hand in marriage and the Marquis had agreed. Now all she could look forward to was the announcement. Joanna scooped a glass of champagne from the tray carried by a passing footman and drank it defiantly before she realised that the Earl of Clifton had entered the room and was being greeted by his hostess. Joanna took a careful step backwards towards a screen but was too late: he must have enquired after her, for Mrs Jameson was scanning the room and nodding in her direction.

Regretting her height, which made her so visible, Joanna slipped her empty glass on to a side table and prepared to make the best of it. He could hardly ask her to marry him in the middle of a crowded reception, after all.

She watched him make his way across the room, critically comparing him to Giles. Rufus was slightly above medium height with an elegant figure and a handsome, slightly aquiline, face. His hair was very blond, his eyes a distinctive shade of blue, and Joanna suspected he knew exactly how attractive he was to look at. He was also always immaculately dressed in an austere fashion.

But compared to Giles's tall, muscular figure, his air of confident command and the quiet humour in his face, Rufus Carstairs cut a poor figure to her eyes, and, although she could not quite decide why, a sinister one at that. His eyes flickered over her rapidly as he approached and once again she had that disconcerting feeling that he was paying more attention to her figure than was proper.

'My lord.' She curtsied slightly as he reached her side.

'So formal, Miss Fulgrave.' He took her hand in his and bent to kiss it. Joanna snatched it away, hoping that this unconventional greeting would go unnoticed.

'*My lord!*'

'Oh, come now, Joanna.' He tucked his hand under her elbow and began to stroll down the length of the room. 'How can you stand so on ceremony with an old friend even if we have only recently been reunited?'

'We were hardly friends, my lord,' she retorted

tartly, wondering if she could extricate her elbow and deciding it would create an unseemly struggle. 'As I recall, you considered me a pestilential brat and I thought you were a bully.'

'But now you are a beautiful young lady and I am but an ardent admirer at your feet.'

'Please, Lord Clifton, do not flirt, I am not in the mood.' She looked around the room for rescue. 'Look, there is Mr Higham. Have you met him? I am sure he would wish to meet you.'

'I have no wish to meet him, however.' Rufus's hand was touching her side, she could feel its heat through the thin gauze of her bodice. Only a few days before Giles's hand had rested there. 'Joanna, when are you going to permit me to speak to you?'

'You are speaking to me now. Oh, good evening, Miss Doughty. How is your mama?'

With a faint hiss of irritation Lord Clifton steered Joanna away from her friend. 'That is not what I mean and you know it, Joanna. Your parents are more than willing for me to address you.'

Joanna wondered if she had the courage to refuse him there and then and risk a scene, but those blue eyes were glittering dangerously and she was suddenly afraid of what he might do. 'Yes, I know, but it is too soon, my lord, we are hardly acquainted again.'

He smiled suddenly, but the attractive expression did not reach his eyes. 'Such maidenly modesty! I know what I want, Joanna, and what I want, I get. I have a fondness for beautiful things and my collection is notable. And I do not think I am going to be fight-

ing off many rivals, am I? I have heard the whisper-
ings since I returned to London. Miss Fulgrave, it
seems, is very picky and turns down every offer. Do
you expect men to keep offering and risking a rebuff?'

'I am surprised that *you* risk it, then,' she retorted,
trampling down the mortifying thought that people
were gossiping about her.

'But I told you, I get what I want and I want you,
Joanna. Just think of the triumph of carrying off the
Perfect Débutante, the young lady who has refused so
many. How lovely you will look installed as chate-
laine of Clifton Hall. I will be calling very soon. Now,
I am expected at Rochester's for cards. Goodnight,
my dear.'

Watching him saunter back across the room and
take his smiling leave of his hostess, she wanted to
throw the glass at the wall, scream, do something utterly outrageous, but only the dark glitter of her eyes
betrayed her innermost feelings. Somewhere, deep inside, the girl she had once been before she had met
Giles was reawakening: older, more socially adept,
polished, but still that rebellious, adventurous spirit
burned, and now it roused itself and stared out at a
hostile world through new and defiant eyes.

The next day while walking in Hyde Park with her
maid, she saw a smart curricle bowling along the tan
surface towards her. At the reins was the petite figure
of Lady Suzanne, a dashing tricorne and veil on her
blonde head, her figure clad to perfection in a deep
blue walking dress. She was laughing with delight as

she controlled the two high-stepping bays at a brisk trot and, with a wrench, Joanna realised that not only was the man beside her Giles Gregory but his right hand was over Suzanne's on the reins and he was laughing too at her uninhibited enjoyment.

They swept past Joanna and for a moment she thought he had not noticed her, then the team was reined in and began to back. Joanna could hear Giles's voice, 'Keep your hands lower, Suzy, for goodness' sake, you are trying to make a team back up, not encourage a hunter over a fence!'

The curricle drew level with her again just as he said, with unmistakable pride in his voice, 'Good girl! There, I told you you could do it. Good morning, Miss Fulgrave, I do beg your pardon, we were past before I recognised you. I hope your family is well?' His eyes asked something else, and Joanna felt a surge of warmth that not only had he remembered her distress, but that he had the tact not to mention it in front of Lady Suzanne.

'Quite well, I thank you, Colonel,' she replied, wondering at her own composure. 'All of us are in good health.'

'Excellent. Are you ladies acquainted?'

'Oh, yes,' Lady Suzanne said with a light laugh. 'We know each other by sight, do we not, Miss Fulgrave? And, of course, I saw you at my aunt's ball.' As did most of the *ton*, her expression said, as her pretty blue eyes rested on Joanna's face. She did not like another woman drawing her Colonel's attention, that was plain.

'Indeed.' Joanna could feel the seams of her gloves

creaking as she clenched her fists. 'And I saw you. Such a lovely gown. Good day, Lady Suzanne, Colonel. Enjoy your drive.'

She forced herself to smile as she turned on her heel and began to walk home. Nothing mattered any more, the only thing left was to immerse herself in whatever diversions presented themselves so that she did not have the opportunity to even think about Giles.

Her mother noted with concern her silence and set face when she came in but within days she found that her daughter's uncommunicativeness was the least of her problems.

At the end of two weeks the list of outrages committed by her lovely, obedient, perfect daughter included flirting heavily with every rake who came within her orbit, being found playing dice with three young gentlemen in a back room at a party, galloping on Rotten Row and eating ice cream in Gunther's with Lord Sutton, having 'lost' her maid. This was on top of her managing, by what stratagems her mama could not establish, to avoid Lord Clifton on every occasion he called. The final straw was to walk up St James's because—as she told her speechless mother—she 'wanted to know what all the fuss was about'.

That exploit led to Mr Fulgrave's involvement, resulting in a painful interview. Joanna was forbidden any parties until they went to Brighton in two weeks' time and had to suffer the ignominy of not being allowed out at all without her mother's escort.

'I do not understand it, I really do not,' Mr Fulgrave said, more in sorrow than in anger. 'At your age dear Grace was married with her first child and was mistress of a large household, while you are behaving like a hoyden of seventeen who knows no better. Lord Clifton will not contain his impatience for much longer my girl, and if these disgraceful exploits come to his attention he will withdraw his suit in disgust.'

Alone in her bedroom Joanna considered these strictures with little sense of remorse. She felt too numb to really care, although the hope that she would drive away Rufus Carstairs gave her a glimmer of pleasure. But disappointingly a course of dissipation did not seem to provide the distraction from the circling thoughts of Giles that she had hoped. Still, it was at least more stimulating than meekly withering into an old maid, which seemed the only alternative to an unwanted marriage.

Nothing, therefore, deterred Joanna from her plans for that evening, which involved leaving the house by the back door after she was supposed to be asleep and meeting her old acquaintance Catherine Marcus. Mrs Marcus, once plain Kate Hampton and now a rich young matron, had informed Joanna three evenings before when they met at a reception that she was getting up a party to attend the masquerade at Vauxhall Gardens. Her dear Joanna, she was sure, would thoroughly enjoy it.

Mama did not approve of Mrs Marcus, whom she considered to be fast and flighty, but, as far as she knew, she and Joanna had never been close at and she was therefore unlikely to lead her daughter astray. The thought that their reacquaintance would involve an expedition to Vauxhall for a masquerade, an activity entirely beyond the pale as far as Mrs Fulgrave was concerned, was inconceivable.

Her mask dangling from its ribbons in one hand, the other clutching her blue domino tightly around her, Joanna made her escape and was picked up by the Marcuses' coach without mishap at the appointed place. No one, she congratulated herself, would know and she had always wanted to experience a masquerade. In the flickering light her friend did not notice the shadows under her eyes and the party set off full of high spirits.

Chapter Three

Vauxhall Gardens seemed an enchanted dream to Joanna. Lights in their thousand twinkled amid the branches and framed pavilions and kiosks in a magical glow. Every twist and turn in the paths opened on to new vistas crowded with party-goers; music and laughter filled the air and Mrs Marcus's party spent the first hour simply strolling, watching the passing throng and revelling in the strange feeling of safety their masks produced.

Mrs Marcus had invited a large group of friends and, although all the young ladies seemed to Joanna to be startling free and easy and the men escorting them more than a little inclined to take advantage of whatever flirtation was on offer, she felt quite comfortable in the company. Everyone seemed to behave towards her as befitted her unmarried status and she rather suspected that Kate had had a quiet word with her friends about their inexperienced new acquaintance.

Joanna firmly refused the offer of a glass of champagne when they retired to a kiosk for shaved ham and other trifles before joining the dancing; as everyone else became gayer and more light-headed, she retained a perfectly level-headed awareness of everything going on around her. Things were certainly becoming a trifle warm but, although she realised her mama would faint away at the sights her younger daughter was coolly observing, she felt only an amused curiosity.

However, she rapidly regretted allowing herself to be taken out on to the dance floor by one young gentleman who proved to be either a very inept dancer or perhaps simply an inebriated one.

'No, no, it is quite all right,' she protested lightly for the third time as he trod on her toe during the boulanger. 'So crowded, is it not? Oh!' His foot found her hem and half dragged the domino from her shoulder. Joanna pulled it back, found she had lost the ties securing it at her neck and that she could not see to untangle the ribbons whilst wearing her mask. 'Oh dear, can we just go to the side of the dance floor?' Her partner, apologising profusely at his carelessness, guided her out of the throng and stood by, helpfully holding her mask while Joanna adjusted her cloak.

'Would you like to dance again?' he asked as he handed back the black satin mask.

'And have her toes completely bruised? I think not, young man.' Lord Clifton appeared at her side, masked, but with his unmistakable blue eyes glittering through the slits. 'May I offer you my escort home, Miss Fulgrave?' He turned abruptly to her partner, who took a step back. 'We need keep you no longer, sir.'

'Yes, thank you for the dance, sir,' Joanna said

hastily. He seemed inclined to square up belligerently
to the interloper and she added pacifically, 'It is quite
all right, I know this gentlemen.'

The young man took himself off with an affronted
bow. 'Would you be so good as to escort me back to
my hostess, my lord? She is over there.' Joanna
forced herself to speak calmly and pleasantly, although her mind was racing. She could hardly make
a scene here.

'The fast young lady in the pink domino? Not, I
am sure, a hostess your mama would approve of, Joanna.' He took her arm and began to steer her away
from the Marcus party. 'And where exactly does your
mama believe you to be at this moment?' Joanna
knew she was colouring, but could not help it. 'Ah,
blamelessly in your bed. I think we had better return
you there.'

'No! I cannot simply walk away from Mrs Marcus
like that.' But from the set of his mouth and the very
firm grip on her arm she knew that, short of screaming
and struggling, she was going to do just as Rufus told
her. 'I must at least thank her and say goodbye or she
will worry.'

'Very well.' She could feel his eyes on her set face
and she tried to look as happy as possible before they
reached her party. 'Do not sulk, Joanna, it does not
suit you. Think what a disillusion it is for me to find
my perfect bride-to-be in such company.'

'I am *not* your bride-to-be!' She broke off abruptly
at the appearance in front of them of a tall figure in
a black domino, a petite blue-clad figure on his arm.

'Joanna!' It was unmistakably Giles, and she realised with a shock that she had not replaced her mask.

She fumbled it back into place, unable to meet his eyes. 'Are you in any difficulties, Miss Fulgrave?'

'No! No, none at all, just rather flustered by the crowd, Colonel, thank you. I was just about to leave. Goodnight.' From being his captive, she almost towed Rufus after her towards Mrs Marcus, leaving Giles Gregory staring at their retreating backs.

'What the…who was that she was with, I wonder?'

'Oh, that was Rufus Carstairs,' his companion said confidently. 'Lord Clifton, you know. I would know those eyes anywhere. Frightfully eligible, but he makes my flesh creep. Well, the perfect Miss Fulgrave *is* behaving badly, is she not?'

Giles Gregory looked down at her. 'Just as badly as you, Suzy, you little witch. Now, come along and let us get home or your papa will cut off your dress allowance and take a horsewhip to me.'

She laughed. 'Not when I tell him you came to rescue me, Giles darling.'

'As well you knew I would, you baggage, considering you left me a note!' he said affectionately. 'Now, do any of your errant girlfriends need an escort as well?' He firmly walked her away from the dancing, but his eyes were scanning the crowd for the tall girl in the blue domino.

Joanna sat in the furthest corner of the earl's carriage apprehensively expecting him to try and kiss her, but to her relief he made no attempt to do so as they rattled over the cobbles and through the night-time streets.

Flambeaux outside town houses cast a flickering light into the interior and she saw he appeared to be thinking. Eventually, unable to stand the silence any more, she said, 'I hope I do not take you away from your own party this evening?'

'Hmm? No, not at all. I was just thinking what best to say to your parents: I would not wish them to be out of reason cross with you.'

'Say to them? Why, nothing! I will let myself in and they will be none the wiser.'

'You shock me, Joanna, you really do! Naturally I cannot be so deceitful, nor can I let you. I will have to tell them for, after all, we are alone in a closed carriage.'

'You mean you…that you think I should…'

'Your parents are, I know, in favour of my suit. Now I imagine they will be only too anxious for the engagement.'

Joanna stared at him speechlessly, then found her voice. 'I would not marry you, Rufus Carstairs, if you were the last man on earth.'

'Hardly an original sentiment, my dear. Now, here is your street. Ah, no need for any surprises, I see, they must already be aware of your absence.' And, indeed, the lights were blazing downstairs as the carriage pulled up. Numbly Joanna allowed herself to be handed down out of the carriage and into the house.

Her mother took one look at her and said, 'Wait in the drawing room please, Joanna,' before vanishing with the earl into the front salon.

How her absence had been discovered she never knew. It seemed hours that she sat in the chilly room, exhaustion dragging at her eyelids, her mind tormented by the thought that Giles had seen her apparently happy to be with Rufus Carstairs.

At last her parents appeared, grim-faced, yet with a subdued air of triumph. 'Well, Joanna,' her father said heavily, 'you are fortunate indeed to so escape the results of your wicked folly. The earl, against all reason, still wishes to make you his wife. He has agreed to wait until the end of the week to allow you to recover from this ill-advised romp but he will be coming then to make you an offer and you, Joanna, are going to accept it.'

'No!' Joanna sprang to her feet, her hands clenched, her voice trembling. 'No! I will never marry him.'

'Then I wash my hands of you,' her father declared, also on his feet. 'You will go to your Great-aunt Clara in Bath. She needs a new companion and, as we cannot trust you to take part in Society, let alone in the more relaxed atmosphere of Brighton, that is the best place for you.'

'To Great-aunt Clara?' Joanna's tired, sore mind wrestled with the shock. 'But she never goes out.'

'Indeed,' Mrs Fulgrave said repressively. 'I am sure she will appreciate your company. You can read to her, assist with her needlework, help entertain her friends when they call. I shall tell the earl that her ill health has meant that we felt we had no choice but to send you. We must just hope that in a few months, when you have come to your senses, he is still interested in making you an offer.'

Joanna contemplated her sentence. Banishment to Bath, to a household of old age and illness, to the care of a formidable relative who, if she were truthful, rather scared her, and no diversion whatsoever to distract her mind from Giles. And at the end of months of incarceration, the only hope held out to her was that Rufus Carstairs might still want to marry her. And she had a dreadful apprehension that he would. He did not seem like a man who tolerated being thwarted. He was a man who would chase the length of Europe to beat a rival to a choice statue.

'Please do not send me away, Mama,' she said, her voice wavering on the edge of tears. 'I will be so miserable.'

'You should have thought of that before plunging into these wild scrapes,' her father said severely. 'Your mother will write to your great-aunt tomorrow. I only hope she is prepared to countenance your presence, considering what she will learn of your recent behaviour.'

He stood up, gathering his dressing gown around himself. As he picked up his chamber candle he remarked with unconscious cruelty, 'Perhaps the contemplation of the loneliness of a single old age will convince you that the rewards of truly happy domestic life with a devoted husband are worth more than the transitory pleasures you have been indulging in.'

Joanna walked slowly up to her bedchamber, well aware that, however late the hour, she could not possibly sleep now. What was she to do? She stood, her forehead pressed against the glass of the window, her eyes unfocused on the darkness outside. Where did she belong now? Probably, she thought bitterly, her role in life would be as the spinster aunt, or cousin or devoted niece. *Dear Joanna, always so good with the children, always available to help with the old ladies...* It wasn't that she did not like old ladies, or children, come to that, it was just that she had hoped to have her own children—Giles's children.

Suddenly she whirled away from the window, propelled by a determination not to be crushed, not to be dictated to. Her life was in ruins: well, no one else was going to rebuild it but she. 'Strategy and tactics,' she said out loud. 'Strategy and tactics.' Then the burst of energy left her and she sank down on the bed. Strategy was no good without an objective.

Resolutely she straightened her spine. She had trained herself to be a soldier's wife—now she had to use the courage she had prided herself she possessed. Her short-term objective must be to decide what to do with the rest of her life, and her strategy would be to go somewhere she could think about this in peace. And that was not Bath, where she would be the disgraced niece to be watched and lectured.

So…Joanna bit her lip and thought. Who could she run away to? Not Hebe and Alex at Tasborough Hall: not when Hebe's confinement was so close. There were Uncle and Aunt Pulborough in Exeter—but they would be scandalised by the arrival of an errant niece—a second cousin in Wales, but he had been recently widowed. One after another Joanna passed her relatives under review and came to the conclusion that the only one who might have helped her, if circumstances had been different, was Hebe. Or, her own sister.

Thoughtfully Joanna picked up a notebook from the night table and wrote, *Grace, Lincoln*. She had no idea how Lady Willington would react, let alone her brother-in-law, Sir Frederick, but perhaps they might serve as a diversion. Her dearest friend from Miss

Faversham's Seminary for Young Ladies in Bath had been Georgiana Schofield; Georgy was now Lady Brandon and living in Wisbech, from where she wrote frequently to say she was utterly bored and was dying for darling Joanna to visit her.

'If I set out on the stage for Lincoln,' Joanna reasoned out loud, 'there is sure to be a point where I can change and go to Wisbech, and everyone will think I am with Grace. And when they realise I am not, I will have vanished into East Anglia without a trace.' She added, *Georgy, Wisbech,* to her list.

Or would her mama suspect she was with Georgy? No, for Mama never asked to see her letters from her school friends and Joanna doubted she even knew Georgy's married name. Something she had just thought touched a chord of memory. East Anglia... Aunt Caroline, of course! Her father's youngest sister, the sister no one was allowed to mention, the one who had made a scandalous marriage.

But Joanna had once overheard a conversation between her parents that she had not dared ask about, yet had never forgotten.

'I am sorry, my dear,' her mother had said firmly. 'But she is your sister when all is said and done, and despite the scandal I will continue to write once a year at Christmas to enquire after her health and to tell her news of the family.'

'The affair nearly killed Papa,' her own father had replied harshly. 'Is she the sort of woman you wish our Grace and Joanna to associate with?'

'Nonsense,' Mama had replied calmly. 'Writing to offer Christmas wishes will not expose our girls to scandal or bad influences. You must do Caro justice, my dear. Has she ever attempted to return to London from East Anglia or to call here?'

Her father's muttered response was inaudible and Joanna, guiltily aware that she had been eavesdropping, had left the study door and had walked on. But somewhere in East Anglia she had a disgraced and scandalous aunt. Would she understand? Could Joanna talk to her and find someone who could counsel her?

But how to find her? Joanna thought hard, then realised that if her mother was writing to Aunt Caroline, then she probably had her direction in her remembrancer where she noted all her addresses, birthdays and other important lists. She got up, opened the door on to the dark and silent house, and went downstairs.

Chapter Four

Three days after Joanna's disastrous masquerade party, Giles Gregory turned his match greys neatly into Half Moon Street, sensing his spirits lift perceptibly as he saw the smart black front door of the Tasboroughs' town house in front of him.

He felt heartsore, anxious and hurt, and the thought of Hebe's warm common sense and Alex's astringent comradeship had seemed like a beacon on the journey from his family home in the Vale of Aylesbury. He had crossed with them journeying up to town from their Hertfordshire estate when he had made his painfully short visit to his parents and, instead of finding refuge at Tasborough, had had to drive back to London to seek out his friends.

He handed the reins to his groom and jumped down. 'Take them 'round to the mews, Mellors, and tell his lordship's man that I am expecting to stay for a day or two. If that is not convenient, come back and let me know and you can take them to the livery stables, but I do not expect the earl has brought more than his carriage horses and one hack up for a short stay.'

The man drove competently away down the street and Giles took the front steps in two long strides. The door was opened by Starling, the family butler, who permitted himself a small smile on seeing who was there.

'Colonel Gregory. It is a pleasure to see you again, sir, if I may be so bold. His lordship is out, but her ladyship is in the Blue Room. She is not generally receiving, but I will venture to say she will be at home to you, sir, if you would care to go up. Will you be staying? Your usual room is free.'

'Thank you, Starling.' Giles handed him his hat and gloves. 'I hope Lady Tasborough will not object to a house guest for a night or two.'

He made his way up to the elegant room on the first floor which was Hebe's favourite retiring room, and opened the door. 'May I come in?'

'Giles!' She was lying propped up against a pile of cushions on a *chaise longue*, a wide smile of delighted welcome on her face.

He strode across to her side, warmed by her delight. There were times when he wondered if he would ever find someone like his friend's wife, someone whom he could love as Alex loved Hebe, someone who would love him back with such passionate devotion.

'Good grief, Lady Tasborough!' He stopped in front of her, his mouth curving into a warm, teasing, smile. 'Just when is this child due? I give you fair warning, I have delivered one baby in my time, and it is not an experience I am willing to repeat.'

Hebe held out her arms to him, giggling as he attempted to kiss her across the bump. Sheets of note-paper scattered unregarded to the carpet. 'It isn't due for six weeks, Giles, so you need not be alarmed. Have you truly delivered a baby? Whose was it?'

'The wife of one of the men. The father fainted, the doctor was away cutting some poor man's leg off, there was not another woman in sight, so it was down to me.' He grinned at her affectionately. *This* felt like coming home. 'Six weeks? Are you sure it isn't twins?'

'Oh!' Hebe stared at him wide-eyed. 'Surely not? There are none in either family as far as I know, and it does follow, does it not?'

'I think so. I'm only teasing you. How are you, Hebe? I am surprised to find you in town just now.'

'I am well, only so tired of feeling like a whale. I cannot recall when I last saw my feet. But never mind me, what are you doing here? Can you stay until we go back to Tasborough? Please do, we would love that so much.'

'Are you sure? It won't be difficult at the moment?'

'Not at all, and you will distract Alex and stop him fretting about me. I am in disgrace because I will not see any of the fashionable *accoucheurs*, which is the excuse I gave for coming up the other day. Alex says if all I want to do is shop, then I must go straight back to the country and rest. But we are here for another two days at any rate.' She settled herself against her cushions and watched him with her wide grey eyes steady on his face. 'The decanters are over there. Pour yourself a drink, then come and sit down beside me.'

Giles did as he was bid, dropping on to a footstool

beside the *chaise* and settling himself comfortably.
'Now, tell me what is wrong, Giles,' she commanded.

'Wrong?' He shifted so that he was sitting with his
back against the side of the *chaise*, his face turned
from her.

'Yes, wrong.' Hebe rested her hand lightly on his
shoulder. 'You look as though someone has been
kicking you—spiritually, I mean.'

Giles put up his own hand and covered hers.
'Clever Hebe. That is exactly how I feel. I went home
to Buckinghamshire two days ago because Mother
has been writing to say that she is worried about Father. The doctor thinks he had some kind of seizure
last month, now one side of his face is stiff and he is
limping. Denies there is anything wrong, of course.'

'How old is the General?'

'Only sixty, but he's had a tough life. Wounded at
least six times, broken bones, yellow fever. He was
never the kind of officer who stayed back at headquarters in comfort. Now he's getting tired, but he
will not admit it, and that's a big estate for one man
to manage. If I had a younger brother…'

'So you came home to see him?' Hebe curled her
fingers within his and gave an encouraging squeeze.

'Yes. I did not want to rush straight there as soon
as I arrived in the country or he would suspect why
I came home. My idea was to see for myself how he
did, and, if he really looked bad, to sell out. I thought
I'd try horse breeding and at the same time take over
some of the estate management. Nothing too much at
first, just the bits that really bore and tire him.'

'And gradually he would let you do more and more
and he would never have to admit he couldn't cope?'

'Yes. At least, that was my plan.' He fell silent. The pain of his father's reaction was almost too raw to speak about yet. 'Where's Alex?'

Hebe laughed. 'At his club, taking refuge because I will not let him fuss over me, and if he stays at home he fidgets himself to death.' Hebe paused, then, 'How did your father react?'

'Badly.'

'Tell me,' she persisted gently.

'He demanded to know what had happened to make me lose my nerve and to want to sell out, like some coward of a Hyde-Park soldier,' Giles said harshly. Hebe gasped.

'He doesn't mean it.' Giles continued more easily now the shaming words had been said. 'He expects me to be a general too—and even younger than he had been. I think in his heart he knows why I am talking of selling out and he is railing against his own weakness, not mine.'

'I shouldn't think that makes it hurt any less,' Hebe said, lifting her hand to touch it softly to his face. Giles turned his cheek against her knuckles, comforted. Lucky, lucky Alex.

'No. And of course he knows he has been unjust and doesn't know how to put it right. So he managed to find yet another sin to throw at my head to justify his anger.'

'What else?'

'He wants to know what I think I'm about, flirting with Lady Suzanne Hall and not making her an offer. *Damn good catch*, the old boy says with considerable understatement, and he isn't going to stand by hearing stories about me trifling with her affections.'

'Are you?' Hebe asked.

'Flirting or trifling?'

'Intending to marry her,' Hebe said tartly.

'None of those things. I've known Suzy since I was ten and she was toddling. She's the sister I never had and I'd as soon marry a cage full of monkeys. I feel nothing but the deepest sympathy for whichever poor idiot marries her. That girl is the most outrageous minx I have ever come across.'

'So you are not in love with her?' Hebe persisted.

'I love the girl—but just as a sister—and she and her parents know it. She has been practising flirting and wheedling on me since she was eleven because she knows I'm safe and her mother likes me to squire her about when I'm in town because *she* knows I'm safe. I scare off the bucks and the fortune hunters and Suzy can play the little madam to her heart's content.

'But she's probably the best catch of the Season, as my father is all too aware. Some old pussy has been telling him I was seen with her driving in the park and dancing with her rather too often and that's enough for him. And that's another thing,' he added bitterly. 'Her father didn't want her to learn to drive because his own sister was hurt in a bad accident, so what must she do but wheedle me into persuading the poor man that I can teach her.'

'Well, you *are* a very good whip, Giles,' Hebe pointed out.

'Yes, and I'm well known for not letting ladies drive my teams, so Father puts two and two together, gets six and then finds no sign of me doing the right thing. And, of course, as he points out, it's about time I was getting married and setting up my nursery and look at Lord Tasborough with one heir to his name already and that pretty little wife of his increasing again…'

'Oh, poor Giles,' Hebe said with indignant sympathy. 'You have been giving your head for a washing, haven't you? What are you going to do? Oh, listen, I think that's Alex.'

The door opened to reveal the Earl, his face breaking into a grin when he saw who was with his wife.

'Giles! No, don't get up, stay there.' He bent down and gave his friend a powerful buffet on the shoulder, wrung the hand that was held out to him, and dropped to the carpet by his side. 'Are you here to stay? Is that why I find you here flirting with my wife?'

'He isn't flirting,' Hebe said, half-anxious, half-laughing. 'He thinks I'm expecting twins.'

'Good God!' The Earl twisted round to regard both his wife and friend. 'Are you serious? And what do you know about it, might I ask?'

'He says he's delivered a baby.'

'But not twins,' Giles hastened to say. 'No, don't hit me! It is merely that kissing your delightful wife is like trying to reach her over a pile of sofa cushions and either someone's mathematics are out, or it's twins. Or triplets…' he added wickedly, ducking away from Alex's punch.

'Oh, stop it!' Hebe cried, slapping at black and blond heads impartially. 'I might as well have two more small boys on my hands as you men. Giles is staying until we go back to Tasborough: he is having a perfectly horrible time at home. Giles, tell him.'

Giles recounted his story again. When he reached his father's reaction to his plan to sell out, Alex went quite still, then simply reached out and gripped his arm. Giles found his vision suddenly blurred and rapidly finished the rest of his tale.

'Just how angry is the General?' Alex asked. No one ever referred to Lord Gregory by his title.

'Angry enough to disinherit me.'

'Can he?' Alex enquired.

Giles shook his head with a rueful grin. The morning's final, painful, interview was beginning to seem less painful and more farcelike now he could talk about it. 'There's the entail, and the money I inherited from Grandmama Ingham—he can't do a thing about either of those. If he really puts his mind to it he can find about sixty acres and a couple of farms—and the furniture, of course—to leave elsewhere. But he doesn't mean it.'

'What will you do?' Hebe was still not reassured.

'I am under orders from Mama to come up to town and embark upon a life of reckless dissipation.' He twisted round to smile at Hebe. 'I'd already taken rooms at Albany as a *pied-à-terre*, but they aren't fitted out yet, which is why I had hoped you'd take me in.'

'*Dissipation?* But why?'

'She says he will soon hear all about it and order me back home to be lectured. At which point he will decide that the best thing for me is to rusticate on the estate for a while.'

Hebe laughed. 'How clever of your mama! Of course, if he thinks you don't want to do it and would rather be in London, then helping with the estate will be just the thing to punish the prodigal, and after a few weeks he'll be so used to it, and will enjoy having you there so much, that you will get exactly the result you want.'

'Has it ever occurred to you that your mother is a better strategist than your father?' Alex enquired.

'Frequently. She always outflanks him and the poor man can never understand how she has done it.' He shifted his position and one hand flattened a sheet of paper, which crackled. 'Sorry, I appear to be crushing the letter you were reading.'

'Oh, goodness!' Hebe exclaimed, taking the crumpled pages. 'I had quite forgotten in the excitement of Giles arriving. It is from Aunt Emily,' she explained to the two men. 'She sent a footman with it this morning, just after you had left, Alex. It is the most incredible thing. She says she is to send Joanna to stay with her great-aunt in Bath because she is in disgrace.'

'I will go into the library.' Giles started to get up. 'You will want to discuss this in private.'

'No, stay, please. You are one of the family, Giles, and besides, you are staying here and will have to know what is going on.' She started to re-read. 'And it is not as though it is anything actually, er, indelicate.'

'What, not an elopement with the apothecary or the unfortunate results of an amorous encounter with the footman?' Alex enquired, earning a look of burning reproach from his wife.

'I still think I had better leave,' Giles persisted. 'I can go to an hotel until my rooms are ready at Albany. Your aunt will want to call and discuss the problem, that is obvious, and she will not feel at ease if she knows I am staying here.'

'Nonsense, Giles. We need you to help us get to the bottom of this puzzle. Aunt Emily says it all began at the Duchess of Bridlington's ball. Joanna got drunk on champagne, flirted outrageously and then went on to commit just about every act in the list of things she could do to be labelled fast. And, to cap it all, she is wilfully refusing an offer from a highly eligible nobleman—discreetly unnamed.'

'*Joanna?* Drunk on champagne?' Alex looked incredulous. 'That girl is a pattern-book of respectability and correct behaviour.'

'The Duchess of Bridlington's ball?' Giles sat down again. 'Oh, lord.' His friends looked at him incredulously. 'Don't look at me like that! I haven't been seducing the girl! But I think I may have started her off on the wine—' He broke off, his eyes unfocussed, looking back into the past. 'You know, she had had a bad shock of some kind: that's why I gave her a couple of glasses of champagne.'

He had forgotten about his encounters with Joanna in the face of his estrangement with his father, but, looking back in the light of Mrs Fulgrave's letter, things began to make sense. 'At the ball I found her sitting outside one of the retiring rooms looking shocked,' he began.

'You mean someone might have said something *risqué* or unkind to her?' Hebe ventured.

'No, not that kind of shock.' He remembered the blank look in those wide hazel eyes and suddenly realised what it reminded him of. 'Alex, you know the effect their first battle had on some of the very young, very idealistic officers who came out to the Peninsula without any experience? The ones who thought that war was all glory and chivalry, bugles blowing and flags flying?'

'And found it was blood and mud and slaughter. Men dying in something that resembled a butcher's shambles, chaos and noise—' Alex broke off and Hebe could see they were both somewhere else, somewhere she could never follow. 'Yes, I remember. What are you saying?'

'Joanna had the same look in her eyes as those lads had after their first battle, as though an ideal had disintegrated before her and her world was in ruins. She was white, her hands were shaking. I asked her what was wrong, but she would not tell me. I assumed it was a man. We talked of neutral subjects for a while. After two glasses of champagne she was well enough to waltz, which helped, I think. Movement often does in cases of shock—' He broke off, remembering the supple, yielding figure in his arms, those wide hazel eyes that seemed to look trustingly into his soul, his instinct to find and hurt the man who had so obviously hurt her.

They discussed the matter a little more, speculating on the spurned suitor to no purpose and, after a while, left Hebe to rest.

Giles went up to his usual room. While Alex's valet unpacked for him he paced restlessly, fighting the urge to drive straight back home to see how his father was. To distract himself from his cantankerous parent, he thought about Joanna Fulgrave. To his surprise he found he was dwelling pleasurably on the memory. He frowned, trying to convince himself that he was merely intrigued by what had turned a previously biddable débutante into a fast young lady. But there was more than that, something that lay behind the desperate hurt in those lovely eyes, something which seemed to speak directly to him.

He shifted in the comfortable wing chair where he had finally come to rest. His body was responding to thoughts of Miss Fulgrave in a quite inappropriate way.

It was two months since he had parted from his Portuguese mistress. There were, of course, the ladies of negotiable virtue who flourished in town. They had not featured on his mother's list of dissipated activities that she had suggested to him. 'Cards, dearest, drink—I know you have a hard head for both, so they are safe. Be seen in all the most notorious places. Perhaps buy a racehorse? Flirt, of course, but no young débutantes, that goes without saying… Do you know any fast matrons?'

'Only you, Mama,' he had retorted, smiling into her amused grey eyes.

After an hour, Hebe, thoroughly bored with resting, summoned both men back to her salon, announcing that she had not the slightest idea what she could do to assist her aunt.

'Send Giles to listen sympathetically,' Alex was suggesting idly when there was the sound of the knocker. 'Who can that be?'

Starling appeared in the doorway. 'Mrs Fulgrave, my lady.' He flattened himself against the door frame as Emily Fulgrave almost ran into the room, 'Oh, Hebe, my dear, Alex… Oh!' Both her niece and the Earl regarded her with consternation from the *chaise* where Alex was sitting beside Hebe who, he had insisted, was to stay lying down for at least another hour. Mrs Fulgrave burst into tears.

It took quite five minutes and a dose of sal volatile before she could command herself again. Giles, his escape cut off by a flurry of hastily summoned maid-servants and general feminine bustle, retreated to the far side of the room, hoping that his presence would not be marked. Hysterical matrons, he felt, were even less his style than fast ones.

Finally Hebe managed to ask what was wrong. Her aunt regarded her over her handkerchief and managed to gasp, 'Joanna has run away.'

Eventually the whole story was extracted. Joanna had vanished from her room, but was not missed until it was time for luncheon because she was assumed to be hiding herself away until her unwanted suitor was due that afternoon and Mr Fulgrave was not in a mood to be conciliatory and seek to encourage her to emerge.

When her mama had finally opened her bedchamber door she was gone, with only a brief note to say she was going 'where she could think.'

After several hours of sending carefully worded messages to her friends in town, all of which drew a blank, her parents were at their wits' end. Mr Fulgrave was prostrate with gout, dear Alex had seemed their only resort.

Alex shot one look at Hebe's white, shocked face and said firmly, 'I am sorry, Aunt Fulgrave, but I simply cannot leave Hebe now.'

'I know, of course, you cannot,' Emily Fulgrave said despairingly. 'I should have thought. It will have to be the Bow Street Runners, but we will have lost a day...'

'I will find her,' Giles said, standing up and causing all of them to start in surprise.

'Oh, Giles, *thank you*,' Hebe said warmly. 'I had quite forgot you were there. Aunt Emily, Giles is staying with us. What could be more fortunate?'

Giles wondered if Mrs Fulgrave would consider that the family scandal coming to the ears of someone else, however close a friend, to be a fortunate matter. 'You may trust my absolute discretion, ma'am, but you must tell me everything you know about what is wrong and where she may have gone,' he began briskly, only to stagger back as the distraught matron cast herself upon his chest and began to sob on his shoulder. 'Ma'am...'

Eventually Mrs Fulgrave was calm, sitting looking at him with desperate faith in his ability to find her daughter. Giles was already bitterly regretting his offer.

Damn it, what else can I do? he thought grimly. Alex and Hebe would fret themselves into flinders otherwise, and the Fulgraves had welcomed him into their family. And the thought of the girl with the pain in her hazel eyes tugged at him, awakening echoes of his own hurt.

Chapter Five

On the thirtieth of June, two days after Mrs Fulgrave had arrived distraught at the Tasboroughs' house, her errant daughter sat up in bed in the best chamber in the White Hart inn at Stilton and decided that, just possibly, she was not going to die after all.

It had been the meat pie she had so incautiously eaten at Biggleswade that had been her downfall. She had known almost at once that it had been a mistake, but she had been so hungry that when the stage had stopped she had eagerly paid for the pie and a glass of small ale.

Up until then the entire undertaking had seemed miraculously easy. She had packed a carefully selected valise of essentials and had donned the most demure walking dress and pelisse in her wardrobe. Her hair was arranged severely back into a tight knot, she had removed all her jewellery and her finished appearance, as she had intended, was that of a superior governess. And governesses were invisible; young women who could travel unregarded on the public stage without the slightest comment.

Finding the right inn from which to depart had taken a little more initiative, but careful study of the London map in her father's study showed her which area the Lincoln stage was likely to leave from, and a shy governess enquiring at six in the morning for the right departure point for Lincoln was apparently an unremarkable event.

In fact, she had felt remarkably pleased with herself and her tactics. Giles would have been proud of her, she caught herself thinking before that fancy was ruthlessly suppressed. Her only worry was how to get from Peterborough to Wisbech and Georgy, but that would doubtless become apparent once she had reached Peterborough.

Joanna pressed her arm against her side, feeling the reassuring bulge of the purse tied to her belt under her pelisse. She had only just received her quarter's allowance and still had, quite unspent, her birthday present from her generous godmother. Of all her worries, how to pay for her journey was the least of them.

Then she had eaten that wretched pie. Goodness knows what it had been made from, or how long it had been sitting in a warm kitchen before she had eaten it. By St Neots she was feeling queasy, past Eaton Socon she knew that at any moment she was going to be violently sick.

The stage had drawn up at the White Hart and she had staggered off, just finding enough voice to request the coachman to throw down her valise before she dived behind the shelter of a barn and was hideously ill. When she emerged shakily some time later the coach was gone, but thankfully the landlady proved motherly and kind to the white-faced young governess who explained that she was travelling back to her employer in Lincoln and had been taken ill.

'I am sure it is something I have eaten,' Joanna explained weakly, 'but I cannot travel like this. Fortunately Lady Brown does not expect me for another week so she will not worry. Is there any possibility of a room?'

The landlady was impressed by the genteel appearance and cultured accents of the young woman before her, and even more reassured by the sight of her guinea-purse. Such a pity that a young lady like that had to demean herself as little more than a superior upper servant.

'You come along, my dear,' she had urged. 'By good luck the best bedchamber is free and I'll have the girl see to you.'

The girl in question was kept more than a little busy over the next night and day. Joanna was thoroughly sick and at one point the landlady considered sending for the doctor, but by the following morning she was pale but recovering and could manage a little plain bread and a glass of water without it promptly returning.

She sat up and considered her situation. It was a setback, for she felt uneasily that until she turned off for Wisbech she was in danger of detection, but otherwise her plan was still holding together. But the delay had made Joanna think, and for some reason a particularly dry and academic book on strategy she had once tried to read came to her mind. She had cast it aside after a few chapters, unable to read further even to impress Giles. What had struck her as so idiotic about it was that the author propounded all manner of cunning manoeuvres without once considering that the enemy would be doing whatever *they* decided was best, thus overthrowing all the plans of their opponents.

It was just what she had been doing: planning her life with Giles without thinking for a moment that he might be doing something entirely otherwise. All at once it dawned on her that she hadn't been thinking about the real man at all, only the object of her dreams, her innocent, ignorant fantasy. Did the man she loved really exist at all?

Giles Gregory meanwhile was finding a perverse pleasure in the hunt. He had never been an intelligence officer, unlike his friend Alex, but no army officer could rise through the ranks without knowing how to hunt down and track the enemy through hostile or strange county.

And this was a foreign country to him, he realised, shouldering his way into the bustling inn yards of London. To a man used to command, and used to the least of his commands receiving instant obedience, the experience of being out of uniform and on the receiving end of the London working man's tongue was instructive.

'Move yer arse!' he was abruptly ordered when he stood too far into the yard of the Moor's Head as the stage swung in through the low arch, then, as he sidestepped out of the way, he was buffeted by a swaggering postilion with his iron-shod boots and aggressive whip. 'Shift yourself, bloody swell cove!'

He swung round to meet the man eye to eye and

the postilion backed off, hands raised defensively, muttering, 'Sorry, guv'nor, no offence meant.'

Giles looked him up and down without speaking until the man was reduced to stuttering silence, then said with a hint of steel in his pleasant voice, 'You will oblige me by telling me the inn for the Lincoln coaches.'

'This one, guv'nor. Let me show you the office, sir!'

Giles allowed himself to be shown the way. He was taking a gamble, but close questioning of a tearful Mrs Fulgrave by her niece and both men had elicited the fact that her sister Grace was the most likely refuge for Joanna. 'Then there is her schoolfriend Lady Brandon in Wisbech,' her mother had said, showing a greater awareness of Joanna's correspondence than her daughter had given her credit for. 'And, of course—' She had broken off, looking guilty.

'Who, Aunt?' Hebe had probed. 'We have to think of anyone she could have gone to.'

'Oh, dear. You must not tell your uncle I mentioned this.' Mrs Fulgrave took a deep breath. 'My sister-in-law Caroline near Norwich.'

'I have never heard of her, Aunt Emily.'

'I know, dear.' Emily had looked round imploringly at her audience. 'You will promise not to tell Mr Fulgrave that I told you? His youngest sister Caroline...' she blushed and went on bravely '...she lived with a married man as his wife. They fell in love, and then it transpired that he had a wife living who had run off with another man. So Caroline and Mr Faversham could never marry. It was impossible, of course, but she went and moved in with him. The family cut her off, even after his wife died, ten years later, and he married her, only to die himself within six months.'

'Oh, poor lady,' Hebe cried. 'How sad!'

'I thought so,' Emily said stoutly. 'And so I told Mr Fulgrave. I have written to her every year, but he would never relent because he says it nearly killed his poor father. But it is foolish of me even to consider Caro—Joanna could not know of her.'

'Are you sure?' Giles pressed. 'Where do you keep her address?'

Mrs Fulgrave had removed her remembrancer from her reticule and held it out, open at the right page. Giles studied the address, then delicately lifted one long black hair from the crease in the page. Silently he held it up, dark against Mrs Fulgrave's own light brown hair. 'I think she knows.' Only Hebe noticed that as he noted the address in his own pocket book he carefully laid the hair in its folds.

However, their supposition that Grace was the most likely choice for Joanna to make appeared to be confirmed at the stage-coach office. Not only did the book keeper assure Giles that this was the right departure point for Lincoln, but he remembered Joanna. 'If you mean the young lady governess, sir? Least, I suppose that was what she was. Remarkable handsome young woman, that I do know. But anxious somehow—that's why I recall her, sir—that and her looks, if you'll pardon me saying so. All dressed so demure-like and those big eyes...'

'Where did she buy a ticket to?' Giles demanded, coming to the conclusion that if he took exception to every man who offended him that day he would not get far.

'Lincoln, she said. At least, first she asked about Peterborough, then she looked confused and said she wanted Lincoln, sir.'

'And what would be the town to change for Wisbech?'

'Peterborough, sir.'

'And what are the stops between here and Lincoln?' Giles dug his hand in his pocket and began to sort coins. The man brightened at the chinking noise.

'I'll make you a list, shall I, sir? All of the stops or just the junction points, like?'

'All of them,' Giles had replied, tapping a gold coin suggestively on the counter.

Within half an hour his curricle, with the matched greys in the shafts and his groom left behind, faintly complaining, swung out on to the Great North Road heading towards Stevenage. Joanna had a full day's start on him and he could not risk simply assuming she was going to Peterborough; he was going to have to check at every stopping place on the list. But then, there were French colonels—some of them still alive to remember it—who had had similar starts on Giles Gregory and who had still found themselves tracked down, outmanoeuvred and defeated. One chit of a girl was not going to elude him now.

Joanna parted with some reluctance from the comforts of the White Hart the next morning. She was anxious to be on her way and to reach Georgy, but the inn and its motherly landlady, Mrs Handley, had seemed safe; although she would never have admitted it, Joanna was feeling lonely and not a little frightened.

Still, she was taken up by the stage without any problem and Mrs Handley had come out herself to see her off and to remind her which inn in Peterborough to get off at in order to pick up the Lynn stage, which would drop her in Wisbech.

She eyed her new travelling companions from under the brim of her modest bonnet and was reassured by the sight of a stout farmer's wife with a basket, a thin young man who promptly fell asleep and a middle-aged gentleman in clerical collar and bands who politely raised his hat to her as she got on.

'I trust I do not intrude,' he ventured after a few moments, 'but I heard the good landlady directing you to the Crown and Anchor and I wonder if I might be of assistance? My name is Thoroughgood, Reverend Thaddeus Thoroughgood, and I am changing at that point myself as I do very frequently. I would be most happy to point out the stage office and so forth when we arrive.'

Joanna thanked him politely, somewhat nervous that he might want to continue talking to her, for conversation with a strange man, even a most respectable-looking clergyman, on a public stage was not what she had been brought up to regard as ladylike behaviour. However, the good reverend did not say any more and she thanked him and leaned back, feeling happier now she knew she had a guide should she need one.

They stopped once on the short distance to Peterborough. What with the exit of the stout farmer's wife whose basket somehow got jammed in the doorway, the Reverend Thoroughgood getting up to assist her, slipping on the step and falling heavily against Joanna, and the thin young man leaping up to help everyone, it proved a somewhat chaotic halt. However, they were soon at the Crown and Anchor and the Reverend Thoroughgood helped her down with her valise.

'Now, I shall go and collect my gig,' he said chattily, 'and be off home to Sister. You just need to go through that door there and you'll find our good hostess and a nice parlour and she'll tell you when the Lynn coach comes in. Now, you do have enough money, do you not, my dear young lady?'

'Oh, yes, thank you,' Joanna replied, confidently. Then, 'My purse! It has gone!'

'Great heavens!' the clergyman exclaimed. 'That young man must have been a cutpurse! Mrs Wilkins! Mrs Wilkins!'

The landlady came hurrying out, wiping her hands on her apron. She smiled at the sight of Hebe's companion. 'There you are again, Reverend. Your gig is all ready for you. But, sir—' she broke off at the sight of their agitation '—what's about?'

'My money has been stolen,' Joanna lamented. 'This gentleman thinks it was a cutpurse on the stage.'

'Well now, miss,' the landlady said sympathetically, 'that's a dreadful thing. Why, there is no stopping the impudent rascals. That's the third time we've seen that happen, is it not, Reverend?' She patted Joanna's arm. 'We had better be telling the magistrate, miss.'

'But that won't get my purse back,' Joanna stammered. 'What am I going to do? I have to get to Wisbech.'

There was a silence, then the clergyman said, 'Normally I would not suggest it, of course, but as I have an open gig, and it is still broad daylight, would you consider riding with me to my home where my sister awaits me? You can spend the night most securely under her protection and then in the morning we can consider what is best. To write to your friends in Wisbech, perhaps? Or I may have a neighbour who is driving that way.'

'There now, that is a good idea,' the landlady said approvingly.

Joanna bit her lip. It did seem the best of the alternatives, for the clergyman appeared well known and trusted at the inn and he obviously kept his gig there frequently. A clergyman's sister sounded a most respectable chaperon...

And there was the benefit of it taking her off the main road in case of pursuit. She made up her mind. 'Thank you, sir,' she said decisively. 'If Miss Thoroughgood would not find it an imposition, I would be most grateful.'

The gig was well kept and pulled by a neat black pony and Joanna felt happier as they progressed at a brisk trot through the lanes. The loss of her money was serious, but at least she was not too many miles from Georgy, who was not only the possessor of a vastly generous allowance but was indulged by her husband as to the spending of it. As soon as she knew of Joanna's predicament, she was sure to send both funds and her carriage at once.

The Reverend Thoroughgood did not seem anxious

to ask personal questions or to make encroaching observations, so Joanna was emboldened to introduce herself. 'I should tell you a little of my circumstances, sir, for I am sure Miss Thoroughgood will not wish to take a total stranger into her home. My name is J…Jane Wilson and I am a governess on my way to my new employer in Wisbech, Lady Brandon.'

It felt shocking to be lying to a man of the cloth, but he would hardly assist her if he knew the truth.

'We must see you on your way as soon as possible, Miss Wilson,' the reverend said, turning down another lane. Joanna was becoming a little confused. The lanes must be more than usually meandering hereabouts, she decided, for it seemed they must be driving in a circle. 'No doubt but that Lady Brandon will be anxious for you to begin to teach her children, and equally your friends and family will be concerned to hear of your safe arrival.'

Joanna bit her lip. It would look odd indeed if the only letter she sent during her enforced stay with the Thoroughgoods was to Lady Brandon. 'I do not have any family,' she said, trying to sound brave but lonely. 'And no close friends. A governess's life is a solitary one, I am afraid.'

'I am sorry to hear that,' the Reverend Thoroughgood said solemnly. 'You must turn for consolation to the thought of the good you are doing and the Christian learning you are bringing to young and tender minds.'

'Oh, yes, quite.' Joanna felt that any further discussion of this would be dangerous. She must recall all she could of her own governesses before venturing into conversation on their lives and duties. 'Are we near your parish yet, sir?'

'I do not have a parish: I have always been a scholar rather than a pastor, although I have many friends in London to whom I minister and attempt to bring spiritual light and succour by correspondence and the writing of tracts.'

'Indeed.' Joanna racked her brains; this was far more difficult than making conversation with a duchess. 'That must be very...satisfying.'

'Indeed it is, my dear Miss Wilson. I feel I myself gain much profit by my efforts in the capital. Now, here we are.'

The gig turned into the drive of a modest yellow brick house set within a somewhat overgrown and dull garden of lawn and laurels. It looked not so much dilapidated as unloved and uncared for and Joanna shivered despite the warm afternoon. A clergyman in modest circumstances could not afford to spend much on external appearances, she chided herself. It was most ungrateful to be critical after he had offered to help her in her difficulties.

No groom came round at the sound of the gig and the Reverend Thoroughgood simply dropped the reins as he helped Joanna down. The pony stood patiently, apparently not inclined to wander off, and the front door opened.

'Lucille, my dear!' The Reverend Thoroughgood took Joanna's arm with one hand and her valise with the other and urged her towards the door. 'I have a young lady in distress who has been cast adrift upon the highway by the actions of some pickpocket. She

is on her way to her new employer and has no friends
or family to turn to.'

The woman who stood on the step, one long white
hand raised to hold open the door, surprised Joanna.
She was tall, dressed with sombre elegance in a dark
gown of excellent cut and, although at least forty-five,
retained striking good looks. In Joanna's experience
ladies of that age were matrons and dressed and appeared exactly that. This lady had a faintly dangerous
and independent air about her.

She looked Joanna up and down, a faint smile on
her well-cut lips, then raised an eyebrow at her
brother, who hastened to complete the introductions.
'Lucille, my dear, this is Miss Wilson. Miss Wilson,
my sister, Miss Thoroughgood.'

Joanna bobbed a curtsy. 'I must apologise, ma'am,
for this intrusion. The Reverend Thoroughgood has
been most kind to me in my predicament and has
offered to allow me to stay for a few days until my
letter reaches my new employer and she is able to
send a carriage for me.'

'Of course. We are delighted you are here, Miss
Wilson. Would you like to come upstairs to your
room?' Her voice was cool, not unpleasant, but Joanna sensed a strange current of amusement under-
lying her words. It made her uneasy, which was ridiculous. She was tired, that was all. Tired, upset by
the theft and still not entirely recovered from her
stomach upset.

'Thank you, ma'am.' She followed her hostess into
a dark hall, up the stairs and into a room. Miss Thoroughgood stood aside as she entered and Joanna
walked forward a few steps before turning to see both

brother and sister standing in the doorway watching her. 'I...' Her voice died away as she took in their cool, assessing expressions and realised that the room she was in was virtually bare except for a bed and a washstand. The narrow window was barred with iron.

Chapter Six

'I must congratulate you, Thaddeus,' Miss Thoroughgood said, eyeing Joanna up and down in much the same way as she might have assessed the points of a horse. 'This one will do excellently. A real young lady.'

'And a *virtuous* young lady,' he replied, tugging off his clerical collar and bands with a grunt of relief. 'You *are* a virtuous young lady, are you not, Miss Wilson?'

Her flaming cheeks were all the answer he wanted and a smirk of satisfaction crossed his nondescript features, which up until that moment Joanna had found reassuringly bland.

The sudden change in tone was completely disorientating. 'I think there must be some mistake,' she said coldly, taking a step towards them. 'I will leave now.'

'Oh no, dear,' Miss Thoroughgood replied. 'You will not leave this room until we are ready to send you to London.' She turned to her brother. 'When is Thomas collecting the next consignment?'

'He has a carriage making the rounds now, he should be with us by the day after tomorrow.'

'London? What are you talking about? Let me go at once.' Joanna tried to keep her voice steady and confident, but it shook despite her efforts. The brother and sister seemed to grow before her eyes until all she was aware of was their assessing looks, their amused smiles, the way their eyes slid over her body.

The woman addressed her frigidly. 'You go where we send you. You belong to us now. In a day or two you will be in the hands of your new master, on the way to your new…home.'

'Belong? What are you talking about? I have an employer…'

'You are about to get an owner. Milo Thomas, the biggest whoremaster in the capital, is going to pay us very well indeed for such an untouched treasure as you, my dear.'

'Whore…*no!*' Joanna backed away, stopping abruptly as the back of her legs hit the bed. 'You are wrong about me! I am a respectable girl, not…'

'Not yet.' Thaddeus sounded amused at her lack of comprehension. 'Not yet, but you will be. You will learn all you need in one of Milo's closed houses, and you will earn him a fortune. Someone is going to pay very good money to deflower such innocence and beauty, and even more are going to pay handsomely to watch.'

'No!' Joanna pressed her hands to her mouth. She was going to be sick, she was going to faint and then wake up and find this was a nightmare. His words made no real sense to her, except to convey a disgusting, terrifying threat. How could they imagine…

She struggled for courage and to think. 'I told you I was a governess, that I was alone in the world. That was not true. I am running away from home and I have a rich and influential family. They will be looking for me—they will pay you to get me back.'

She broke off, panting, and watched the expressions on the two predatory faces opposite her. There was calculation going on and for a moment she dared hope, then Lucille said, 'No. She would, of course, say that to buy time. But even if it were true, if we released her, she has seen us. As it is, a few months in Milo's care and her family, if they exist, will not want her back to shame them.'

She took the valise from her brother's hand and opened it, sorting roughly through its contents. She removed a nail file and a pair of scissors, then tossed it into the room. 'There. Now, rest and do not try to make a noise. There is no one to hear you and you will not want to annoy Thaddeus. He would not leave a mark on you, naturally, but you would be sorry none the less.'

The door closed and Joanna heard the sharp click of a lock, then the further sound of two bolts being drawn. Shaking in every limb she sank down on the bed and tried to think, tried to plan, but all that was in her head were those obscene words. Someone was going to pay to…to… No! She buried her face in her hands and still the Thoroughgoods' words invaded her mind, a rape in themselves. Pay to watch…pay handsomely to watch…

It was impossible. Of course, men went to brothels, she knew that. But surely they went because they wanted women who knew what they were about, who would know how to give them pleasure? How could they want to watch a terrified girl being raped, let alone carry out the act? The sheer perversity and wickedness of such a thing steadied her as she applied her reason to it. There were people who got pleasure from being cruel to animals, there were bullies, people who maltreated their servants; perhaps this was an extreme example of that. But that there should be so many men that a brothel keeper could grow rich from them was appalling. Had she met such men? Could they go about in society hiding such evil behind a mask of respectability?

The thought brought her back to her own fate and, for all her courage, she suddenly gave way to racking sobs, curled up on the musty counterpane where, she supposed through her misery, other girls had sobbed in despair before her. Other girls. Joanna sat up, scrubbing the back of her hand across her wet eyes. Other girls. If she did nothing, not only was she damned to this hell, but all the others who followed her would be. Under no circumstances was she going to be worthy of Giles if she gave up now.

Joanna blew her nose, got to her feet and examined the room. Her legs felt like string, every now and again a sob escaped her, but she forced herself to search. There was nothing that could be used as a weapon. The bed was screwed to the floor, the sheets were thin with age and would tear easily. The washstand was bare of ewer or basin and under the bed the chamber pot was of such thin china that it would hardly bruise a head if she struck someone with it.

The door, as she expected, did not even move when she pressed against it and there was no handle on her side. The window was barred, not with wood, but with iron set into the frame, and the opening sash had been screwed up.

Joanna stared out down the front drive to the glimpse of road at the gate. Could she attract attention if someone passed? No, she would have no warning of their passing, the hedge was so high.

So, she could not escape from here. Then it would have to be the carriage when it came. From what the Thoroughgoods had said, there might be other girls in it, girls in the same predicament. That seemed too easy—a carriage full of frantic, healthy young women would be difficult to control. In the Thoroughgoods' shoes, if it were possible to imagine inhabiting them, she would drug the prisoners. Which meant she must not eat or drink anything, dispose of what she was given, and then feign the right kind of reaction to an unknown drug.

Difficult…Joanna paced away from the window. The practical problem of escape was mercifully blocking out the true horror of her situation, but it lurked in the back of her mind, surfacing every now and again to send shocks of paralysing terror through her before she could wrestle control back again.

Giles…what would Giles do if he were captured? The thought steadied her again, gave her courage, something to fight for. If she never saw him again, if these evil people defeated her, she would at least know she had done all she could and had not been a feeble victim.

There was the sound of carriage wheels on the drive outside and she ran to the window. Surely this was not the threatened Milo Thomas so soon? But all

she could see was a curricle, the reins looped around
the whip, a pair of handsome matched greys in the
shafts standing steaming, their heads down.

Probably a friend of the Thoroughgoods. But what
if it were not? What if this were some innocent neighbour or passer-by? Joanna looked around the room
wildly. Faintly from below came the thud of the
knocker sounding. How could she open the window?
The door below must have opened, for she could just
hear the rumble of masculine voices. Desperately she
snatched a sheet from the bed, wound it around her
fist and punched a hole through the glass.

'Help! Oh, help!' she screamed, hitting the glass
again until it showered down on to the front step below. 'Help!' There was a scuffle from below, then
silence.

Joanna snatched up a long sliver of glass from the
floor and ran to the door, standing at the hinge edge,
desperately trying to quieten her gasping breath.
There was a noise on the landing and the sound of
bolts being dragged back. The visitor? Or Thaddeus
Thoroughgood? If it was Thaddeus she was going to
stab him, she had no doubt about it, not even the
slightest qualm. The back would be the place...

The door swung open, she took a step forward and
a voice she could not believe she was hearing said,
'Joanna?'

'*Giles?*' She must be hallucinating, delirious, the
whole thing was a dream. Then he came into sight
around the door and she was stumbling forwards and
into his arms, the lethal glass dagger falling unregarded to the floor. She was saved: and saved, miraculously by the man she loved. 'Giles, oh, Giles...how

did you find me? These people...oh!' Over his shoulder she saw Lucille, a poker clenched in her fist, her arm upraised to strike. 'Behind you!'

Naturally Joanna had never seen a fight, let alone men boxing, but even she could appreciate the economy and power of the single blow that Giles delivered as he swung round. It took Lucille perfectly on the point of the chin and she went down with a thud, quite still.

'Damn it!' Giles knelt beside the recumbent form. 'I've never hit a woman before.'

'I hope you have broken her neck,' Joanna said vehemently, startling him. He had expected tears, fainting, but not such fierceness. She must have been terrified: he recollected the feeling of her quivering body as she hugged him so fiercely. 'Where is her brother?'

'Unconscious on the hall floor. Joanna, never mind them, are you—'

'Yes, I am fine, thanks to you,' she said, regarding Lucille with a wary eye. She did not appear to understand what he was really asking, and he did not persist. Time enough for that. 'Giles, we must not risk these two escaping before we can get the magistrate. I cannot begin to tell you how evil they are.'

Giles had formed a very good suspicion of exactly what he was dealing with as soon as he heard the landlady's tale of the kind clergyman and the string of unfortunate young ladies who all had their pockets picked on the stage. The last few miles, springing the already tired horses, had been a battle between his imagination and years of disciplined calm under extreme pressure. Now he simply nodded, accepting what she said without questioning her. 'Is there a room where we can lock them up?'

Joanna put her head around the adjacent door. 'This one, the window is not broken. Oh—' She broke off, turning to him, her eyes wide with horror. 'Oh, look.' The room had manacles bolted to the wall at the bed head.

She had gone so white that Giles thought she was about to faint. He put an arm around her and she looked up into his eyes, her own dark with, he realised with a jolt, burning anger. 'Put them in here,' she said fiercely. 'Shackle *them* to the bed.'

Before he could respond she was running downstairs, the poker in her hand. 'Joanna, stop!' For a horrible moment he thought she was going to strike the unconscious man who sprawled on the dingy tiled floor, but she was only standing over him, watchful for any sign of returning consciousness.

Giles crouched, hauled Thaddeus over his shoulder and stood up in one clean movement, only a slight grunt of expelled breath revealing the effort it took. Joanna ran upstairs after him, and, when he turned from dropping Thoroughgood on to the bed, she was already dragging his sister into the room by both arms.

He picked up the unconscious woman and laid her on the bed beside her brother, then snapped a shackle around one wrist of each. 'Now, where are the keys, I wonder?'

'Here.' Joanna, who had been carefully checking the room for anything that might give the Thoroughgoods assistance, picked up the key from the bare washstand. She bent over Lucille, pulling the hair pins from her head and the reticule from her waist. 'They might pick the lock,' she said tersely. 'What has he got?'

Giles raised his eyebrows at this ruthless practicality, but if it was helping Joanna he was not going to try and distract her. He removed Thaddeus's tiepin and patted his pockets, coming up with a roll of banknotes, a leather wallet and a pretty guinea purse.

'That is mine!' Joanna reached across and took it, clutching it tight in her fist. 'He stole in on the stage.'

'I know,' Giles said, keeping his voice low and calm, sensing that it would take very little to tip her over the edge. 'Come downstairs now, they are quite secure.'

'Lock and bolt the door.'

'Yes, of course.' He reached up and pulled across the topmost bolt, allowing her to turn the key and shoot the lower bolt. Let her be certain her nightmare was safely shut away.

'Now, come downstairs and I will see if there is anything for you to eat or drink in the kitchen.' Joanna let him guide her down the stairs, her arm quivering under his hand. All at once she stiffened.

'Miss Thoroughgood! Miss Thoroughgood, ma'am!' A thin voice was calling from the back of the house, coming closer, accompanied by the sound of shuffling footsteps.

Giles pushed Joanna firmly behind him and called, 'Who is there?'

'Just me, Mrs Penny, Mr Thoroughgood... Oh! Who are you, sir?'

It was a woman, perhaps in her fifties, perhaps older, skinny in a shabby hand-me-down dress covered by a large sacking apron, her straggling grey hair pulled back into a bun. She stood wringing her hands in front of her, obviously completely unable to cope with the unexpected sight of two strangers in the hallway. Giles noticed with a pang how red and sore her hands looked.

'Do you work for Miss Thoroughgood?'

'Yes, sir. I comes in three times a week and does the rough cleaning.'

'Does she have any other servants?'

'No sir, just me.' She did not seem able to ask what they were doing there, just stood and stared at them.

'Well, Mrs Penny, I am sorry to tell you that Mr and Miss Thoroughgood are a pair of rogues of the worst kind and are going to be handed over to the Justices and will come to a very bad end.'

'Gawd, sir!' Her eyes widened. Giles could not believe for a moment that she had any idea what had been going on in the house.

'I am Colonel Gregory, and this young lady is my...my sister. Now, Mrs Penny, where is the sitting room?'

'In the front, sir...Colonel, sir.' She threw open a door on to the most comfortable and well-kept room they had seen so far. Giles steered Joanna firmly towards the sofa. She moved when he pushed her, but made no effort to sit.

'Can you make the young lady a cup of tea, Mrs Penny?' The woman nodded, but he saw the anxiety in her eyes and how her hands were twisting in the apron again. 'Now, you are not to worry. No one will think you have had anything to do with this. What are you paid?'

'Sixpence a week, sir.'

'And when were you last paid?'

Her brow wrinkled with the effort to remember. 'Three weeks ago, sir.'

Giles fished in his pocket. 'Here,' he handed over a coin which made her gasp. 'That will pay your back wages and is some extra for your trouble today. Now, the tea?'

'That was kind,' Joanna observed faintly as he pushed her gently onto the sofa.

Giles sat down beside her, but did not try to touch her. He was puzzled that she showed no surprise at seeing him: perhaps the shock was just so all-encompassing that she would not have questioned any familiar face.

'Joanna, did he touch you?' he asked, and this time he saw she understood him.

'Oh, no. There was no danger of that.' Her voice was calm and, although faint, quite clear. 'He wanted a virgin, you understand. He made it very plain what for, and that was where my value lay.'

Giles had suspected that as soon as he realised that there was a woman in the scheme. Thoroughgood was not a solitary pervert, kidnapping girls for his own gratification. No, he was a trader in a very specialised commodity. But he had hoped that Joanna had not realised and that nothing had been said to shatter that innocence. He wanted to take her in his arms; even without touching her he could see the fine tremor running through her entire body. Her skin was so pale it seemed translucent and her eyes appeared unfocussed. But how would she react to being touched by a man now?

She did not respond when Mrs Penny came in with the tea. Giles nodded thanks to the woman and told her to get on with the tasks she normally carried out but not to venture upstairs, whatever she heard.

He pressed a cup into Joanna's hand, but she could not hold it steady so he put it down again to let it cool. After a moment she turned and looked at him, although he could not tell whether she really understood who she was talking to.

'He said that they would get a very good price from the man who…from the man—' She broke off, biting her lip. 'And money from those who would pay to watch. They said a man called Milo Thomas would come and collect me in a coach. I think there will be other girls in it.'

'How can that be?' Joanna asked him, her face reflecting her desperate need to understand. 'I know men go to brothels, have mistresses. Of course I do. And I am not so foolish as to believe that women would not turn to such a way of life if they had better alternatives. But surely men want someone who knows how to make love? Is that not more pleasant? Yet there must be many men like those he was talking about, otherwise how could the brothel keepers and people like the Thoroughgoods make money from them? How could it be worth the risks?'

Giles wished vehemently that he was not the one having to answer her questions. In fact, he would rather have found himself surrounded by French cavalry at that moment. If he got this wrong…

'The vast majority of men are perfectly decent and normal,' he said, keeping his voice as steady and quiet as he could. 'Just as you imagine, they want to enjoy themselves, and they want the woman they are with to enjoy herself as well, whether it is within marriage, or outside it. Normal men,' he added, with a hint of a smile, 'would feel it a slur on their manhood if the lady did *not* find pleasure in their attentions.

'But there are some who like cruelty, like to inflict pain. I think it must be about feeling powerful, that men who do not feel assured of themselves like to dominate someone weaker. Some stick at bullying their families and servants, others maltreat their horses. Some, just a few, go further. It is not many, Joanna, you must not assume that half the men you meet and know socially are like this, hiding a wolf's teeth under a human smile. But the ones who enjoy such things can usually pay for it, and pay very well to get exactly what they want.'

She looked at him, and he could see her eyes were beginning to focus a little and knew she had listened and understood. As he watched, her rigid calm began to falter and the tears started to well up in her eyes, which had turned a dark, dull brown.

'Joanna, come here.' Without stopping to think whether she might fight him, he leant forward, took her in his arms and lifted her on to his knee, holding her tight against his chest. 'Most men are decent men who respect women. Men like your father, like Alex, like William will be when he grows up.'

He could feel the front of his shirt becoming wet. She was crying almost silently. Then she nodded and he heard her voice, muffled. 'Like you.'

'Yes. Like me. I would never hurt you, Joanna.' For some reason that seemed to make things worse:

in the tightness of his embrace he could feel her sobbing fiercely. Not knowing what to say, or whether it was better just to let her weep, he simply held her, his face buried in the silk of her hair, his body shaken with the force of her sobs. Never, in his entire thirty years, had he felt so violently protective towards a living creature, nor had he ever known himself to be in such a killing rage. He could not trust himself to open that door upstairs without a restraining presence or there would be murder done.

Finally the sobs died down and he tentatively let his arms fall away from her. Joanna sat up a little, but otherwise made no attempt to move from his knee.

'Would you like some tea?' She nodded and reached out for the cup, sitting there sipping it like a trusting child in his lap.

She put it down at last and turned to face him, her eyes still drowned in tears. 'He did not touch me, but it still feels like...' she struggled with the word '...like rape.'

'Because he forced those words into your mind, he forced that image into your imagination?'

'Yes, exactly that. You understand so well. Now I cannot make them go away.'

Giles thought carefully before he spoke, then simply trusted to his instincts. 'They were only words. They were only images, they were not reality, because you would not let them be. You were fighting back, you were not a victim. Those things would not have happened because you were never going to give up.'

'You saved me,' she pointed out.

'Only because you helped me. If I had not come

today, you would have been scheming, plotting, resisting.' He smiled at her. 'Where did you find the courage, Joanna?'

'Thinking of the other girls,' she said simply. 'And thinking of what...of what someone who is very important to me would have expected of me.'

For some reason Giles felt that he had been punched in the solar plexus. Of course—this mysterious man who had so upset her at the Duchess's ball that this entire train of events had been set in motion. He could hardly cavil at anything that had given Joanna the strength to resist, but why was she wasting her emotions on this damned man? She was worth more, this pattern-book débutante who had kicked over the traces.

'Remember that you had the courage to fight,' he said, when he had trampled on his anger. 'And talk about it, don't bottle it up.'

'Who can I talk about it with?' she asked.

'Me. Hebe. Alex.'

'*Alex?* Goodness, no!' Joanna sounded almost normal again. 'I am scared of Alex.'

'Why on earth? He usually has to fight the ladies off—or at least he had to until he had Hebe to do it for him.'

'He looks so...sardonic,' Joanna said. 'Hebe told me that her maid on Malta said he looked like "a beautiful fierce saint". He was furious, apparently.'

Giles grinned, saving that one up to torment Alex with on some future occasion. It was enough that talking of their friends had restored Joanna a little. 'Will you be all right if I go and talk to Mrs Penny? I want to find out where the nearest magistrate is.' She nodded, so he placed her carefully back on the sofa, found a clean handkerchief in the depths of his pocket for her and went in search of the charwoman who was scrubbing the kitchen floor.

'Magistrate, sir? The nearest one is the Squire.'

Patiently Giles extracted the information that Squire Gedding was a good man, firm but fair, and his lady was as nice as you could find anywhere.

'When my Jimmy had a bit of trouble with a pheasant—out of work he was, on account of him having hurt his arm—Squire had him in front of his desk and was right fierce. Told him he was a bloody fool and ought to have come to see him, not go trampling about in his coverts scaring the birds. And he gave him a job in his stables, and Mrs Gedding, she went right 'round with food for the little ones, and medicine for Susan, that's my daughter-in-law...'

Giles let her ramble on, feeling a considerable relief washing over him. A country squire with a firm hand but some imagination and a kindly wife were exactly what he had need of just now. 'How far away does Squire Gedding live?' he asked, cutting into further reminiscences of the Geddings' goodness.

'Less than two miles, sir. In the middle of the village.'

'That close?' Giles said with considerable relief. The sooner he got Joanna into the hands of a respectable lady, and the Thoroughgoods into the grip of the forces of law and order, the happier he would be. There were muffled shouts from upstairs and Mrs Penny started nervously. 'Do not worry, Mrs Penny, they cannot get out. Will you come with us in my carriage and direct us to the village? I will drop you off at your home.' She nodded, obviously anxious. 'If you go and make sure the fire in the kitchen is banked down,' Giles continued firmly, 'then I will lock up and we will be on our way.'

The three of them were soon outside. The greys stood patiently, too tired to show any inclination to wander. Giles helped both women up and then squashed into the seat beside them, thankful that Joanna was slim and Mrs Penny positively skinny.

The journey to the village did not take long despite the tired horses and the fact that dusk was falling rapidly. The charwoman indicated a cottage by the side of the road and was helped down, much to the amazement of the younger woman who came to the door, one child in her arms, another clinging to her skirts. 'There now, Mrs Penny. Thank you for your help. Squire will probably want to talk to you about this, but, in the meantime, be sure not to gossip about it.'

Giles glanced anxiously at Joanna, who was beginning to sway now that Mrs Penny's skinny form was no longer supporting her. Fortunately the Squire's house was as easy to find as Mrs Penny had said, and as he drove on to the gravelled apron at the front a groom came round from the side of the house. 'Good evening, sir, may I take your horses?'

'Thank you. Is the Squire at home?' Giles put a steadying arm around Joanna, whose eyes were fluttering closed.

'Yes, sir, and Mrs Gedding, sir. Will you be staying, sir? I can stable the team and give them a good rub down and a feed.'

Giles was too concerned to get Joanna inside to pay much attention to the niceties such as introducing himself to the Squire first. 'Thank you. Just hold their heads while I help the lady.'

Between them they lifted Joanna down safely. Giles was not sure whether she had fainted or was simply asleep, but her head fell against his shoulder as he carried her and her face was buried in his coat front. A wave of fierce protectiveness swept over him, startling in its intensity: somehow he was going to make this all right for her.

A sensible-looking maid opened the door to him, took one look at his burden and said simply, 'You'll be wanting Mrs Gedding, sir.'

He followed her across the hall and through the door she held open and saw a big, grizzled man sitting on one side of the hearth, a plump, cheerful lady opposite him, obviously in full flow of speech. She broke off at the sight of the apparition on her threshold, then jumped to her feet and hurried over.

'Ma'am, I apologise for the intrusion,' Giles began. 'My name is Colonel Gregory and—'

'You need help,' she finished for him. 'Bring the poor lamb in, everything will be all right.'

And Giles, who could not remember feeling so relieved since he had seen a relief column of cavalry cutting their way through to his bridgehead at Vittoria, decided it probably would be.

Chapter Seven

Joanna stirred, yawned without opening her eyes and snuggled down into the bed again. She felt completely drained, she realised, sleepily beginning to wake up, but that was no wonder after such a dreadful night made hideous with nightmares. How had she imagined such appalling creatures? That clergyman, his sinister sister, their unspeakable plans for her...but her imagination had at least conjured up Giles to rescue her.

Then a cold, queasy hand gripped her stomach and she woke fully, remembering the day before, realising that it was all true, that it was no nightmare. 'Giles!' Joanna scrambled up against the pillows, searching the room with wide, frightened eyes, but it was not the shabby, dark room with its barred window. This was an airy, pretty chamber with delicate furniture, white muslin curtains stirring gently at an open window and a bowl of tumbling roses on the sill.

The door opened and a smiling lady looked in. 'Are you all right, my dear? I am Mrs Gedding and this is my home. You are quite safe here.' She came further

into the room and Joanna saw she was a motherly-
looking person with an air of commonsense kindness
about her. She relaxed back against the pillows, her
panic ebbing. 'My husband is the squire and a magistrate, and he and your young man are off dealing
with those dreadful people,' she added reassuringly.

'My young man? Oh, you mean Giles? Oh, no, he
is not…I mean…' Joanna was afraid she was blushing
and when she saw the twinkle in Mrs Gedding's eyes
she was sure of it. 'He is a friend of the family,' she
added hastily, then realised with a shock that she had
no idea how it was that Giles had saved her. How on
earth had he come to be there? It had seemed so right,
so perfect that it was the man she loved who had
rescued her from that nightmare that it had never occurred to her to question it.

She recalled, as though from a long time ago, her
fierce anger with her captors and Giles's calm han-
dling of her fears. 'Are they, the Thoroughgoods, I
mean…?'

'Off to Peterborough gaol last night,' her hostess
said firmly. 'Two armed constables with them in a
locked carriage. They'll be out of harm's way now,
and there they'll stay until Quarter Sessions. The
Colonel and my husband have gone back to the house
today to search it for more evidence and to see if they
can set an ambush for that Milo Thomas you told the
Colonel about.'

She smoothed the bedcovers and watched Joanna
for a moment, her head on one side like an inquisitive
robin. 'You'll do better knowing all there is to know,
I can tell. Some people don't want to know, other
people need to. You've got too much imagination to

be sheltered with half-truths. The Colonel told us how brave you were. Now, would you like a bath and some breakfast? Or would you like to talk to me about anything?'

Joanna smiled back. In the absence of Giles's arms around her, she could not have felt more secure than she did with this frank, friendly lady. She hugged the comment about Giles's opinion to herself and considered the question. 'Not at the moment, thank you,' she said. 'I asked Giles about why, and that sort of thing. That was what I could not understand. Why? And what made men like that? He explained it all.'

'Did he, indeed!' Mrs Gedding's eyebrows shot up. 'Well, he is an extraordinary young man if he could do that without turning a hair.'

'I think I could talk to Giles about anything,' Joanna said thoughtfully, then remembered exactly what they had been discussing and smiled faintly. 'He is *very* kind—and brave,' she added. 'I expect he had rather have faced a cavalry charge!'

Mrs Gedding smiled back. 'Bath and breakfast? I have no idea what has happened to your luggage; probably it is still at the Thoroughgoods' house. Even the most thoughtful and courageous man may be relied upon to forget such essentials as clean undergarments and tooth powder in a crisis. Never mind, my younger daughter's things are here—she is staying with her married sister, and she will not mind at all if you borrow whatever you need.'

A bath and clean, pretty clothes restored Joanna's spirits and she sat down to breakfast ravenously hungry. 'I do beg your pardon, ma'am,' she apologised

when she realised she had finished the entire plate of
toast, 'but I have eaten hardly anything since I left
home but a meat pie at Biggleswade, and that made
me ill.'

'Ah, yes, your home.' Mrs Gedding refilled her tea
cup. 'The Colonel has written to your parents, and I
have added a note. I have left the package open, so
if you would like to add something of your own we
will get it sealed up and off to Peterborough to catch
the post as soon as may be.'

'Oh. Yes. Thank you.' Joanna bit her lip. She had
meant to be with Georgy at least two days ago, with
a reassuring message on its way to London as soon
as she arrived—without any direction for finding her,
of course. 'I should never have done it,' she blurted
out, suddenly acutely conscious of the anxiety she
must have caused. 'I was so miserable and confused.
I cannot imagine what you must think of me.'

'That you were very unhappy, Joanna dear, and not
thinking very clearly,' Mrs Gedding said prosaically.
'We all do stupid and thoughtless things at least once
in our lives. Now, in his letter the Colonel has explained a little of what has happened—not the worst
of it, naturally—and has told your parents that he
must stay a day or so until the evidence is all collected together and you have rested. I have promised
your mama that I will look after you and that we will
find you a suitable chaperon before you travel back
to London. All that remains for you to do is to rest
and get stronger. But write your note first.'

'Yes, ma'am,' Joanna said meekly. The letter was
hard to compose. In the end she managed a few lines
to say how sorry she was, and that she was quite safe

and that Mrs Gedding was very kind. But it was more than she was capable of to apologise for running away before Lord Clifton called to make his offer. The ink was blotted here and there with large teardrops, but she did not want to ask for more good notepaper and she hoped Mama would recognise tears of real regret.

Her hostess was bustling about with lists when she brought her the note. When it was sealed with the others and the groom dispatched with it, she asked politely if there was anything she could do to help.

'It won't do you any good to sit and brood, will it, my dear? No, I did not think it would. But you must not exert yourself too much yet.' Mrs Gedding thought for a while then said, 'I know, *pot-pourri*. Come along.'

Joanna found herself shown out into the back garden, a basket over her arm and a pair of scissors in her hand. 'Oh, how beautiful!'

The garden was a mass of roses, of old-fashioned flowers, of weeping trees and winding paths scythed through the grass. The scent was magical and almost took her breath away.

'I love it,' said Mrs Gedding simply. 'It has taken me twenty years to make it look as though it just happened by accident. Not many people appreciate it.'

'It is Sleeping Beauty's garden,' Joanna declared. 'Is there a turret hidden in the midst of it?'

'No, but that is an excellent idea. I must ask Mr Gedding to have one built as a summer house. Now, my dear, the sun has dried the dew off the roses, so if you will be so good as to start picking heads from the ones that are just open, they will be perfect for drying.'

Joanna spent an idyllic morning exploring the garden. The maid brought out a chair and a rug and some larger baskets and she wandered up and down the paths, snipping rose heads into her basket, smelling the other scented bushes, thinking about the perfect place to position Sleeping Beauty's turret. Occasionally she would tip her basket into the bigger one by the chair and sit and rest for a little.

Mrs Gedding came out with some lemonade and they talked of their families and the contrast between village and town life, then her hostess went back inside and Joanna sat, surrounded by her baskets brimming with roses, and finally let herself think about the previous day.

She probed her memory like someone exploring a sore tooth, very cautiously, wincing as she realised just how careless and gullible she had been and what dreadful danger she had escaped. Giles's words of praise were balm to her self-esteem, but her conscience continued to prick her when she thought of her parents' anxiety.

And how, of all the miracles, had it been Giles who had found her? On the thought he appeared from the back door, carrying a chair and a folding table, the maid with a loaded tray behind him.

'Hello.' Joanna's heart gave a sudden, hard thud and she found that all she could do was to smile back at him. 'Mrs Gedding thought we might like to picnic out here. The Squire has come back to arrange for a clerk to assist us this afternoon: there is so much paper we are unearthing that we are going to have to get it listed and ordered before we can start to make sense of it all, let alone mount a court case.' He set down the chair and unfolded the table. 'May I sit down?'

'Oh, yes, of course, I am sorry, my wits are gone a-wandering.' He looked exactly as she remembered him from London. This morning she had been half-afraid that it was all a delusion and it wasn't the real Giles. Now, sitting beside him, watching the dappled shade from the tree cast patterns over his dark blond hair and returning the smile that crinkled the corners of his grey eyes, she knew he was real and a ridiculous, hopeless wave of love swept over her.

'Gi...Colonel Gregory...'

'Giles will do very well, Joanna.' He leaned forward and poured two glasses of lemonade. 'How are you today?'

'Much better than I deserve,' she replied ruefully. 'I cannot thank you enough. I was praying for a miracle, and there you were! But I do not understand how you came to find me.'

'Well, your father is laid up with gout and your mama hurried round to the Tasboroughs' town house in a fine state of alarm, as you might expect, hoping that Alex would be there. But, of course, she had not stopped to think about Hebe's condition. Fortunately I was staying and I knew Alex would not want to leave his wife, so I offered to hunt you down. You gave me a fair run for my money.' He lifted a plate and offered it to her. 'Ham? A slice of bread and butter? Or I think that is a slice of raised pie...'

'Ham and bread, please.' Joanna cut up her food, thinking over what Giles had said. 'Hebe is well?'

'Oh, perfectly, but she doesn't rest as much as she should, and I put the idea into Alex's head that she is expecting twins, so you can imagine the state he is in. I should imagine he and your mama between them are exercising Hebe's powers to calm and reassure to the utmost.'

Joanna digested this information, decided she could not possibly ask why Giles thought Hebe was expecting twins and said, 'How lucky you were still in London. I thought I heard someone say you had gone to see your father. Is the General well?'

Giles shrugged and Joanna saw the anxiety in his eyes, although he kept his voice light when he said, 'Not entirely. He does too much, will not admit he is not in the best of health and drives my mother distracted.'

'But you came back to town despite that?' Joanna bit her lip, wondering if she had overstepped the mark and was being intrusively curious, but Giles did not appear to find her question impertinent.

'We had a blazing row and he disinherited me,' he said with a smile that did not reach his eyes.

'Oh, Giles! How dreadful!' Joanna's bread and butter dropped to the plate unheeded as she stared at him. 'But why on earth?'

'I told him I intend to sell out. Oh, and there is the question of my marriage, of course.'

'Giles, you should not jest about it,' Joanna said, shaken to the core. 'Of course you are not going to sell out. Why, you are going to be a general—'

'Not you, too!' He got up and took two angry

strides across the grass, then turned back with a shake of the head. 'I am sorry, Joanna, I did not mean to shout at you. My father is a sick man who is not getting any younger. He needs my help and support with the estate, even if he won't admit it. And we are at peace now: I do not want to spend the rest of my career as a peacetime soldier, always on parade, or worse, putting down industrial unrest in the north of England. I did not join the army to ride down starving mill workers or hungry farm labourers.'

Joanna put a hand on his arm as he sat down again, his lips tight, his eyes shadowed. 'I am sorry. That was very stupid and thoughtless of me. Of course, you must do what is best for your family. But has he truly disinherited you?'

Giles smiled, this time with real humour. 'He doesn't mean it. He will be regretting it now, although I doubt if he is regretting the strip he tore off me and the lecture I got on doing my duty and settling down with a conformable, suitable wife!'

Joanna took a drink of lemonade as the best way of hiding her reaction. So, the old general did not consider Lady Suzanne a suitable wife. Why ever not? She seemed eminently eligible to Joanna, but perhaps he thought her too flighty to make his son a good match. A faint glimmer of hope stirred in her breast. Would Giles heed his father? Would the General's opinions make him reconsider?

But, no, surely if he loved Suzanne he would not give her up, and much as it hurt, Joanna would not want him, too. She could only think less of him if he was the sort of man who could turn from true love under pressure.

'You are looking very serious,' he said after a moment. 'How do you feel?'

'Much better, truly,' Joanna reassured him. 'I was just worried about you and your father. Now you are even further away, and it is all my fault. What if he wants to contact you and make peace?'

Giles laughed. 'My mama, who packed me off back to town to indulge in a course of carefully calculated dissipation, assured me it would be at least two weeks before he would admit to any regrets in the matter and another two after that to digest the rumours of my behaviour, which my assorted well-meaning aunts would send back.'

'Dissipation? But what...?'

'The plan, according to Mama, is that he will summon me back in order to engage me in some salutary hard work and will then get accustomed to having the prodigal around and will be reconciled to my assisting with the estate.'

'Goodness,' Joanna said rather blankly. 'Do you think it will work?'

'Mama has been winding my father around her little finger for thirty-five years and I have never known her wrong yet.'

'Yes, but you are hardly engaging in dissipation, are you? What sort of dissipation, anyway?'

'Cards, horses, um...'

'Um?'

'I do seem to be having the most improper conversations with you, Miss Fulgrave! Wicked widows and fast matrons is what my outrageous mama had in mind, I think.'

'More than one mistress at once?' Joanna asked,

trying to imagine her own mother recommending such a course of action to William in fifteen years' time and failing utterly. 'Isn't that terribly expensive and complicated?'

'As I have never had more than one at a time I have no idea. Expensive, certainly. But complicated?'

'I shouldn't imagine they would take very kindly to sharing you,' Joanna said, frowning over the practicalities. 'You would have to keep them apart and remember what you had said to each… Have you had many?'

Giles sank his head in his hands with a groan. 'Oh lord, what have I let myself say! Your mama would have fits if she knew. Yes, I have had mistresses, in Portugal and in Spain, and only one at a time, and we parted very amicably in every case, before you ask! And, no, I am not going to tell you about any of them.'

'I am sorry,' Joanna said penitently. 'I did not mean to put you to the blush, but I feel that I can ask you about things that no one else will explain. I mean, it is obvious that lots of men in society have mistresses, and even I can guess that some ladies are, well…not entirely faithful to their husbands. But no one ever says anything about it and it seems a bit late to find out after one is married.'

'I cannot imagine,' Giles said, putting one hand over hers and squeezing it reassuringly, 'that any husband of yours would contemplate setting up a mistress for one second. Especially this mysterious suitor you are so imprudently fleeing from. He seems most devoted!'

Joanna ignored the reference to Lord Clifton, for

she was fighting the urge to curl her fingers into his and return the pressure. Somehow it hadn't hurt to know there had been other women in his life: she had expected it, the man was not a monk. But being so close to him, his kindness, almost overset her.

'I don't expect to marry,' she said, attempting to laugh it off and freeing her hand to reach for an apple, 'so it really doesn't arise. I meant, it was a bit late for young ladies in general to find out about that sort of thing.'

'Not marry? Why ever not?' Giles took the apple from her hand, picked up a knife and began to peel it, the ribbon of red skin curling over his hand.

Joanna shrugged, trying not to look at his long fingers dexterously wielding the knife. What would it be like to be caressed by them? She shivered. 'My *mysterious suitor*, as you term him, is not someone whose regard I return—in fact, I dislike him excessively. My affections are engaged elsewhere, but the man I love, loves someone else.'

'Is that what upset you at the Duchess's ball?' He handed her back the apple. 'You found out about it?'

'Mmm.' Goodness, how had she let herself talk about this?

'But just because one man has let you down, it doesn't mean you should give up on the entire sex,' Giles said, watching her with a frown between his straight brows. 'There are many other men—the one who is attempting to make you an offer, for example. Are you sure you know him well enough to have formed such a negative impression?'

'Quite sure! I dislike the way he looks at me—and he tried to blackmail me after I had got into a scrape.'

She caught his quizzical expression and nodded, 'Yes, that night at Vauxhall. And, yes, it is Rufus Carstairs, I suppose you have already guessed. But as for marrying someone I do not love—how can you say that?' Joanna was hurt and surprised that he could fail to understand. 'If the lady you love spurned you, could you just shrug and walk away and think "I'll find someone else"? Of course you could not, not if it were true love! I will never feel like this about anyone else, and I will not marry anyone I don't love.

'Imagine being tied to someone you did not hold in the deepest affection! I know some unfortunate women find themselves having to accept distasteful suitors, or men have to make duty marriages to restore their family fortunes, and I truly pity all of them. I would rather remain a spinster than marry anyone other than…him. And,' she added vehemently, 'I *cannot* like or trust Lord Clifton.'

Giles appeared taken aback by her vehemence, but, although he had raised his eyebrows on hearing who her suitor was, he said nothing, so she asked, 'Will you obey your father in the question of *your* marriage?'

'No!' he retorted hotly. 'I will not!'

'You see? In matters of the heart, feelings run very deep.'

He regarded her thoughtfully over the rim of his glass. 'You are sure that this unfortunate experience has not made the entire business of marriage distasteful to you?'

'Oh, no,' Joanna looked directly into his concerned grey eyes and smiled ruefully. 'Oh, no, not if it were marriage to the man I love.'

Chapter Eight

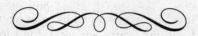

That evening brought a report that Milo Thomas had been intercepted near Lincoln and three distressed young women rescued. Joanna wondered anxiously about the reception they would receive when they returned to their homes and whether they would have the reassurance and support she was enjoying from Giles and from the Geddings.

'And what about the ones who are already in those dreadful places?' she asked vehemently as they sat down to dinner. 'What is going to happen to them?'

'I will be laying evidence with the Bow Street magistrates,' the Squire said reassuringly. 'They will check all of the addresses in Thoroughgood's notebooks and ensure that every young woman there is free to leave. If any have been kidnapped and, er…forced, then the justices will take the appropriate action.'

'Yes, but what becomes of the women?' Joanna persisted. 'What on earth happens to them?' There was an uncomfortable silence around the table. 'When

I get back to London I am going to *do* something about this.'

'My dear,' Mrs Gedding said gently, 'there is nothing that an unmarried girl of good family *can* do about it.'

Joanna knew that was likely to be only too true. 'Oh, I wish I were a rich widow!' she declared vehemently. Giles sat back in his chair with a gasp of laughter and she caught his eye, defiantly. 'Well, I do! Not that I would wish anyone dead, of course not, but it seems to me that the only women who have any freedom of action at all are rich widows.'

The Squire looked faintly scandalised and, although Mrs Gedding sent her an amused look of understanding, Joanna thought it best to take herself off to bed as soon as possible at the end of the meal.

When she woke the next morning, it was to the feeling that she had been ill, in a fever, and that now she was back to normal. The spectres of the Thoroughgoods and her terrifying experience had become less nightmarish, although her determination to do something about the plight of the girls forced into brothels was no less ardent. Perhaps Hebe, when she had recovered from the birth, would be able to help.

But with the sense of recovery came the anxiety about how her parents would react and the more pressing realisation that not only was she in the same house as Giles but that she had been having conversations of quite shocking frankness with him. As she dragged the brush ruthlessly through her hair, she thought it was only by some miracle that he had not guessed the identity of the man she loved, the man whose presence she was fleeing from.

She was so preoccupied with these thoughts that she walked straight into Giles in the hall outside the little parlour that did service as a breakfast room. Joanna knew she was blushing frantically, but could think of nothing to say, other than to stammer, 'Good morning.'

Giles opened the door for her and ushered her through. The room was deserted. 'Good morning, Joanna. May I pour you some coffee?'

Joanna sat down abruptly, making a business of shaking out her napkin so as not to meet his eyes. 'I…yes, thank you.'

Giles put the cup in front of her and took a seat opposite. 'Might I trouble you for the bread? Thank you. You are feeling more yourself this morning, I think.'

'What?' Joanna looked up, startled, and saw he was regarding her with an expression halfway between amusement and sympathy. 'I am feeling better, yes, but how do you deduce that?' Her heart was beating irregularly: did he really understand her so very well?

She waited, biting her lower lip, while he buttered his bread, a slight frown between his brows. 'How do I know? Well, yesterday we were having extremely frank conversations without you turning a hair. In fact, you were quite unnaturally calm, which convinced me you were still suffering from shock. This morning you react as any gently bred young lady would at the realisation that the man she has just bumped into was the very one with whom she was discussing mistresses, houses of ill repute and the perils of the married state only the day before.' He smiled as she bowed her head in confusion. 'You blush very prettily.'

'Oh!' Joanna gasped indignantly. 'You are just saying that to make me blush more! Really, Gi…Colonel Gregory…'

'That is better,' he said approvingly. 'I would have hated to see you revert entirely to—what was it your mama called you? Oh, yes, the "perfect débutante".'

'I was never that,' Joanna said sadly, 'although I did try so hard. Colonel, was Mama *very* angry?'

Giles stood up to carve a slice of meat from the joint on the sideboard. 'Cold beef? No? I do wish you would stop calling me *Colonel*. What is wrong with Giles? After all, I am a family friend, almost a friend of your childhood.'

'It seems hardly proper.'

Giles's expression was so comical that Joanna burst out laughing. 'Oh, Giles, do stop looking at me like that! I realise that after everything that has occurred it must seem finicky of me to cavil at first names, but believe me, I truly am trying to behave myself as I should. But do tell me about Mama.'

Giles flipped open the lid of the mustard pot and looked round for the spoon. 'She was not angry at all when I saw her, but you must remember she was very much shocked and upset and anxious to have you found. I cannot vouch for her mood when she knows you are safe. And, of course, she was most anxious to keep the news from your highly eligible suitor.'

'Hmm,' Joanna murmured, depressed. 'I know exactly what you mean. When one is frightened for someone the fear is all there is. The moment they are safe you can be angry at how foolish they have been. I remember how I felt when William was stuck in the big oak in Green Park. Once the keepers had got him down safely I could have boxed his ears, yet only a minute before I was frantic with worry that he would fall out and break his neck.'

'Well, I think it is unlikely that you will escape without a lecture,' Giles said kindly, 'but I am sure your parents will soon forgive and forget. And no one else in society but the Tasboroughs knows of this adventure, so you will be able to emerge next Season as though nothing had occurred. Although,' he added frankly, 'do you not think it would be a good idea not to strive to be quite such a pattern card of perfection? It must be very wearing for you, never allowing yourself to kick over the traces.'

'Young ladies are not permitted to kick over the traces, as you put it,' Joanna retorted. 'Look at the fuss it causes.'

'I meant indulging in the odd bit of mischief and high spirits, not running away and being kidnapped,' Giles countered. 'Suzanne is always up to something or another and it does her reputation no harm.'

'I am sure if I were as beautiful, well connected and rich as Lady Suzanne,' Joanna snapped, 'I could get away with almost anything. We lesser mortals have to be more careful.'

'But not to the point of becoming a by-word for your virtues! It is a testimony to your character that your reputation does not result in jealousy amongst the other débutantes and that you have so many friends.'

'I am sure those who do not think so well of me

will be most amused to see me take part in a third Season, still unspoken for,' Joanna said bitterly. 'I never intended to behave in any way to make other débutantes seem less...correct. I was only trying—' She broke off. It was so easy to talk to Giles that she was in danger of saying far too much and betraying herself to him.

'Trying?' he prompted.

'Trying to make sure I would be a perfect wife for...him.' *For you, only for you*, her inner voice repeated.

'Ah. The mystery man. Are you so sure he wants perfection?' Giles appeared annoyed rather than curious.

'He deserves it!' she said hotly. 'He needs a wife with perfect social skills: it is very important in his position.' Only now, of course, Giles had voluntarily ended his glittering career. Now he had no need of a Society hostess who also understood the army, only a well-bred, suitable wife and in Lady Suzanne he most certainly had that, whatever his father thought.

'Who on earth is he, this paragon who must have such an impeccable wife? A duke? A leading politician? A diplomatist?'

'I am not going to tell you. It is hopeless now, anyway.' Joanna took a mouthful of her cooling coffee and refused to look at Giles.

'Then stop trying to be perfect. Relax and enjoy next Season for a change.'

'To what end, pray? To put off being on the shelf for a few more months?'

She realised that they were glaring at each other across the table. It hurt so much that Giles seemed to care about what was troubling her; his indifference would have been easier to bear. And he must care to become so involved and angry about it.

Then his face lightened and he smiled at her. 'Come now, it is far too nice a day to be inside squabbling. Squire Gedding has no need of me this morning and I have a treat for you. You do ride, I assume?'

'Why, yes, I love to ride. But ride what?'

'Did I tell you that part of my scheme now is to breed horses on the estate? No? Well, that is what I intend to do; it will mean that I am not spending all my time breathing down the General's neck, and I think it might be a satisfying undertaking. I was talking to the Squire about it and he tells me a neighbour of his has a fine mare he wants to sell. He is bringing it over this morning for me to look at; I thought you might like to ride it so I can see its paces.'

'Oh, yes, please!' Joanna jumped up, then recollected her small stock of clothes. 'But I have no habit. And what about a saddle?'

'Mrs Gedding tells me her daughter's old habit is here, and the saddle she herself used when she still kept a riding horse is in the stables. Listen—I imagine that is the neighbour now.'

The breakfast parlour windows opened out on to the side of the house where the carriage drive led to the stables and, sure enough, Giles's sharp ears had picked up the sound of hooves. A man on a black hunter came into sight leading a pretty grey mare on a long rein towards the yard.

Mrs Gedding appeared in the doorway. 'Good morning, my dear. Have you had enough breakfast? I expect the Colonel has told you all about James

Pike's grey mare. If you would like to ride her, the girl has put out Jennie's old habit on your bed.'

With a smile Joanna thanked her hostess and ran upstairs to change, her heart pounding. The encounter with Giles over the breakfast table had left her feeling flustered and almost frightened. But she had no opportunity to reflect alone, for the maid was waiting and Joanna had to submit to being unbuttoned and undressed, standing patiently while the habit was tossed over her head. The girl discovered with a cluck of displeasure that a section of hem had dropped and one button was loose. Joanna nodded absently as the maid asked if Miss would mind waiting while she fetched the sewing things and did a hasty repair.

She sat on the edge of the bed while the maid rapidly whipped stitches along the hem and shrugged out of the jacket for the button to be replaced, without really being aware of what was going on. Giles, and her feelings for him, seemed to fill her mind to the exclusion of all else. She found she liked him so much it was a shock. She had known almost from the moment she met him that she loved him, but now she knew that she had fallen in love with the *idea* of the man, not the man himself. Perhaps if she had never seen him again after that evening at the Duchess's ball she would have gradually fallen out of love with her memory of him. But now fate, and her own foolishness, had thrown them together so closely that there was no escaping the impact of his personality on her.

And not just his personality. Joanna had never felt so aware of a man before—even the thrilling sensation of being held in his arms as they waltzed paled

beside the effect of being so close to him daily. She
was getting to know the tiniest details: the impatient
way he pushed his hair off his forehead, the black
flecks in his grey eyes that turned them dark when he
was angry, the way he would tug at one earlobe when
he was thinking, the way he would throw his head
back and laugh, the scent of Russian Leather cologne...

She had fallen in love with an heroic ideal of a
man, now she was in love with the real thing. And
not just in love: she *wanted* him, she realised with a
sudden shock, which sent the colour flooding into her
cheeks. Wanted his kisses, wanted to be held in his
arms.

'Oh, I'm sorry, Miss, I've kept you waiting in this
warm room,' the maid said apologetically. 'You're
quite flushed, Miss.'

Joanna cast a harried glance at the mirror and
tugged down the veil on her hat. 'It will soon pass,
thank you.' She took the gloves the girl handed her
and ran downstairs to where Giles was patiently waiting in the hallway, talking to Mrs Geddings. 'I am
sorry to have kept you,' she apologised. 'The hem
needed a few stitches.'

The mare had been saddled up and was standing
quietly in the little paddock that opened off the stable
yard, a groom at her head. A short man in a buff coat
was talking to the head groom, but broke off when
he saw Mrs Gedding and her guests. Introductions
were made and Giles and he ducked under the rails
to look at the mare.

Joanna watched as Giles ran his hands down her
legs, checked her teeth, lifted a hoof, which the ani-

mal allowed without fuss, and asked the groom to remove the saddle. He ran his hands down her back, making her withers twitch, but otherwise provoking no reaction. Then he vaulted neatly on to her back and gathered up the reins.

He was far too big a man for the mare, but she walked on obediently, stopping when commanded, and standing like a rock even when Giles dropped the reins on to her neck and clapped his hands loudly. One dark grey ear swivelled back, but that was all.

He swung down and led her back to Joanna, who was leaning on the fence. 'She seems steady enough, if you would care to try her. The question is, will she prove too steady? I'm not looking for an armchair ride. I want to breed a line with spirit.'

Joanna smiled as the mare pushed her soft muzzle into her hands, looking for caresses and tidbits. 'Oh, no, you must earn your apples! What is her name, Mr Pike?'

'Moonstone, ma'am,' he replied, looking embarrassed. 'That's what my youngest daughter called her when she was foaled. Seems a bit fancy-like.'

'It suits her. No, stop it, there is nothing for you in my pockets!' She gathered up the reins and glanced round. 'Please will you give me a leg up, Mr Pike?'

He cupped his hand for her booted foot and tossed her up into the saddle. Joanna concentrated on adjusting her skirts and the reins, not looking at Giles. She wanted, very badly, to impress him with her riding and it was making her nervous.

Moonstone responded promptly to the pressure of her heel and Joanna circled the paddock once at a walk, then at the trot and finally shortened the reins and urged the mare into a canter. She responded willingly and Joanna soon forgot she had an audience. The paddock was dull riding though, but at one end the fence bordered a larger meadow and as she cantered past Joanna could see no sign of a ditch or other obstacle. When they reached the far side she wheeled the horse and set her direct across the field towards the fence.

The mare's ears pricked forward and she lengthened her stride, anticipating the jump. There was a shout behind them, which Joanna ignored, and then the mare was bunching the muscles of her hindquarters and leaping smoothly over the rails, Joanna balanced lightly on her back. They landed safely and Joanna let her have her head.

The exhilaration of galloping was wonderful. At the end of the meadow she turned the mare, took her back at the same pace, only collecting her up before the jump, and returned to the waiting onlookers with face flushed and veil all awry.

'She is a beautiful ride, Mr Pike!' Joanna pushed back her veil and saw that although Mrs Gedding was looking pleased at her performance, Giles's expression was positively thunderous. He stalked into the paddock to her side and she leaned down and whispered, 'I am so sorry! Was I sounding too enthusiastic? I should not have done so before you had agreed a price—but she is a lovely ride, such even paces and so willing.'

'It is not that at all,' he ground out. 'Are you completely careless of your safety? There might have been a ditch, a fallen tree, goodness knows what on the other side of that fence and to jump a good five

foot before even trying her at a smaller obstacle—
what folly!'

'Of course I looked first,' Joanna said pacifically.
It was wonderful to realise that he was so anxious for
her. 'And I think I ride well enough to manage such
a jump, do you not agree?'

Giles looked up at her, the anger fading out of his
face. 'You ride extremely well,' he conceded. 'But I
was having visions of explaining to your mama just
how you had come to break your neck while in my
care.'

Mr Pike walked out to take Moonstone's head
while Joanna let Giles lift her down. His hands fastened firmly on her waist, but the moment her feet
touched the ground he let go and she was left chiding
herself for being so immodest as to want his hold to
linger.

The two men strolled away, the mare following behind. Joanna went to join Mrs Gedding, who was ful-
some in her praises. 'What a good seat you have, my
dear! I was never in the slightest fear for you, although you should have heard the Colonel's language
when you took that jump!' She chuckled. 'On second
thoughts, perhaps it was best that you did not. I believe he had no notion he was swearing until I
laughed.' She regarded Joanna, who was carefully
gathering up her skirts to keep them out of the long
grass. 'Would you care to keep that habit, my dear?
It is an excellent fit and my Jennie will never get into
it again, not after two babies. I am sure you have far
finer at home, but perhaps the Colonel will let you
ride while you are here.'

'Why, thank you, ma'am, that is most kind, I would

be very grateful if you are sure your daughter would not mind. Oh, look, they appear to have reached agreement.' The men were shaking hands and Mr Pike ducked back under the fence to remount his hack.

'Good day, Mrs Gedding, ma'am! My compliments to the Squire.'

'Good day to you, Mr Pike! You and Mrs Pike must dine with us soon.'

Giles rejoined them, looking pleased. 'A good morning's work, I believe. Would you like to take her out on to the roads for a while, Joanna? I'll have the gelding the Squire has loaned me saddled up and we can explore a little.'

'If you do not need me, ma'am?' Joanna tried not to look too enthusiastic, but could not help her wide smile when Mrs Gedding shook her head.

'No, dear, thank you. Off you go and get some fresh air, it will do you good.'

Joanna had never seen Giles on horseback and could not help watching from under her lashes as he rode out of the yard on the raking bay the Squire had found for him. For a big man he rode lightly, his hands relaxed on the reins, but Joanna could tell that the gelding knew exactly who was in command and that at the slightest sign of trouble those long, well-muscled legs would close and quell it.

The enclosures of recent years had left long, wide grass verges bordering the quiet roads and the two riders found plenty of opportunities to canter and many ditches to hop over. Giles made no comment about her riding, but Joanna was aware that he was watching her. A pheasant erupted from under Moonstone's nose sending her skittering across the road, but he made no effort to catch her rein, merely steadying the gelding until she had soothed the mare and brought her back alongside him.

'What will you do when you get home?' he asked after they had reined in from a long canter and were walking the horses up a slight incline.

'I doubt I will have much say in it,' Joanna responded ruefully. 'Go to Bath as Mama says, I suppose. I would prefer that we all went to Brighton, which was what was planned, but if Papa's gout is bad, I have no idea what will be decided. In any case, that might be regarded as too much of a treat after my behaviour.'

'Could you go to Hebe?'

'Of course, under normal circumstances. But the baby is due, and Alex will be cross with me for worrying Hebe and making all this to-do, and I expect I would find myself looking after little Hugh the whole time. And,' she added gloomily, 'no doubt there would be all sorts of gossip about why I'm not in Brighton with the family.'

'Chicken pox?' Giles suggested half-seriously and received a reproachful look.

'Where will you go?' Joanna thought it was a reasonable question in response to his and one unlikely to make him suspicious of her motives for asking.

'Well, unless there is a message saying that the prodigal is forgiven and I'm to hasten home, then my campaign of dissipation will best be advanced in Brighton, I imagine.' He reined in and pulled his pocket watch out. 'I thought so, we had better turn and make our way back or we will be late for luncheon and I promised the Squire some more help at the Thoroughgoods' house this afternoon.'

'There must be a lot of paperwork,' Joanna commented.

'Yes. We believed we had it all, but I thought it worth checking the panels in the study and, sure enough, we found a concealed cupboard with another stack of ledgers and letters.'

Joanna rode in silence for a while, firmly biting back the question on the tip of her tongue. Finally it got the better of her. 'Will Lady Suzanne not be in Brighton? I should imagine that might restrict your efforts to create a mild scandal. Your father will hardly believe you have plunged into a life of dissipation if he hears that you are squiring her about in Brighton.'

'Indeed it would, and I have absolutely no desire to end up with another argument with Papa over Suzy and my intentions in that quarter! No, fortunately Lord Olney disapproves of Brighton. He will probably be taking the whole family up to stay with his mother in Harrogate.'

'And what,' Joanna said tartly, 'will Lady Suzanne say when she hears about your activities in Brighton?'

'Darling Suzy will no doubt tease me unmercifully.' He grinned. 'That young woman understands me very well indeed. Come on, let's canter or we will be late.'

Darling Suzy! Joanna dug her heel into Moonstone's flank and gave the mare her head. Giles was so relaxed about Lady Suzanne, so confident about her reactions. His voice when he spoke about her was warm, affectionate, caressing. What she would not give to have him speak to her in that way. She closed her eyes for a moment against the tears that stung her lids and followed the big bay hunter.

Chapter Nine

After luncheon Joanna spent the rest of the day with the rose petals she had collected for the *pot-pourri,* separating them and spreading them on muslin to dry in the stillroom.

It was a pleasant occupation in the cool, scented room, but one which gave her far too much time to think. Would her parents allow her to go to Brighton? And if they did and Giles was there, was that better or worse than being separated from him entirely? And what about Lord Clifton? Was he going to persist in his suit?

Her thoughts went round and round like a dog in a turnspit. She had run away, wanting time to think. But now, when she had it, it seemed she was no further forward in planning her life.

Dinner time passed with no sign of the men, only a note from the Squire saying that they had decided to work on and finish all there was to do that day. They had sent out to the nearest inn for food, he assured his wife, and he thought he would probably go direct to Peterborough that evening to ensure that all the evidence was safely delivered, so she was not to expect him home that night.

By ten Giles had still not returned and Joanna found she was restless and quite certain that if she went to bed she would not sleep. The ladies had retired to the sitting room with its big window on to the garden and the scents of the sun-warmed flowers still drifted in through the open casement, mingling with the song of the nightingale in the long hedge.

'May I sit up, ma'am?' Joanna asked as Mrs Gedding put down her sewing at last, got to her feet and announced that she was for her bed. 'I am not tired and I am sure the Colonel will lock up if you want to send the servants to bed.'

'Very well, my dear. Everything will be secure except for this window and the front door, if you will be so good as to ask him to attend to those and to make sure all the candles are out. The decanters are there, on the sideboard—I am sure the Colonel will welcome a drink when he returns.'

She hesitated, drawing her shawl around her shoulders. 'Or should we close the window now? It is just becoming a little cool.'

'May I leave it? I am quite warm and the evening is so lovely. Or...' Joanna glanced at the grate with its fire basket full of pine cones '...might I light the fire? It will just keep the chill off.'

'Of course. The tapers are on the mantel shelf. Just make sure the embers are raked right out before you go to bed, dear. Goodnight.'

Joanna found some old papers in the log basket and after one false start managed to light a small fire. She heaped on pine cones, enjoying the crackle and the bright blue light they produced. The fire was not so much a source of warmth as of company and she sat on the floor, leaning against the arm of one of the wing chairs, close enough to the hearth to toss on cones as they burned up.

The longcase clock in the hall chimed eleven and then the quarter before she heard hoofbeats on the carriage drive. She got up and put the front door ajar, leaving the sitting-room door open as well, and set the tray of decanters and a glass on the side table next to the wing chair. The candle on the mantelshelf was guttering so she trimmed it and lit another. With the firelight they cast a soft glow in the room and a few moths blundered in from the garden.

When she heard his step she called, 'Giles! Will you lock the front door, please? Everyone has gone to bed.'

There was the sound of the lock and of bolts being shot, then Giles appeared in the doorway. 'Joanna! Still up?' Even in the dim light she could see how tired he looked.

'Come in and let me take your coat,' she urged. 'See, the decanters are here. Sit down and have a drink—you look too tired just to go to sleep.'

Obediently he shrugged out of his riding coat, stretching with a sigh as he did so. Joanna took it and hung it carefully over the back of a chair, smoothing out the creases with a hand that lingered on the cloth, warm from his body.

When she turned back to him he was standing, a tall figure in his shirtsleeves, by the window where the moonlight was just beginning to spill on to the boards. 'God! Those nightingales! Heartbreakingly beautiful, isn't it? They would sing on the battlefields, you know. Some of the soldiers were superstitious about them, said they were Death's bird.'

Joanna shivered at the thought. 'Come and sit down. Have you and the Squire finished now?'

He sank into the wing chair and lifted the brandy decanter, stretching long booted legs out in front of him. 'Yes, all complete, thank goodness. I fancy we have cooked the Thoroughgoods' goose for them.' He splashed some spirits into the glass and raised it to his lips. 'Ah! That is good. What are you doing up at this hour with everyone else in bed?'

Joanna came and sat down again in her place by the hearth, leaned against the arm of his chair and tossed a handful of pine cones into the blaze. 'I wasn't tired and the scents and the sounds from the garden are so lovely I stayed up.'

Giles did not seem to want to talk, and Joanna was too content just sitting with him in the firelight to disturb the mood. Gradually she relaxed until her head rested against the chair and after a few minutes she was conscious of a light touch on her hair which she had twisted into a crown on the top of her head. Giles seemed to be stroking it gently as he might a cat that had settled in his lap and she realised that he was probably quite unaware he was doing it.

Unlike the cat, which would have stretched and curled tighter to his caressing hand, Joanna kept as still as she could, willing him to continue.

'That smell of burning pine cones,' he said, almost to himself, his voice deep and quiet. 'It reminds me of campfires when we were in the foothills of the Pyrenees.'

'Tell me about it,' she said softly, as though speaking to a sleepwalker.

'Memory is a strange thing: the bad times, the nights when it was raining or snowing, or when the enemy was close and no one could relax or sleep, the nights when we were all hungry and cold or wet and the wolves were howling and the wounded moaning—all those nights seem to blur into one nightmare. But the good times, the nights when it was dry and warm and there was no alert, I can remember almost every one quite clearly. It was best in the foothills; we had clean water and there was plenty of wood to burn and trees to shelter amongst.

'The men set the tents out in lines, each with its fire in front. It was like a village, people wandering up and down, the women gossiping, sitting in front of the tents in the firelight mending or cooking, the smell of the burning wood and the pine cones, someone singing, a sleepy child crying.'

Joanna could tell from his voice that Giles was smiling at the memory. The caressing fingers in her hair had found the pins and one after another they fell out on to the floor or into her lap until the mass of black hair fell softly around her shoulders.

'They were happy times?' she asked.

'Yes. They had a simplicity, an honesty. It was like a big family: one with its rogues and its problem children for sure, but still a family tied together with intense loyalties and one purpose.'

'And what would you be doing on those evenings?' He was running his fingers through her loosened hair now, lifting it and letting it fall. It was hypnotically sensuous and reassuring. Joanna could feel her eyelids drooping, although she had no desire to sleep.

'If I were not on duty I might walk along the lines, visit men who had been wounded, talk to anyone who wanted a word. Sometimes I'd eat with a group of them, sometimes sit and listen if they were making music. Other times I would sit outside my own tent, talk to my servant, write my journal or letters. Be thankful for the peace and the stillness. As I am now. You are very tranquil company, Joanna.'

She smiled, her eyes on the dancing blue flames. It had been one of her dreams of when they were married, to be a restful presence for him at the end of a long, hard day. It would never happen again, but now she could savour it.

One of the pine cones exploded with a sharp crack and landed on the hearthrug in a shower of sparks. Joanna bent forward, but Giles was before her, going down on one knee and reaching out to scoop the burning fragment back with a deft flick of his long fingers. He pinched out the remaining sparks and half-turned, finding himself face to face with Joanna as she knelt beside his chair.

Her hair flowed over her shoulders and down the curves of her breast and as she regained her balance the last of the pins fell to the ground.

Giles put out a hand and lifted a heavy lock of hair. 'Did I do that?'

'Yes, of course you did. You were sitting there, stroking it as if it were a cat, and all the pins fell out.' Joanna tried to keep her tone lightly amused, but her breath was tight in her chest. He was so close that she could see the firelight catching the golden stubble on his chin. He smelt of leather, a faint scent of brandy and the indefinable masculine smell that was simply *Giles*.

'You have beautiful hair,' he said simply, then leaned forward and kissed her on the lips.

His mouth was warm and gentle and for a moment Joanna froze, not with alarm but in pure shock. Then she put out a hand to his shoulder to steady herself and tentatively leaned into the kiss. Giles's hand cupped the back of her head, pulling her to him, and the pressure of his lips increased, parting her own slightly. He tasted of brandy and his body, so close to hers, was hot.

No man had ever kissed her like this and she was conscious of her ignorance and inexperience. What should she do now? What would he do? The answer made her gasp as his tongue insinuated itself between her parted lips, touched the tip of her own tongue with a fleeting, startling intimacy and then she was hard against his chest, one of his hands in her hair as the other caressed her neck, sliding sensuously down to her shoulder where the sensitive skin was exposed by the lace of her fichu.

His mouth now was firm, demanding things that her body seemed to half-understand but did not know how to respond to. She seemed to have stopped breathing and to be both freezing and burning at the same time. Her entire world was focused on the sensation of his mouth on hers, the invasion of his tongue and she was unaware that her fingers were clenched tight in the thick linen of his shirt.

Then, as suddenly as he had kissed her, he released

her. Joanna opened her hands and sat back on her heels with a bump, her lungs filling with a deep, racking breath.

Giles got to his feet in one swift, violent movement and stood beside the chair opposite her, his face stark. 'Damn it! I am sorry, Joanna, I don't know what came over me. No, what am I saying? I know perfectly well what came over me and I should not have let it happen.'

'I...' Her voice seemed to have vanished along with all the strength in her legs. Her skin seemed unnaturally sensitive and a hot, disturbing feeling burned inside her.

'I am sorry I frightened you, Joanna. Of all the stupid things to do when I imagine the last thing you want is a man so much as laying a finger on you. I had forgotten where I was, who I was with. You look so...so hauntingly different in the firelight with your hair down like that.'

Even in the gloom Joanna could see the tension in Giles's face, the way he was gripping the chair back until his knuckles showed white. It was incredible, impossible, but it seemed that kissing her had affected him as profoundly as it had affected her. And yet, he did not love her. As a glimpse of the power of physical desire, it was disturbing and enlightening.

'Giles—' she swallowed and managed some control over her voice '—you did not frighten me, I promise.'

'You are too innocent, too—'

'No,' she interrupted sharply. 'I may be inexperienced, but I am not innocent of what has just happened. You kissed me, that is all. We were alone, it

is late, neither of us was concentrating on the proprieties. It happened, and I am sure I should not say so,
but it was very…interesting.'

He made a sound which Joanna thought was a
choked laugh. 'You see,' she persevered, 'I have
never been kissed before, not properly, and I do not
expect to be again, so it was interesting to find out
what it was like.' There, that should explain why she
had not slapped his face, or shrieked or done any of
the other things a well brought-up young lady ought
to have done.

'Joanna, you simply cannot go around allowing
yourself to be kissed because it is *interesting!* How
many other experiences do you think you might sam-
ple out of interest? You are playing with fire…'

'Nonsense!' Joanna got to her feet shakily. She felt
as though her legs were going to give way at any
moment and she grabbed hold of the chair back.

'Nonsense? Joanna, I do not believe for one moment that you have any idea of the danger you are in
when you trustingly let yourself be kissed like that.
And *don't* stand there looking at me like that with
those big hazel eyes: there is just so much a man can
take.'

'You are trying to scare me for my own good,' she
retorted. 'I don't believe for one moment I am in any
danger from you, Giles. I trust you.'

Giles stood looking at the defiant, piquant face. Her
eyes were huge in the firelight and the shadows flickered over her mouth, swollen from the pressure of his
mouth. Her hair fell like black silk, rising and falling
with her rapid breathing and she said she trusted him!

He took a deep breath and said, 'Joanna, will you please go to bed. *Now*.'

'Very well.' Anyone who did not know her would have missed the slight tremor beneath her composed tone, but Giles caught it. He did not believe now that he had frightened her, but he knew he had not been in any way restrained, that he had simply followed his instincts in a way that left him feeling utterly shaken at his own indiscretion. He was no rake, never had been. He was no monk, either, but he had never trifled with virgins, and he had no intention of starting with this one.

'Go on,' he said again, making his tone light with some effort. 'And leave me to contemplate exactly what your mama would say if she knew about this.'

Joanna, who had been making her way to the door, stopped in her tracks and stared at him, her eyes wide. 'You would not tell her!' He realised with a shock that she was truly alarmed at the prospect, far more alarmed than she had been by the kiss itself.

'I ought to,' he said ruefully, 'but I will not, unless you wish me to confess.'

'No! She would be so angry.'

'At me, with full justification; not with you.' It seemed incredible that Joanna should appear so worried at the prospect of her mother's displeasure. Mrs Fulgrave had always seemed a most amiable and reasonable woman.

'Oh...well, you do not deserve her censure for such a thing, after you have rescued me and looked after me. You are a friend of the family, I would not want to put any barrier in the way of that continuing,' she finished formally, apparently getting control of her feelings with an effort. 'Goodnight.'

Giles, finding himself alone, stood staring at the fire for a long moment before, with a little shake, pulling himself together and raking out the dying embers. He shut and bolted the window and snuffed out one of the candles. Picking up the other with one hand and his coat with the other, he walked slowly upstairs to his bedchamber, trying to sort out his feelings.

Colonel Giles Gregory was not a man who was given to self-doubt or lengthy introspection. He was self-confident, assured, used to being in command of himself, his emotions and those around him. If he felt himself in error, he had no trouble owning to it and when he confronted a problem he would apply his intellect and experience to it, asking advice when that seemed the best course of action.

He shut the chamber door behind him and tossed his coat on to a chair, tugging off his cravat with an impatient jerk. There was no problem about what to do in this situation: he simply had to make sure he did not allow himself to relax to the point of care-lessness when alone with Joanna and to see she got home, suitably chaperoned, at the earliest possible op-portunity.

No, he thought, glaring at his reflection in the glass with as much irritation as he would if he was lecturing a subaltern caught in some indiscretion, the problem was that his normally well-regulated emotions were now decidedly disordered.

Giles sat down and began to tug off his boots. 'Pull yourself together and apply your brain,' he muttered, leaning back in his shirtsleeves, his stockinged feet propped on the fender.

He was feeling aroused—damnably aroused. It hardly required any intellectual effort to deduce that. Giles trampled firmly on the demands his taut body was sending him, and, beyond resolving to seek out some accommodating feminine company when he returned to town, did his best to ignore it.

Joanna had got under his skin in a totally unexpected way. How long had it been since he'd thought about that time in Spain, relived the sounds and smells and emotions? A long time, he realised. And when he had, there was no one to talk to about it. His father and Alex would understand, they had the same experiences, but it was not something you discussed with another man. And yet…it had been curiously comforting to do so. How had she managed to so disarm him, to take him so far off guard and out of himself?

He had thought her an unhappy girl, hurt by some man she would soon forget, but he had been wrong. Joanna was not a child with an infatuation. She was a young woman who had experienced two Seasons and who had devoted herself to becoming the perfect wife for some insensitive lout who had hurt her by rejecting that dedication, that love. What had she said just now? 'I have never been kissed before, not properly, and I do not expect to be again.'

At least that man had not seduced her and then cast her off. Giles winced, remembering the matter-of-fact way she had announced that she did not expect to experience another kiss. What was she going to do with herself now? Return home and dwindle into an unpaid companion to an elderly relative? Become the spinster support of her mother? What a waste!

Giles wearily got to his feet and began to shed the remainder of his clothes. It was as he pulled his shirt over his head that he realised there was another element to that evening's encounter, which was fretting him like a stone in his shoe. He stood, one hand on the bedpost, trying to analyse it.

Joanna had been so trusting when he had imprudently kissed her, so calm in the face of what should, after her terrifying recent adventure, have been an alarming experience. She trusted him, she had said so. Suzy trusted him, too—her 'darling Giles'. Trusted him enough to kiss him and flirt with him, wheedle and flutter her eyelashes, without a thought in her pretty head that he might step over the line and take advantage of what she was so charmingly offering.

'You're getting middle-aged, my boy,' Giles told himself, casting a disparaging glance down at an admirably flat and well-muscled stomach. 'That's what it is. You're no longer a devil with women, just a nice, reliable, safe friend to flirt with.' With a wry grin at his own self-pity, he blew out the candle.

In a bedchamber at the other end of the landing Joanna was also wrestling with her emotions. The memory of the kiss itself seemed to warm her whole body and to fill her with a dull yearning ache. She knew she had added a physical desire for Giles to what had always, in her inexperience, been a purely spiritual longing. But how could she not have let him kiss her? How could she not have responded? The pressure of his lips on hers was still tangible: would she feel it still when she woke in the morning or would it become like a dream?

But wonderful though that simple kiss had been, she treasured more the way Giles had let her share his memories, his recollections of ordinary life with his troopers. Not the glory or the tragedies, just the scents and smells, the music, the rough camaraderie. That was what she had always hoped for, that as his wife she would be someone to whom he could talk without reservation about whatever mattered to him, the big things and the most trivial.

Like the kiss, his voice describing the firelit camp was a door opening into a world of intimacy and trust. A door that she must shut again. Neither his kisses nor his trust belonged to her: they were another woman's and she must learn to do without either.

Chapter Ten

If Mrs Gedding noticed that her guests were somewhat constrained the next morning she gave no sign
of it and carried the burden of conversation at breakfast with her usual cheerful good humour. Had she
been privy to the very different preoccupations of
Miss Fulgrave and the Colonel she might have been
apprehensive, but both managed to give the impression of merely having slept badly.

Giles was trying to concentrate on what his plans
should be once he had safely delivered Joanna back
to her mama, but was finding the thought of escorting
a disturbingly unpredictable young lady preying on
his mind. He gave himself a brisk mental shake. What
possible problems could one young woman present to
an experienced senior officer?

On one occasion he had simultaneously delivered
a general's temperamental Spanish mistress, fifty
French prisoners, a wagon train of army pay and six
field guns through enemy territory and had arrived
with every coin, gun and prisoner intact. And he had
achieved this without offending the lady, who had

made it quite clear that she was offering to make the journey very pleasant indeed for him.

That aspect of the experience made his mouth quirk in a reminiscent smile and Joanna, watching him covertly over the rim of her coffee cup, caught her breath. Was he remembering last night? The sensual smile faded, leaving her back with her circling thoughts.

What was she going to do? It did not help that she had no idea what she wanted. She must give up all hope of Giles, that she understood very clearly. His flat refusal to bow to his father's disapproval of the match with Lady Suzanne was clear enough indication of that.

Surely Mama would not be too angry now she knew she was safe? Surely she would understand that only real unhappiness would have driven her daughter to such extremes? Joanna, hating the thought of being estranged from her parents, felt utterly miserable that they would feel she had let them down and behaved badly.

Show some backbone! she lectured herself silently. *Mama will write soon and be forgiving, surely. And then we can all go to Brighton and no one will know I am in disgrace and I will be able to think about what to do with the rest of my life once I have got rid of Lord Clifton...* Having some sort of plan made her feel better and by the time the maid brought in the morning post the heavy look had vanished from her eyes.

'A letter for you, Joanna.' Mrs Gedding passed it across with a sympathetic smile at the sudden flare of apprehension in her eyes. 'Your mama, I expect. One for you, Colonel...two, no, three for Mr Gedding.

Thank you, Anna. From Mrs Thwaite by hand? Ah, good, I hope this is the reply I was expecting. Do, please, both of you read your letters, if you will excuse me perusing this.' She bent her head, crowned with its frivolous cap, over the note and Joanna nervously slit the seal on her letter.

She ran her eyes rapidly over the page unable to focus at first, then phrases and words jumped out at her with the force of blows. *Your poor father...Dr Grace...William quite distraught...wicked, wicked girl...*

Papa! Joanna took a shuddering breath, willed her hand to stop shaking and made herself read the letter from the beginning. After the first few sentences she realised with relief that it was her father's gout that was so severe that the doctor had been called and not, as she had first feared, that her disappearance had brought on a seizure of some kind. William, apparently, was distressed at the absence of his sister and the fact that no one knew why she had gone and as for her mother...

Words, Mrs Fulgrave declared, quite failed her. This fact did not, however, prevent her from writing at length of her opinion that Joanna was the gravest disappointment to her parents, that she had behaved in a way which was incomprehensibly wicked and wilful and that her poor mama had been at a loss to know what to do with her. It was only the intervention of Providence in the shape of Colonel Gregory that had prevented the most appalling consequences and it was to be hoped that she was fully repentant and thankful.

Naturally she could not be inflicted upon her el-

derly relative in Bath after such behaviour. Dear Hebe
had begged that Joanna be allowed to go to her at
Tasborough and the Earl had assured Mrs Fulgrave
that she would be kept under the strictest watch and
that she would be able to make herself useful. The
last word was underlined several times with some
force.

Blinking back the tears, Joanna looked up and met
Giles's eye. He raised one eyebrow. 'Mad as a wet
hen?' he enquired.

'Really! Colonel!' Mrs Gedding chided, failing to
hide the fact that she was amused.

'Mama is displeased,' Joanna agreed with dignity,
swallowing hard. She was in no mood to be teased.
Presumably Mama had found Giles's actions com-
mendable throughout—as indeed they had been. 'She
says I must go to Tasborough and that she has told
our acquaintance, including Lord Clifton, that she
cannot refuse her dear niece's request for my company.'

'Ah. She expects that Alex will keep a strict eye
on you, I imagine?'

'Yes,' Joanna agreed drearily. 'She also says that
she is taking Papa and William to Bath to take the
waters. Papa, I mean; William will not be taking the
waters. Mama points out that William will be very
much bored in Bath and it is all my fault that they
are not going to Brighton.'

'How can that be your fault?' Giles enquired.
'Surely you cannot be blamed for your father's
gout—she tells me in her letter that that is what con-
tinues to trouble him.'

'The doctor informs her that anxiety and strain all

aggravate a naturally gouty tendency,' Joanna said, scanning the letter again for the lengthy description of poor Papa's sufferings, all of which were made infinitely worse by thoughts of his undutiful daughter. 'She quotes Shakespeare, something about a thankless child.'

'*King Lear*,' Mrs Gedding supplied helpfully. '"How sharper than a serpent's tooth it is to have a thankless child".' She regarded Joanna's white face. 'She is very upset, I fear, my dear. But never fret, once she has you home safe all will be forgiven, you will see.'

'I do not know when that might be. If I am to go to Tasborough for the summer it could be weeks before I see her.'

'Good thing,' Giles said briskly. 'By the time she does see you again this will all be ancient history. And you will enjoy being with Hebe.'

'And Alex, and little Hugh, and the new baby,' Joanna said bitterly. The last thing she wanted just now was to be in the heart of a happy young family, especially with a new baby about to arrive. She wanted her own babies—Giles's children—not to be a doting nurse for little relatives.

'You really are going to have to get over this antipathy towards Alex, you know,' Giles said casually, spreading preserves on his toast. 'You'll enjoy yourself once you are there.'

For the first time since she had known him Joanna found herself staring at Giles with real anger in her heart. She had confided in him! She had believed he understood how she felt; surely he would know, instinctively, why she was so upset at this banishment?

No, apparently he did not. This man she loved was proving to be very much a human being, she realised. He kissed young women he was not in love with, he quarrelled with his father, he did not understand how she felt after all she had told him…

'Don't glare at me,' he said with a grin, which only added fuel to her anger. 'I have to escort you all the way back to Hertfordshire, always assuming we can find you a chaperon.'

'Now there I think I have the perfect solution,' Mrs Gedding announced, flourishing the note she had received. 'Mrs Thwaite, our vicar's wife, has dispensed with the services of her governess now that her youngest daughter has left the schoolroom. Miss Shaw is returning to London to stay with her sister whilst seeking a new post. She would be quite happy to assume charge of Joanna and is ready to leave at your convenience. Mrs Thwaite says…' Mrs Gedding peered closely at the foot of the note where the vicar's wife had almost run out of paper '…she says Miss Shaw will call today at eleven to discuss the arrangements.'

'What have you told Mrs Thwaite about me, ma'am?' Joanna asked apprehensively.

'Only that owing to family circumstances you find yourself stranded here without the female company you were expecting. I referred to your papa's poor health and the fact that you had a sister in Lincoln, and I flatter myself that without uttering one untrue word I have managed to give the impression that various plans have simply come adrift.'

Mrs Gedding might have thought she had pulled the wool over her neighbour's eyes, but as soon as

Joanna was introduced to Miss Shaw she was convinced that the governess was not deceived for a moment.

Miss Shaw was an acidulated woman in her mid-thirties, and if Joanna had wished to find a spinster unhappy with her lot and soured by her experiences, she could not have hoped for a more depressing example. The governess appeared to find some satisfaction in appearing as downtrodden as possible in her severe grey wool gown, her hair dragged back from her thin face and not so much as a piece of mourning jewellery to ornament her bodice.

She kept her hands clasped together throughout the interview, casting sidelong glances at Giles and answering Mrs Gedding in a respectful undertone. But the looks she sent in Joanna's direction were sharp and judgemental and it was quite apparent that she guessed her temporary new charge was in disgrace.

She agreed that she could be ready to set out the next day and that she had not the slightest objection to going into Hertfordshire, provided that she returned to her sister in Holborn eventually. 'It must be an object with me,' she announced primly, 'to assist Mrs Gedding in any way within my power.'

I am sure it is, Joanna thought rebelliously, *especially if that involves a comfortable journey in a private chaise with a handsome gentleman to look after all the arrangements, and not a bumpy journey on the public stage!*

The arrangements were finalised and Mrs Gedding took Miss Shaw to the kitchens to collect a recipe she had promised to Mrs Thwaite. Joanna, her vision a blur, got abruptly to her feet and walked out of the room. Giles caught up with her in the garden.

'Are you sulking, Joanna?'

'*Sulking!* No, I am not sulking! I am trying not to cry, if you must know,' she stormed at him, suddenly finding it incomprehensible that she had even liked Giles Gregory, let alone loved him. 'My mother has all but cast me off, my father is unwell and angry with me, my little brother is upset, I am being sent off in disgrace and that horrible woman with a face like a weasel is going to be smug and superior all the way to Hertfordshire.' She took a gulping breath. 'And I will soon be learning all about being the poor spinster relation who is the very person to call in to look after things when one or other of my female relations is confined, or the children have measles or…or…'

'Joanna!' He was laughing at her! The wretched man was actually laughing! 'Calm down, for goodness' sake. I agree Miss Shaw closely resembles a weasel. I agree that your family is distressingly angry with you, but all you need—you and your parents— is a few weeks to get over this. No one, yet, has died of a broken heart and this man who has so cruelly disappointed you is not going to achieve that, or even ruin your life as you are so convinced he has.

'I would be prepared to wager that in six months you will have recovered sufficiently to take an interest in the new Season—and without the impossible task of living up to this paragon you will have much better time of it—' He broke off, looking down into her stormy, upturned face. 'Believe me, Joanna, he is not worth this anguish, whoever he is.'

'I have already come to that conclusion, I thank you,' she snapped, turning on her heel and stalking off into the shrubbery. Giles made no attempt to follow her.

Joanna emerged wan-faced at luncheon and took the opportunity, while Mrs Gedding was out of the room greeting her returning husband, to apologise to Giles. 'I am sorry I snapped at you,' she said stiffly. 'I have everything to thank you for, I should not be so ungrateful.'

He looked up with a smile. 'There is nothing to thank me for—it was only what anyone would do for a lady in such distress as your mama.' He regarded her downcast, heavy eyes and added, 'And you had a terrifying experience; it is no wonder you are feeling somewhat vapourish just now.'

Well, that has put me firmly in my place, Joanna thought, compressing her lips firmly on a tart retort. *I need not think he had any particular concern for me, only for Mama! And I am suffering from the vapours, am I?*

Her lacerated feelings suffered a further blow after the meal when, returning to the dining room to retrieve her shawl that she had left on her chair, she overheard Mrs Gedding in conversation with Giles. It was apparent at once what they were discussing and Joanna listened with growing indignation from behind the door.

'Miss Shaw is very sensitive, it seems,' her hostess was saying. 'Although I had said nothing to her or Mrs Thwaite of Joanna's true predicament, she appears to have guessed that we are returning a runaway to her home. I suspect that several years as a mistress in a girls' seminary in Bath has given her experience of young ladies overreacting to emotional situations. But she assures me that she will keep a very strict eye upon Joanna, and promises that she will not leave her side, by day or night.'

'I am sure that will not be necessary,' Giles answered. 'Joanna appears resigned to returning home—or at least, to her friends in Hertfordshire.'

'I am sure she has realised the errors of her ways,' Mrs Gedding agreed comfortably. 'But Miss Shaw tells me that she has a number of improving tracts suitable for young ladies and will do her utmost to engage Joanna's interest in them during the journey.'

Joanna did not wait to hear Giles's opinion of improving tracts, but ran out into the sunshine and took refuge in the stables.

'Hateful, hateful woman!' she said vehemently. Moonstone, who had put her head over the half-door at the sound of her approach, shied away with a snort. 'To be dragged back, not just in disgrace, but shut up with her, having to share a bedchamber with her and being lectured morning, noon and night as though I had run away from school with the drawing master!'

She thumped her fist on something, then realised it was the side saddle she had been using with Moonstone, the bridle hanging beside it. Slowly Joanna ran her hands over the hard leather, an idea slowly filling her mind. Dare she? Just how far away was Georgy's house?

The Squire's study was empty and Joanna soon found where he kept his atlases, for one already lay open on a stand. She located Wisbech, then traced the roads back to the village. There were several options, all of them straight, with sharp turns every now and again as they crossed the dykes and canals that drained the flat fenlands. After ten minutes' rapid scribbling on a sheet of notepaper she found on the desk, and some careful measuring with the ruler, Joanna came to the conclusion that even going by the smaller roads, it could not be more than thirty miles to Wisbech. Once she was there, surely everyone would know where to find Lord Brandon's house.

Tactics and strategy, she murmured to herself. Once she was with Georgy, surely Mama would be content to let her stay, for no one could doubt that Lady Brandon, however featherbrained she might be, was not eminently respectable. But with Georgy she would be able to plan and her friend would not be trying to dissuade her from whatever course she decided upon. In fact, now she thought about it, Georgy had been encouraging her husband to take her on a continental tour. Surely she would want a female companion for that adventure? And once Joanna had some experience, perhaps she could find a position with another lady wanting to travel...

Joanna's rosy daydream was clouded somewhat by the thought of the anxiety this new escape would provoke, but she knew she would be at the Brandons' within the day and she could immediately send news of her safe arrival to Mrs Gedding. It would be far too soon for Mama or Hebe to be alerted. The only danger would be capture by Giles.

Tactics, tactics, she murmured, gathering up pen, ink and paper and retiring to her bedchamber to compose the most reassuring and grateful note she could to Mrs Gedding. That took some time and when it was finished there were her route notes to arrange carefully and to con and a selection to be made of the absolute essentials to pack into a small portmanteau.

By dinner time her stomach was full of butterflies and she had little appetite, although she made herself eat as much as possible; it could be a long and hungry day tomorrow.

The Squire was in excellent spirits and Joanna was able to keep up the appearance of normality with an odd comment or question while he recounted how he was writing to London magistrates about the Thoroughgoods and their associates and how he had every confidence in them all receiving their just deserts.

After dinner she sat and helped Mrs Gedding with some sewing until the tea tray was brought in, then made her excuses and went up to bed.

'Goodnight, my dear,' Mrs Gedding said placidly. 'It will be as well to get a good night's sleep, for the chaise has been ordered for ten and we must have you all packed and ready before that. I do hope the men will not keep you awake; I believe they are set on a game of billiards tonight, and once the Squire finds a willing opponent he is quite likely to play into the small hours.'

Joanna was delighted with that news, for after a late night she hoped that Giles would sleep in and she would be well on her way before he was awake to miss her. She catnapped restlessly all night, too worried about oversleeping to drop into a deep slumber.

At last she heard the longcase clock strike four and in the grey dawn light scrambled into her habit, pulled on her boots and gloves and picked up the small portmanteau. The note to Mrs Gedding she left on her pillow.

The house was silent and the parlour window opened easily under her nervous hand. She pushed it to and ran across the grass to the stables. The old dog opened an eye as she passed, but he was used to her by now and made no attempt to bark, and then she was inside.

Moonstone stood patiently while she heaved on the saddle and struggled to tighten the girth. The bridle was more difficult, but by dint of standing on a crate she managed it. Then she carefully unbuckled the girth from every saddle in the tack room and the bit from every bridle, dropped them into a sack and hid them under some hay in an unoccupied loose box. That should slow down any pursuit until she was well away and if the hired chaise was not ordered until ten, even that could not hope to catch her.

Joanna walked Moonstone out of the box and across the yard to the mounting block. With a last, anxious, glance up at Giles's chamber window, she turned the mare's head and rode quietly off down the drive into the lifting mist.

Chapter Eleven

Giles woke to a violent pounding on the door. He had swung his legs out of bed and was reaching blindly for where his sabre always used to be before he remembered where he was and that he was not being woken to meet a surprise French dawn attack.

He flung the door open to reveal the Squire clad in a gaudy dressing gown, his nightcap askew on his grey hair and his boots protruding from under the hem. 'She's gone!'

'Who...?' Giles shook the fumes of the Squire's excellent brandy from his head and forced himself to think. 'Joanna? Where?'

'I don't know!' Mrs Gedding appeared from behind the bulk of her husband. 'Look, this was in her room.'

Giles took the note and scanned it rapidly. 'There is only one place she can hope to reach today if we are to take her at her word and believe that she is going to a "respectable friend" and that is Lady Brandon in Wisbech.'

'Oh, I am sure she would not deceive me,' Mrs Gedding said anxiously. 'Poor child, she must have been far more frightened of returning home than I guessed!'

'Poor child!' Giles said grimly. 'I'll give her poor child when I catch her. Have you any idea when she left?'

'It was before five-thirty, for the undergroom went into the stables then,' the Squire said. 'He saw Moonstone was gone, but the fool assumed Rogers had turned her out and it wasn't until I ran out just now that he thought to check.'

'What time is it?'

'Half past seven.'

'I will get dressed immediately,' Giles said. 'Squire, can you get your man to put the greys to? And, if you could give some thought to jotting down the fastest route to Wisbech, I would be grateful. I will be down directly.'

He deliberately kept his anger under control as he pulled on his clothes. There was time for that, and time for the anxiety that was roiling in his stomach, later, after he had found Joanna. That mare was steady, he reassured himself. Joanna was a good rider and the roads were dry and clear. Surely there was nothing that could befall her in a day's ride in the English Fens?

He was met at the bottom of the stairs by the Squire with a sketch map and notes and Mrs Gedding with a bulging napkin and a flask. 'I have no hope of you sitting down to eat your breakfast,' she said resignedly. 'But you can eat this one-handed.'

'Thank you, ma'am...'

'Squire! Squire!' It was Rogers the groom, bursting into the hall without ceremony, a bridle flapping in his hands. 'Every girth's missing from every saddle, sir!'

'Damn it, I'll drive then.'

'No good, sir,' the groom cut in. 'All the bits have gone, too. I've got the lad tearing the place apart now.'

'From my driving harness as well?' Giles demanded before the squire could speak.

'Yes, Colonel.'

'The little witch! I could almost admire her ingenuity if I was not so angry with her. Squire, have you a horse which would tolerate a rope bit? I can ride bareback.'

Followed by Mrs Gedding clutching the food, the men headed for the stables. Ten minutes' careful work with a thin rope and Giles was astride the Squire's raw-boned black hunter, who stood quietly enough, although mumbling his tongue over the unfamiliar feel of rope and not metal in his mouth.

'He'll do you all the way to Wisbech, never fear,' the Squire said, slapping the muscled black neck affectionately. 'Send word as soon as you have news.' He took a satchel from the groom and stuffed the food and flask into it. 'Here. Have you money enough?'

Giles patted his coat pocket. 'More than enough, unless I find she's taken boat for the Low Countries,' he said, with a smile for the look of sudden alarm on Mrs Gedding's face. 'Do not worry, ma'am, I'll have her safe soon enough. In fact, I have no doubt I'll find her snugly ensconced with Lady Brandon drinking tea!'

All she has to worry about, Giles thought grimly as he sent the hunter down the drive at a controlled canter, *is the tanning I'm going to give her backside the minute I lay hands on her.*

Far from suffering any of the alarms or discomforts that Mrs Gedding feared for her, or which Giles, growing increasingly angry the further he rode, might have wished on her, Joanna had an uneventful journey to Wisbech. The roads were just as she had noted, there were ample finger posts and milestones to reassure her she was on the right route, the sun shone and the only people she encountered were well disposed and friendly to a passing rider.

The last five miles or so were, admittedly, difficult, for Moonstone was tired and Joanna felt it would be a long time before she could sit down again with any degree of comfort. But her flagging spirits lifted at the sight of Lord Brandon's charming house set in its landscaped park and the gatekeeper, respectfully touching his hat, was able to inform her that her ladyship had only returned from a drive a little while before.

She slid stiffly from the saddle at the front door and surrendered the reins to a groom, who was understandably surprised at the absence of an escort. At the front door she was received by a superior butler who regarded her dusty skirts and solitary state with hauteur. 'I could not say whether my lady is at home, Miss.'

'I know she is,' Joanna said wearily. 'Please just tell her that Joanna Fulgrave is here.'

'If you would care to wait in here, Miss, and I—'

'Jo!' With a shriek of delight the lady of the house ran down the stairs and enfolded Joanna in a comprehensive embrace. 'Darling Jo! Where have you sprung from? Did you write and the letter hasn't got here? Rooke, do not stand there like that—refreshments in the Chinese Salon at once! Bring in Miss Fulgrave's luggage.'

Joanna was swept in a swirl of chatter, silks and scent into a pretty room hung with Oriental paper. Her friend pushed the door to with a bang and, seizing Joanna by the hands, stood back to regard her from head to toe.

'Darling, you are covered in dust, your nose is pink and I have to tell you that that habit is quite three Seasons' old, but I am enchanted to see you. Where have you sprung from? How long can you stay?'

Joanna smiled at Georgy, knowing that until she ran out of breath it was hopeless to try and answer her. Lady Brandon was a handsome brunette with a voluptuous figure, wide mouth, endless enthusiasm and rather more kindness than common sense. Her doting husband, a good fifteen years older than she, maintained her in considerable style and indulged her in all her whims except that of living in London or whatever fashionable resort the season of the year demanded. Visits to London certainly, his lordship agreed. Prolonged stays, no.

Georgy, ever optimistic, was convinced that by next Season she would have worn him down; meanwhile she seized upon any diversion from their rural idyll with enthusiasm and the surprise arrival of her dearest friend from their Bath schooldays was a treat indeed.

She finally fell silent and Joanna said simply, 'I've run away.'

'Aah!' Georgy plumped down on the sofa, eyes wide. 'How wonderful! Who is he?'

'Who?' Joanna asked, making rather a business of settling her skirts as she sat opposite.

'The man involved, of course. Is he handsome and dashing and hopelessly ineligible so your cruel papa has forbidden him to offer for you? Or is he taking you for granted, so you have vanished in order to pique his interest? Or…'

'Well, if you must know, he is in love with someone else and is going to marry her.' It was hopeless trying to hide anything from Georgy. She had the instincts of a terrier and the staying power of a running footman.

'That is too bad! You mean the wretch has been flirting with you and then went and offered for someone with a bigger fortune?' her friend demanded indignantly.

'He has not the slightest idea I have any feelings for him at all,' Joanna said drearily, all the exhilaration of escaping falling away and leaving her feeling bereft and anxious. What would Mrs Gedding be thinking now? What was Giles doing? 'Georgy, might I ask you to send a groom with a message? It is all of twenty miles or so, I am afraid, and he must not, on any account, reveal where I am, but my kind hostess will be so worried if I do not write.'

'Yes, of course. Henry is not at home, so half the grooms are sitting around with nothing to do, I dare say. There, use my writing desk.' She managed to contain her questions while Joanna scribbled a note and addressed it, sitting silently until the butler came in with a tea tray.

'Rooke, please see this is taken by one of the grooms immediately. It is very important it goes at once and he must take a good horse. And, Rooke...'

'Yes, my lady?'

'On no account is he to say where he comes from. He is to leave the note and return at once.'

'As you say, my lady.'

'Oh dear, he will think it very odd,' Joanna said, closing the tambour front of the writing desk and returning to her seat. 'I am afraid he regards me in a very suspicious light altogether.'

'Well, he regards me as being completely unsatisfactory,' Georgy said with a twinkle, 'so he probably expects all my friends to be as well. Now, never mind Rooke, tell me all about this horrid man.'

By the time the ladies went upstairs to dress for dinner Joanna had poured the entire tale into Georgy's receptive ears. At first she kept the identity of the man she loved secret, presenting Colonel Gregory simply as an old family friend who had gallantly come to the rescue, but Lady Brandon knew her far too well.

'It is no good, Jo,' she declared, 'You blush every time you mention him: this Giles Gregory is *him*, is he not?'

'Yes,' Joanna admitted. 'But, please, Georgy, do not breathe a word of it to a soul. He loves someone else and I would die of mortification if he so much as suspected how I feel.'

'I can see that,' Georgy agreed, snuggling back into the sofa cushions. 'It would be the most humiliating thing. But tell me all about him—what does he look like?'

'Tall, very soldier-like, broad shoulders, grey eyes with the most fascinating black flecks, thick hair like dark honey which he should have cut more often...'

'Oh! He sounds *wonderful!*' Georgy's own, much-beloved husband was only a head taller than her, already slightly corpulent and the possessor of a hairline that could only be described as receding. Fond as she was, Georgy could not help but thrill at the description of the gallant Colonel. 'Go on, then...'

She listened with many exclamations and demands for detail to the account of how Joanna had discovered that her love was lost to her, her subsequent misbehaviour, the odious attentions of Lord Clifton and her decision to run away. But when Joanna began to haltingly recount what had befallen her at the Thoroughgoods' hands, the sparkling excitement left her eyes and she stared aghast at her friend.

Only the triumphant rescue restored her spirits. 'Oh, what a hero he is,' she murmured, dabbing her eyes with a fragile scrap of lace. The chiming of the clock recalled her to the time. 'We must dress for dinner in a moment; hurry and tell me how it all fell out.'

Joanna came to the end of her tale as they climbed the stairs. 'Well,' Georgy exclaimed, 'what an adventure! I am sure you have left out lots of important details, but we will have a comfortable coze after dinner. Now, what can we find you to wear? I declare you are more than a head taller than I am. Butterwick! Here is Miss Fulgrave come to stay and hardly a stitch to her back. I rely on you entirely...'

They returned downstairs again half an hour later, Joanna prettily clad in a gown that was somewhat too short but, as Georgy said, 'Who is to see it, my dear? Butterwick can let some things down tomorrow; meanwhile, Rooke and the footmen will have to take a care not to stare at your ankles.'

Joanna was just suppressing a giggle at the thought of the awe-inspiring butler so far forgetting himself as to ogle her ankles when there was a thunderous knocking at the front door. She gave a squeak of alarm. 'Giles!' and retreated rapidly upstairs to the landing.

Georgy, agog, her heart beating with excitement, continued to descend slowly while Rooke opened the door. Her eyes fell on a tall, travel-stained figure whom she had no difficulty in identifying as Joanna's colonel. Behind him she could see a big hunter, mysteriously saddleless, its head drooping and sweat staining its neck and flanks.

'Sir?'

'I wish to see Lady Brandon.'

Georgy shivered. The voice was deep, perfectly polite and with a bite of utter authority. It was also the voice of a very angry man who was reining in his temper hard.

'I will ascertain whether her ladyship is At Home,' Rooke responded with sublime disregard for the fact that his mistress was in plain view behind him. 'Who should I say is calling, sir?'

'Colonel Gregory. I regret to say I do not have my card case with me.'

Georgy felt it was time to take a hand. The Colonel's patience appeared to be wearing thin, which was understandable if he had just ridden almost thirty miles bare-backed. Although why he should be reduced to such straits…

'Thank you, Rooke. I am Georgiana Brandon.' She held out her hand, tipping her head back to look up at Giles as his large, capable grasp closed around her pampered plump fingers.

'I sincerely trust you know why I am here, ma'am.'

'Really, I cannot—'

'Lady Brandon, I implore you not to play games with me.' The firm grip did not release her. 'If Miss Fulgrave is here safe with you, that is one thing. If she has not arrived, it is most serious and a search must be undertaken immediately.'

Georgy could feel Rooke at her side bridling with indignation that she should be so abruptly addressed, but the look in those dark grey eyes was one of such concern that she could not prevaricate. 'Yes, Colonel. Joanna is here, and quite safe.'

He freed her fingers and for a fleeting moment his eyes closed. His hand reached out for the doorpost and Georgy wondered if he was dizzy with exhaustion, then the grey eyes snapped back to her face and all she could read there was anger.

'Then would you be so good as to allow me to speak to her?'

At the head of the stairs Joanna gripped the banister and strained her ears. Giles's voice came clearly to her and under the controlled cadences of his voice his rage was all too plain for her to hear. She had never heard him speak so levelly. *No, Georgy*, she pleaded inwardly, *do not let him in!*

'I am sorry, Colonel. Joanna is far too tired to receive visitors tonight.'

'Then perhaps you would be so good as to give her a message, Lady Brandon. I will return here the day after tomorrow with a chaise and a chaperon and I expect her to be ready to travel back to Hertfordshire without further prevarication.'

'That is not necessary, Colonel. I have invited Joanna to stay.'

'I am sorry to contradict you, ma'am, but Joanna's parents have charged me with returning her to her home.'

'She does not wish to go.'

'Oh, brave Georgy!' Joanna whispered under her breath.

'What Miss Fulgrave wants is, I regret to say, neither here nor there. She is under age and unmarried and therefore under the authority of her father, who has entrusted me with her safe return. I am sure I do not have to tell you what an outrageous risk she took, riding all this way alone?'

'Well, yes, of course, it was most imprudent...'

'And I may rely upon you to ensure she remains here safely until I return for her?'

'I...well...yes, very well, Colonel.'

'Oh, Georgy, how could you?'

'Thank you, Lady Brandon. I wish you good evening, ma'am.'

The door had hardly shut behind him when Joanna came running down the stairs. 'Georgy! I cannot have heard aright! You have never promised to let him take me away?'

'Shh, Jo dear.' Georgy cast a speaking glance at the butler and swept her indignant guest into the dining room. 'Thank you, Rooke, we can serve ourselves, I will ring when I wish the courses removed.'

The butler bowed himself out, followed by both footmen, and Georgy plumped herself down in her chair. 'Don't glare at me so, Jo! What could I do? If I had said no, he would have marched in here and dragged you off, I feel sure of it.' She shivered delicately. 'He was magnificently angry—I am half in love with him myself.'

'Well, you may have him,' Joanna retorted furiously, splashing water into a cut-glass flute with scant regard for its fine rim or the polish on the table. 'He is angry because I defied him and he is used to people obeying his every order.'

'Now, Jo, do calm down and be reasonable. He was angry because he was worried about you, and exhausted. Do you realise he had ridden here bareback? Goodness knows why.'

'I hid all the girths and the bits from the bridles, too.'

'That was clever—although it has done nothing for his temper, I fear. But, Joanna, truly, he was so anxious about you—he only became angry when he was sure you were safe.' She regarded Joanna's stormy face. 'Have some smoked trout, or a little of this chicken; no wonder you are so fractious, you must be starving.'

Joanna reluctantly accepted the food, then began to eat ravenously. 'Oh, I had no idea I was so hungry! But, Georgy, you cannot truly mean to let him take me away when he comes back?'

'I really have no choice, dearest. But Jo, why is

that so dreadful? You will have to spend the summer in Hertfordshire with the Tasboroughs—'

'Baby sitting and being disapproved of by Alex. And that horrible man Clifton will call and try and make me marry him.'

'Then tell him "no". This is not the Middle Ages and your father cannot lock you up in some tower until you relent. And quite frankly—' Georgy helped herself lavishly to spiced prawns '—you could hardly be in any more disgrace than you are already.'

'Georgy.' Joanna put down her knife and fork with some emphasis. 'I am in love with Giles Gregory. You are telling me that I have to spend days in his company and that of a disapproving old puritan with a face like a weasel being sent home in disgrace with nothing to look forward to but the attentions of a loathsome man and the news that Giles's wedding has been announced.

'And when Lord Clifton has finally given up and Giles is safely married to his rich, eligible, lovely wife I will have nothing to do with my life than to dwindle into an old maid.'

'But how would staying here help?' Georgy said imploringly. 'It would save you the journey in the Colonel's company and the stay with the Tasboroughs' but you would still be no better off.'

'You told me that you were going to persuade Lord Brandon to take you abroad. You will need a lady companion. I could perform that role, and when we returned I could find employment with other ladies who wish to travel, for you could recommend me and my languages are excellent. I learned them for Giles,' she added bitterly.

'Oh, Jo, I am so sorry.' Georgy put down the serving spoon, which she had just loaded with yet more spiced prawns. 'I was going to tell you, only your news was so exciting. I am increasing and it will be at least a year, if not more, before I will be travelling on the Continent.'

Chapter Twelve

Giles walked stiffly across the gravel to where the Squire's hunter stood, its head low. 'Come on, boy.' He picked up the reins and started to lead the tired animal down the drive. 'We'll find a good inn in Wisbech with a warm stable for you, a bucket of oats and a good rub down.' The thought of the human equivalent—a hot bath, a thick beefsteak and the depths of a feather bed—were powerfully attractive.

He had been right the other evening to think he was getting middle-aged, he mocked himself grimly. A thirty-mile ride across country, even bareback, was no excuse for the weariness that gripped him. But he had not felt like this until he knew Joanna was safe: then the exhaustion had gripped him.

'Damn it,' he remarked to the horse, which cocked one ear in response, 'she's turned me into a worrier. Do you think I am overreacting?' The horse snorted and butted him gently with its nose. 'Hmm? You are right; I have absolutely no confidence that Lady Brandon could stop Joanna doing precisely what she wants, when she wants to, however good her ladyship's intentions are. Joanna has run away twice now because she thought she was about to be coerced; I am afraid she is quite capable of doing it again.'

With a resigned sigh he veered off the main carriage drive and made for the stables, the low roofs of which were just visible behind a high brick wall. The yard Giles found himself in had a faint air of neglect, then he realised that a larger and more impressive block in bright new brick and stone was visible through an arch. A groom emerged from a doorway, stopped at the sight of a stranger and then came forward knuckling his forehead.

'Can I help you, sir?'

'Yes, you can.' Giles continued forward, ending up leaning on the half-door from which the man had emerged and able to see through it to a line of large loose boxes. All were apparently empty except one where a dappled grey rump could be seen over the door.

'I have called to see my...ward, Miss Fulgrave, who is staying with Lady Brandon. You have her mare safely stabled there, I see.'

'Yes, sir. Were you wanting to look at the animal, sir?'

'No, no. I had not realised Lord Brandon was from home, and obviously it is quite ineligible for me to stay at the house with only the ladies there. Can you recommend an inn in Wisbeach with a good livery stables?'

The man waxed lyrical on the numerous excellent establishments, ending with some skill at the one owned by his uncle. 'Used to be a head groom, sir, your horse couldn't be in better hands. And my aunt cooks a powerful good beefsteak if your fancy was that way, sir.'

Giles noted the name and direction of the inn, gazing round the yard with apparent indifference as he did so. 'Thank you.' A coin changed hands, to the obvious pleasure of the groom. 'Your master has had new yards built?' He nodded towards the archway.

'Yes, sir. And a fine new lodging over the tack room for the grooms, sir,' the man enthused, usefully providing Giles with the information he had been willing to spend another ten minutes in conversation to extract. 'Why, thank you, sir,' he added as another coin exchanged hands and Giles turned to lead the hunter back out of the yard. *Wonder why he don't ride it?* he mused, watching man and horse disappear.

Giles, from years of military service when keeping one's horse in prime condition was both a humane and a possibly life-saving priority, fell into an automatic marching step and applied his mind to strategy. In the big house behind him he was acutely aware that another mind was also setting itself to counter whatever plans he had. The sight of Giles's grim smile might have given Joanna pause if she had chanced to observe it.

Five in the morning dawned clear and chill. Joanna's footsteps sounded hideously loud on the gravel as she hastened around to the old stable block, but she consoled herself that no one was about to hear her. In the quiet house Georgy was sleeping soundly, just as her doctor and doting husband ordered, without a thought that her errant friend was escaping yet again.

She paused in the yard, her eyes flicking over the empty space, her ears alert for any sound, but it was silent with no sound from the new stables beyond to suggest an early-rising groom was about his business. The double door into the stables with the loose boxes was shut, although above it the door into the hayloft stood open. The interior was in deep shadow and the hoist beam jutted out from it. With its dangling hook and chain it had an unpleasant look of the gallows about it.

Suddenly edgy, Joanna tugged back the bolts and set the door open, hesitating on the threshold at a sudden noise. But it was only the sound of Moonstone shifting round in her box to see who had arrived. The relief at seeing the alert head watching her was so great that the descent of a wisp of hay from above went unnoticed and it was not until a second fell, tickling her nose, that Joanna glanced upwards. And froze.

Giles was looking down at her from the hayloft door overhead. He was sitting with his back against the door frame, one leg dangling over the edge. He appeared relaxed and mildly interested at seeing her. Joanna was not deceived in the slightest. 'Good morning,' he observed pleasantly. 'Somewhat early for a ride, perhaps?'

'I...I...what are you doing here?'

'Waiting for you. I had every confidence that you would come.' Giles got to his feet in a smooth motion that belied the fact that he had been sitting motionless in the cold dawn air since three o'clock. 'No, do not run back to the house,' he ordered sharply as Joanna gathered up the trailing skirts of her habit and turned back the way she had come. 'I have no desire to have this conversation in Lady Brandon's presence, but if you insist, we will.'

With hope draining out of her, Joanna watched as Giles leaned out, caught the trailing chain and hook and swung himself down to the ground. Even in the midst of her mingled humiliation, anger and despair she could not but admire the grace with which he moved. 'You must have been very uncomfortable,' she ventured. He was certainly dusty and, knowing him as she did, she could see the tightness around his eyes from tiredness. But the grey gaze watching her was alert and watchful, not at all the gaze of a tired man.

Giles shrugged. 'One gets used to night watches. A roof over one's head is a luxury.' He glanced around. 'Come, in here. I do not want an early stable boy to see us at this hour of the morning.'

With a sigh Joanna allowed herself to be guided into the interior of the stables. A textured floor with a drain at its centre ran between two rows of large loose boxes, each surrounded by a high wooden partition topped with iron grilles and with double doors at the front. All of them were closed and apparently empty save for Moonstone's stall at the back, where she still watched them over the half-door, and the box behind Giles, which appeared to be used as a store by the stable boys.

Both its doors were open, a carelessly abandoned pitchfork was propped in the entrance and inside were piled boxes and bales. A sudden glimmer of a plan struck Joanna and she hastily dropped her eyes in case

Giles should see either her change of mood or the direction of her interest.

'Just what do you think you are about?' he began, giving Joanna a very fair idea of how he might sound to a subaltern who had been out on the tiles to the neglect of his duty. 'Setting out alone, into God knows what, on a tired horse…'

'Oh, Giles!' she said softly, not having to act in the slightest to produce the quavering note in her voice. She risked a glance upwards from under her lashes and willed the production of two large, glistening tears.

Giles, who was quite used to this sort of outrageous play-acting from Suzanne, entirely failed to recognise it in Joanna. 'Joanna…damn it, there is no need to cry…'

'Oh, Giles,' Joanna said again, on a falling note of despair. Quite unused to this sort of behaviour herself, she was at a loss as to what more to say, but her performance appeared to be working, for a second glance revealed that the Colonel's harsh expression had softened.

She took a stumbling step forward and cast herself with considerable energy on Giles's broad chest, catching him around the neck. Taken by surprise he took a step backwards for, whilst slender, Joanna was tall. Before his arms could close around her to steady her, she thrust out her right foot, catching it neatly between his ankles and threw her weight forward against him.

Off balance, Giles took another unguarded backwards step, the pitchfork caught him behind the knees and he fell back into the loose box.

Joanna was at the door in a second, dragging both top and bottom sections across, bolting them both to the door frame and to each other. Now she must saddle Moonstone up and be away before either Giles managed to scramble up and squeeze through the narrow gap between the top of the railings and the rafters, or his shouts attracted the attention of the grooms.

It was ominously quiet: he must be assessing the best way to climb out. Her heart thudding so loud that it seemed to drown out any other sound, Joanna ran down the aisle and dragged the saddle and bridle off their stand outside Moonstone's box.

'Good girl, steady girl. Stand nicely for me,' she pleaded as the grey sidled and stamped, alarmed by her haste and the urgency of her movements. It seemed to take an hour but, in fact, the horse was saddled in minutes and Joanna led her out into the yard with a scared glance at the box where Giles was imprisoned. There was still no sound: he must be building the boxes and bales into a heap to climb up. He would be so angry… Joanna clutched to herself the memory of that moment when she was in his arms, against his chest. Then she found the mounting block and was up and away, spurring the mare down the carriage drive with scant regard to the noise she made.

It was an hour later when a bemused footman opened the front door to a thunderous knocking and found a large, coldly furious and bloodstained man on the step. A second, incredulous glance identified the gentleman who had called the evening before. 'Sir?'

Giles scrubbed at the trickle of blood that kept blurring the vision in his right eye and snapped, 'Kindly inform Lady Brandon that Colonel Gregory requires urgent speech with her.'

'But, sir...Colonel...it is quarter past six in the morning!'

Giles simply stepped firmly into the doorway and shouldered him aside. At which moment, to the young man's undying gratitude, Rooke appeared. The butler was not best pleased at having had to struggle into his tail coat in haste and had an uneasy suspicion that his neckcloth was well short of his usual standards. His tone as he addressed the importunate visitor was less than subservient.

'Colonel! I really must ask you to withdraw, sir! I will naturally inform her ladyship that you called.'

'When will you do so?' Giles produced a large pocket handkerchief and attempted to staunch the flow of blood from the cut on his forehead. It did nothing to make his appearance any less villainous.

'At her ladyship's normal breakfast hour, naturally.' He took in Giles's expression and added, 'At ten-thirty, sir.'

Giles regarded him with an expression that had routed more strong-willed men than the butler. His voice, however, was pleasant as he remarked, 'You will go to her ladyship now and you will inform her that either she receives me in the room of her choice in fifteen minutes or I will do myself the honour of calling upon her in her bedchamber. Do I make myself plain?'

'Certainly, Colonel.'

'Indeed. Then go and do it—and if you are consid-

ering scuttling down the backstairs and summoning
support in the shape of a number of grooms or footmen, let me promise you that you will regret it. As
they will,' he added thoughtfully.

Rooke eyed the large right fist that was flexing and
unflexing and decided that discretion was the better
option. 'Philips! Get the Colonel some warm water
and a bandage for his head and brush his coat. Her
ladyship must not be discommoded—any more than
is inevitable.'

It was twenty minutes, not fifteen, before Georgy
sent Rooke to say that she would receive Colonel
Gregory and his expression as he strode into her boudoir was not conciliatory. Georgy gave a squeak of
alarm and shrank back against her maid, but to her
relief he merely bowed from the doorway and said,
'My apologies for inconveniencing you at this hour,
ma'am. If you will tell me where Miss Fulgrave has
gone, I will remove myself immediately.'

'But I have no idea! Surely she is in her chamber?'

'I can assure you, ma'am, that at half past five this
morning she was riding away from this house. Are
you telling me that you had no idea of what she was
planning?'

'No! None at all,' Georgy protested indignantly,
pushing back her lace nightcap, which threatened to
slip over one eye. 'She was cross with me last night
when I promised you I would let her go with you
tomorrow, and she was disappointed when I explained
that I would not be travelling abroad for some
months.'

'Then where will she have gone?'

'I do not know, she has no acquaintance in the

area—all I can think of is that she will try and reach her sister, Lady Willington, in Lincoln.' She looked distractedly at Giles, then appeared to notice for the first time the rough bandage around his temples. 'Are you hurt, Colonel? Will you not sit down?'

'Thank you, no, ma'am. A cut and a bruise merely, but head cuts bleed like the dev…very badly. Have you heard of an aunt of Joanna's? A Mrs Faversham?'

'Faversham? No…but how did you come to cut your head, Colonel? And if you knew what Joanna was about at five o'clock, why did you not stop her then?'

'Because,' Giles said grimly, 'she tripped me up with a trick I would have expected—and might have suspected—from a street urchin and locked me in one of your loose boxes. To be fair, I think she had no idea she had knocked me out.'

'Oh, how clever of Jo!' Georgy clapped her hands in delighted admiration, then broke off, biting her lip at his expression. 'I wonder where she learned to do that?'

'I shudder to think. Lady Brandon, I am going to gamble on Joanna attempting to reach her aunt in Norwich. May I ask you to write to Squire and Mrs Gedding—I will give you their direction—reassuring them that she reached you safely and that I am still on her trail? And can I ask you to return Squire Gedding's hunter to him? It is too tired to go on at the pace I must set.'

'Of course. But you cannot waste time hiring another horse in Spalding,' Georgy said. 'Rooke! I know you are out there! Send to the stables and have them saddle up his lordship's best hunter—that new one he justified to me by saying it would go all day.' She turned her brilliant smile on Giles. 'He won't mind, and in any case he is not due back for two weeks.'

By the time Lady Brandon had seen her husband's black stallion vanish through the gates and swing southeast, it was half past seven. Joanna was already realising that there was all the difference in the world between setting out on a fresh horse on a comparatively short journey, well armed with maps and taking off into the unknown with only the haziest idea of the distance and direction and with a tired horse under her.

By nine she was weary, hungry and beginning to doubt her recollection of simple navigation that her military reading had given her. The sun rose in the east, she knew that. Norwich was to the east of Spalding, so she had to travel towards the sun. But the sun moved. And none of the milestones yet showed Norwich on their carved faces. Soon she was going to have to ask, and she suspected that it was no use asking a yokel who had never travelled beyond his nearest market town. It would have to be someone of more sophistication—a yeoman farmer, perhaps—and someone of that sort would be very suspicious indeed of a young lady out by herself asking such a question.

Then Moonstone pecked and stumbled. Joanna reined her in and gazed around. Was there anywhere she might safely rest for a while? At least Giles would have no idea where she was going and would probably assume she would be trying to reach Grace in Lincoln.

An open gate slumped on its hinges and gave easy access to a flower-spangled meadow. The tempting expanse of grass sloped to a line of willows, giving the promise of water at their feet. Joanna turned the mare's head into the mead and at the water's edge slipped off her back. It was a perfect spot: the grass was lush and soft, the brook sparkled hardly an inch deep over bright pebbles and the willows cast a welcome shade.

She loosened Moonstone's girths, let her drink then hooked her reins over a branch and left her standing in the shade while she wandered through the long grass to where an old stump made a welcoming seat. An hour would rest Moonstone and give her a chance to think of what she would say to her Aunt Caroline. Would she help her? What would Joanna do if she did not? However uncomfortable, those thoughts were better than the alternative, which was to think about Giles, recall that strong, lithe body swinging down from the hay loft, the anger in his eyes, the feel of his chest under her flattened palms as she fell against him…

Worn out, Joanna dozed where she sat in the meadow, undisturbed by the buzzing bees, bird song and the ripple and plash of the stream as it hastened across the pebbles. Moonstone grazed placidly until the distant sound of hoofbeats made her raise her head.

Joanna smiled in her sleep, for Giles had come and was striding across the field towards her, his arms held out to embrace her, a look of tenderness on his face that made her start to her feet…

Chapter Thirteen

Jerked awake, and finding herself half-slipping from her perch, Joanna blinked in the sunlight, unsure where she was. 'Giles?' He had seemed so real, so close. Moonstone stamped her hoof and Joanna saw that her head was up, her ears pricked and she was watching the far side of the field.

A tall black horse appeared in the gateway, passing at the canter, then it was reined in and the rider pulled its head round to urge it into the field. The horse was unfamiliar, but the tall figure on its back was not. Suddenly filled with unreasoning panic, Joanna picked up the skirts of her habit and began to run, stumbling towards her mare. She glanced back over her shoulder; Giles had spurred the horse into a canter and it was gaining on her. He was riding one-handed, leaning sideways over the pommel, obviously intent on scooping her up as she ran.

Mindlessly, panting with exertion, Joanna dodged to the right, but the great hooves hardly broke stride as he turned the black after her. She twisted round, held up her hands in a futile effort to fend him off and was caught around the waist, dragged off her feet and up against Giles's leg as he fought to bring the animal to a halt.

There was a confused sense of plunging chaos as the horse, resenting the sudden kicking, struggling creature who had seemingly attached itself to its side, fought back against its rider. Giles dragged one-handed on the reins until it stood, then swore as Joanna wriggled out of his grasp and fell to the ground.

Sobbing, she took to her heels again, only to be brought down by a flying body that sent her headlong into the lush grass and landed painfully half on her back, knocking the breath out of her.

Unable to move, unable to do more than fight to regain her breath, Joanna realised that she was pinned down by Giles's body lying along her right flank. His left arm was thrown over her shoulders and his breath was hot on her nape. As rational thought returned to her, she wondered if he had knocked himself out, then realised that the sound she could hear was him swearing, very quietly, under his breath.

'Giles?' she ventured after several seconds when it seemed he was going to make no effort to move. 'Giles!'

'I am trying to decide whether to put you over my knee and give you a well-deserved thrashing and then strangle you,' he remarked conversationally, 'or whether simply to strangle you.'

'Giles!'

Abruptly she found herself turned so that she was on her back and he was over her, pinning her even more effectively than before. His body was hard and heavy and, from where his legs straddled her to the pressure of his elbows, pinioning her own arms as he raised himself to look down at her, she was aware of his every muscle, every breath.

'What the hell do you think you are doing?' he demanded and she realised that he was furiously angry. His eyes seemed almost black as he glared down at her, his breath, for all his control, was short and his mouth was clamped into a hard line.

'I couldn't let you take me back, Giles. I...I will not tell you where I was going, but I did have a plan.'

'You had a plan,' he repeated flatly. 'So you take off into the wide blue yonder all by yourself. Have you forgotten what happened to you before, damn it? Have you forgotten the Thoroughgoods?'

'No, of course not, how could I? But you told me that very few people were like that, that I shouldn't—'

'Give me strength!' He closed his eyes for a moment, and released from their dominance Joanna noticed the stained bandage around his head and the dried trickle of blood on his temple.

'Are you hurt—?' she began, only to be cut off by the glare of those angry dark eyes as they snapped open again.

'Be quiet and listen to me and try, just try, to behave like the sensible young woman I know you to be. You are unlikely ever to come across anyone like the Thoroughgoods again in your life; agents for specialist breaking-houses are thankfully very rare indeed. But men who would insult, assault or very probably rape some undefended, innocent, empty-headed chit of a girl, wandering around the countryside without the slightest idea of where she was going or how she was going to get there—now I would say that men like that are to be found in every town and many a village.'

'Oh!' Joanna gasped at the stinging frankness of his words, even as she recoiled from the volume of his voice. She had never heard Giles raise his voice or lose control of his temper, now she was experiencing both at very short range indeed. 'I wouldn't let anyone take liberties,' she began, wincing at the vapid euphemism even as she used it.

'Like you are not letting me take liberties now?' Giles enquired, his voice suddenly silkily quiet. Joanna realised that she could not only feel the weight and lines and heat of his body, but that also the fact that he was powerfully aroused. Without conscious thought her untutored body shifted, accommodating itself more closely to his and instantly he snarled at her, 'Lie still.'

Shaken beyond words by the reality of his arousal, Joanna froze. After her marriage Grace had been asked by Mama to talk to Joanna about married life. She had given some indication of the changes necessary in a man's body to allow lovemaking to take place, but she had been very reticent. Giles was so very…but then he was a big man—obviously everything was in proportion.

Blushing hectically at her own thoughts as much as at the shocking intimacy, she closed her eyes and waited for what would happen next. Then opened them abruptly as she realised just what she was thinking, what she was hoping. Her body was beginning to ache very strangely, not with his weight, but from the inside with an unfamiliar hot yearning. She wanted to move against him, wrap her arms around him, incite him to kiss her again, but the expression in his eyes was so darkly fierce she dared not. 'Giles, you said I could trust you!'

'Damn it, Joanna, if you could not, neither of us would have a stitch of clothing on by now. And stop looking so scandalised. Your dream lover, whoever the bloody man is, is a man too and if you think you can behave with such recklessness with him without provoking a reaction, then you are deluded, my dear.' The hard stare softened. 'If I let you go, will you promise not to run away again?'

'What, not run away now, or not run away again ever?' she temporised, forcing herself to think about anything but the immediacy of his body, of the thin barrier of clothing between them. About the fact that he undeniably desired her and that she wanted nothing more than for him to prove just how much.

'Never again. I warn you, Joanna, you have run the length of my patience. Any more and you will discover exactly what that means. Promise me.'

'No.' She shut her eyes, the only defence against his will, which overwhelmed her, mastered her as surely as his long hard body had subdued hers beneath it.

'Promise me.' He was speaking against her lips, his breath feathering the sensitive flesh like a kiss, his hands cradling her head. She could feel the pulse in his wrists beating strongly and the rhythm of her blood leapt to echo it. 'Promise me.' It was a whisper, soft yet compelling. Her lips parted to deny him, but no words came. There was only the heat of his mouth over hers, the insidiously gentle pressure of his fingertips tangling in her hair, the utterly dominant male weight of him fitting so perfectly to her slender frame stretched beneath him.

Time stopped. Around them the flowers opened to the warm sunlight, to the thrumming bees that pillaged each golden heart for its pollen. Overhead a lark spiralled upwards into a cloudless blue sky, singing as though its heart would break, rising, rising, until the human figures below it were a dot in the green of the meadow.

They breathed with one breath, shared the same heartbeat. Without conscious thought Joanna breathed, 'I love—'

And found herself free of Giles's weight, jerked upright, shaken until her eyes snapped open. *'I know you love him!'* She was kneeling, facing Giles, his hands hard on her shoulders. 'I know you love him,' he repeated quietly. 'But how does running away help? What were you going to do?'

Her breath was coming as though he were still riding her down. His own, despite the control she could feel vibrating through his hands, was short. Shaken out of all attempt at pretence, she gasped, 'I was going to my aunt near Norwich. I knew you would never find me there.'

He smiled at her wryly. 'In fact, I know all about Aunt Caroline; your mama suspected you might go to her. But even without that knowledge, did you think I would give up? Did you really believe I would rest until I had found you again? Joanna, look at me.'

She shook her head, bending her neck until her hair, loosened in the struggle, shielded her expression from his eyes. Giles lifted his hand from her right shoulder, smoothing back the curtain of black silk that slithered over his fingers with its own caress. Joanna found her chin raised inexorably and met his gaze.

The anger had gone, and with it the blackness, leaving once again the cool grey stare that seemed to transfix her. 'You have no hope of eluding me, Joanna. Believe it.' She nodded, resisting the impulse to turn her cheek against the hard, gentle palm with its calluses from years of riding and weapon-handling. 'Promise me you will not try to escape and I will take you to Tasborough and Hebe. No chaperon, no carriage. We will ride, stay at out-of-the-way inns.'

'And…' It was difficult to speak, her voice cracked. Joanna swallowed hard. 'And if I do not promise?'

'I will tie you to the horse and there will be no inns. I will find barns to sleep in.'

She met his eyes, met the implacable resolve in them and believed he would take her back, trussed and thrown over his saddle bow if that was what it took. 'But if we are together for days I will be compromised…'

'I am escorting you with your parents' permission. This is not what they had envisaged, but I can assure you, as I will assure them if necessary, you are going to be delivered into Hebe's hands in as perfect condition as you left your own home.'

Her gaze shifted under his. 'Being alone is enough. Spending nights alone, however blamelessly, is enough if it is discovered.'

'Then we had better be sure we are not discovered, because believe me, Joanna, I have no wish to find myself married to you.' He smiled grimly at the sudden flare of feeling reflected in her wide green eyes. 'I find myself strangely sentimental: I require love in marriage, Joanna.'

'So do I,' she snapped back, hating herself for the jealousy that flooded through her.

'Then we are agreed.' She stared back into the inimical eyes and nodded. 'You do not try to escape? You give me your word?'

'Yes. I give you my word.' Joanna held his gaze long enough for him to read the truth in what she said, then twisted away to sit with her profile to him.

Giles let out his breath in a long exhalation and let his long body topple back on to the lush grass beside her. Joanna was conscious that he was letting the tension ebb out of him like a big cat relaxing in the sun as he lay on his back at her side, his eyes narrowed against the glare of the summer sky. He turned his head to look at her, crushing buttercups under his cheek. 'Did I frighten you? I am sorry if I did.'

'You meant to frighten me,' Joanna said without rancour. After the almost unbearable closeness and emotion of the past few minutes there was a sense of release. She felt very comfortable with him all of a sudden, just as long as she did not let herself think with her body. 'It worked. I should not have run when you came into the field, but I had been asleep, you see, and you seemed like someone from a dream that had suddenly become a nightmare.'

'You were dreaming about that damn…that man?'

'Yes,' Joanna admitted shortly. 'Oh, look, you like butter—the buttercups are reflecting all gold on your face.' She smiled as he brushed the flowers away, then added, 'But I wish you would tell me about your head. How did you hurt it.'

'Ow! Stop touching it,' Giles protested, pushing her hand away. 'I hope you are proud of the damage you did when you pitched me into that loose box.'

'*I* did that? But how?'

'Well, you tripped me up with a trick I would have expected from any street urchin, but not a young lady—more fool me—and then I fell over a pitchfork, landed on a bale, rolled off it and hit my head on a crate. A most effective attack.' He studied the mingled horror and shameful pride on her face and added, 'You make me feel middle-aged, Joanna Fulgrave.'

'Middle-aged! Oh, no—that is preposterous! How could I make you feel middle-aged?' she protested, laughing at him.

'You and Suzy between you.' Giles sighed, getting to his feet with the careless grace of a youth of sixteen and reaching out hand. 'You make me feel middle-aged and sensible.'

Joanna was very certain that whatever Lady Suzanne made Giles feel, it was not the onset of middle age. The feeling that had swept through her, and which she could only compare to the sensation of having had one glass of champagne too many, left her abruptly. She scrambled to her feet without taking his hand and stalked off towards Moonstone who was making friends with the black hunter.

'Well, if we are to travel in easy stages because of your age, we had better get going again,' she threw over her shoulder, then dodged laughing behind Moonstone's dappled hindquarters as Giles made a mock-threatening grab for her.

Once mounted, Joanna asked, 'How long will it take us?'

'Two days, three possibly.' He squinted up at the sun, appeared to do a rapid mental calculation and turned left out of the gate. 'You really were going to go to your aunt this morning? You did not have some other bolt hole you haven't told me about?'

'No, really,' she admitted ruefully. 'I knew that if she would not take me in I had run out of options, other than to go to my sister Grace. But she would have only sent me home and, in any case, I have no idea how to get there. Not like when I ran away from the Geddings. I had worked out my strategy and made notes from atlases…do not laugh at me!'

Giles was failing to suppress a grin, but he apologised solemnly in the face of her indignation. 'And where did you learn all about strategy, might I ask?'

'Er…I read about it because of William,' she said hastily, crossing her fingers. 'When he was army-mad, you remember. He kept wanting to talk about famous battles and marches and so I read some books so I could talk more sensibly to him.' Well, it was partly the truth, although the person she wanted to have the conversations was not her young brother. 'And I remembered about having an objective and then working out one's strategy for achieving it, and what tactics one needed to employ.'

'I am impressed: most people get in a muddle over the difference between strategy and tactics. Shall we canter? I think we cannot be far from March.'

The long, fine July day passed for Joanna in un-alloyed happiness. She was with Giles, riding in easy companionship, and although they spoke little it seemed as though they had no need to and understood each other without words. He would glance at her and she would nod and urge Moonstone into a canter, then just as she was feeling a little tired, he would rein in and they would walk along the quiet lanes, heavily fringed with white clouds of cow parsley, occasionally pointing out to each other a view, a picturesque ruined church or a deer grazing at the edge of a coppice.

They found an inn on the outskirts of Chatteris where the landlady served them thick slices of ham and wickedly vinegary pickled onions with slabs of crusty bread and fresh churned butter. When they had finished Giles pushed aside his tankard and pulled out his notes, gleaned from Lord Brandon's head groom.

'Can you face another twenty miles?' he asked. 'If you cannot, we will stop for the night at Huntingdon, but if we can make it to St Neots we will be that much further on our way tomorrow.'

Joanna was beginning to feel both tired and stiff, but she nodded firmly. 'Of course, that sounds far the best thing to do.'

To her surprise Giles reached out a hand and caught the point of her chin in his fingers. 'Brave Joanna,' he said softly. 'I know you are tired, I know you cannot help but be apprehensive about how all this is going to turn out, and I do believe you when you tell me your heart is broken—even if you don't think I take it seriously. Any other young woman of my acquaintance would be treating me to tears, sulks or tantrums by now.' The strong fingers gently ca-

ressed the soft skin of her throat and Joanna swallowed hard at the feeling it evoked.

'Even Lady Suzanne?' she queried tartly in an effort to suppress the desire to turn her cheek into the
palm of his hand, to beg for caresses.

'Suzy?' Giles snorted with laughter, the all-too-
familiar expression of tender forbearance coming into
his eyes. 'Suzy would have decided to run away with
her maid, her lapdog, at least two portmanteaux of
garments and a courier to enable her to secure the
most comfortable accommodation at every stop. Under these conditions she would have burst decora-
tively into tears fifteen miles ago, called me the
greatest beast in nature and insisted on a detour into
Huntingdon for some shopping to soothe her fractured
nerves. The temptation to elope with Suzy, just to
watch the havoc she would wreak along the way, is
almost irresistible.'

'But doubtless the thought of your father's disapproval prevents you?' Joanna said sweetly, her nails
digging into her palms.

'It would certainly greatly distress him,' Giles
agreed. The General would have another seizure, just
at the thought of such a scandalous occurrence, Giles
reflected with grim humour, although of all the things
that he might do to incur his father's wrath, eloping
with Lady Suzanne was about the least likely.

As they walked back to the horses, Giles reflected
on just why it had never so much as crossed his mind
to offer for Suzy until his father had demanded it and
why, when the idea was raised, he was so very certain
she was entirely wrong for him.

He loved her, faults and all; he admired her beauty

and charm and wilful spirit. She made him laugh, she took his breath away when she was attired for a grand ball, he forgave her whatever pranks she played. And yet he could never recall her arousing the slightest desire in his breast, not the faintest stirring of longing to possess her, either for passion or as his wife. He really must love her like the sister he had never had, he realised.

Whereas the young woman beside him was stirring emotions in him that were far from brotherly. She was less pretty than Suzy, she employed none of her ladyship's tricks of flirtation, none of her winsome, charming ploys to attract and amuse. But she had courage far beyond what that shallow, adorable little madam possessed. Courage and an innocent, passionate nature that was making it harder and harder for him to feel towards her as he should.

Giles came to himself with a start to find Joanna waiting patiently for him to give her a leg up into the saddle. He lifted her swiftly, anxious not to linger, aware of a new scent—something of her friend Lady Brandon's, perhaps. He swung up into the saddle and tried to make himself forget the long moments when he had lain across her body in the meadow. The feeling of her trembling, warm form against him, the new scent in her hair as it clouded around his nose and mouth.

And then the even more arousing sensation of her stretched out beneath him, supple and yielding and innocently reacting to the demands of a male body pressing down on hers for the first time. It had taken all his self-control not to lower his mouth to hers, to kiss her until she was dizzy with passion and then…

'Giles?'

'Mmm? Sorry, I was thinking.' *Thinking!* Damn it, he was working himself up into a thoroughly uncomfortable state and he must stop it immediately. Unfortunately Joanna's next hesitant question did nothing to turn his mind from the heated image of what she would look like naked.

'What are we going to do tonight…I mean…when we get to the inn? I have no baggage, and it is going to look very odd, is it not?' She broke off, blushing slightly and Giles administered a sharp mental kick and set himself to reassure her.

'We must agree our story and stick to it. Let's think: you are my sister. We set out on a foolish whim from St Ives to visit our great-aunt in Sandy, not considering how far it was in this heat. Then Moonstone lost a shoe and we had to find a blacksmith and you are far too tired to ride on to Great-aunt Julia's so we are having to spend the night in St Neots. How is that?'

'That is very convincing,' Joanna agreed approvingly. 'It accounts for everything neatly. What a deplorable turn for invention you have!'

Giles smiled back at her teasing, but his mind was racing. With that story they might find a respectable inn with two bedchambers available and hope their tale would cause no impertinent comment. But he was less sanguine about it than Joanna appeared to be. For a start, they looked not the slightest bit like brother and sister. Even if that went unnoticed, how would she feel when the reality sank in that she was spending a night alone in a strange place with a man? And one who only that morning had tumbled her in the meadow grass and had spoken frankly of male desire to her?

'Yes, quite deplorable,' Joanna continued brightly. Her mind too was racing with thoughts of the night ahead, although she had no intention of insulting Giles by allowing him to think she did not trust him. But his story, ingenious as it was, could perhaps be improved upon. Not for anything would she have him embarrassed by impertinent assumptions about his motives.

'However, it does not account for your bandaged head. How would it be if we say you had a fall— quite early on, to account for it not being fresh blood—and you thought we could carry on, but you had a worse headache than you expected so we have been riding slowly?'

She saw his frown and added, 'I know that you have not regarded it in the slightest, however much it is paining you, but can you not dissemble a little? And we must bicker, too—brothers and sisters do that.'

'Nonsense,' Giles said briskly. 'This is not a dramatic performance. I will deal with the landlord, you remain as unobtrusive as possible and we will brush through this as well as may be.'

Chapter Fourteen

Giles reckoned without an unexpected flair for the dramatic on Joanna's part. From the moment they wearily dismounted in the yard of the Grey Horse in St Neots, she began nagging gently with the air of someone speaking more out of habit than real anger.

'I told you we should have taken the carriage, Giles, now here I am without a hairbrush to my name. What Great-aunt is going to say when we arrive on her doorstep with you looking like a scarecrow, and me hardly any better... Thank you, my man. Where is the landlady to be found, if you please? Giles, stop scowling, you need to see an apothecary with that head, I do not care what you say.

'Ah! Mrs...? Mrs Henderson, good evening to you. Now, tell me at once, do you have two bedchambers for my brother and myself? You do? Excellent. Giles! Let the groom help you down, I really think you should go to bed immediately. Perhaps you should be bled as well, but doubtless the apothecary...'

The landlady blinked at the relentless, soft on-slaught as Joanna walked firmly into the inn. 'This seems very pleasant, Mrs Henderson. I will see the rooms directly. Can someone go for the apothecary at once, if you please? My poor brother—such a fall, and of course, a large man like that falls harder—he is my half-brother, as you have no doubt guessed, Mrs Henderson—did you say something, Giles? Ah, this room will be admirable for you, dear, in you go and lie down until the apothecary arrives.

'Now, Mrs Henderson, you are saying to yourself, what are these two people doing descending upon my inn without servant or luggage to their name? You may well ask. Our name is Pontefract, Miss and Mr Pontefract, and we are on our way to visit our great Aunt Julia in Sandy. Well, I say our great-aunt, but actually she is my half-brother's great-aunt…'

Joanna's voice continued its penetrating prattle, clearly audible to Giles through the wall from the bedchamber beyond. He lay down on the bed and gave way to barely suppressed laughter. He was still gasping gently and mopping his eyes when Joanna peered around the door, then came in, eyeing him disapprovingly.

'What *are* you about, Giles? Do pull yourself together. Mrs Henderson is an admirable woman and has entirely believed our story. Oh, stop it, you will set me off! She has sent for the apothecary, and the maid has gone round to knock up Mr Watkins at the haberdashery shop. Apparently he can provide such necessities as hairbrushes, tooth powder and, she gives me to understand, nightgowns. I do hope you have enough money. We must pay Mr Watkins, and our shot here, and the apothecary, and I will have to tip the maid I have engaged.'

Giles sat up against the pillows, sobered at last. 'You have engaged a maid? To sleep in your room?'

'Yes. I hope you do not mind, but it seemed just the sort of thing I should do, and I can't for a moment think Mrs Henderson will suspect anything untoward with me insisting on a girl to sleep on a truckle bed. I have assured her I never sleep alone, but always with my maid, and she appeared to think that showed a refined respectability.'

'Excellent. But why should I mind?'

'Well—' Joanna broke off and blushed. 'I thought you might think I did not trust you.'

'But you do?'

'Of course! Now quiet, here comes the apothecary, if I am not much mistaken. I am afraid you will have to endure my interference, for I am sure Miss Pontefract would want to supervise everything.'

Fortunately the apothecary showed no inclination to bleed Giles, and politely turned his 'sister' out of the room before cleaning up the cut, inserting two stitches and rebandaging it.

To Joanna's indignation, Giles called for supper to be eaten in a private parlour and then sent her up to bed before settling down with a London news sheet and a bottle of the Grey Horse's excellent brandy.

Despite her indignation and the presence in the truckle bed of Polly the maid, Joanna fell into a deep sleep almost immediately.

When she woke with a start it was pitch dark and Polly was snoring loudly in her corner. Muttering, Joanna turned over and pulled a pillow tight around her ears, but the rasping penetrated the goose feathers with an infuriatingly regular rhythm. She found she was lying there listening, counting the seconds until the next predictable snore.

Gradually she became aware of other sounds: the building cooling and settling for the night, the distant sound of a baby crying, a restless sleeper near at hand tossing and turning. It was difficult to orientate herself in the dark, but Joanna realised that it was coming from the room next door and that the sleeper in question was Giles.

Was he just dreaming or had he developed a fever from the blow to his head? Perhaps the cut was inflamed. For perhaps fifteen minutes Joanna lay undecided in the dark, expecting at any moment for the restless sounds to die away as Giles fell into a deep sleep, but they did not. Eventually she slipped out of bed and tiptoed out of the room. Behind her Polly's snores continued unabated, muffled as she cautiously closed the door and cracked open the one to the next room.

The shutter was open, admitting just enough moonlight for her to discern Giles laying on the narrow bed, the sheets tossed and rumpled, one pillow half on the floor. He was muttering; as Joanna hesitated in the doorway, he turned restlessly, flinging out an arm. Despite the nightshirt provided by the shopkeeper, he appeared to be naked under the twisted bed linen.

She should not be there, she knew, and certainly she should not be standing there letting her eyes stray over the muscular planes of his chest as though caressing him with her gaze.

There were so many reasons why she should not

be there and only one possible excuse for her presence—that Giles was ill. Joanna inched across the floor, bit back a cry of pain as her bare toes stubbed against a stool leg, and finally reached Giles's bed. She laid the back of one hand on his brow and to her surprise it was as cool as her own, with no hint of fever.

Puzzled, but relieved, Joanna reached down to pull the sheet over the distractingly bare chest and found her wrist gripped suddenly.

'Darling,' Giles said clearly and drew her down on to the bed on top of himself. 'My love.'

For one startled, wonderful moment Joanna thought he was awake and knew her, then she realised he was still deeply asleep, obviously in the toils of a dream into which her fleeting touch had intruded. And it did not take much imagination to guess that Giles was dreaming of Suzanne as his arm tightened around Joanna and his free hand drifted across her breast in a lingering, sensual caress.

Joanna gasped and lay still, her entire body tingling with a surge of heat. His hand flattened against the soft curves of her left breast, stroking until his fingers found the nipple which tautened in response, sending an aching arc of pleasure through her. Her entire body seemed to cry out for his touch as the drifting fingers conjured up sensations not only in her captive breast but, shockingly, down through her belly to her thighs.

Her entire body wanted to move under his hands, stretch itself along the length of his, savour the touch of his bare skin against hers, yet she knew she could not, must not move or she would wake him.

Giles's face was buried in the sweet curve of her

neck, his lips tasting the warm skin with tiny kisses, his tongue flickering lines of desire across the pounding pulse at her throat.

Joanna forced back a groan of desire and tried to push back the clamouring demands of her body long enough to think before it was too late. If she stayed where she was, it could only be a matter of moments before she lost all will-power, all self-control and simply allowed herself to be swept along on the tide of sensation his hands and mouth were orchestrating within her inexperienced body.

If she woke him, Giles would be appalled at having compromised her beyond redemption. Somehow she had to free herself from his arms, get away from the bed without rousing him. She caught his roving hand in hers and raised it to her lips, nibbling the fingertips while she slipped from the mattress. Giles reached for her blindly, but she placed his hand lightly on the rumpled sheet and almost ran to the door.

Safely outside, she leant back against the panels and drew a long shuddering breath, willing the cool of the draughty corridor to steady her quivering limbs, calm her ragged breathing. That it could be like that! That she could feel so transported, so utterly possessed when all he had done was to caress her breast, kiss her neck. Why had nobody warned her? Her sister and Hebe both obviously enjoyed the marriage bed, that much was discreetly obvious in the warmth of exchanged looks with their husbands, the fleeting caress in passing. But *this!* What would it be like to make love to completion, to be joined utterly to his strength, to know Giles's as intimately as it was possible to know another human being?

Then the heated fervour began to fade, leaving her shivering and bereft in the bare corridor. She would never know what that ultimate experience was like because all she had done was to steal his kisses and caresses from another woman, one who was so close to him that she haunted his dreams and racked his nights with desire.

On the other side of the panelled door Giles turned his head restlessly on the pillow and murmured, 'Joanna?' then lay still as the dream faded and was gone.

The next morning the landlady was concerned to see that her guests appeared to have slept badly, a worrying matter for a woman who prided herself that her feather beds were the best of any of the town's hostelries.

Giles, who had experienced a torrid night of powerfully erotic dreams, managed to produce a smile and the assurance that it was only the remains of his headache that had disturbed his sleep. Joanna, equally heavy-eyed and subdued, confessed that she had found the church clock disturbing as she was unused to having one so close.

It was true enough. She had lain awake, her mind endlessly recreating those moments in Giles's arms until her body roused into restless desire again and she was forced to get out of bed and pace up and down the room in the chilly dawn light, willing the chiming hours to move faster and release her from the prison of her memory.

Nor did the fresh air and stimulus of being mounted and on the road again appear to lighten their mood.

Giles assumed that Joanna was anxious about the journey and her reception when she reached the Tasboroughs, she that he was missing Suzy. Yesterday's camaraderie had quite vanished and they rode almost as two strangers, forced together by circumstances and awkwardly having to make the best of it.

Joanna let her glance flicker across to Giles, to be met by a guarded look in his grey eyes. *He is tired of having to look after me,* she thought miserably. *He is worried about his father and missing Lady Suzanne. I should never have run from Georgy's house. I should never have entered his bedchamber last night.*

Oh, but her body still vibrated from his touch in the strangest way. Once, she had tried the harp, thinking that she should improve her musical performance, and she could still recall the humming vibration of a plucked string taut under her fingertips. Her body felt like that all through. And worse, she seemed to ache deep inside as though something was missing...

Joanna did not glance at Giles again unless he spoke to her and tried to focus instead on what she could possibly do with her life when the summer was over. Could she face another Season?

After what seemed like an hour of silence Giles said abruptly, 'We can make it to Tasborough by this evening if you feel up to it. I would prefer not to risk another night on the road.'

'I would prefer it, too,' Joanna agreed fervently. She was determined to ride until she dropped if there was the chance that they could spend the night somewhere where they did not have to pretend, watch every word and action. And somewhere where she could sleep in a chamber far from Giles.

'Colonel, sir, and Miss Joanna, good evening.' Starling greeted the pair of them calmly as they stood on the threshold of Tasborough Hall, apparently unconcerned by the unheralded arrival of his lordship's best friend and her ladyship's cousin at ten of the clock, without baggage or attendants and distinctly travel-stained.

'You were expecting us, Starling?'

'Indeed we were, Colonel, although upon which day or time we were not certain. I will inform her ladyship of your arrival immediately, she was about to retire. His lordship is out, but is expected back shortly. Mrs Fitton will show Miss Joanna to her room.'

Joanna was old friends with the housekeeper, who showed not the slightest surprise at her arrival with Giles as she ushered her to her usual chamber. 'There is hot water on its way, Miss Joanna, then I hope you will go down to her ladyship directly. She's been that anxious about you and I have no doubt will not go up to bed as she should until she has seen you with her own eyes.'

'How is her ladyship?' Joanna asked, not a little anxious of the effect her disappearance and the subsequent hue and cry might have had upon a lady so close to her confinement.

'Blooming!' The housekeeper clapped her hands together in barely suppressed excitement. 'Blooming! She says it might be twins, and you only have to look at her to think she might be right.' A cough from the maid bringing the hot water recalled her to the fact that she was speaking to an unmarried girl. 'She's in the Panelled Parlour, Miss.'

Joanna hurried down, not realising, until she pushed open the door and saw her cousin, how much in need of some feminine support and comfort she was. 'Oh, Hebe!' And then she was clasped in her arms on the sofa, being kissed and patted. For almost a minute the two of them clung together, both fighting back tears, then Joanna sat back and managed to produce a watery smile.

'Are you well, Hebe? And Alex and little Hugh?' Reassured on these points, she asked, 'Have you heard from Mama or Papa?'

'At length, dearest, they sound... Oh Giles, how well you look!' She held out her arms as Giles strode into the room and bent to kiss her, then added, half-seriously, 'And if you say one word to Alex about twins I will never speak to you again. He has been intolerable ever since you suggested the possibility to him; I have been fussed to death and it is all your fault, you wretch. But I forgive you everything for rescuing Joanna.'

She glanced at Joanna, taken aback by the bleak look in her cousin's eyes. 'Oh, my dear, I am sorry, I was telling you about what your parents said and now you are worried. There is no need, they sound positively *forgiving*. Yes, I know, I was surprised too, but Aunt Emily has sent all your best clothes over and has begged me to keep you for as long as I wish. All she asks is for me to write the moment you arrive. There is a note for you, and one for Giles. There, on that little table.'

Joanna took the folded paper and regarded it dubiously. That she had been so easily forgiven seemed highly unlikely; no doubt Mama had not wished to sound too angry in her letter to Hebe so as not to worry her. 'I will read it in my room,' she said. 'We must not keep you from your bed, Hebe.'

'No, nor I from yours.' She allowed Giles to help her to her feet and tucked Joanna's hand under her arm as they walked from the room. 'Goodnight, Giles dear.' When they were out of his hearing she remarked rallyingly, 'I have to tell you, Joanna, that not only do you look extremely tired, you are positively brown from the sun. I can see all our cucumber frames being stripped before we can restore your complexion.' This sally produced nothing but a faint smile and she turned to catch her cousin by her forearms, holding her so she could study her face properly. 'Go to bed, Joanna darling, and sleep well. In the morning I can see we are going to have to have a long talk.'

Joanna climbed wearily into bed, the soft imprint of Hebe's kiss on her cheek both a comfort and a reproach. Hebe was obviously concerned for her and would want to help. Yet how could she begin to tell her anything of the truth behind her scandalous escape or Giles's capture of her?

Chapter Fifteen

Joanna slept so deeply that when she finally roused it was several moments before she could recall where she was. When she finally realised that she was safely at Tasborough, she lay rubbing her eyes and watching the play of sunlight through the gap in the drawn curtains. Images and memories of the past few days ran dreamily through her mind. Eventually she roused herself sufficiently to tug the bell-pull beside the bed.

The maid who usually looked after her when she stayed at Tasborough popped her head around the door with a speed that made it obvious that she had been waiting in the dressing room.

'Good morning, Miss Joanna.' She threw back the curtains with both hands, letting in a flood of light and a view across the beech woods towards the Vale. 'I'll have the hot water brought up, miss. The hip bath is all set out in the dressing room. The Colonel said you would be wanting a hot, deep bath.' She whisked out again as rapidly as she had entered, leaving Joanna staring after her.

'*Giles* said I would want a hot bath? Why on

earth...ouch!' She struggled to sit up against the pillows, every muscle and joint complaining. 'My word, I am stiff,' she said to Polly as the maid came back, holding out a pale cream wrapper. 'I had forgotten just how far we rode yesterday. What a pretty wrapper, Polly. Is it one of her ladyship's?'

'No, miss. It is one of the new things Mrs Fulgrave sent over for you,' the maid explained, leaning over the bath to check the temperature of the water. 'There are some lovely gowns, Miss Joanna, and a parasol and all sorts.'

New clothes? Joanna's brow furrowed as she shed her nightgown and climbed into the steaming, herb-scented water. She must be well and truly forgiven if Mama had sent what sounded like a complete new wardrobe. The gift itself was wonderful, but she was far more thankful for the forgiveness: being at odds with her family had been one of the hardest things to bear about the entire situation.

'What time is it, Polly?'

'Nine o'clock, miss. Her ladyship said, would you care to take breakfast with her in her room? She usually has it at half past the hour.'

'Please will you send to say I would love to join her. Does anyone go down to the town with post in the morning? I really must write to my parents.'

'John will go down at ten, miss. There'll be just time after your bath.'

Clad in one of three charming new muslin gowns with a pair of wafer-thin kid sandals on her feet, Joanna sat down to pen the second note to her mother since she ran away. This one had just as many tear-stains as the first, but they were happy tears. Having seen the wardrobe her mama had sent, Joanna could not be in any doubt she was forgiven, even if she had not read the short affectionate note Hebe had given her.

And please give my most dutiful love to Papa and assure him that I am all too aware of the distress and anxiety I must have caused you. I will do my best to make myself useful here at Tasborough and look forward to seeing you all again very soon. With all my love, your affectionate daughter, Joanna.

She conned the two pages of closely written words and hoped that they conveyed her regrets. And yet… She folded the pages and wrote the address of the Bath hotel on the front before handing it to Polly to seal. And yet…she would do it again if she had to. She would most certainly not allow herself to be coerced into a loveless marriage, that was for certain, whatever the next Season held for her.

Hebe looked up from the fashion magazine she was scanning as Joanna walked into the room and said immediately, 'My dear! You look so fierce, whatever is the matter?'

'Good morning, Hebe.' Joanna bent to kiss her cousin's cheek and joined her at the little table set in the wide bay window of Hebe's bedchamber. 'I am sorry if I was scowling: it was simply that I am resolved not to allow myself to be pushed into marriage, however grateful I am that I appear to be forgiven.'

'The clothes?' Hebe rang the silver bell beside her plate. 'Yes, I wondered about those. They are a notable peace offering indeed. You may serve breakfast now, Starling, thank you. Has John taken the post? Miss Joanna will have a letter.'

'I have already given it to Polly, thank you, Starling.' Joanna took ham from the proffered plate and allowed Hebe to pour her a cup of coffee.

When Starling had left the room her cousin asked bluntly, 'Why did you not come to me in the first place, Joanna? You know I will do everything I can to help.'

'I thought…Mama said your confinement was very near, and from something she said it sounded as though you were very tired and perhaps Alex was a little worried about you—' She broke off and eyed Hebe anxiously. 'You are all right, are you not?'

'Absolutely fine,' Hebe assured her, buttering a roll. 'It is just that this seems to be the biggest baby in the world and the weather is so hot. And Alex will fuss so. If only Giles had not put the idea of twins into his head! I am delighted to see you and I want to do everything I can to help.'

'I am not sure anyone else can,' Joanna said ruefully. 'I ran away to think, but all I succeeded in doing was putting Giles to a great deal of trouble, inconveniencing some complete strangers—the Geddings, who are delightful people, by the way—almost ending up in a London brothel and distressing my family.'

'*A brothel?*' Hebe dropped her bread roll and stared aghast at Joanna. 'I wondered what she was so very tactfully avoiding in the letters I had from your mama.'

'I had better explain.' Joanna recounted the tale of her adventures from the moment she crept away from Charles Street in the dawn light to her rescue by Giles and arrival at the Geddings. 'And, Hebe, we must do something about those poor girls who have been already forced into prostitution in those places. I cannot, as an unmarried girl, but you could…'

'Yes, of course, we must discuss it soon, after the baby,' Hebe said distractedly. 'Joanna, I had no idea you had been in so much danger, it must have been terrifying. But why did you run away in the first place? And why did you not come to me from the Geddings? Your mama had agreed to that, after all.'

'I did not come because…because Mrs Gedding had found a horrible chaperon who guessed I was in disgrace and who was going to read me religious tracts all the way here. And I knew Alex would be furious with me for worrying you and I could not bear…' Her voice trailed away as she bit back a sob.

Hebe leaned over and took her hand. 'Could not bear what, darling? Surely you did not think I would lecture you?'

'You and Alex are so…so happy. And there's little Hugh and the baby coming and now I am never…'

Hebe reached for her reticule and passed over a square of fine linen. 'So it is a man? The reason behind all this?'

Joanna nodded, not meeting Hebe's eyes.

'What has he done to you? You can tell me, dearest. I will not be shocked, whatever it is. When you imply that now you cannot have a family of your own…'

'Oh, nothing like *that!* He has done nothing at all, except be in love with someone else.'

'But he made you promises, led you to believe…'

'No. He is quite blameless and he has not the

slightest idea I love him. But I do love him, and for ever. And when I found out that it was hopeless, that he loved someone else and wanted to marry her, I just could not think what to do with the rest of my life, and Mama insisted that I marry Rufus Carstairs, whom I hate. So I ran away to think.'

Hebe put down her knife and stared at her cousin. 'But when did you meet this man, Joanna? You have always been so…I mean, we used to joke that you were the perfect débutante.'

'I cannot tell you where I met him. The only reason I wanted to be ''perfect'' was for him,' Joanna said bleakly. 'Everything was for him. And, yes, it was a very foolish thing to do, for I never thought about the real man at all, only about my thoughts and my plans and my feelings. He was a dream, an ideal. Nothing you can say will reproach me any more than I reproach myself.'

'Then if you recognise that,' Hebe said, eagerly seizing on Joanna's realism, 'then you know it is not real and you can hope for another person to enter your heart and your life.'

'No.' Joanna shook her head sadly. 'I may have fallen for an ideal, and I know the real man is not a pattern book of virtues. But I still love him. I love him even more for being flesh and blood. And there will never be anyone else. Not while he lives.'

'Who is it, Joanna?'

'I will not tell you.'

'Do I know him?'

'I will not tell you.'

Hebe sat back, one hand on the swell of her stomach and winced. 'Stop kicking, Frederick!'

'Frederick?'

'It is what I call the baby—just in jest, you understand. I am sure he has eight feet, and all of them booted. Joanna, how can I help you if you will not confide in me?'

'You cannot help me, no one can. I must simply find my own way through this. If only I were an heiress, at least I could become an eccentric spinster and do something about those unfortunate women. As it is, I suppose I must become the typical unmarried daughter. I am sorry, Hebe, I cannot expect you to understand.'

'But I do. For several long, horrible weeks I thought that Alex was going to marry someone else. If that had happened, I do not know what I would have done or whether I could ever have contemplated marrying another man. It came right for me, Joanna; we must make it come right, somehow, for you.'

'I wish I had your confidence.' Joanna took a long sip of her coffee. 'But I am not going to repine, for that will not help me. Nor will running away, I know that now. I am here, I have your support, my parents appear to have forgiven me and I hope I can be of some use to you for a while.'

Hebe looked doubtful. 'Promise you will tell me if there is anything, anything at all...'

'I promise. Where is Alex?'

'He rode over to Giles's family home with him first thing. Giles is very worried about his father, as I am sure you know. Alex has promised to support the fiction that Giles is spending a summer of wild indulgence—you know about that as well, I expect?'

'I do. His mother sounds a most unusual lady, does she not?'

'She is charming, but very unconventional. When you get to know Giles really well you can see her in him. But I expect all you saw was the perfect cavalry officer!'

'Er…yes. He is certainly used to his orders being carried out, is he not?'

'Alex says he is the best officer of his acquaintance. It is so sad he is selling out, he would have had a glittering career.'

'He said something about not wishing to be a peacetime officer,' Joanna said indifferently. The pleasure of speaking about Giles was insidious. She was terrified of saying too much, yet to avoid the subject of her rescuer would seem suspicious. Or so she told herself. 'He is going to stay there—his home, I mean?'

'Oh, no. Would you pass the conserve. Thank you.'

'Of course, I was forgetting, he was planning on going to Brighton.'

'No. He is going to stay here—unless he finds things much worse at home with the General. I think he realised I would appreciate him distracting Alex and he said something about buying horses as well. Anyway, he seemed quite content to stay for a few weeks. And it will be company for you.'

'Oh, possibly,' Joanna said forcing an air of vagueness into her voice. 'Although I am sure the poor man has had quite enough of my society to last him a lifetime!'

Inside her heart was beating like a drum. Giles at Tasborough for weeks, Giles at meals, Giles every evening in the relaxed atmosphere of a family home. It had been difficult enough hiding how she felt from him, but now she would not be able to relax for a moment. How was she going to hide her feelings in front of Hebe's anxious, intelligent eyes?

To her relief, Hebe did not appear to want to know the details of their journey. Even the most tolerant cousin was going to baulk at the news of an unchaperoned night in an inn and long rides across country with no escort whatsoever. Joanna caught Hebe easing her position in her chair to give her back more support and guessed that, having got her safe and sound, she was just too preoccupied to think of delving deeper.

Giles and Alex did not arrive back until late afternoon, finding both ladies sitting under the shade of a spreading cedar of Lebanon on the back lawn. To Joanna's loving eye, Giles looked serious but as though a weight had been lifted from him. When Starling brought a tray of lemonade and cakes out, she changed position under the pretext of passing glasses and sat beside him.

'How did you find the General? Is his health still causing Lady Gregory concern?'

'I found him much better. Mama is very pleased with him and I could see the difference immediately. The stiffness has gone from the side of his face and, although he still has a hesitation in his step, it is much improved.'

'I am so glad,' Joanna said warmly, putting out a hand and squeezing Giles's without thinking. 'To be so worried about him at a time when there was an estrangement between you must have been difficult to bear.' She would have been pleased to hear that any person who had been unwell was recovering, but the relief on Giles's face made her feel as though she had received good news of one of her own family.

Giles placed his other hand over hers and smiled at her. 'You are a darling, Joanna.'

Her heart fluttered as though it were a bird he had captured with that strong gentle hand, which held hers within it. He was so large, so masculine close to and yet his voice was tender as he spoke the endearment. Joanna knew she was staring transfixed into his eyes, knew that Hebe and Alex were within feet of them, yet she could not move, could hardly breathe.

Then Giles's gaze shifted and his hand moved and the spell was broken. Joanna tried not to glance round guiltily to see if anyone had observed them. 'And is your father reconciled on the subject of your marriage and you selling out?'

'To the latter, a little perhaps. Not that he will admit it. He lectured me on wasting my substance around town. When I said mildly that on the contrary I had been out of town on an errand for a friend he snorted and said, ''Chasing some petticoat, more like!'', which was rather too close for comfort and I suspect I may have looked a little conscious of it.'

'And your marriage?'

'Now there, at least, we are now thinking as one. Lord and Lady Olney visited last week, which settled matters and put all misunderstandings to rights. They gave out that they had heard he was unwell, but I suspect Mama had said something to Lady Olney. If he is feeling strong enough, they have invited my parents to visit in August.'

'How wonderful. What good news for you,' Joanna said hollowly. Now every barrier in the way of Giles marrying Lady Suzanne appeared to have been swept away. 'Lord Olney's seat is near Bath, is it not? Will you accompany your parents?' Giles nodded, his expression suddenly unreadable, and Joanna guessed he was thinking about idyllic summer days spent courting the girl he loved.

'Joanna?' It was Hebe calling to her across the grass. 'Should you not move more into the shade? It is very hot and you look quite pale.'

'Thank you, but I am quite comfortable,' she called back, inwardly cursing her own lack of self-control. If she were to change colour every time Giles said something to her, she might as well make a public announcement of her feelings for him here and now.

Beside her Giles was also brooding inwardly although, with more practice than Joanna at concealing his feelings, very little showed on his face. He should never have held her hand like that just now. Certainly he should not have allowed that warmth to creep into his voice when she reacted with such sympathy and understanding to the news of his father. She was sweet and open and had come to be used to him, trust him. And then he did something to remind her of the intimacy she yearned for with that confounded man and she froze and turned from him.

If I knew who he was I would drag him here on his knees and make him beg for her, he thought fiercely. Did Hebe know his identity? How much had Joanna confided in her cousin? Not that he could ask.

He watched from under heavy lidded eyes as Joanna got up and ran to met the nursemaid who was bringing young Master Hugh out to his parents. The child saw Joanna and ran to her chuckling with delight, his podgy arms held up for her hug.

Joanna caught him and swung him up into her embrace, teasingly chiding him for being such a big boy. And something inside Giles caught with a sudden stab of pain. It was gone almost as soon as it hit him. With a soft exclamation under his breath he got to his feet and strode over to Joanna, lifting the child from her arms, but holding him close so she could continue the nursery rhyme she was chanting with the child.

'He is too heavy for you,' Giles said.

Hebe, who had turned to watch her son, broke off what she was saying to Alex, an arrested expression on her face as she looked at the little tableau. Then she turned back to her husband and asked urgently in a low voice, 'Is Giles engaged to be married? Or has he his eye on any young lady to ask?'

Alex, inured to his wife's rapid changes of topic, merely raised a dark brow and murmured, 'Doubt it. Hasn't said anything to me, and I think he would. He hasn't been home long enough surely—and most of that time he's been chasing round the countryside after Joanna.'

'That is what I thought,' Hebe replied, a frown marring her forehead. Under her breath she added, 'In which case either I am wrong or what Joanna said makes no sense at all.'

Chapter Sixteen

For the next three days Joanna kept as far out of Giles's way as she could contrive without appearing to avoid him. It proved unexpectedly easy and she found she hardly had to make excuses, for Giles was absent from breakfast to dinner, reappearing only to report visits to local horse breeders and farmers and successful purchases of breeding stock for his new project.

'Have we said anything to upset Giles?' Hebe asked Alex bluntly on the evening of the third day as he stood behind her at the dressing table, fastening a double string of pearls around her neck.

'No. What makes you think that?'

'He is out every day. Are you sure he is buying horses?'

'Well, if the animals occupying the south paddock are anything to go by, he is. Nice bay hunter he found over Tring way. I'm thinking of making him an offer for it.'

'He isn't courting someone, is he?'

'He's working exceptionally hard if he is managing

to do that and visit as many farms as he appears to be doing.' Alex laid his hands lightly on his wife's white shoulders and met her eyes in the mirror. 'What are you thinking?'

Hebe would only shake her head. She wished she knew.

But the next morning it was Alex who left home early to settle some boundary problems on his most distant farm and Giles who was alone at the breakfast table when Starling came in.

'I am sorry to disturb you, Colonel, but Hickling, his lordship's head groom, is outside and wishful to speak to you. I told him to wait until you had finished your meal, sir, but he says it is urgent.'

The problem was apparently his lordship's best mare, who was due to foal any day and who appeared to be in sudden difficulties. 'I daren't leave her until his lordship gets back, but I think the foal's the wrong way round and ought to be turned. None of the lads have any experience of that sort of thing and to tell you the truth, Colonel, sir, I don't like to attempt it on my own. Seeing what an eye you have for horses, sir, and knowing you are a cavalry officer, I thought mayhap…'

'Of course, I'll come and have a look at her, Hickling. Starling, if anyone wants me I will be in the stables. Oh, and, Starling, if her ladyship asks, there is no need to tell her why. Not a subject to worry her with at the moment, I think.'

Half an hour later the two men finished examining the sweating, distressed mare and exchanged grim looks across the loose box where she was circling restlessly. 'You are right, Hickling. The foal's all round the wrong way: I can see we've a long morning ahead of us.' Giles shrugged off his coat and waistcoat and threw them carelessly over the stable door before unbuttoning his shirt. 'No point in ruining good linen either. Now, what do we need? Hot water…'

'Plenty of soap… Ned! Run to the kitchens and ask Cook to put water on the range. Well, sir, are you going to take her head, or shall I?'

Unaware of the drama unfolding in the stables, Joanna finished breakfast with Hebe, who announced that she was going along to the housekeeper's room to discuss the deplorable state of the household linen. 'What are you going to do, dear?'

'I thought I would take my sketch book and go down to the south paddock to try my hand at drawing the horses. I flatter myself that I can draw a bowl of fruit or a landscape with tolerable ease, but I have never tried to draw an animal.'

'Are you sure it is not that you want to have a look at that little mare Giles was so pleased about at dinner last night?' Hebe teased.

'Well…of course, Moonstone is lovely, and Giles is most kind to let me ride her, but the new mare sounds very spirited.'

Hebe laughed. 'Well, try and see if you can wheedle him into letting you try her this evening. If he has another successful day, he will be in a good mood.'

Joanna found her sketch book in the drawer where she had left it on her last visit to Tasborough, picked up a wide straw hat by its almond-green ribbons and ran lightly down the stairs without bothering to set it on her dark hair. Despite everything she could not but feel happy this morning. The sun was shining, Giles seemed content with the way his plans were progressing and she had put on the most becoming of her new muslin gowns. The skirts were simple white fabric with a subtle figuring of white rose buds in the weave. The bodice was the same almond green as her hat ribbons, with puff sleeves and a narrow satin trim around the neck.

Humming quietly to herself and letting her mind wander dangerously towards daydreams of what Giles would think when he saw such a fetching ensemble, Joanna reached the bottom of the front steps and turned away across the lawn towards the corner of the complex of stableyards and the way to the paddocks. Out of the corner of her eye she saw a curricle turn between the high brick pillars of the front gate far off down the drive, but ignored it. A visitor for Alex and Hebe, no doubt.

She reached the entrance to a little yard, unused except for hay and feed storage, and would have walked past but for a pitiful mew from inside. One lost kitten, its eyes just open and its legs scarcely under control, was staggering across the cobbles, squeaking its distress.

'Oh, you poor little thing! Where's your mother?' Joanna dropped hat and book on to a low wall and went to pick up the protesting scrap of fur which immediately attempted to suck her finger.

'What a charming picture,' a voice remarked from the entrance to the yard. 'Quite the subject for a sentimental print.'

'Rufus!' It was Lord Clifton. His driving coat was carelessly open, he carried his gloves in one hand and, as she stared at him, he swept his hat from his blond head and made her an elegant bow. 'What on earth are you doing here? Have you come to visit Lord Tasborough?'

'Joanna, my dear, how low you rate your own attraction. I am here to see you, of course, and to continue the discussions we were having about our impending nuptials before you were so inconveniently summoned to your cousin's bedside. That is the excuse your parents are putting out, is it not? I would not like to get it wrong and cause embarrassment. It is always so difficult to recall in these cases what the story is. Chicken pox? The needs of an aged aunt? How convenient to have a cousin in the country.'

He strolled towards her as he spoke and Joanna backed away, still clutching the kitten which sank needle claws into her unfeeling hand. 'I do not know what you mean. My cousin asked for me to stay, and I am most certainly not going to discuss her health with you. As for our *nuptials*, I have told you before, I would not marry you if you were the last man...'

'On earth, yes, I remember.' His eyes glittered blue. Joanna backed away further then stumbled as her foot found the central drain. She regained her balance, but the few seconds brought him closer. 'But, you see, your parents do want you to marry me, and beside my title and my fortune I have the other inestimable advantage in their eyes of being willing to marry you despite whatever havey-cavey activities you have been up to the past few weeks.'

'If that is what you think of me, I wonder that you

care to offer for me.' Joanna continued to back, her
eyes never leaving his face. She had been so right to
mistrust him on sight, she thought, desperately racking her brains to recall whether this yard was entirely
enclosed or whether there was a gate through into one
of the others. But the sapphire gaze held hers like a
stoat with a rabbit and she could not turn her head to
look.

'As I told you before, Joanna, I desire you. You
are very beautiful: a collector's piece. And somehow,
whatever scrape you have got yourself into, I think
you are untouched. Ah, yes, you blush so prettily.'

Another man for whom a virgin was a prerequisite,
Joanna thought wildly. 'Perhaps, perhaps not,' she
said as casually as she could and saw his eyes narrow.

'I would not joke about it if I were you, Joanna.
Now, where was I? Oh yes, the list of your advantages. Respectable breeding, lovely manners when
you try and, of course, it would please my mama to
have me marry her old friend's daughter.'

She backed into something solid. Looking down,
she realised it was the mounting block. Carefully she
set the complaining kitten down on the bottom step
and straightened up. To either side the walls were
uninterrupted by anything but loose-box doors standing open to reveal bales of hay or sacks of feed. No
escape that way.

'How did you know I was here now?'

'Why, Mrs Fulgrave told me, of course.' He tossed
his gloves onto the mounting block. 'Now, come here,
Joanna, let me kiss you and we will discuss plans for
our honeymoon. Italy I thought. You will like Italy.'

Mama! How could you? Joanna realised with a

burning sense of hurt just why the lovely new clothes
had been sent. And she had fallen neatly into the trap
by putting on the most becoming gown that morning.
Her mother simply could not know what a hateful
man her best friend's son had become or she would
never have schemed for this meeting.

'Rufus, go away. I have absolutely no intention—'
He took one stride forwards and seized her, his hands
clamping hard on her upper arms as he jerked her
towards him.

'No! Stop it! *Giles!*' The last word was wrenched
out of her as Rufus pulled her hard against his chest
and fastened his mouth on hers. Joanna struggled
wildly, but the folds of his caped riding coat flapped
around her, confusing her, his hands were too strong
and then the sensation of his open mouth crushing her
lips against his was too overwhelming. She was
vaguely aware of being pushed backwards, of her heel
catching painfully on a threshold and the sense of
surrounding walls, then all of her being was concentrated on struggling against the hands that were on
her body and the mouth that seemed intent on dragging the breath from her until she surrendered.

Giles exhaled deeply and leaned back against the
cobwebbed stable wall. 'We've done it, Hickling!'
The groom grinned back, his face as sweat-begrimed
as the Colonel's. At their feet a filly foal lay in a wet
jumble of legs, the mare already licking and nuzzling
it, urging it to stand on its impossibly long limbs for
its first suck. Giles dragged his wrist across his forehead and stopped as the groom exclaimed, 'Don't do
that, sir! You're a right mess as it is.'

Giles looked down at his filthy torso and then across at Hickling. 'Do I look as bad as you?'

'Worse, Colonel. Better be putting yourself under the yard pump, if I can be so bold. Won't be doing for any of the ladies to be seeing you in that state, sir.'

Giles reached for his shirt, thought better of it and opened the half-door. 'Can you manage now, Hickling?'

'Aye, sir, thank you. I'll find you a bit of towel, sir.'

Giles stretched and strolled across to the pump. The sun was hot on his bare back and the sudden shock of cold well water made him gasp as he stuck his head and upper body under the flow. He emerged running wet with his hair sleeked down dark and scrubbed his head vigorously with the piece of rough linen the groom handed him.

'Thank you. I'll send my valet over to pick up my clothes, if he ever speaks to me again once he's seen these leathers.' Giles strolled out of the main yard, intending to lean on the paddock rails and admire his new bloodstock. Alex would be pleased with his new addition, and soon the Gregory stables would be full of mares carrying the new lines he hoped to breed.

There was a sound, abruptly cut off from further down the stable range. He raised his head, suddenly alert.

'Giles!'

Joanna wondered hazily how much longer she could struggle, and even if there was any point. Some instinct told her that Rufus was kissing her more out of frustration and anger than desire or even lust. She had spurned him, rejected him and his normally cold and calculating collector's instinct had turned to thwarted fury. If she stopped resisting, he would probably let her go: she had no real fear he was about to rape her. But every nerve in her body refused to submit to him or to let him think even for a moment that he could overcome her.

The violence with which he was wrenched from her sent her staggering against the wall. Dazedly she stared at the figure that appeared to fill the doorway. A figure out of some Norse legend: a tall, hard-muscled, half-naked warrior, the light gleaming off wet shoulders, his face and chest in shadow.

Rufus twisted in the man's grip on his collar then managed to fight his way out of his long coat to stand, fists raised defensively in front of him. There was nowhere else to go, his assailant seemed to block out the light. The man made no move to raise his own hands or to ward off any attack from Lord Clifton. There was contempt in the lack of care he took to watch his opponent as he shifted his attention to search the shadows until he could see Joanna, her dress pale against the brick walls.

Giles. She spread her hands against the rough surface to stay upright. She was not going to let herself collapse in front of him.

'How dare you!' Joanna felt a slight flicker of admiration for Rufus that he could summon up speech in the face of this elemental force. 'How dare you lay a hand on your betters, you clod! I'll have you dismissed.'

'Be quiet. You will apologise to this lady.' The

deep, quiet voice neither promised nor threatened. But Joanna saw Rufus take a step back.

'Who…I thought you were a groom…you are mistaken…'

'I told you to be quiet.' Now Joanna could hear the anger beating under Giles's unnaturally calm voice. 'Now, apologise.'

'I'll be damned if I do!' Rufus blustered. 'She led me on, the little hussy. Lures me in here, then screams the place down when I try and take a little kiss…'

The punch was so hard and so fast that Rufus did not even appear to see it coming. It lifted him off his feet and sent him across the box to land sprawled over a hay bale. As he lay there gasping, Giles hauled him to his feet by his collar and spun him round to face Joanna.

'Apologise or I will fetch a horse whip to you.'

She met Rufus's unfocused gaze with contemptuous green eyes.

'I…I'm sorry, Joanna—' He broke off gasping as Giles twisted his grip tighter. 'Miss Fulgrave. I misunderstood…I will not trouble you again.'

She closed her eyes and heard the sounds of Rufus being summarily propelled out of the box and across the yard. Footsteps came back, into the loose box, slowed, halted. Her eyes remained closed, all her concentration seemed to be taken by the friction of her fingertips on the rough brick keeping her upright.

'Joanna?' He seemed to be very close. She could feel the warmth of him in the cool, dim room. What did she look like? Her fingers crept to the torn neck of her gown, then up to her swollen lips. What must he think of her, struggling in the stables with a man?

Would he think her a flirt who went too far? Or worse, the hussy Rufus had called her?

The pain in her fingertips was suddenly worse. She was slipping down, the darkness behind her closed lids was full of lights and she was caught up, pressed hard against a chest that was bare and, puzzlingly, wet.

Joanna pressed her cheek against the flat planes, sharply aware through the dizziness of the crisp kiss of hair, the surprising softness of male skin over hard muscle. She turned her face a little and the touch of hair on her sensitised lips forced a gasp from her throat.

The movement stopped. Joanna forced herself to open her eyes a little and discovered that Giles had sat down on a hay bale and had her cradled on his lap, facing the doorway so the light fell on her face. He was studying it with painful intensity, his eyes almost black with the emotion she had seen in them before.

'I am sorry, Giles.'

'You are sorry?' His brows drew together sharply.

'I was not expecting him. I did not realise how foolish it was not to leave the yard immediately. Mama must have told him I was here. That is why she sent me all those new clothes, I expect,' she finished, her voice trailing away. 'I do not think he would have...forced me. I made him angry by rejecting him.' The expression of sudden fury on his face made her gasp.

'Never, *never*, apologise for this! Nothing you could have done justifies the way he behaved to you. Nothing.'

He tightened his arms around her and she flinched as he unwittingly touched the places on her arms where Rufus had gripped her.

'Let me see.' Shakily Joanna stretched out her arms. Already the bruises were darkening on the tender flesh of her inner arm. 'Oh, my God.' Giles closed his arms around her and pulled her gently against him, cradling her so that he did not touch the savage marks, rocking her gently until the pain of his accidental grip ebbed.

Joanna let her body mould to his, reaching around his body as far as she could until her palms were flat on his back, her breasts crushed against his chest. Her head seemed to fit exactly into the angle of his neck so that against her mouth she could feel the hard pulse beat in his neck. Through the thin muslin of her gown, dampened by his wet skin, she could feel the tantalising tickle of chest hair.

Her body, roused into fear by Rufus, changed insidiously until it was desire, not fear, that animated her, sent the blood tingling through her veins, started the deep, mysterious, intimate ache inside her. She wanted to arch into his body, twist in his grasp until she could press her lips to his, fall back on to the soft hay with his hard weight on her.

Her fingers flexed and spread, sensing the matt satin of skin under their pads, exploring the lines of muscle, the hard strength held in check. He was so taut under her palms, so still except for the slow, controlled rhythm of his breathing, the steady beat of his heart and a scarcely discernable vibration that seemed to resonate through her like a note of an organ when it has reached the point beyond hearing.

'Giles,' she murmured against his throat, not knowing whether it was a question or a simple word of thanks. 'Giles.'

Chapter Seventeen

'Giles.' He felt rather than heard the soft whisper against his throat. Could he let her go? He doubted it. He thought about opening his arms, releasing her, gently urging her to her feet and helping her inside to Hebe's care. And could not do it. His arms would not obey, his mind was not ready to exert its will.

She felt so right, curled trustingly against him, as though some sculptor had made a mould of his body and had created this being to fit within the curve of his arm, the shelter of his torso.

He thought about that first glimpse over Clifton's shoulder. Her wide defiant eyes, the bruised mouth, her hands spread against the wall to support her. Those eyes were closed now, he could feel the lashes caressing the tendons of his throat. The slender fingers were spread over his back muscles, unconsciously flexing in a way that made him want to roll her over into the hay, feel her beneath him as he had in the meadow, kiss that bruised delicate mouth into flowering response.

And he could not. He could do none of those

things. She was clinging to him out of shock and reaction and because he was familiar and she trusted
him. He had to start thinking again with his head, not
his body, not with that newly awakened part of him,
which was still unsure of what it was feeling but
which was intent on turning his will from iron into
fragile porcelain.

Joanna felt Giles's grip relax and his arms open.
Unsteadily she sat up away from his chest, letting her
hands slide round to his sides to steady herself.

'How do you feel now?' he asked, his palm gently
cupping her chin so he could tip up her face and look
into her eyes.

'Much better, honestly. Oh, Giles, thank you so
much. And do not be angry again if I say I am sorry,
but I *am* sorry that you have to keep rescuing me.'

She was relieved at his sudden grin and the fleeting
caress of his hand as it left her chin. 'No need to
worry. Dragon slaying is my speciality.'

Joanna smiled back, then stiffened as her palm felt
a sudden change from the hard muscled smoothness
of his side. She twisted in his lap and ducked her head
to see better. 'Giles, what a dreadful scar.'

He bent his head to look. 'Oh, that. Shell fragment.
They leave very untidy wounds.'

'As opposed to what?' she demanded.

'Lances leave a nice tidy hole, if they don't drag.'
He lifted her hand to his shoulder. 'And a sabre—'
he moved her fingertips to the long thin scar running
down the back of his right arm '—now that can be
positively neat.'

Joanna looked at him aghast. 'You might have been
killed by any of these!'

'I suppose so. But what did you expect a soldier's body to be like?'

Joanna knew she was blushing furiously, but she was too intrigued to be distracted. 'But this sabre cut—how could you defend yourself afterwards? You are right handed.'

Giles extended both arms, clenching his fists until the muscles stood out. 'You train until you can fight with either hand.' He went still as Joanna put her hands on his forearms.

'Do that again!' Obligingly Giles clenched and unclenched his fists. Joanna gasped, then put her right hand over her own left forearm and made a fist. 'There is hardly anything there and I always thought I was quite strong.'

'You are, look at the way you handle Moonstone. But a woman's muscles are more slender. See.' He traced his index finger down the back of her forearm. It was Joanna's turn to go still. For a long moment they looked at each other, then Giles said lightly, 'As I said before, I appear to be having the most improper conversations with you, Miss Fulgrave.'

'I expect it is because I seem to get myself into such improper situations,' she said with equal lightness. 'Giles, you haven't said why you have no shirt on and are so wet.'

'I was helping Alex's head groom, Hickling, with a mare who has just foaled.'

'Oh, how lovely! May I see?'

Giles stood her on her feet and got up. 'Not today,' he said drily. 'Anyone looking at you would have the impression that you have just been kissed, rolled in the hay and then pressed up against a very wet sur-

face. Somehow I do not think this is a picture Hebe
would wish you to present to the outdoor staff. I am
afraid that hiding you from all of the indoor staff is
going to be impossible. My only hope is that I am
going to feature in belowstairs gossip as the rescuer,
not the ravisher.'

'You are teasing me,' Joanna said stoutly, well
aware that Giles was trying to make light of the possible embarrassment awaiting them. 'I am sure Starling will not permit any gossip.'

Even so, the butler's professional imperturbability
was hard pressed by the appearance on the doorstep
of Colonel Gregory in a deplorable state of semi-
nakedness and grime accompanying Miss Joanna,
who appeared to have been...

'Miss Joanna has had a most unfortunate encounter,
Starling, although she is thankfully unharmed. If Lord
Clifton should call she is not, under any circum-
stances whatsoever, at home. Regardless of who Lord
Clifton is with. Now, if we can just get her upstairs
before her ladyship...'

'Starling, what are you whispering about out here?'
Hebe emerged from the dining room, a large lace tablecloth in her hands. 'Oh, my goodness!'

'I am absolutely fine, Hebe...'

'No need to worry, I know it looks...'

'I am quite sure, my lady...'

'Oh, be quiet, the three of you.' Hebe regarded
them severely. 'We will go upstairs, Joanna, and you
can tell me all about it. Giles, put some clothes on,
for goodness' sake. You will frighten half the housemaids into hysterics and the rest will fall in love with

you. No, Starling, do not fuss, I promise I am quite all right.'

She placed the tablecloth in Starling's hands, linked her arm through Joanna's and proceeded up the shallow stairs. Joanna sent Giles a rueful look and allowed herself to be borne away.

Once away from the men and in the seclusion of her own room, Hebe proved to be far more worried than she had let herself appear. She sat Joanna down and held her hands, gazing anxiously at her bruised mouth.

'Whatever happened, darling? You and Giles have not…?'

'No! Certainly not! As if Giles would do such a thing.'

'Well, no, of course not, although sometimes men just do not know their own strength.' Hebe's voiced trailed into silence in the face of Joanna's furious indignation. She watched her cousin's face for a moment, then added, 'I am sure Giles is always the perfect gentleman,' and hid her own inward enlightenment at the sight of Joanna's rosy blush.

'But if you and Giles have not been, er, romping in a hay stack, what on earth has happened?'

'It was Rufus Carstairs.'

'Lord Clifton? But he has not been here today. Starling would have told me, even if he had told Lord Clifton that we were not receiving.'

'He did not go to the house. I think he must have seen me in the grounds and followed me without announcing himself.'

'Disgraceful! Had you told him you were here?'

Hebe was obviously adding general bad manners to Rufus's sins.

'No.' Joanna twisted her handkerchief tight in her lap. 'I think Mama must have done that.'

'Aunt Emily. Of all the misguided things… Try not to be so upset, dearest. He is very eligible and I am sure she thought she was acting for the best.'

'I know. But that is why she sent me all those clothes, you see, Hebe. And I thought it was as a present to show me she had forgiven me.' Joanna tried to stifle her misery, but the tears were running down inside her nose and she ended up producing a pathetic sound between a sniffle and a sob.

Hebe wrapped her arms around her and hugged her tightly. 'I shall write to Aunt Emily today and tell her just how she is deceived in the wretched man. And I shall threaten to keep you here for ever unless she promises never to allow him close to you again.'

She received a watery smile and a murmur of thanks, but Joanna would not meet her eyes and a sudden unpleasant thought hit her. 'Joanna, he did not do anything other than kiss you, did he?'

'No. He hurt my arms holding me so tightly, but all he did was kiss me until I could not breathe. I honestly do not think he would have done anything else, Hebe. He was just so angry with me for not behaving as he thought I should. He is a collector, you see, and he has decided he wants to collect me for some reason. Statues and paintings do not answer back or try and run away, so he is not used to rejection.'

She hesitated, glancing sideways at Hebe. Now was, perhaps, the only opportunity to ask a question that was intriguing her. 'Hebe, why do men set such a store on virginity? He was obviously very concerned that I had not lost mine in the course of whatever scrape I had got myself into. And the horrible couple who kidnapped me were most adamant that that was the most important thing.'

'Joanna! What a question to ask me. Well, I suppose men want to be certain that their children really are their children—at least the first born,' she added scrupulously with a thought to many a society marriage. 'And those horrible brothels—perhaps that is rarity value, or power, or wanting to hurt someone powerless.'

'And the wedding night, of course, I suppose that is something special,' Joanna mused and was startled at the rosy blush that stained her cousin's cheeks. 'Hebe! You don't mean that you weren't?'

'We were shipwrecked in France,' Hebe said defensively. 'This is thoroughly improper and we are not going to discuss it any more and you are most certainly not going to do what I did.'

'I doubt I would ever be shipwrecked with—' Joanna started with a giggle and suddenly broke off, appalled at how close she had been to saying Giles's name.

'With…?'

'We are definitely not going to discuss this any more,' Joanna said firmly. 'I am quite all right and I will be very grateful if you would write to Mama and tell her about Rufus. Now, are you not going to ask me why Giles had no shirt on?'

Hebe gave up her attempt at luring Joanna into revealing the name and said with a laugh, 'I am not sure I feel strong enough to know, but you had better tell me. Did it all end with a fight?'

Joanna told her about the foal, which Hebe appeared to find a tame explanation, and then described what had happened when Giles had burst into the loose box.

'He only hit him once? I find that very disappointing. I was hoping that you would say he had knocked out his front teeth and broken his handsome nose for him.'

'How bloodthirsty you are.'

'Only when wretches like that hurt my family. Now, I am going to ring for my maid, have my stays unlaced, put on a wrapper and take a light luncheon up here. Why do you not do the same?'

In the event the cousins spent an indolent afternoon in a state of *déshabillé* in Hebe's room, glancing at fashion plates, gossiping, discussing whether the latest hair styles could possibly flatter anyone under the age of thirty and catnapping.

It was therefore two well-rested, enchantingly gowned and frivolous young women who came downstairs when the dinner gong was rung and it was quite twenty minutes into the meal before they realised that they were sharing the table with two unusually silent men.

Hebe broke off an amusing tale concerning a neighbour and her trials with an unsatisfactory governess and regarded her husband, her head on one side. 'What is the matter, Alex? I declare you are positively dour and you have not touched that terrine, which is usually your favourite. Are you not pleased about the new foal?'

'Nothing is the matter, my dear. I have just got rather a lot on my mind. The new foal? Yes, excellent news, she is one of the Starlight line so I have high hopes of her. I must see about a bonus for Hickling.'

'And for Giles,' Hebe teased.

'Nonsense. He is eating us out of house and home, it was time he earned his keep.'

Giles, who was making substantial inroads into the roast goose, raised a quizzical eyebrow at his friend but did not say anything.

Hebe rolled her eyes expressively at Joanna and announced, 'Well, coz, I can see we must bear all the burden of the conversation ourselves. Let us discuss hemlines.'

Even this dire threat did not appear to register with the men who spoke when spoken to, assisted the ladies punctiliously to whichever dish they required and otherwise remained silent.

'They are communicating with each other, you know,' Hebe said in exasperation as she and Joanna retired to the panelled chamber, leaving Giles and Alex to their port.

'I have seen them do it before,' she continued, sinking on to a *chaise longue* and thankfully putting her feet up on the footstool which Joanna fetched. 'They lapse into long silences, occasionally make eye contact and grunt. Then the next day they have apparently planned a journey, or decided what to do about poachers or announce they are going to a prize fight. I challenged Alex about it once. He just said that when men know each other really well, as he and Giles got to do in the army, then they don't need to talk. Or prattle, as he rather unkindly put it.'

'Then what are they planning now?' Joanna asked.

'I do not know. I just hope it isn't—'

The door opened and the men walked in. 'Would you mind if we play billiards?' Alex said.

'No, of course not.'

Alex got as far as the door before turning. 'Oh, yes, I almost forgot. I will have to go up to town tomorrow. Some slight matter of business.'

'I thought I would go with him,' Giles added. 'We will be back on Wednesday.'

'No!' Hebe said with such emphasis that Joanna jumped. 'No, you will not do anything so foolish, either of you.'

'What?'

Hebe turned to her, anger sparkling in her eyes. 'Ask them why they are going.'

'But Alex said, a matter of business.'

'Ask them what business.'

Joanna had never seen Hebe so furious. More out of anxiety to keep her calm than a desire to interrogate her host, she said, 'Please explain, Alex. Hebe seems rather upset.'

Alex's face wore the darkly severe expression that had led others to describe him as looking like a member of the Spanish Inquisition. 'We have to talk to a man, that is all.'

'Which man?' Hebe asked Joanna between gritted teeth.

Feeling as though she was caught up in the midst of a farce, Joanna dutifully repeated, 'Which man?'

and was met by two equally stony and uncommunicative faces.

'Nothing you need worry about,' Alex said, fatally misjudging his wife for once.

'In that case, Joanna and I are coming with you.'

'I forbid it.' A shiver of awed excitement ran down Joanna's back. Alex in a towering rage was a force to be reckoned with.

'And I forbid you to fight duels,' Hebe snapped back.

'I am not...'

'But Giles is, is he not? And you are going to stand his second. And, if he kills that wretched Carstairs, the pair of you will have to leave the country. And if you think I am going to have a baby all by myself, Alex Beresford...'

'I am not going to kill him,' Giles said, managing to get a word in between the furious married pair.

'But you are going to fight him,' Joanna stated, cold gripping her heart.

'Yes.'

'And if he kills you? Do you think I want that on my conscience, Giles Gregory?' She found she was standing toe to toe with him, glaring up into his face. Behind her Alex and Hebe had fallen silent.

Giles laughed contemptuously. 'Kill me? I hardly think so.'

'Oh, you arrogant, infuriating, pig-headed...' Joanna struggled to find a bad enough word and finished '...*man!*'

Giles's laugh turned into one of pure amusement. 'I will admit to the last charge. Ouch! Stop that!'

Joanna, infuriated beyond words, had begun to hit

his broad chest with her clenched fists, ignoring the tears running down her face. 'Please, Giles, do not do it. He isn't worth it...'

Giles caught her pummelling fists in one hand and held them just tight enough to stop the blows. 'Shh, little one. There is nothing to worry about.' Joanna blinked back her tears and looked up at him through soaked lashes. His expression was so gentle the breath caught in her throat.

'Please,' she whispered.

As he bent his head to catch the word, Hebe said sharply, 'The risk to Joanna's reputation is too great. There is no saying who he has told he was coming here. He reappears in town with, I presume, a bruised face and the next day her cousin's husband and his friend descend and call him out. Do you think the gossips will have no difficulty putting that puzzle together and making a very pretty picture of it?'

Giles raised his head and looked across to Alex, then at Hebe. His grasp remained tight around Joanna's trembling hands. At last he said, 'You may be right. I just hate to think of him getting away with this.'

'He has not,' Hebe said with conviction. 'The word will go round that he is not to be trusted with young ladies. Soon he will find that he is not welcome to pay his addresses when he seeks a wife of the eligibility his pride demands. No one will know quite why, just that his perfect reputation will be ever so slightly tarnished. He will hate that.'

'Good,' Joanna said, her voice sounding distant even to her own ears. Something very odd was happening. Surely she was not going to faint? She never fainted. Even that dreadful night at the Duchess of Bridlington's ball she had not fainted. Even this afternoon in the stableblock she had only been dizzy....

She came back to consciousness to find herself being carried in Giles's arms. He seemed to be climbing. 'Where am I?'

'On your way up to bed.' He glanced down at her and his arms tightened. Joanna fought the instinct to wrap her arms around his neck and bury her face in his chest. 'You fainted.'

'I never faint. Where is Hebe?'

'Downstairs making up with Alex. She sent Starling for your maid to meet you in your chamber, so there is no need to worry about the proprieties.'

'I was not,' she protested. 'Giles, please promise me not to fight Rufus.'

'Very well, I promise. Why are you so against it? Surely you don't think I would either kill that fool or let him kill me, do you?'

'I have caused you more than enough trouble,' she mumbled against his shirt front.

'You have certainly caused me trouble,' he agreed. 'Can you stand? I had better set you down here.' Then, to her amazement, as he put her on her feet outside her chamber door he bent and kissed her forehead lightly. 'Whether it is more than enough trouble remains to be seen.' On which enigmatic note he strode off down the corridor.

Chapter Eighteen

For three of the residents of Tasborough Hall breakfast the next morning was an uncomfortable meal.
Hebe was pale with dark shadows under her eyes, but
although Alex tried to insist she go back to her room
she protested that she was too restless to settle.

Alex ate with a darkly severe eye on Joanna, who
was convinced he blamed her for the previous day's
alarms and arguments and therefore for Hebe's discomfort. Uncomfortably torn between meeting his
judgmental gaze, flustering Hebe by looking at her
and appearing to fuss and catching Giles's eye, which
for various reasons she was reluctant to do, Joanna
kept her eyes on her plate.

Only Giles appeared to be in good humour. Seeing
the reddened and grazed knuckles of his right hand,
Joanna assumed he was pleasurably satisfied at having delivered such a devastating blow to Rufus Carstairs. Men, she gathered, set a lot of store by that
kind of thing. At least he did not appear to be repining
at not challenging him to a duel.

Joanna had lain awake half the night worrying that

Giles might slip away up to London, even if Alex could not for fear of upsetting Hebe. He had promised not to call Lord Clifton out, but she was certain there were ways in which he could turn the tables and publicly provoke Rufus into issuing a challenge.

And during those long, restless hours Joanna had found her memory was all too vivid and awake. Rufus's assault troubled her not at all. What kept her tossing and turning was the memory of Giles's body sheltering hers, his anger for her, the tenderness in his eyes as he looked at her cradled in his arms. And that enigmatic remark as he had left her outside her room; almost as though he *wanted* her to cause him more trouble. But that was absurd.

Hebe crumbled a roll and said, 'That is a very fetching habit, Joanna. I like the pale revers.'

Thankful for something to talk about, she replied eagerly, 'Yes, it is nice, is it not? Mama sent it. The skirt is lined with the same colour as the revers so it shows a little when I am mounted and the hat and veil are *very* dashing.'

'Is it not too hot to ride?'

'I was going to go after breakfast. I was only going to get a little fresh air in the paddock. Unless you would like me to stay?'

'No, dear, you go out, the fresh air will do you good.'

That appeared to exhaust everyone's capacity for conversation. Joanna glanced round the table and saw Giles was smiling at her. He raised one eyebrow and glanced sideways at Alex and Hebe with a rueful expression. She could not help but smile back, wonder-

ing if she dared give into temptation and ask if he
would ride with her.

No, it was not safe. It was so wonderful to be alone
with him, so painful when they parted or something
reminded her that he could never be hers. And it was
increasingly difficult to keep her feelings from showing. She kept catching herself looking at him, then
did not know whether to look away rapidly which
might look self-conscious or risk being seen staring.

He was getting to know her too well, that was the
trouble. It was the only explanation for the oddly
tender look in his eyes sometimes and the almost possessive way he protected her. Giles was obviously a
man who was fiercely protective of 'his' people,
whether they were his family, his men or, in her case,
a stray young woman he had offered to help. It must
be one of the characteristics that made him such a
good officer: his men would sense his concern and
interest, even if he never allowed it to show in the
way he did with Hebe, or his father, or herself. How
was she going to cope with this ache inside once he
was no longer with her?

'A penny for your thoughts,' he said suddenly, startling her into unwary speech.

'I was just wondering how on earth you are going
to fill your time now you can stop rescuing me.'

Giles grinned. 'I do not anticipate being bored.
Quite the contrary. I have…plans.' There was a note
in his voice of mischief, and something else that Joanna did not recognise, but which caught Alex's
brooding attention.

'Indeed? And what is her name?'

Before Giles could reply Hebe said, 'Alex!' sharply
and Starling came in with a silver salver.

'The post, my lady.'

'Give it to his lordship, please, Starling. My goodness, what a pile of letters. All our acquaintance no
doubt telling us how much happier we would be in
Brighton or Bath, I expect. I hope they have some
interesting gossip. Oh, how I wish I could go sea
bathing right this minute.'

'Really?' Joanna was startled.

'Yes, truly. I do not understand it. I feel so restless,
as though I could walk for miles.'

'You'll do no such thing my darling, but if you are
good and rest I will take you to Brighton the moment
the doctor says you may go. Here you are, three letters for you, that should keep you occupied.' Alex
passed them across and tossed one letter to Giles.
'One for you, Joanna.'

Joanna slit the seal on her missive, which by the
handwriting was from her sister Grace. No doubt she
was now fully informed by their mama of her younger
sister's shocking behaviour, dangerous adventures
and also Mama's hopes of a proposal from Lord Clifton despite all this.

She skimmed the letter but it was exactly as she
feared—shock, surprise, gentle chiding and a strong
hint that good fortune was going to smile upon her
despite it all. Joanna folded it crisply and set it down
beside her plate. She was in no mood for lectures or
sermons, however softly delivered.

Giles had unfolded the wrapper on his letter to reveal what appeared to be at least three sheets of expensive paper covered in a swirling hand. A cloud of

attar of roses' scent wafted across the table, making Hebe cough.

He was reading with some difficulty but with an all-too-familiar expression on his face of loving amusement.

'A letter from Lady Suzanne, I collect,' Joanna enquired, attempting to keep the sharp note out of her voice.

'Yes. I have not written for *an age*, so she says, and she is taking the opportunity to chide me for that and to remind me, with very little subtlety, that it is her birthday in ten days. I suspect that all this hinting is because she knows I am buying horses and she would like a showy hack to ride in town.'

'How old will she be?' Hebe asked.

'Twenty.'

'And no offers yet? I am surprised. Surely she is an exceptionally eligible young lady.'

'Exceptionally,' Giles agreed. He hesitated, then added, 'It is not yet spoken of, so I am sure you will not say anything, but there will be an announcement very soon.'

'A lucky man,' Hebe said.

No one except possibly Alex noted the sharp tone of Hebe's comment. Joanna stopped breathing, her every nerve seemed to be alive and shuddering with pain. She was unaware that she had gone white, was unaware that she had put her cup of tea down so sharply that it slopped into the saucer. All she was aware of was the loving expression in Giles's grey eyes as he looked at the letter in his hand.

Suddenly she found she could move. In fact, it was almost more than she could do to control her instinct to spring to her feet and run. She stood up abruptly, causing both men to rise rapidly also. 'Please, don't.' She gestured for them to sit. 'I think I will go for my ride now.' She was at the door before Starling could collect himself to open it and there was an awkward shuffle as they both reached for the handle, then she was out and the door closed behind her.

In the long silence that followed Hebe watched Giles with such concentration that his eyes dropped from hers. He sat looking at the fallen sheets of paper in front of him, then got to his feet. 'Excuse me, Hebe.'

Left alone in the dining room with only the discreet figure of Starling moving chafing-dishes on the sideboard, Alex said with an air of sudden discovery, 'Hebe, are Giles and Joanna…?'

'Yes,' she said tightly. 'The trouble is, I don't think they both know it yet.' She broke off, an arrested expression on her face. 'Oh! Oh, Alex, I do believe the baby has started.'

At which point the question of his friends' relationships suddenly ceased to interest Lord Tasborough in the slightest.

Joanna arrived somewhat precipitously in the stableyard to find Hickling in earnest discussion with an undergroom who was just tightening the girths on Moonstone's saddle. She set her hat rather more firmly on her head and pushed in the pins.

'Miss Joanna, Robbins says you sent to have the grey saddled this morning.'

'Yes, Hickling. Is there a problem? She isn't lame, is she?'

'No, miss, nothing like that. It s just that the Colonel ordered her rested and to have extra oats because of the long journey when you arrived here.'

'Yes?'

'Well, miss, now she's as fresh as paint and ready to jump out of her skin, I don't know as how you really ought to be riding her, miss. Perhaps I ought to send one of the lads out on her today, shake some of the mischief out.'

'Nonsense, I can manage her,' Joanna said, walking firmly up to the mare and pulling on her gloves. 'I am only going to ride in the paddock.'

She gathered up the reins and stood waiting for Hickling to give her a leg up. 'Thank you.'

Giles arrived in the yard just as she was hooking her right knee over the pommel and flicking her skirts into order. Apparently he had come straight from the breakfast table for he was hatless and appeared to have been running. Joanna pulled down her veil and made a business out of gathering her reins.

'Hickling, is that mare fit to be ridden?'

'Fit? Yes, Colonel. I was just saying to Miss Joanna, she's jumping out of her skin after all that rest and oats.'

'Jo…Miss Fulgrave, I think you had better dismount. Perhaps we can find another horse for you this morning.'

'You think I am an incompetent rider?'

'You know I do not, but Moonstone…'

'But Moonstone is about to become a birthday—or is it a bride-gift—is she not? Surely you would not deny me one last ride on her, Colonel?'

'I am not giving Moonstone to Suzanne, if that is what you mean.'

'No? Then you will have no objection to me riding her, will you?'

'Joanna…'

But as she spoke Joanna dug her heel into Moonstone's side. The mare needed no encouragement. From a standing start she was cantering as they reached the stableyard arch. Joanna took her under it in a sweeping turn towards the front drive and disappeared.

'She said she was going to ride in the paddock, Colonel,' Hickling said, 'I'd never have got her mounted if I'd known.'

'She was going to, until I interfered,' Giles responded grimly. 'What have you got in the stables? I don't want to waste time having something fetched up from the paddocks.'

'Just Black Cat, sir. I'll get him saddled up.'

Hickling ran for the box and dragged back the bolts. Giles joined him inside, pulling the saddle off its tree as Hickling reached down the bridle. An intelligent Roman-nosed head swung round to regard them with mild interest.

'Damn it, he's big!'

'Up to your weight, Colonel. He'll go all day, agile as the cat he's called for over wall and ditch, but he's got no great turn of speed. Long stride, though. Coom up, Cat!'

Thus encouraged, the big horse allowed himself to be led out into the yard where he stood placidly while Giles swung himself up into the saddle. He broke into a steady canter as they left the yard, but to Giles's grim amusement his ear flicked back as though in amazement as he was asked to gallop. 'Come on, Cat,' he encouraged him. 'We've got a little grey mouse for you to catch.'

Luckily the fine weather had given way to showers during the night and had softened the ground just enough for the marks of Moonstone's passing to be visible. Giles checked as three long rides split off from the carriage drive. Each headed deep into the dense beech woods, but only one showed the cut turf left by elegant sharp hooves. Cat wheeled neatly and followed Giles's guiding hand down the left-hand ride, the one which followed the very scarp edge of the Chilterns before they plunged down into the Vale below.

As she rode Joanna caught glimpses through the trees of the fields and hedges, the curls of smoke over the villages, but her attention was far too concentrated on Moonstone to admire the view. The mare was proving just as much a handful as Hickling had warned and Joanna was aware that she was riding at the very limit of her skill and strength.

Not that there was any spite in the mare, but she had been bored standing in a strange paddock and the sensation of a familiar rider and wide open rides stretching before her was too much to resist. Joanna sensed that if she was allowed her head she would calm down of her own accord after a mile or two and there was no point in indulging in a fight.

The concentration needed to keep balanced and maintain at least the illusion of control helped blot out the memory of Giles's face as he read Lady Suzanne's letter, but try as she might Joanna could not stop the words *announcement...very soon* repeating themselves over and over again to the rhythm of the hoofbeats.

Then Moonstone burst out of the ride into a small clearing where four ways met and straight into a herd of fallow deer that had been grazing on the clipped turf. The hinds bounded away but the stag, his spread of antlers broad and menacing, stood his ground, head lowered.

Moonstone stopped so abruptly that Joanna almost went over her head. Somehow she scrambled back into the saddle, groped for the reins and thrust her foot back into the wildly swinging stirrup. The mare tossed her head, allowing Joanna to grab a handful of mane and rein, then took off down a ride at a flat-out gallop.

Joanna had never ridden so fast. Hauling on the reins did nothing to stop the panicked animal and only threatened to unseat her. At this speed a fall could be fatal. She gave up and clung to mane and pommel and prepared to hold on until Moonstone calmed down.

Behind her Giles was making ground, for although Black Cat had no great turn of speed his stride was immense and his steady canter ate up the distance. Then they reached the clearing and Giles reined in hard at the sight of the welter of hoofprints dug deep into the ground. For a moment he circled, his face set, then leaning over he tore a hazel switch from a bush and applied it to the black horse's flank. 'Come *on*, Cat, gallop!'

With an indignant snort the big animal gathered his

hindquarters under him and took off. Giles's mouth twitched in a humourless smile. Now he had her.

The chase took longer than he imagined. By the time he caught a glimpse of dappled grey hindquarters ahead of him, the Cat's neck was flecked with foam. Joanna and her mount had reached a point where the ride curved in to skirt the edge of a deep dell. At some time long ago the farmers far below had hauled chalk from it for their heavy clay soils, now it was simply a deep depression lined with years of fallen beech leaves, crisp and tan in the sunshine.

Joanna had regained the reins as Moonstone slowed and had begun to pull on them, talking to the mare as she did so, 'Come on, girl, steady, steady now, that's enough.' Moonstone slowed, halted, then, hearing the hoofbeats behind her, put back her ears and reared. They were on the edge of the dell. Under her hooves the chalky soil crumbled. The mare slipped, recovered, twisted and Joanna went over her shoulder, tumbling head over heels through the thick leaf mould to the bottom as Moonstone bolted into the depths of the wood.

Black Cat was coming on so fast that he reached the point where Moonstone had reared before Giles could pull him up. Despite his legendary nimbleness the big horse stumbled, pecked and stopped with a suddenness that jolted Giles in the saddle.

Joanna looked up from where she lay flat on her back in a deep mattress of leaves and saw the plunging animal and then Giles swinging down from its back. 'I am all right!' she called. 'Just give me a moment to get my breath, there's no need...'

But Giles was already over the side of the dell and

half-sliding, half-jumping down towards her. He reached a shelf in the slope where grass grew thick and checked the slope for a moment, then stepped forward again.

The sound—a crack, then a thud—was so strange that it made no sense to Joanna. Then with a gasp that she realised with horror was a choked-off cry, Giles fell sideways on to the ledge, clutching at his leg.

She got to her feet, scrambling frantically up the slope, clawing at roots and scrubby branches until she reached the ledge. 'Giles?'

He was lying awkwardly and for a long moment Joanna could not understand what was wrong. Then she saw the cruel iron jaws clamped around his right calf and realised that he had stepped on a mantrap.

'Giles!' She fell on her knees beside him, ineffectually trying to find a point where she could grip the trap to pull it apart, but it bit tight into the leather of his boot cutting deep into the flesh beneath and the gap either side of his leg was too close to the hinges for her to be able to exert any leverage.

Joanna stopped her frantic, futile efforts. Her gloves were torn and stained red with blood and rust. She wrenched her gaze from them and forced herself to look at Giles. He was white, his mouth a tight line and his eyes dark. How he was conscious Joanna had no idea: the sight of his leg was enough to make her feel sick and dizzy; she could not begin to imagine the pain.

'I will go for help,' she said as steadily as she could manage with tears trickling down the inside of her nose. *I will not cry, I will not!* 'Moonstone has bolted, but your horse is still here.'

Giles focussed his eyes on her with an effort. The first stunning blow as the jagged teeth closed around his leg had been replaced by a burning agony that seemed to fill his consciousness. He could not tell whether any bones were broken, all he was aware of was a sensation as though something was gnawing the flesh from them.

The image of Joanna blurred and then cleared. She was sheet white, her eyes filled with tears, but there was a fierce determination about her from the set of her jaw to her clenched, stained fists.

'Black Cat,' he managed to say. 'He's steady, he'll know his way home.' He saw her look at his leg and wondered with a strange sense of detachment if he was going to lose it. 'Is it bleeding much?'

'Oozing,' Joanna replied, bending over to look closely. Her hat had come off in her fall and her hair was loose. He half-lifted a hand to touch it, then let it fall back again. 'I think the trap is so tight around it that it is stopping much blood.'

And stopping much blood going to his lower leg and foot, Giles realised grimly. 'Do not try and hurry,' he said as she got to her feet. 'Get there safely. Alex will know what is needed.'

'I cannot believe he would be so barbarous as to allow these things,' she said, her voice shaking with anger.

'Not his land,' Giles managed to grind out. He was damned if he was going to pass out in front of her.

Joanna turned to clamber up the slope, stopped, turned back suddenly and stooped to drop a kiss on

his forehead. 'Lie still, I will be as quick as I can.'
Then she was gone. He could hear her scrambling
progress, then, 'Here boy, here, Black Cat.' Silence.
A gasp. 'Oh...oh...hell!'

Giles twisted awkwardly in an attempt to see up
the slope behind him, failed and fell back sweating.
There was the sound of someone slipping and sliding
down again and Joanna reappeared in front of him, a
saddle over her arm.

'He is dead lame,' she said furiously, falling to her
knees and turning the saddle over.

Giles felt a flicker of amusement run through him.
'Your language, Miss Fulgrave!' he murmured.

'Do not joke,' she retorted. 'I can't...can't...just
don't, that's all.' She broke off and swallowed. 'I
thought that if I could get the saddle under your thigh
and knee it would support it and take some of the
strain off the muscles.'

Giles watched her from between eyelids that felt
dangerously close to closing. She was so shocked and
frightened, yet so determined to cope that her own
weaknesses were making her furious.

She got the saddle into position and began to slip
it underneath, breaking off to take his thigh between
both hands in an attempt to straighten the angle. He
bit back a gasp of pain and saw her anguished face
as she glanced at him, then she set her lips tight and
carried on. The relief as the padded lining of the saddle took the strain from his leg was so immense that
it almost undid his resolve to stay quiet and stay conscious.

'I am sorry I hurt you,' she said stiffly and he realised with a twist of his heart that tears were running

unchecked down her cheeks now. 'But I think it will help.'

'So much courage,' he whispered but she did not react and he realised that his voice was so quiet she had not heard him.

'Right, now then, I will start.' Joanna said with brisk determination. 'It will take longer, of course, on foot, but I will go as fast as I can.'

She scrambled to her feet again and Giles saw with a pang that she was scrubbing the tears from her face with the back of her hand like a tired child.

'No.' His voice sounded oddly remote and he cleared his throat and concentrated on making her attend to him.

'What did you say?'

'I said no. You are not travelling through these woods alone on foot.'

'Giles, I cannot just sit here and do nothing! It is broad daylight, I am unhurt and it is all my fault that you are—' Her voice cracked and she stumbled to a halt.

'You do not win battles by sitting around apportioning blame,' Giles snapped. He hated speaking to her like that, but her chin came up again and he saw she was listening to him. 'You lost your temper and I...I realised I hadn't been looking beyond the end of my nose,' he finished. Joanna looked mystified, but he knew what he meant and he was not about to explain it now.

'Well, I am going anyway,' she retorted defiantly, turning on her heel.

'Stop!' It was the voice he used in the heat of battle

to reach troops around him and it halted her in her tracks. 'I *order* you to come back here.'

Their eyes met: implacable pain-filled grey clashed with tear-soaked, anguished hazel. Giles put every ounce of authority he possessed into that look, knowing that he had no hold over her whatsoever beyond that which she chose to let him have. Their eyes clung for a long minute, then,

'Yes, Giles,' Joanna said, and came back to sit beside him.

Chapter Nineteen

Joanna sank down beside Giles, feeling as though she had fought a battle, and in some obscure way had managed to both win and lose it. Her every instinct screamed at her to go for help, but the part of her she had tried to train to be the perfect wife for a soldier told her that this was a dangerous situation and that Giles knew what to do far better than she.

The struggle of wills seemed to have exhausted him and he lay back awkwardly, his eyes closed. Joanna wriggled round until she could take his head and shoulders into her lap and cradle them in the deep folds of her habit.

Giles's eyes opened with a hint of his wicked twinkle in their depths. 'Now that is nice,' he remarked.

'Giles, is there anything I can do?' she asked, trying to sound practical and down to earth. The last thing he needed to be coping with was a watering pot of a female.

'No. Hickling saw us leave and he will be on the watch for us returning. If Moonstone gets back to the stables he will be alerted at once, if not, I am sure he will go to Alex by midday.'

'How will they find us?'

'The ground is soft—I was able to track you easily. Given the size of Cat's feet, they will have no trouble following us.' He was speaking calmly to her and she recognised that he was deliberately pitching his tone to reassure her. How many frightened young subalterns had he spoken to in just such tones before now?

He moved slightly and Joanna felt the shock of pain that went through his body. Her hands tightened on his shoulders and she bent over him, desperate to do something, anything to stop this torture. Watching his pain, his efforts not to show it, was an agony in itself and one she suddenly felt she could not bear. Then the vein of reality and self-knowledge that ran deep through her came to her aid. *If he can bear it, and he has no choice, then I can certainly bear it*, she told herself grimly.

'Talk to me,' he said, eyes closed.

'Of course. What about?'

'Tell me about this man you love so much that losing him has left you with nowhere to go, no direction to take.'

Joanna hesitated, her heart thudding. The need to talk, to confide, was an almost physical thing. Yet how could she do so to the very man concerned? 'I will not tell you his name,' she said at last.

'Very well.' Giles's eyes were shut. She could sense through every quivering nerve in her body responding to his that he was husbanding his energy to withstand what was happening.

'I…met him when I was…before I came out. I fell in love with him almost at once.'

'Why?'

The stark question took her aback. Why did she love Giles? Had she ever thought about it, analysed it?

'Because he has the power to inspire devotion,' she managed at last.

'Hmm.' Giles murmured. 'I distrust that.'

'What? An officer distrust leadership?'

'Ah, now that is different. You do not have to inspire devotion in order to lead. Sometimes you have to be hated, but they must still follow you.'

Joanna pondered this. Was what she felt for Giles devotion, or a response to a natural power to lead? Just now she had subdued every instinct in order to obey him. No, she had done as he had asked—as he had commanded—because deep down she trusted him.

'Trust then,' she amended. 'He inspires trust.'

'Very well, I will accept trustworthiness. But was that all?'

'He is very good looking, very…male,' she confessed, blushing.

'So, what then?'

'I knew he would not think twice about me,' she said ruefully. 'I was a harum-scarum schoolroom miss. But I knew what I had to do if I was to be the perfect wife for him. I applied myself to every lesson in manners and deportment, I practised my languages, I studied to please anyone of any rank and influence. I read everything I could about…about his profession.' She paused to pull a handkerchief from her pocket and gently wiped the sweat from his forehead.

'He was destined for very great things, all I could do was to make sure I was as fitted as possible to support him.'

Giles stiffened in her arms. 'Listen!'

Joanna strained her ears to catch the distant sounds. 'Deer, perhaps, not horses, I think.'

'Go on.'

'I was such an innocent fool,' Joanna said abruptly. 'He was gone for thr…years. Every day I studied the announcements and felt myself safe because there was no notice of his engagement. It never occurred to me that he was living his own life, finding his own love.'

'When *did* you realise it?' Giles was sounding increasingly distant. Joanna willed him to give up and to slip into merciful unconsciousness until rescue came.

'I realised when I saw him with the woman he loves at the Duchess of Bridlington's ball. I did not face up to just what an idiot I had been all that time until after I had run away and had time to think about it.'

'Tell me about the ball…what…?' Joanna felt Giles's tense body relax into her arms and let out a deep, answering, sigh of relief. He had gone at last. But now she had begun to talk it was difficult to stop. Anxiously she studied his unconscious face. The traces of pain still marked it, a thin line of blood at the corner of his mouth marked where his teeth had closed in agony on his lip. But his breathing was deep and regular and the strong torso in her arms had the weight of oblivion.

Reassured she continued speaking as though by telling herself the story she could staunch the wounds that evening had left.

'I went to the Duchess's ball, even though I was in disgrace with Mama and Papa for not receiving Lord Clifton. I had no expectation of seeing...seeing *him* there: after all, I had looked for him night after night, day after day for three years.

'But he *was* there, like some wonderful, inevitable miracle and I started to make my way up the ballroom to meet him. It was going to be perfect, I knew it. Then he went into a retiring room. I never even thought to wonder why, I simply followed him and there she was in his arms, that beautiful, eligible young lady. And he was telling her he was going to speak to her father, telling her she was his first and only love. I saw his face: I could not doubt him. His eyes betrayed just what he felt.'

Joanna was hardly aware she was speaking aloud. Her arms cradled Giles, rocking his body against herself in a gesture as old as time. 'I got away somehow, and then you came and looked after me. Nothing mattered after that. What was I to do? Not marry some man I detested, that was all I was certain of. I had to get away, and you know the rest.'

The soft sigh of his breathing was all the answer she received. Joanna bent her head silently to study every line of Giles's face and set herself to wait.

How much later it was before she heard the sounds of hooves approaching, then the blessed sound of voices raised and calling, Joanna had no idea. The sun had moved almost overhead, her mouth was dry and her stomach grumbled at her.

'Giles! Giles, they are here!' She shook him gently by the shoulder, then raised her voice and shouted, 'Here! Help! Help, down here!'

It seemed like dozens of men who came crashing down the slope as she arched protectively over Giles's body. Then it resolved itself into Alex, his face like thunder, Hickling and three grooms.

Alex fell to his knees beside Giles, his eyes appalled as they took in the bloodied and mangled leg and the cruel trap around it. He reached out one hand and pressed his friend's shoulder, then snapped at Joanna, 'Get away from here.'

'No! Why...?' She was hauled to her feet and dragged to one side, still protesting. 'Giles needs...'

'Giles would not be in this state if it were not for you.' Alex's face was drawn and furious. 'When we release the pressure of those jaws the pain is going to be infinitely worse than it is now as the blood begins to flow again. He is going to want to swear or throw up or faint—or all three—and he does not need to have you hovering around clucking and making him feel he cannot do any of those things in front of a lady.

'Now get out of here and find Peter. He'll take you up and you can ride with him back to the Hall. Tell the doctor what has happened and get Giles's room ready.'

'The doctor? The doctor is at Tasborough?' Joanna pushed Alex's angry, hurtful words to the back of her mind and clutched at the one thing that mattered.

'Hebe went into labour after breakfast,' Alex said grimly.

'She is all right?'

'How the hell would I know? The last person they tell is the father. It all seems to be taking a damn long time.'

No wonder he was so angry with her! Joanna reached out and gave Alex a swift, hard hug. 'She will be fine, Alex. Now, look after Giles. I will go and do just as you say.'

Resolutely she pushed the thought of what was happening in the dell out of her mind and ran to the ride where one of the undergrooms was waiting with a farm cart and three horses. Black Cat, his off-hind cocked up, was standing dolefully, nose to nose with one of his stablemates.

'Peter? His lordship said that you are to take me up and we are to return to the hall to alert the doctor. The Colonel has been hurt.'

The ride back, clinging to Peter's rough jacket, was little more than a lurching blur. As they reached the steps Joanna slid from the horse and ran for the front door which opened as she reached it.

'Miss Joanna! What has happened?' It was Starling, shaken right out of his usual imperturbability.

The ride back had given her enough time to order her story and what she must do. 'The Colonel has been caught by a mantrap and his leg is badly injured. His lordship is bringing him back in the wagon. We must tell the doctor and make the Colonel's room ready.' She was already running up the stairs towards Hebe's chamber. 'We will need hot water and bandages,' she tossed back over her shoulder.

She got no further than the dressing room before being firmly turned away by the housekeeper. 'You cannot go in there, Miss Joanna!' she said, scandalised.

'I do not want to,' Joanna managed to pant out. 'I need the doctor for Colonel Gregory. How is her ladyship?'

'As well as might be expected, considering, miss.'

Considering what? No wonder Alex was getting so agitated! 'May I speak to the doctor?'

Eventually that harassed gentleman put his head round the door long enough to listen to Joanna's tale. 'Hmm. Let me know when the Colonel arrives: it will definitely need seeing to at once and nothing is moving at any speed here, that is for sure.'

Joanna retreated to hover at the head of the stairs, giving orders to a distracted butler and harassing the maids who she sent scurrying for bandages, basilicum powder and extra pillows. At the sound of the arriving wagon she hastened for the doctor, only to find herself put very firmly outside the door as Giles was carried in on a hurdle.

Starling appeared with a sandwich and a glass of wine, which he insisted she ate. It tasted of straw, but she sensed that looking after her was all that Starling was able to do at the moment and so she ate it to please him.

It seemed an age before the doctor reappeared, wiping his hands on a towel. After a sharp look at her white face he took pity on her and stopped long enough for a rapid bulletin. 'He won't lose the leg and nothing's broken. But the muscle is severely crushed and bruised: he'll be in a lot of pain for some days and then will need careful exercise to get the strength back in it.'

He strode off to his other patient, leaving Joanna leaning against the panelling too relieved even to cry. Eventually she pulled herself together sufficiently to open the bedchamber door and look in.

Giles was alone in the room, stretched out on the big bed under a single sheet. He looked alarmingly still, but as Joanna tiptoed forward he opened his eyes and smiled at her. She smiled back, opened her mouth to speak, then found her throat was too tight.

'Stay with me?' He turned his head on the pillow and glanced towards the armchair standing beside the empty grate. Joanna went to pull it over to the bedside, but when she had it in position and looked back to the bed he was asleep again.

It was a big old leather-covered chair, deep and sagging comfortably. Joanna curled up in its depths and settled down to watch Giles. At first she was inclined to be anxious that he slept so deeply, then she recognised it for what it was: the utterly relaxed reaction of a strong, fit man whose body knew what it had to do to heal itself.

She closed her eyes, and against the lids saw again his warm, sleepy smile as she had entered the room. *Stay with me.* That spoke volumes for his trust in her that he should want her with him while he was vulnerable, unconscious. They had become very close over these past days: perhaps these few hours alone with him were all that were left to her of that intimacy before the demands of marriage and Lady Suzanne and his family took him away from her.

Joanna opened her eyes and simply sat looking at him, letting her gaze rove slowly over the long form outlined by the thin sheet, the breadth of his shoulders, bare where the linen folded down, the stubble golden on his skin, the fading scar on his forehead.

She catalogued each characteristic in her memory to last forever. The fact that his hair needed cutting and that where it was overlong at his nape it was beginning to curl. The sweep of his eyelashes, darker than his hair, ridiculously long for such a masculine man. The precise, complex, curl of his ear. The way his neck was strapped with muscle, the firm line of his jaw, determined even in sleep.

And his mouth. Expressive, flexible lips that she knew could firm into anger, part in uninhibited laughter, soften, then harden into a demanding, thrilling kiss. Her fingers curled and flexed with her longing to touch his mouth, to trace the sculpted upper line, the fuller, sensual lower swell.

Time passed and Joanna did not move as the clock in the hall below struck the hour. When it struck again Giles opened his eyes and looked directly into hers. Time stood still as grey met hazel gaze and locked in wordless communication in a language that she did not have the key to.

Then Giles moved slightly and caught his breath at the pain in his leg and the moment shattered.

'Damn it,' he muttered, raising himself on his elbows in an effort to sit up. Joanna jumped to her feet and shook the pillows behind him into a pile to support him, stepping back sharply to avoid touching him as he managed to draw himself up the bed and lay back.

'How does it feel?' What a stupid question!

'Sore,' Giles admitted in what she felt must be a massive understatement. He saw her face and grinned at her expression. 'Truly, not that bad, I've had far worse, and far worse conditions to recover in, let me tell you.'

Joanna, reassured, stopped hovering at the bedside and resumed her seat. 'That wound in your side?'

'Hmm? I had forgotten you had seen that. Yes, they picked me up, tied my sash round it tightly, slung me over an army mule and carted me back to camp like a sack of potatoes. I then spent two weeks in a flea-infested barn. And no beautiful nurse, only my batman, whose ideas of medical care were, to put it mildly, rough and ready.'

Beautiful. Joanna hugged the word to herself and asked, 'Is there anything you need? Something to drink?'

'Yes, please.' He ran his tongue over his lips. 'Would you ring for a footman?'

'I can get what you need.'

Giles cocked an eyebrow. 'I think I would prefer a footman.'

Joanna opened her mouth to protest, then realised that there might indeed be reasons why he would prefer to be attended by a footman. 'Oh, yes, of course. I'll send someone up.'

Starling was pacing distractedly in the hall. Joanna felt a pang of sympathy: he was probably unconsciously echoing the Earl's own restlessness on the floor above.

'Could you send a footman to the Colonel, please, Starling? He has woken up and says he is feeling much better.'

Starling hurried off and Joanna was about to go upstairs to see if Alex had any news when she glimpsed the fine array of walking canes in the hall stand. She selected one which looked long enough for Giles and went to find Alex.

To her relief he was at least sitting down and demolishing a pile of sandwiches and a tankard of ale. He gestured Joanna to a chair and pushed the plate towards her.

'Is there anything to drink?'

In answer he poured ale into a spare tankard and Joanna cautiously tried it. To her surprise it was surprisingly good and she also found her appetite had returned. Goodness knows what Hebe would say if she saw her cousin sitting quaffing ale out of a tankard, elbows on table and ham sandwich in hand.

'Is there any news yet?'

'The doctor emerged about fifteen minutes ago, told me not to be such a damn fool and stop worrying and went back in again. How is Giles?'

'He's been sleeping and has woken up saying he feels better and asking for a footman. I'll go back in a while if there is nothing I can do here.'

Alex's mouth twisted into a rueful smile. 'Unmarried girls and husbands are apparently of no use whatsoever at a childbed, so I suggest you go back to Giles. I am sorry I shouted at you, Joanna. By the way, Moonstone is quite unharmed and Black Cat will be fine—Hickling sent to tell me a while back.'

'I do not blame you for being angry,' Joanna said.

'You must have hated to leave Hebe and to find Giles like that…'

They sat in companionable silence for a while, then Joanna went back to her room, washed and changed. The clock was just striking five as she tapped on the panels of Giles's chamber and heard him call, 'Come in.'

Chapter Twenty

Giles was sitting up in bed, looking so much better that she could hardly believe it. Her surprise must have shown on her face for he remarked, 'Shave, wash, clean shirt, ale and a sandwich.'

'Me, too—all except the shave, of course.'

'Ale?'

'I know, Hebe would be shocked. I have been keeping Alex company for a while. I think everything is all right, he is just finding the waiting, and the fact that no one will tell him anything, very trying.' She recalled the walking stick and held it up. 'See what I found for you.'

'Thank you! Do not tell me this means you are not going to cluck over me?'

'Of course,' Joanna said briskly. 'If you were William I would be clucking like a flock of hens, but you are far too old to need that. Besides, you have been wounded enough to know exactly what rest you need and when you should exercise.'

Giles regarded her, a quizzical look in his eyes. 'Tell me, this man you love…'

'Yes?' Joanna felt instantly defensive. Now what was he going to ask her?

'Would you do whatever he told you to?'

'Yes…no. No, I would not, only if I agreed with him.'

'Good. Would you mind locking the door?'

Joanna looked at him, realised that her mouth had dropped unbecomingly open and shut it with a snap. To be in a man's bedroom was shocking enough, though probably even her mama would approve of her being with Giles in view of his injury. But a locked door was enough to compromise her utterly.

She turned the key. 'Why?'

'Because I need to talk to you and I do not want to be interrupted. You locked it before asking why.'

Joanna ignored that observation and went towards her chair.

'Would you mind moving this pillow for me?' It seemed perfectly well positioned to her, but she went to do as he asked, was caught neatly round the waist and swung on to the bed beside him.

'Giles!' She wriggled but found herself firmly held.

'I want to talk to you, and I do not want you to interrupt…'

'I do not interrupt!'

'…interrupt me. Now, sit there where I can see you and I will tell you the story of *my* evening at the Duchess of Bridlington's ball in return for your tale this morning.'

'The Duchess's…' *No! He couldn't have heard what she'd said in the woods, he was asleep, unconscious…*

'Shh.' Giles placed one finger fleetingly on her lips. 'No interruptions, remember?

'I had hardly been back in London two days, but I met the Duchess in Piccadilly and she invited me. So I went: it was as good a way of taking my mind off what I knew was going to be a difficult interview with my father as any other.

'I was not expecting to see her, but before I knew it Suzy had lured me into a retiring room and was wheedling me into teaching her to drive.'

'To drive?'

Giles's finger pressed on her lips again and this time lingered for a moment. 'To drive—which her father was adamantly opposed to because a female relative had been injured in a carriage accident. However, as Suzy knows only too well, she has been able to wind me round her little finger since I was ten years old. Like a fool I agreed to ask the Marquis and, of course, the little madam was instantly immensely grateful—as only Suzy can be.

'So there I am, faced with the unenviable task of persuading her father to let me teach her to drive. I only agreed because if I hadn't she would have prevailed on someone else to teach her and at least her parents trust me to keep her out of trouble.'

Complete confusion was blurring every certainty in Joanna's mind. He was speaking of Lady Suzanne with deep affection, but in the most unloverlike terms. He had known her since he was ten, her parents trusted him to keep her out of trouble...

'She...'

'Shh. At least the minx has good hands—you saw her in the Park. But as you may have gathered when

we met at the masquerade, she also uses me to rescue
her from the endless pranks she gets up to. She went
to that romp with a quite ineligible party and made
sure I got the message about where she was in suf-
ficient time to come and remove her before things
became too hot.'

Joanna ducked away from under his hand and demanded, 'But you love her!'

'Like a sister,' Giles agreed amiably. 'But I am
most certainly not in love with her. I would as soon
marry a cageful of monkeys and I have only the deepest sympathy for Lord Keswick. You will not repeat
that yet, please, it will not be announced until the new
Season.'

'But…'

'Anyway, as I said, no sooner had I arrived back
in England than Suzy had embroiled me in her usual
battle of wits with her father. Off she flits and I
emerge from the retiring room to find you…'

Joanna twisted right away until she was crouched
on the furthest side of the bed. 'You were not unconscious in the woods, you heard me and now you are
saying that because I… Oh!' She buried her face in
her hands, too humiliated to continue.

'Joanna.' She remained huddled, her face hidden.
'Joanna!' She looked up, white-faced, and saw Giles
was regarding her patiently. 'Did you believe I was
asleep?'

'Of course I did! Do you think I would have said
what I did otherwise?'

'Exactly. I congratulate myself it was as good a bit
of acting as the time I had to pretend to be dead while
being prodded by a French bayonet. So, if I was in

love with darling Suzy, there was not the slightest reason for me to tell you this, was there? I could just have tactfully removed myself.'

'Even so, I have embarrassed both myself and you.' Joanna forced herself to speak calmly, although she could not meet his eyes. Somehow she had to get out of this room before the floor opened up and swallowed her. 'I am sorry, I will go away now and go back to Mama and Papa tomorrow.'

'You know very well that you cannot run away from me, Joanna. I have captured you before, I will have no difficulty doing so again.'

'Why do you want to humiliate me like this?' she whispered, swallowing back the tears.

'Joanna, darling, come back over here.'

'No. And do not call me that. Just because you feel sorry for me because I have made a complete fool of myself, there is no need to patronise me.'

'Joanna, at least look at me.'

Reluctantly her head came up and she met his eyes. He was regarding her ruefully. 'I am making a compete mull of this. Joanna, *I love you.* I thought you were in love with someone else: so in love that you would defy your family, risk ruin rather than compromise that love. How could I even admit to myself how I was beginning to feel about you?'

'You love me?' she whispered. This was not real, it must be some dream, some hallucination. Perhaps she had struck her head when she fell and had not realised. 'How? When?'

'I think, looking back, from the moment I came out of that room and you looked up at me with huge, pain-filled eyes. You were beautiful, brave and I wanted to hit the man who had made you feel like that.

'Then when I found you at the Thoroughgoods something should have told me. I have never felt such killing rage before; I knew I was not safe to be alone with them, I just did not realise why.' He regarded her, his face more calmly serious than she had ever seen it. 'I told myself it was simply what I would feel about any young woman trapped like that and I told myself that the way I found myself thinking about you, the effort it took not to touch you, kiss you—I told myself that was desire, impure, but simple.

'When I kissed you that evening after I had talked to you about life in camp, I should have known then but I kept denying it to myself. How could I fall in love with you when all you thought about was that man? God, but I wanted you. When you ran away from me and I caught you in that field it was all I could do not to take you there and then on the grass amidst those flowers, under the sun.'

'When did you realise?' Joanna could not make herself believe this was happening.

'When I found that lout Clifton mauling you. I held you afterwards and you fitted—not just fitted into my arms and against my body, you fitted my heart and my soul. I told myself it was hopeless, but something, some instinct gave me hope. I do not know what.'

'Perhaps the shameless way I kissed you, the way I clung to you,' Joanna said shakily. Feeling was beginning to come back to her limbs, she was conscious of breathing again. This was not a dream. Giles was saying these things to her. *He loved her.*

'I thought you were lonely, that you were innocent

and curious and trusted me. I hated that. I would have rather you thought of me as dangerous than as safe.' He laughed harshly. 'Male pride. Then I got that letter from Suzy this morning. I was a fool, I had no idea that I was hurting you, I was just so relieved that everything had been agreed about her marriage, for there is some history between the two families and for a while it looked as though it might not happen.

'Then you swept out of the room and Hebe was looking at me as though I had just sworn at you and suddenly I realised what she had seen. *I* was the one you loved and you thought I loved Suzy. Such a coil and such an easy one to resolve, I thought—until I saw your hurt and anger.'

He lay back against the pillows, his grey eyes steady on hers, waiting for her to speak. Joanna drew a long shaking breath and stared back, reading his soul in his eyes, reading the truth. Against all the odds, despite her foolish, romantic, unrealistic dreams, the lengths she had gone to to try his patience, Giles loved her.

Carefully avoiding his injured leg Joanna returned to kneel beside him and reached out her hand. Her fingertips grazed down the side of his face and he turned into the caress until his cheek lay against her palm. 'I love you,' he murmured against the delicate skin.

'Oh, Giles!' Joanna hesitated no longer. Somehow she was in his arms, cradled across his knees and his mouth was hard on hers, possessive, demanding, rough with an urgency she returned as she curved her arm around his neck and kissed him back.

They fell apart breathless, laughing with relief.

'Oh, Giles, what will the General say? He wanted you to marry the daughter of a marquis.'

'He wanted me to be a Field Marshall as well. He won't ever have that, but he is going to have a daughter-in-law he and my mother will adore. And what about your parents? They wanted you to marry an earl.'

'They already know and love you—and from what Hebe tells me she wrote to them, they will be so thankful you saved me from him they will fall upon your neck.'

They sat there handfast, too overwhelmed to even want to kiss for the moment. Then Giles said, 'They are going to want a big wedding, you know. After all the risk of scandal with you running away, they are going to expect banns and weeks of planning. There will be hoards of guests, a magnificent wedding breakfast... I will not see you for weeks because you will be buying your wedding clothes—' He broke off to caress her face. 'I am going to miss you so much. Still, it will give me time to sort out where we are going to live.'

Before she thought Joanna said, 'I do not want to wait,' then blushed crimson.

'We have waited a few weeks, sweetheart, a few more...'

'You might have waited a few weeks, Giles Gregory—I have been waiting for you for three years.'

A wicked sparkle came into his eyes. 'You want to make love?'

Joanna tried to drop her gaze, found she could not and admitted bluntly, 'Yes. Giles, I am sorry if that makes me sound wanton and shocks you, but I thought I had lost you for ever and it has been torture being so close to you every day and when we touch—' She broke off in confusion, only to be caught hard against his chest.

'Are you sure?' he said harshly.

'Yes. I want to be yours. I do not want to wait for weeks and have Mama explaining things to me the night before. I do not want to worry that I will not be perfect on our wedding night.'

Giles laughed, a suppressed chuckle against her hair. 'I rather think you are going to have to endure the pre-wedding talk from your mama, unless you want to explain it is rather late.' He tipped her head back and looked down at her. 'Nothing would give me more pleasure than to make love to you now, my darling. I cannot help feeling this is all a dream and I need to have you in my arms to make it real. But only if you are quite sure.'

He sounded very calm, very controlled, very reassuring. Then Joanna saw the banked fires burning in his eyes, felt the tension in his body and knew he was far from calm and the control was achieved only by exerting his will to the utmost.

'Make it real, Giles,' she murmured, letting her fingers tangle in his hair, pulling him down towards her. He shifted to hold her more easily and she felt rather than saw the stab of pain that ran through him. 'Oh, your leg, I am so sorry, I had forgotten.'

'To hell with my leg,' he said. His lips were nuzzling down the sensitive line of her neck until they found the edge of her dress where it touched her collarbone. His hands came up and searched for the fastening even as his mouth continued to explore the

area where lace and skin met. Joanna wriggled round
to let his questing fingers find the buttons then, overcome by shyness, hid her face against his neck as he
slid the bodice from her shoulders. Somehow the
dress was off before she realised it, leaving her clad
only in her thin summer cambric shift and petticoat
and her silk stockings.

She was still curled on his lap and his fingers
seemed to find their way to her garters and be rolling
down her stockings before she could have time to
wriggle away. He rolled each one down, taking his
time, letting his fingers linger on the soft skin behind
each knee, the sharp point of her ankle bones, the arch
of her foot. As he pulled off the second stocking he
tickled her instep, making her giggle despite her tension.

'Giles! That tickles,' she protested, trying to evade
his fingers and was silenced with a kiss.

'Making love can be fun, you know,' he remarked.
He released her lips and bent his head to wrestle with
a bow fastening her chemise, which had pulled tight.

'Fun?' Joanna was feeling so taut with nerves and
desire that it was difficult to speak.

'It isn't all high passion and intense, serious pleasure.' He moved on to another bow without Joanna
realising that the chemise was slipping from her
shoulders. 'Can you remember that meadow where I
found you after you had run away from Lady Brandon's?' She nodded, intent on his words, on watching
his face. 'Can you imagine making love naked in that
long grass, tickled by those flowers, seeing just where
buttercups would reflect gold on each other's body?

Then bathing in that shallow stream afterwards,
splashing in cold, clean water?'

'Oh, yes! I see what you mean about fun: Giles,
can we find a meadow and…oh!' She fell silent,
blushing as the chemise slipped off, leaving her
breasts bared. Her hands went up to shield herself and
were caught in one of Giles's, held while he bent his
head and kissed the tip of one nipple. The sensation
seemed to flow through her body from the gentle
touch of his lips, down to become a unfamiliar ache
low in her belly.

She closed her eyes as his lips were replaced with
his tongue tip, then a gentle teasing nibble that made
her gasp and arch against him. Giles bent her backwards to lie beside him and began to stroke the fullness of her other breast as his mouth continued to
play havoc with the first.

Joanna shifted restlessly, her feet tangled in petti-
coats and the sheet, trying with what rational thought
was left to her to recall which of Giles's legs was
injured so she did not knock against it.

'This is like trying to make love in a laundry basket,' Giles remarked, his mouth still against her
breast. He raised his head and smiled wickedly at her
and she found she could breathe again. This was not
at all how she imagined losing her virginity. Grace's
careful description of the process had sounded em-
barrassing, alarming and downright painful— 'But no
worse than having a tooth pulled, and it is never as
bad as that again.' It had definitely seemed to be
something that should be got over with and then one
could hope for some pleasure from the marriage bed.
But Giles's lovemaking was leisurely and, while star-

tling in the effects it was producing, certainly not alarming.

She smiled back at him, suddenly realising that she was no longer embarrassed and that he was right, this was *fun. So far*, a cautious inner voice warned her.

'I think we are getting rather tangled up,' she observed. 'If we get rid of the sheet—'

'And all our clothes,' he finished for her, dragging his shirt over his head and tugging at the edge of the sheet. As he was under half of it and Joanna was on top of the other half, removing it involved her getting off the bed before she could turn back. The sight of Giles stretched out completely naked stopped her in her tracks, the colour mounting hectically into her cheeks.

She had seen him stripped to the waist in bed at the inn, had been held against his bare chest after he had hit Lord Clifton, she had been aware of his body as he had trapped her in the meadow. But the naked reality of a man in the throes of lovemaking was still a shock.

Giles lay there unselfconsciously while she swallowed hard and climbed back on to the bed. 'It is all right, you know. Everything is designed to work together.'

This insight into her thoughts made her blush more deeply. Giles caught her round the waist and pulled her down against him again and kissed her with such thoroughness that she stopped thinking again and simply clung to him, drinking in the scent of him, letting the heat of his mouth envelop her as his tongue teased hers and his teeth caught at the sensitive fullness of her underlip.

Somehow he had managed to undo the tapes at the waist of her petticoat and Joanna found herself as naked as he was. Her immediate instinct was to curl against his flank, hiding herself against him, but he stopped her, easing her back against the pillows and raising himself on his elbow to look down at her.

'You are so lovely.' He reached out a hand and freed her hair from the pins that held it and it tumbled down, black against her white skin. Giles caught up one lock and used the ends to caress her breast, his eyes never leaving hers as he did so.

She saw his pupils widen as he watched her, knew hers were dilating too, feeling that if the subtle caress did not stop soon she must seize his hand and press it to the flesh that seemed to be becoming heavier, tauter with every whispering stroke of the fine hair over it.

He bent his head to recapture the nipple and with a gasp she closed her eyes, reaching blindly to caress his hair, hold him closer to her. His hand slid down her side, paused at the point where her hip curved, then ran over the gentle swell of her stomach. The warm palm spread and flattened over soft skin that seemed to quiver under the pressure.

Joanna moaned softly, her head moving restlessly on the pillow, her hands tangled in Giles's hair. His mouth on her breast was creating strange feelings deep inside her close to where his palm stroked across her stomach.

'Giles, I don't…I don't know what…'

'I know, sweetheart, I know. Just trust me.' His fingers slid lower into the triangle of black curls and she stiffened, her thighs tight together in instant re-

jection. Giles's mouth left her breast and she almost
sobbed, convinced she had displeased him. Then his
lips found hers again and he murmured, 'Shh, my
darling, just relax, let me love you.'

His fingers moved down, parted her, slipped gently
into secret, sensitive places that made her gasp against
his mouth. Then the ball of his thumb found and caressed her in a way that stopped the breath in her
throat. Without conscious thought her body arched to
press against his hand. The amazing sensation went
on, on, until she thought she could not bear it any
longer, then his finger slipped into the moist centre
of her and through her delirium she heard him whisper, 'Open your eyes, Joanna, look at me.'

Her lids fluttered open. Her eyes widened, found
his tender, watchful gaze on her. 'I love you,' he said
as everything gathered inside her into one imploding
firework that burst through her veins and nerves,
made her cry out with amazed joy, then fall trembling
back against the pillows.

Giles caught her against him and held her until the
trembling stopped. Gradually some sort of coherent
thought came back and she found herself resting
against his chest, hearing the reassuring beat of his
heart under her ear. 'Giles?'

'Yes, sweetheart?'

'That was…that was wonderful.'

'Good.' He sounded gently amused.

'But that wasn't…I mean, you didn't…'

'No, you are still a virgin. I just wanted to give you
pleasure, that is all.'

'You succeeded,' she said shakily, wondering if

she had the courage to lie back and look at him. 'But what about you? I mean, don't you want to...?'

'We do not have to take this to its conclusion Joanna, not unless you are sure. You can give me pleasure, just as I pleasured you. Look.'

Shyly she lifted her head from his chest and watched as he guided her hand on to him. For a moment she kept it still, then the heat and hardness under her fingers, the sensation of soft skin, fascinated her and she closed her grasp. 'Oh!' To find that she could provoke a reaction just by a touch was a revelation. Biting her lip in concentration, she tentatively moved her hand and was rewarded by a soft groan from Giles. She glanced up at him, saw he had closed his eyes and let her hand move again.

'Giles, am I doing this right?'

He caught her caressing hand in his and opened his eyes. 'You are doing it so right that I think you had better stop.' He hesitated, his eyes dark with passion. 'Joanna, do you still want to do this? Do you still want me to make love to you?'

'Please, Giles.' She slid her hands up across his chest, pausing to savour the unfamiliar feeling of his nipples hardening against her palms, then cradling his face between her hands. 'Please love me.' This time it was she who bent to kiss him, discovering the intriguing difference of being the one on top, of being able to vary pressure and contact. Greatly daring, she let her tongue flicker out to trace the line of his upper lip then caught his lower lip in sharp teeth, teasingly threatening to bite.

For a few seconds he let her lead, then with an

easy strength rolled her over until his weight lay on her, his knee pushing hers gently but inexorably apart.

Joanna struggled against the desire to surrender utterly to the sensations flooding through her and managed to gasp, 'Your leg?'

'Just give me a moment,' Giles shifted his position, winced, then smiled down into her wide, anxious eyes. 'Provided you don't kick it we will be fine.'

She fitted against him so well, Joanna realised hazily, burying her face against his neck, feeling the reassuring strength of his shoulders under her hands, which were trembling with nerves. Lower, where she still tingled from the pleasures his fingers had wrought, she was overwhelmingly conscious of his aroused body and tried desperately not to think, simply to trust Giles and endure the next few minutes.

He nudged against her and she found with a shock that he had already entered her a little. It felt strange but good and she let herself relax. Then he stopped and she was aware of a tightness, a constriction, as though her own body was barring the way. Giles bent his head to whisper against her lips, 'Trust me, sweetheart', then he thrust into her. There was a fleeting sensation of pain, more of discomfort and tightness, then he was lodged deep within her and she realised that they were joined, that this was Giles whose body was cradled within hers and that her own body was opening around him, caressing him, holding him.

Her eyes fluttered open and she found his, a mixture of awe and anxiety in them. 'Giles.' Her voice was an unsteady whisper.

'Sweetheart, are you all right? Did I hurt you?'

'No, yes—just a little. Oh, Giles, I do love you.'

Her body was telling her to move so she tried, tentatively. In answer Giles began to move too, the rhythm of his passion overtaking her caution, sweeping her along on a building crescendo of sensation that she recognised from his earlier lovemaking. But this was fuelled, driven, by his body, too. She was part of it, swept up in it, unaware that her head was moving restlessly on the pillows, her fists were clenched against Giles's chest or that she was crying out with pleasure. It reached a point where she could not withstand the tension any longer, her body arched into his, driving him deeper, convulsing around him as he cried out and the two of them collapsed back on the bed in a tangle of entwined limbs, their mouths locked in a final, desperate kiss.

Chapter Twenty-One

Joanna came to herself to find that Giles was still lying above her, his weight on his elbows, his forehead resting against hers. Her wide open eyes were so close to his that their eyelashes tangled and he smiled and raised his head to look at her better.

'Thank you,' he said simply.

'It was all right? I...'

'You were perfect. I could not have dreamed of anything more perfect. That you want me, that you trust me—I cannot imagine a more wonderful gift.'

'I loved it, too,' Joanna said, uncaring how brazen that sounded. 'Giles, I had no idea it would be like that. I thought perhaps you would find me clumsy: everything I did was just instinct.'

'Mmm.' He bent his head to kiss her slowly along the line of her collarbone. 'Your skin is like silk. Instinct? You have the most wonderful, sensual, loving, natural instincts, Joanna. Just think how good we are going to be together the more we practise. I foresee the need for a lot of practice.'

He rolled carefully over on to his back and stretched like a cat. 'I feel so good.'

'Even your leg?' Joanna sat up rather unsteadily and looked at the bandage that appeared, by some miracle, to still be in place.

'I wouldn't want to go on a route march,' Giles admitted, cautiously flexing the foot and grimacing as the damaged tendons stretched. 'I am going to have to make love to you at least three times a day simply to get enough exercise.'

'Oh,' Joanna feigned a pout. 'Only three times?'

'Minx,' Giles said appreciatively. 'If you carry on sitting there looking so utterly delectable I will just have to...'

He broke off at the sound of the door handle being rattled. Then they heard Alex's voice on the other side raised in what Hebe always referred to as his 'parade-ground shout'. 'Giles! This door is jammed.'

Giles shouted back at the same volume. 'It's locked, you idiot.'

'Then open it!'

Joanna pressed her hands over her mouth to suppress the giggles.

'How can I?' Giles demanded. 'I can't walk.'

Joanna hissed, 'Ask him if everything is all right. He sounds drunk.'

'Lord, Hebe! I had forgotten.' Giles raised his voice again. 'Is everything all right? How is Hebe?'

'Couldn't be better!'

'He *is* drunk,' Giles commented, grinning. 'The baby has come?' he shouted back. 'Really,' he added, dropping his voice again, 'this is a ludicrous way to have a conversation.'

'Then make him go away and I'll open the door,' Joanna said, hopping out of bed and searching frantically for her stockings. 'I can hardly let him in now, can I? Look at this room.'

'Indeed,' Giles drawled, regarding the havoc from under sensual, hooded lids.

'Of course the baby's come! We want you to come and see. I'll get Starling to fetch the spare key and a couple of footmen with a chair.'

On this threat he appeared to leave. Joanna gave a muffled shriek, scrambled all her clothes together and bolted into the dressing room, only to be recalled by Giles.

'Unlock the door, quickly, and throw that sheet back on the bed!'

Joanna closed the door of the dressing room and pulled on her clothes with as much calm as she could manage given a mixture of giggles over their predicament, joy at hearing that Hebe and the baby were both well and a complete sensual daze engendered by Giles's lovemaking.

At the sound of Starling and what sounded like at least four footmen arriving in the bedroom, she sat down at the dressing table and regarded her image in the glass. Dragging Giles's comb through her hair restored some order to her appearance but did little for the flush in her cheeks or the crimson swell of fiercely kissed lips.

'He loves me,' she whispered. *'He loves me.'* It was a miracle, but it was no dream, not with her body throbbing with the knowledge of his, not with the proof of his love in every tender word, every skilful caress.

When the room outside fell silent she risked a peep around the edge of the door to find Giles sitting in the chair clad in a gorgeous Oriental silk dressing gown, the walking cane she had fetched him by his side.

Giles grinned. 'Starling says that he trusts that his lordship's natural joy at the ''Happy Event'' did not disturb my rest, but he fears that his lordship cannot have tried the door handle properly in his ''understandable excitement''. He quite understands that I do not wish to be carried through the halls of Tasborough in the manner of a Roman emperor and will make my own way to her ladyship's suite when Miss Fulgrave returns from her own room.'

'Thank goodness. Giles, have you any idea where my hair pins ended up?'

'All over the bed, I imagine. That *will* cause the chambermaid to speculate in the morning.'

'No, it won't,' Joanna was determinedly shaking out pillows and smoothing the under sheet. 'Six, seven…eight. That's all of them. Now I'll just put my hair up and we'll go and see Hebe.'

With the aid of her arm and the stick, Giles managed to get to his feet and hobble painfully along the corridor. 'Can't put any weight on it, otherwise it's fine,' he ground out in answer to Joanna's attempt at a calm enquiry as to how his leg felt, but the beads of sweat on his forehead said rather more than he was willing to reveal and Joanna could only be thankful that there were no stairs to negotiate.

To Joanna's anxious gaze Hebe seemed very small and far away in the big bed, but although her voice was tired it sounded strong as she cried, 'Joanna,

Giles! Come in. Giles, sit down at once—Joanna, why did you let him walk?'

Joanna pressed Giles firmly into the nearest chair and ran to Hebe's bedside. 'How on earth do you expect me to stop him? He is as stubborn as a mule. Oh, Hebe, how lovely! Is it another little boy?'

'Meet young Giles,' Hebe said with a smile which lit up her tired, pale face. 'Here, take him.'

'Oh, may I? He is so tiny! Giles, look...'

She turned to find Giles still sitting in the chair, an identical shawl-wrapped bundle in his arms and Alex by his side looking not drunk, just utterly dazed and happy.

'Twins! Giles, you were right!'

'This one is little Joanna,' Alex said, smiling as Joanna had never seen him smile. 'We thought you both might be willing to be godparents.'

Giles looked up at his friend. 'Very happily, on one condition: you stand as my groomsman.'

'Joanna!' Hebe threw her arms wide and, handing little Giles to his father, Joanna went and cast herself into her cousin's embrace. 'Thank goodness, I was beginning to think the pair of you would never work it out.' She looked closely at Joanna and said, low voiced, 'If there is anything you want to talk to me about, you only have to say.' Joanna blushed hotly and Hebe's eyebrows rose. 'I see, perhaps I am a little late. *What* a bad chaperon I am.'

'Dreadful,' Joanna agreed solemnly, 'but a very good friend. Oh, Hebe,' she whispered, 'I love him so much it hurts.'

'I know,' Hebe agreed. 'And it never gets any better, thank goodness.'

They were interrupted by Nurse bringing Hugh down to meet his new brother and sister and Joanna helped Giles to his feet and out of the room.

'This is a truly wonderful day,' Giles said, gathering Joanna against his side and hugging her tight. 'Shall we go back to my room and discuss exactly how many children we plan to have?'

'It is very tempting,' Joanna smiled up at him, 'but first I must write to Mama and the Geddings and Georgy, and you must write to your father.'

'No, that is the second thing,' Giles said, seeing Starling advancing in a stately manner down the corridor. 'Starling! Break out his lordship's best champagne and find me those footmen and their chair. I intend to be carried in state to the dining room and there to consume lobster and champagne with my affianced bride.'

Starling rose to the occasion. 'Congratulations, Colonel. I will place the wine on ice at once and set out the very best crystal. As to the lobster, I will ascertain whether one is to be found upon the premises.'

As the butler swept down the staircase, summoning minions to his side, Joanna rested her cheek against the heavy silk of Giles's sleeve. 'I do not think I would ever have had the courage to rebel as I did if it were not for that champagne you gave me at the Duchess's ball. Do you remember? I had a dreadful hangover the next day and as far as Mama was concerned that started my disgrace.'

Giles pulled her tight against him. 'I just want to see your eyes turn green and sparkle with that same fire I saw in them that night. I want to kiss your lips to taste the wine on them as I could not then. And I never, ever want to part from you again as long as I live.'

'You want to hold me captive?'

'Chained to my heart and my soul for ever.'

At the head of the stairs Starling held up a restraining hand to four stalwart footmen who were carrying a chair between them. They obediently turned their backs and waited patiently while Colonel Gregory satisfied himself that his runaway love perfectly understood the terms of her surrender.

'For ever,' Joanna whispered against his lips. 'For ever.'

* * * *

Look out for Ivo Trenchard's story!
Lord Trenchard's Choice
by Sylvia Andrew
is available next month in
Regency High-Society Affairs, Volume 5

Regency

HIGH-SOCIETY
AFFAIRS

BOOK FIVE

These charming scoundrels will be tamed by their ladies

Beloved Virago by Anne Ashley
Lord Trenchard's Choice by Sylvia Andrew

On sale 3rd July 2009

Regency

HIGH-SOCIETY AFFAIRS

Rakes and rogues in the ballrooms — and the bedrooms — of Regency England!

6th March 2009
A Hasty Betrothal by Dorothy Elbury
A Scandalous Marriage by Mary Brendan

3rd April 2009
The Count's Charade by Elizabeth Bailey
The Rake and the Rebel by Mary Brendan

1st May 2009
Sparhawk's Lady by Miranda Jarrett
The Earl's Intended Wife by Louise Allen

5th June 2009
Lord Calthorpe's Promise by Sylvia Andrew
The Society Catch by Louise Allen

8 VOLUMES IN ALL TO COLLECT!

Regency

High-Society Affairs

Rakes and rogues in the ballrooms – and the bedrooms – of Regency England!

3rd July 2009
Beloved Virago by Anne Ashley
Lord Trenchard's Choice by Sylvia Andrew

7th August 2009
The Unruly Chaperon by Elizabeth Rolls
Colonel Ancroft's Love by Sylvia Andrew

4th September 2009
The Sparhawk Bride by Miranda Jarrett
The Rogue's Seduction by Georgina Devon

2nd October 2009
Sparhawk's Angel by Miranda Jarrett
The Proper Wife by Julia Justiss

8 VOLUMES IN ALL TO COLLECT!

Immerse yourself in the glitter of Regency times through the lives and romantic escapades of the Lester family

Miss Lenore Lester was perfectly content with her quiet country life, caring for her father, and having no desire for marriage. Though she hid behind glasses and pulled-back hair, she couldn't disguise her beauty. And the notoriously charming Jason Montgomery – Duke of Eversleigh – could easily see through her disguise and clearly signalled his interests.

Lenore remained determined not to be thrown off-balance by this charming rake. The Duke of Eversleigh, though, was equally determined to loosen the hold Lenore had on her heart.

www.mirabooks.co.uk

MIRA

Immerse yourself in the glitter of Regency times through the lives and romantic escapades of the Lester family

Jack Lester had every reason to hide the news of his recently acquired fortune: he wanted an attractive, capable bride who would accept him for himself, not for his new-found riches.

But he had to make his choice before the society matrons discovered the Lester family were no longer as poor as church mice. He must convince Sophie, the woman of his dreams, to marry him as poor Jack Lester.

*Immerse yourself in the glitter of
Regency times through the lives
and romantic escapades of the
Lester family*

Now the news was out that the Lester family
fortunes had been repaired, Harry Lester knew the
society matrons would soon be in pursuit, so he
promptly left London for Newmarket.

Fate, however, proved more far-sighted, having
arranged for a distraction in the person of
Mrs Lucinda Babbacombe. Lucinda is a beautiful,
provocative but unwilling conquest – who
to Harry's irritation cannot be ignored.

Immerse yourself in the glitter of Regency times through the lives and romantic escapades of the Lester family

Miss Antonia Mannering and Lord Philip Ruthven had been childhood friends who had not seen each other for years. And although considered a very eligible bachelor, Philip remained unmarried.

With Philip's close friend Harry Lester recently married, Antonia only hopes that she can convince Philip of the bliss marriage brings, that she can run his home and not disgrace him in Society. But is Philip ready to set up his nursery… with Antonia as his wife?

www.mirabooks.co.uk

MIRA

Regency romance…and revenge
by bestselling author Nicola Cornick

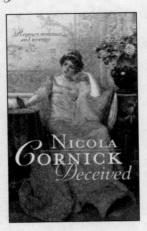

Princess Isabella never imagined it could come to this. Bad enough she faces imprisonment for debts not her own. Even worse that she must make a hasty marriage of convenience with Marcus, the Earl of Stockhaven.

As the London gossips eagerly gather to watch the fun, Isabella struggles to maintain a polite distance in her marriage. But the more Isabella challenges Marcus's iron determination to have a marriage in more than name only, the hotter their passion burns. This time, will it consume them both – or fuel a love greater than they dare dream?

Available at WHSmith, Tesco, ASDA
and all good bookshops

He could marry her — or ruin her!

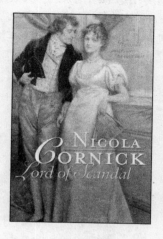

London, 1814

Scandalous and seductive, Hawksmoor is a
notorious fortune hunter. Now he has tasted the
woman of his dreams, Catherine Fenton, and
he will do anything to make her his.

Though heiress to a fortune, Catherine is trapped
in a gilded cage and bound to a man she detests.
She senses there is more to Ben, Lord Hawksmoor,
behind the glittering façade. She believes he can
rescue her – but has she found herself a hero, or
made a pact with the devil himself?

Wanted: Wife

Must be of good family, attractive but not too beautiful, but calm, reasonable and mature... for marriage of convenience

Spirited Charity Emerson is certain she can meet
Simon "Devil" Dure's wifely expectations. With
her crazy schemes, warm laughter and loving heart,
Charity tempts Simon. However, the treacherous trap
that lies ahead, and the vicious act of murder, will put
their courage – and their love – to the ultimate test.

Widow Eleanor Scarborough is out to shock Regency London!

Eleanor has always been looked on as
'the bossy American' by London society. Now,
at the death of her husband, she has been
appointed trustee to his estate.

Infuriated, her mother-in-law sends Lord Anthony
Neale to end Eleanor's gold-digging ways and they
clash immediately. He thinks she's a siren who
uses beauty to entrap men; she thinks he's
a haughty, cold English snob.

But someone is threatening Eleanor, and as the
malicious activities begin to pile up, it's Anthony
who tops the suspects list!

A sumptuous and seductive
Regency novel

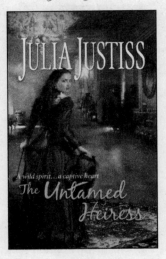

Despite being imprisoned as a child by her
spiteful father, Helena Lambarth journeys to
London to enter society – and becomes a reluctant
houseguest of the dashing Lord Darnell.

Saddled with his father's debts, Adam, Lord
Darnell, must win the hand of wealthy Priscilla
Standish. If only she weren't so ordinary compared
to the unconventional Helena – who has
transformed into a bewitching young woman…

"To say that I met Nicholas Brisbane over my husband's dead body is not entirely accurate. Edward, it should be noted, was still twitching upon the floor…"

London, 1886

For Lady Julia Grey, her husband's sudden death at a dinner party is extremely inconvenient. However, things worsen when inscrutable private investigator Nicholas Brisbane reveals that the death was not due to natural causes.

Drawn away from her comfortable, conventional life, Julia is exposed to threatening notes, secret societies and gypsy curses, not to mention Nicholas's charismatic unpredictability.

MIRA